CRAZY LADY

Also by James Hawkins

INSPECTOR BLISS MYSTERIES

Missing: Presumed Dead
The Fish Kisser
No Cherubs for Melanie
A Year Less a Day
The Dave Bliss Quintet
Lovelace and Button
(International Investigators Inc.)

NON-FICTION

The Canadian Private Investigator's Manual

*1001 Fundraising Ideas and Strategies for
Charities and Not-for-Profit Groups*

CRAZY LADY

A Chief Inspector Bliss Mystery

James Hawkins

A Castle Street Mystery

THE DUNDURN GROUP
TORONTO

Editor: Barry Jowett
Copy-editor: Andrea Pruss
Design: Andrew Roberts
Printer: Marquis

Library and Archives Canada Cataloguing in Publication

Hawkins, D. James (Derek James), 1947-
    Crazy lady : a Chief Inspector Bliss mystery / James Hawkins.

ISBN-10: 1-55002-581-3
ISBN-13: 978-1-55002-581-1

    I.Title.

PS8565.A848C73 2005   C813'.6   C2005-904873-5

1   2   3   4   5   09   08   07   06   05

Conseil des Arts du Canada   Canada Council for the Arts   Canadä   ONTARIO ARTS COUNCIL CONSEIL DES ARTS DE L'ONTARIO

We acknowledge the support of the **Canada Council for the Arts** and the **Ontario Arts Council** for our publishing program. We also acknowledge the financial support of the **Government of Canada** through the **Book Publishing Industry Development Program** and **The Association for the Export of Canadian Books**, and the **Government of Ontario** through the **Ontario Book Publishers Tax Credit** program.

Care has been taken to trace the ownership of copyright material used in this book. The author and the publisher welcome any information enabling them to rectify any references or credits in subsequent editions.

                                        J. Kirk Howard, President

Printed and bound in Canada
Printed on recycled paper⊛
www.dundurn.com

Dundurn Press	Gazelle Book Services Limited	Dundurn Press
3 Church Street	White Cross Mills	2250 Military Road
Suite 500	Hightown, Lancaster, England	Tonawanda, NY
Toronto, Ontario, Canada	LA1 4X5	U.S.A. 14150
M5E 1M2		

CRAZY LADY

Every man deserves to know one true love in his lifetime.

This book is dedicated with love and gratitude to Sheila, my true love, and is in loving memory of her sister, Elizabeth Khanna.

With particular thanks to all the wonderful women in my life, especially my publicist and mentor, Sandra Baird, and her sister, Barbara.

chapter one

"In the beginning was the Word, and the Word was with God."

"Yes, I'm aware of that, ma'am."

"And the Word became flesh and lived amongst us ..."

"If you say so."

"... and we have seen his glory."

"Well, you may have seen it, lady. But all I see is a busload of ticked-off passengers who wanna go home to their wives and kiddies. Now have you got the fare or not?"

"The Lord Saviour says it is better to give than to receive."

"Look, lady, I'm a bus driver, not a charity. Now either pay the fare or get off."

"Peace is my parting gift to you. Set your troubled heart at rest."

"Get off! Freak."

Now what? It's pouring and it's getting dark. Oh, God. Mummy'll be cross if I'm late for tea again.

"*You'll have to walk,*" the woman's God tells her. "*Do you know where you're going?*"

Yes. It's 255 Arundel Crescent, Dewminster, Hampshire, England, The World, The Universe —

"Have you got any spare change?" A voice breaks into Janet Thurgood's musings, and she leaps. The sixty-one-year-old's eyes dart around, seeking escape from Vancouver's near-deserted Chinatown and the dull-eyed, prickly-haired youth who has cornered her in the bus shelter.

"Turn to Our Lord Saviour and he will provide —" she starts, but the panhandler backs her against a glazed advertisement featuring a busty perfume vendor.

"Get a life, lady. I just wanna buck for a coffee, not a freakin' lecture."

The Lord Saviour is my shepherd. Yea, though I walk through the valley of the shadow of death, I will fear no evil, Janet prays inwardly, saying, "I'm sorry. I haven't got any —"

"Don't give me that crap. I've got a knife."

It's a poor excuse for a knife, stolen, like everything else in Jagger Jones's world — including his name. But the ten-cent table knife, filched from Giorgo's Corner Coffee & Souvlaki, has been honed to a stiletto by Jagger (a Hollywood substitute for Davy, the forename thoughtlessly given by his teenage mother while she had more pressing matters on her mind than registering the birth of an unwanted child).

Janet Thurgood turns to her faith for defence, but her words are hollow as she warns, "The Lord Saviour's sword will protect me ..."

"Oy. Punk. Leave the lady alone," cautions a scurrying businessman with his head down against the rain. But he has no more clout than Janet's God, and he's not big enough to step in to ensure that his instruction is heeded.

"I said, don't give me no crap," continues Jones, unfazed by the warning, as his knife goes to his victim's throat.

"My Lord Saviour is with me," chants Janet with the certainty of a televangelist as she is stretched onto her toes. "His rod and staff comfort me …" she continues as her eyes go to the darkening heavens and the palms of her hands join in supplication.

"I mean it," threatens Jones as the sharpened blade hollows a dimple in Janet's neck.

"… and I will dwell in the house of the Lord Saviour forever."

"Shuddup, you crazy old bat. Shuddup and give me the money," spits the young addict as he flattens Janet against the wall on the end of his knife and rubs her down. However, his anticipation turns sour as he realizes that beneath the rain-soaked mackintosh the aging woman is wearing only a flimsy nightdress, and she clearly has no purse. Despite the four decades between them, the youth's hand momentarily idles on Janet's naked thigh, and his face and tone soften as he sneers, "Mebbe you've got something else to give me, eh?"

"Help me, my Lord Saviour," intones Janet as she feels the hand sliding between her legs. "Help me resist this," she is saying as the brake lights of a passing police cruiser shimmer brightly on the rain-slick asphalt. Jagger Jones, ever-watchful, spies the slowing vehicle, pockets his knife, and melts into the gloom, leaving barely a pinprick on his victim's neck. Janet slowly opens her eyes with the realization that she has been spared, spots the police car, now quickly reversing in her direction, and scurries out of the shelter.

"Are you all right, ma'am?" shouts Constable Montgomery from the dry comfort of his cruiser, but Janet slips into a laneway and wades through a mud puddle, while constantly reminding herself of her intended destination. "255 Arundel Crescent, Dewminster, Hampshire, England," she mutters repeatedly as she runs barefoot through the garbage-strewn back alley.

The flashing red and white lights of the pursuing cruiser spur her on as she jinks through the labyrinth of Chinatown's narrow lanes. However, as Constable Montgomery catches glimpses of the fleeing woman, he questions his motives. Was that a knife at her throat? It was just a glint of streetlight — perhaps a cigarette lighter that Jones was holding up for her to light a toke. And knowing Jones as well as Montgomery does, it would certainly have been a toke.

She's probably just another hooker working for a fix, the street-hardened cop wants to believe, but he can't escape the feeling that something is different. The lack of stiletto heels — of any heels — is certainly unusual for a sex worker, as is her drab raincoat, but there is more, although Montgomery can't put his finger on it and would be loath to admit it to his colleagues. It was a feeling of fear — vibes coursing through the ether — that had alerted him to the woman's plight. But now she is running.

"Wait a minute," yells Montgomery as he skids to a halt and cuts Janet off at the exit from a narrow lane, but she spins and is headed back down the lane as he leaps from his cruiser while calling into his radio for a missing person's check.

"Five foot, six inches … Caucasian … late fifties … no shoes … grey raincoat and brown head scarf …"

Blood pours from Janet's shredded feet, but she feels no pain. She's an adrenaline-driven vixen with a baying pack on her tail as she streaks through the maze with Montgomery's laboured footfalls pounding through the mire in her wake.

"255 Arundel Crescent, Dewminster, Hampshire, England," she incants continuously as she runs blindly through Vancouver's tight laneways, but she is nearly five decades and an entire continent from her childhood home. However, Janet views the foreign landscape through the eyes of an eleven-year-old and seemingly recognizes familiar features through the miasma of rain and murk.

Not far now, she thinks, mistaking a dark alleyway for the overhung Dewminster lane where, it was rumoured amongst her pre-teen peers, Jack the Ripper kept a spooky cottage and lay in wait to deflower young virgins.

"Don't be silly. Mr. Smeeton is a very nice man," Janet's mother told her when she tearfully insisted on taking the long way home from school to avoid passing the disabled soldier's thatched cottage. "And he always goes to church," her mother added to bolster her assertion, but she sidestepped the question of "deflowering," and for several years Janet had an image of herself as Red Riding Hood creeping past the veteran's front gate with a basket of roses, desperately praying that the old man wouldn't leap out and steal them.

Latent fear of the lane drives Janet blindly into a tight cul-de-sac, and she's taken a dozen steps before she realizes her blunder. She hesitates momentarily as she seeks an escape route, but Constable Montgomery is gaining ground and his bulky figure is already filling the narrow passageway behind her.

"Wait up," he wheezes after the fleeing woman, but he's conscious that his words barely carry from his lips. However, the prospect of being outrun by a barefoot, middle-aged woman spurs him on, though his rain-sodden clothing and beer belly are weighing him down — so is the pack of Marlboros in his pocket. "I'm getting too old for this," he gasps as he's forced to a walk by an iron band clamped around his chest, but the end of the alley is in sight and he has his quarry backed against a high brick wall.

I just want a few words, dear, he is practising mentally as he advances slowly on the cornered woman, but five more paces and he's wading through treacle. *What's going on?* he questions when a pain as incisive as lightning courses up and down his left arm. Comprehension comes when the blade of a red-hot poker stabs through his chest and enters his heart.

"Help," he cries, lurching to a halt and doubling in agony, but Janet takes advantage of the hiatus and tries to squeeze past in the gloom. Montgomery reaches out and gets a desperate hold on her coat.

"Vengeance is mine. I will repay," screams Janet as she frees herself by scything the officer's hand with her fingernails.

Lights from the basement kitchen of the Mandarin Palace restaurant offer the ailing constable sanctuary as Janet runs off, but as he reaches for the banister of a steep iron staircase, the lights fade, and he knows that he is falling into an exceedingly deep hole.

"255 Arundel Crescent, Dewminster, Hampshire, England," Janet reminds herself as she streaks back towards a busy road and charges into the path of a zippy Volkswagen Jetta.

"What the …?" questions the driver, Trina Button, as she spies the ghostly grey apparition through the murk and slams on her brakes. The car fishtails on the slick surface, and the fleeing woman throws herself to the ground to avoid the skidding vehicle.

Oblivious to the blaring of horns, Trina leaps from her car to aid the sprawled woman, but Janet sees only another persecutor and is quickly on her feet, readying to take off.

"Get thee behind me, Satan," she cries out as Trina tries to grab her, but the young driver manages to snag the sleeve of the woman's raincoat.

"My Lord Saviour will protect me," claims Janet as she slips out of her coat and runs.

"Rats," says Trina as she drops the coat to take up the chase. The young homecare nurse may be fitter and fresher than the escapee, but Janet, wearing only a saturated night-dress, seems to have God on her shoulder as she flies fearlessly through three lanes of speeding traffic. Trina is more judicious and waits for the semblance of a gap before racing across the road in pursuit. Behind her, the abandoned Jetta is clipped by a heavyweight truck and is spun into the path of a taxi. "Shit!" exclaims Trina at the *crunch*, and she dances in deliberation for a few moments before continuing the chase.

"What do you mean, you've lost the car again," sighs Rick Button, Trina's husband, twenty minutes later when she phones breathlessly from a pay phone. "You were only taking the guinea pig to the vet."

"Oh no. I forgot the guinea pig —" Trina is saying as Rick cuts her off to answer another call. Seconds later he's back with Trina.

"That was the police," he says sternly. "They want you at the police station to talk to you about a pileup."

"Oh dear …"

However, the multi-vehicle accident on Hastings Street has taken second place to the discovery of a body in the basement courtyard behind the Mandarin Palace.

Most of the patrons of the restaurant have no idea of the ruckus going on in the kitchen as Charley Cho, the head chef, together with the rest of the staff, clamours for a view out of the basement's condensation-misted window. Outside, the shabby yard is ablaze with emergency lights and jammed with officers readying to raise the body of Constable Roddick Montgomery from the giant fish tank into which he has crashed head first.

"He kill half the fish," complains Cho bitterly as a rope is looped around Montgomery's ankles; two members of the police team, together with a burly fireman, stand in the laneway above, preparing to haul.

"Christ he's heavy," mutters the fireman and receives black looks from the others as the waterlogged body begins to rise from the tank. The blue-faced cadaver begins to slowly rotate as it's hoisted into the air, then a stupefied trout slips out of the officer's tunic and plops back into the tank, making everyone jump.

Sergeant Dave Brougham's face falls as Trina Button rushes the inquiry desk at Vancouver's central police station.

"I might have guessed," grumbles the officer, recognizing the bouncy homecare nurse from a previous encounter, but Trina recognizes him as well and grabs him by the lapels, demanding, "Where's my guinea pig? What have you done to him?"

"He's all right," says Constable Hunt, stepping forward with a battered cage. "I rescued him. You're lucky he wasn't flattened in the wreck. He's just a bit shaken up."

"Leaving the scene following an accident is a serious offence," cautions the sergeant as Trina lifts the shivering creature from the cage, but Trina launches at him boldly.

"I didn't leave *after* the accident," she protests. "You should get your facts straight before you accuse innocent people."

"But you dumped your car in the middle of Hastings Street."

"Give me a parking ticket then. Anyway, I only went to help the poor woman."

The question, "What woman?" leaves Trina without an answer. Janet's wraithlike figure somehow dissolved by the time the concerned nurse worked her way to the far side of the street and scoured the numerous laneways and potential hidey-holes.

"So you did have an accident then," persists the sergeant, once Trina has explained the incident.

"No. She was the one who had an accident. I didn't hit her," explains Trina precisely. "I just stopped to help her."

"Help who? No one mentioned a woman," continues the sergeant, and he turns to PC Hunt for backup. "Did anyone else report seeing a woman?"

"No, Sergeant."

"Sounds like a pretty convenient story if you ask me," the sergeant sneers, but Trina spits back in defence.

"She dropped her coat."

"OK. Now we're getting somewhere. Can you describe it? Where is it?"

Trina shakes her head. "It was raining … she was running … I'm not sure."

"According to the witnesses, the only person running was you," steps in PC Hunt. "They say you ditched the car and ran."

"But … the grey lady …"

"Precisely, Mrs. Button," mocks Sergeant Brougham. "A grey lady. Sounds like a bit of a ghost story to me."

Trina is still concerned about the missing woman as she prods Brougham with the guinea pig, insisting, "You've got to find her. She'll freeze to death. She's only wearing a nightie."

Rick steps in to rescue the animal as Brougham sarcastically explains. "One of my officers has been murdered, you've screwed up the downtown rush-hour traffic, and you want us to look for a nutcase in a nightdress."

"Yes."

"Stop wasting my time, lady," he says, turning away. "We've had no reports of a missing woman. Anyway, she obviously didn't want to be caught."

"In that case we have a responsibility to find her ourselves," proclaims Trina loftily and loudly as she snatches the guinea pig back from Rick. "This lot couldn't find the hole in a donut."

"Are you quite sure you saw a woman?" asks Rick once Sergeant Brougham has angrily ushered them outside, where they shelter under a dripping arbutus tree to await the arrival of the remnants of Trina's Volkswagen. "Only it was raining and almost dark. Perhaps it was a deer or a —"

"It was a woman," cuts in Trina defiantly. "She dropped her coat. She even said something about being saved by someone or other."

Janet Thurgood is still leaning on her Saviour for protection as she huddles from the cold dampness of the British Columbian autumn in a dark doorway. The lost coat should concern her, but she has sunk inside her mind, seeking answers from the past as well as the road that will lead her to the present. But there is a gaping hole in her memory — someone has ripped the centre out of her life's scrapbook — and the hole is growing, and has been growing for sometime.

"255 *Arundel Crescent* ..."

I know that. I know where I used to live. But it's gone. Can't you see that? Everything's gone.

"*What came after then?*"

I can't remember.

"*Think ... think ... think. First there was 255 Arundel Crescent ...*"

With Mummy and Daddy ...

"*Yes. Now go back. What do you remember?*"

Daddy hated me.

"*He wanted a boy. He would've liked that.*"

Joseph liked me.

"*Yes ... yes ... yes. Now go deeper. Who was Joseph? What did he look like?*"

I can't remem ... was he ... I can't remember. I can't remember.

"What's up, lady?"

Janet's eyes open in alarm. A bagman leaning over a loaded supermarket buggy waits for a reply.

It's nearly eight o'clock, and the homeless have taken over: ghostly cloaked figures drifting soundlessly through the alleyways of Vancouver as they scavenge the detritus for a bottle of nirvana. Janet scrunches herself further into the corner and watches several men — grey-bearded cadavers of men all similarly beaten into the same haggard, hunched form — wanting to question, "Are you Jesus?"

"I asked, like, who are you?" continues the bagman, then he drags a black garbage bag of clothing from his buggy. "Try these. They'll keep you warm."

"Are you Jesus?" she asks, peering deeply into his lifeless eyes. He grins — a single-toothed grin that turns him into a caricature of a leering maniac — then laughs at the alarm on Janet's face. *There was a time ...* he thinks to himself, vaguely recalling an earlier life in a better world, but his memory is as clouded as Janet's and, as he shuffles away, his laughter turns to a harsh cough.

The clothes were a teenager's donation to Children's Aid until the vagrant did his daily round. Janet's withered frame doesn't overly stretch the modern garments, although the sight of a skinny sixty-one-year-old in baggy cargo pants, ripped Nike running shoes, and a T-shirt screaming "Eminem Fuckin' Raps" turns a few heads as Janet resumes her search.

The roadway to her past is there, she's certain, but her mind is as fuzzy as a blurred windshield and she sees only isolated visions — visions that are startlingly clear, frighteningly clear, and she's always running: running, terrified, from a perpetually angry father; on the run from her first Girl Guide camp after two tear-filled days and nights; running from schoolyard bullies; from unbelievers; from boys; from responsibilities. And at eighteen, running from her parents into the arms of a man — a married man. Then running back home in tears, pregnant, to a father who slammed the door in her face. On the run again, knocking on the door of a church — a church unsympathetic to harlots and home wreckers, and another door slammed in her face.

Nothing makes sense as Janet wanders the grimy side of Vancouver that is kept out of the tourist brochures and off the tour guides' schedules. If only she could find Mrs. Jenson's sweet shop or even St. Stephen's in the Vale parish church. But the twenty-first-century Canadian streets confuse her. The cars, quiet and fast, flow like a river of molten steel. Lights, bright and flashing, remind her of Christmas, and a store full of televisions mesmerizes her: movies, she assumes, though she's not seen one in nearly forty years — not a real one, not like the ones they showed at The Odeon in Dewminster Market Square in her youth.

"A window on Hell," Janet's mother told her whenever she protested that all her friends spent Saturday afternoons with Roy Rogers and Buster Keaton.

The nearest she came to a movie in those far-off days was when a church missionary set up a flimsy screen in front of the altar, annoying a crusty churchwarden who considered it sacrilegious to block God's view of His congregation, and showed grainy images from a 35-millimetre projector: little black boys wearing starched white shirts with ties, and skirted girls with spindly black legs and bright head scarves, their toothy grins showing delight as they marched down the aisle of a palm-roofed hut to signify their conversion to God. But which God? Whose God?

"Why doesn't God like seeing girls' hair?" earned Janet a rap on the knuckles from Mr. Gibbons, the Sunday school teacher, and she seriously considered becoming a Roman Catholic until she discovered that their God seemed to have a similar aversion.

Janet spots her reflection in the television store window and instinctively checks her head scarf. "Thank God," she murmurs, though she questions the identity of the waiflike woman wearing it. "Who are you?" she asks and is surprised to see the woman's lips moving in unison. "Mother?" she questions.

In many ways, Janet has become her mother, a fearful woman devoted to God but lost to the world who slaved in the service of a man as required by her marriage vows.

"Listen to your father ... Do what your father says ... Your father knows best ... He must be obeyed," Janet's mother always said, using the same words her mother drilled into her as a child, and her mother's mother before her. And then: "Listen to your husband ... Do what your husband says ... Your husband knows best ... He must be obeyed."

And after that: "Listen to God ... Do what God says ... God knows best ... He must be obeyed." In Janet's childhood world, political correctness was a thing of the future — God was still indisputably a man.

With the growing feeling that her God was no longer on her side, and with a baby swelling inside her, Janet had thrown herself on the mercy of another man: Joseph C. Creston, a shy, pious young man, a man — a pimply youth, really — who, she was well aware, had lusted after her from the choir stalls throughout puberty.

"That's the third one this year," complains Rick Button an hour later as he and Trina survey the debris of the Jetta in the police pound.

"Wasn't my fault," she is protesting as she begins rummaging through the wrecked vehicle to retrieve her personal belongings, then she spots an unfamiliar garment bundled onto the back seat by the tow truck driver. "Yes!" she screeches triumphantly as she drags out Janet's sodden raincoat and examines it in the headlights of Rick's car.

"Yes what?" inquires Rick.

"I told you she dropped her coat," Trina says as she fingers the wet material, searches the pockets, and comes up with a bronze crucifix bearing a figure worn smooth by years of veneration.

"We'd better give it to Sergeant Brougham," suggests Rick, taking a look at the aged icon, but Trina is shaking her head.

"Not likely. Remember what happened when I turned in a stray goat."

"That was different," protests Rick. "It was a wild animal."

But Trina doesn't agree. "They still had no right to do that to it. And then there was the time I warned them about the anthrax in Wal-Mart."

"It was just a leaky packet of talcum powder."

"Yeah. But they had no right to strip-search me."

"Decontamination. They stripped everyone, Trina ... mainly because you were running around shouting, 'I'm a nurse — we're all gonna die.'"

"Look. It comes apart," says Trina, anxious to move on as she unscrews the base of the small metal crucifix and spots the end of a paper cylinder tucked into the upright of the cross.

"This belongs to Janet Thurgood. 255 Arundel Crescent, Dewminster, Hampshire," she reads once she had slipped the sepia roll from the inside.

"What's that?" asks Rick, looking over her shoulder.

"Our first case."

"Whose case? What case? What are you talking about?"

"Lovelace and Button, International Investigators," she says, as if Rick should have remembered the zany scheme she cooked up with her elderly English friend following an escapade in the mountains of Washington State. "I'd better phone Daphne and let her know we're in business."

"In business? I thought you were joking."

"No joke," says Trina as she flicks open her cell-phone, but Rick clamps his hand over the keypad and points to his watch.

"Whoops!" exclaims Trina realizing that it's four in the morning across the Atlantic in sleepy Westchester, home of retired wartime agent Daphne Lovelace. "I'd better wait till tomorrow."

"Surely you need a licence or something to be an investigator," protests Rick. "You can't just go around snooping ..." But he knows he's wasting his time; Trina has spent her life delving through other people's garbage, both physical and psychological, and will leave no stone unturned to get at the truth.

Answers are also being sought in the untimely death of Constable Roddick Montgomery. The suspected murder of a serving officer has galvanized the police community with as much fervour as the threat of an overtime freeze. Cruisers have been drawn from all over the city. The area surrounding the Mandarin Palace has been sealed off for several blocks, while officers trudge through the muddy back alleys rounding up the usual suspects: pimps, panhandlers, hookers, and dealers. The fact that the officer's demise occurred in a seedy back alley of Chinatown is sufficient confirmation of foul play. The possibility that it could have been natural causes is not even considered by his colleagues.

Montgomery's final radio message describing Janet Thurgood has yet to be associated with his death. Indeed, if Charley Cho hadn't phoned to complain that someone had dived, headfirst, into his fish tank, the death of Montgomery might have gone unnoticed until shift handover at 10:00 p.m.

"Come on," says Rick, peering at the shivery creature in Trina's arms. "Let's get you home."

"But what about Janet?" demands Trina as they drive away.

"Who?"

"Janet. The woman."

"Forget it, Trina. Like the sergeant said, she obviously didn't want to be caught."

"That's not the point. Now that I've got her coat and I know her name I kinda feel responsible for her."

"You've got to get over this idea that everyone needs your help. Some people manage quite well on their own."

Droplets of tears glisten on Trina's cheeks, her lips quiver, and she clutches the guinea pig tightly — too tightly, but she's determined not to say anything. Then Rick comes to his senses.

"All right," he concedes, U-turning, "where did you last see her?"

"Yes!" she exclaims triumphantly, and the furry creature makes a break for freedom and heads for the dark corner under Rick's feet.

chapter two

Janet is prowling Trina's luxurious basement suite, keeping pace with the guinea pig in the cage on the corner table, though she doesn't realize it, and she's thinking of running again; if only she could remember how to get home. The sopping clothes given to her by the bagman have been replaced by dry ones from Trina's closet, but while the lost woman is about as meaty as a wire clothes hanger, Trina is only a notch or two short of voluptuous, and Janet is forced to hold both the clothes and herself in place with folded matchstick arms. She has slept little and eaten less.

"You have to keep up your strength," Trina insisted the previous evening as she laid out a smorgasbord of delicacies filched from the Christmas goodies that she has been laying away since Thanksgiving.

Janet eyes smoked salmon sandwiches, banana cream chocolates, and marzipan fruits, muttering, "The Devil's poison," and her brow is furrowed as she warily glides a hand over the television, computer, and stereo, as if she is a time traveller beamed in from the past or, possibly, the future.

"Where am I? Where am I?" she repeatedly intones as she searches the room for anything to give her a grounding.

Janet's temporary domicile is also a concern for Trina.

"Just make sure she's gone by the time I get home from the office," Rick said on his way out of the door. "I've warned you before about bringing your work home and filling the house with strays."

"She's not one of my patients," declared Trina angrily, then she softened and gave him a placatory kiss. "Don't worry. I'll call Mike Phillips again. He'll know what to do."

"He'd better, Trina. Either she goes by this evening or I will."

"Just remember," warned Trina with a finger in Rick's face, "you said that about the goat, and look what happened to him."

"How could I forget," said Rick, laughing. "But if a Vancouver cop slits Janet's throat and sticks her on a barbecue we'll report him to the humane society. OK?"

Inspector Mike Phillips of the Royal Canadian Mounted Police has never swallowed the force's mantra, and he has just as many failures as successes to show for his twenty-year career. And although it is barely eight-thirty, today looks like another check in the negative column as he scrutinizes the pathologist's preliminary report into the sudden death of Constable Roddick Montgomery.

"Heart attack," he mutters with a tone of disappointment, though the marks on the dead man's hand left by Janet's fingernails caught the mortician's eye and suggest that the deceased officer was engaged in some kind of struggle prior to his dramatic plunge.

"If someone attacked him and he died as a result," explains Sergeant Brougham on a technicality, "it would still be homicide."

"That's true —" begins Phillips, but he's interrupted by his personal cellphone.

"She seems to be a bit of a stray," explains Trina Button once the pleasantries are over.

"You could try the pound, then," jokes Phillips and catches a rebuke. "All right," he relents, grabbing a pen. "Give me her name. Who is she?"

"An angel."

"What? Come along, Trina, I don't have time to play. The Vancouver City boys have called me in to investigate one of their officer's deaths."

Trina stalls for a second, knowing that she's about to stretch. "OK, Mike. She says her name is Daena the fifteenth, though she insists it has to be written in roman numerals, like Daena XV."

"And you believe her?"

"It's what she believes."

"Sometimes I believe I sing Verdi's *La Traviata* just like Pavarotti — just don't ask my wife."

Trina laughs. "Knowing how much Ruth loves you she probably thinks you sound better than him, but actually I think the woman is Janet Thurgood, originally from England, though she denies it."

"Okay. Now we're getting somewhere. Date of birth?"

"Ah … I don't …"

"Look, Trina. Missing persons in Vancouver are the City police problem. Sergeant Brougham is with me now. Give him the details —"

"He'll reckon he's too busy dealing with accidents and things," Trina sneers, as if she was in no way responsible for the previous evening's snarl-up. "Anyway, his lot couldn't detect a bad smell in a bathroom."

"Trina!"

"I suppose I could try Raven. She'll know."

"Raven?" queries Phillips.

"You remember — the psychic who told your wife she'd won the lottery."

"And she was right."

"I know. But she also told me I wasn't gonna get hit by a bus."

"And were you?"

"No. But I was bowled over by a kid on a bike. It's just as painful."

"I'll see what I can do," promises Phillips once he's elicited a brief description of Janet. "But you really should hand her over to the Vancouver authorities."

"Not likely. I handed over a lost goat once and they ate it," Trina says snidely. "Anyway, she's scared of authority. She'll probably run again."

"Trina, be careful," warns Phillips, suddenly concerned. "Maybe she's on the lam from a loonie bin."

It's a good job I kick-box, thinks Trina as she puts down the phone. And she takes a practice leap at the kitchen door as fifteen-year-old Rob throws a cereal bowl on the table and heads for the fridge saying, "Who's the skeleton in the basement, Mum?"

"Oh. You mean Sister Mary?" jests Trina, straight-faced. "She's the new animal trainer: guinea pigs and uncouth teenagers."

Rob stops in thought, just for second. "Grow up, Mum."

"Touché. Anyway, what were you doing in the basement?"

"Watching television — Ky took mine."

"Right. That's it," seethes Trina, then she screeches to the ceiling, "Kylie Button, you're grounded."

"Mum. Forget it," says Rob. "She's already grounded, remember? No TV, no boys, no emails, cellphone, or texts. So she just takes mine."

"OK. So what's our visitor doing?"

"I think Bart Simpson freaked her out."

"Trust you," mutters Trina, picking up Janet's crucifix and making for the basement. "And tell your sister to get a move on or I won't drive you to school."

"Fine with me," replies Rob as Trina heads downstairs wondering whether or not it might be more sensible to give her teenagers a day at home as backup.

Janet leaps up from the television like a kid caught with his hand in his pants, and Trina switches it off, lightly saying, "It's all a load of garbage" as she tries to calm the woman with a hand, but Janet backs away until she hits the wall. The fearful woman's salt and pepper hair, scraped sternly back from her forehead, hangs like a frayed sisal rope down her back, although it is more knotted than plaited. And her pinched features and faded brown head scarf, as tight as a tourniquet across her forehead and around her face, have Trina thinking of a bald-headed buzzard.

"I'll do your hair if you take off your scarf," she tries warmly, but Janet's frightened eyes back her off, so she attempts bribery. "I could ask my hair girl to stop by and give you a snazzy style …" she starts, but Janet tightens the scarf and quickly butts in.

"Our Lord Saviour wouldn't approve."

"God wants you to have lovely long hair, but he doesn't want anyone to admire it?" Trina questions disbelievingly.

"He sees everything," explains Janet in a reverent whisper. "And he scorns vanity."

"Would you like some breakfast?" inquires Trina as she dances around the basement, keeping Janet at arm's length. But Janet is doing her own dancing.

"I can't pay you."

"I don't want —"

"Our Lord Saviour says …" begins Janet, then she spots her crucifix in Trina's hand, roughly snatches it, and grips it to her chest as if trying to force it into her heart. "Where did you get it?" she demands.

"I just want to help you get home," tries Trina, but Janet drops to her knees and raises her crucifix and eyes to the ceiling.

"I shall dwell in the house of Our Lord Saviour for eternity."

"With any luck we all will. But where do you live now?"

"255 Arundel Crescent, Dewminster, Hampshire, England," intones Janet by rote.

"That's a long walk."

"255 Arundel Crescent, Dewminster, Hampshire, England," she repeats as if stuck in a loop.

"But how did you get here?"

"255 Arundel Crescent, Dewminster, Hampshire, England," she reiterates, pacing with agitation, and Trina takes refuge behind the guinea pig's cage. "Time for his morning walk," she says, grabbing the cage, and she quickly slips out and closes the suite door firmly behind her with the growing feeling that she has a very restless cat loose in the basement — but is it a Blue Persian or a white tiger?

With the television off, Janet seeks comfort from her God as she caresses and kisses the smooth face of Jesus, while above her in the marble-floored kitchen Trina telephones Margaret, her dispatcher, to say that she will be unable to visit her regular clients today.

"Mr. Hammett needs a new colostomy bag," she explains as she whips through her daily to-do list. "And I told Mrs. Williams that I'd pick up a bouquet of white carnations at the florist's. It's her friend's ninetieth …"

"Will do," says the dispatcher. "Has she paid?"

Trina hesitates. "Ah … actually the old dear hasn't any money, so give me the tab. And make sure she gets the best, OK, no gas station grunge."

"Hey, I could use flowers," jokes Margaret. "How come there's no one in my life like you?"

"You just wait until the most exciting thing in your life is a soft-boiled egg and a clean diaper and you may get lucky."

"I know, I know. So, is that it?"

Trina takes a deep breath. "Actually, it's Wednesday."

"And?"

"I usually give old Mr. Sampson an enema on Wednesdays."

"OK. If it's essential?"

"It's not really," admits Trina reluctantly. "But it gives the poor old guy a bit of a thrill."

"Shit, Trina, you're supposed to be a homecare nurse not a freakin' sex worker."

"I know, I know. But sometimes I think it's the only thing he lives for."

"Well, I know what I live for, and no one ever gives me that," sighs the dispatcher pointedly, and Trina is considering suggesting the other woman might have more success if she were to lose a couple hundred pounds when Margaret asks concernedly, "You're not sick or anything?"

"No, I'm fine," explains Trina before detailing Janet and her symptoms.

"Sounds like me when I'm pissed," suggests Margaret, "although it could be that she's subconsciously blocking out some traumatic experience by returning to a time before it happened. You should get her to a shrink."

"Yeah. I know," replies Trina. "But she's so scared she'll probably run if I take her out of the house. Anyway, I have some ideas."

Trina's first idea involves Daphne Lovelace, a long-time resident of Westchester, England, with a propensity for getting involved in situations that should properly be left to the authorities. But in a way, Daphne still considers herself to be a part of the authorities, and despite more than thirty years on the pensioner's list at Whitehall's Ministry of Defence, she has never fully retired. A twenty-five-year stint as the cleaning lady at Westchester police station before her compulsory departure from the workforce merely reinforces her belief that she is still a servant of Her Majesty. The Order of the British Empire, awarded to her for unspecified acts of national importance during and after the Second World War, proves conclusively, in her mind at least, that despite her advancing years she has the full backing of the British government.

"Janet Thurgood from Dewminster," Daphne muses aloud once she's digested the information from her Canadian friend. "Doesn't ring a bell, but it's only about ten miles. I could get a bus over there tomorrow afternoon and make some inquiries. What was the address again?"

"Yes! Lovelace and Button are back in business," shrills Trina in delight as she punches the air, and Daphne laughs at the younger woman's exuberance.

"Just don't tell David what we're doing or he'll have me arrested by Interpol for interfering in international investigations."

"Roger, wilco," says Trina in a passable English accent, knowing that Daphne's friend Detective Chief Inspector David Bliss of Scotland Yard has good reason to complain about civilians meddling in police affairs. He still walks with a limp from a flesh wound inflicted on him the last time that Daphne and Trina decided to do a little sleuthing on their own and wound up uncovering a CIA operation in the mountains of Washington State.

Bliss is not in a position to complain about any extra-judicial inquiries this time. Despite several attempts to resign from London's Metropolitan Police Service to begin his writing career, and to avoid further confrontations with a slippery senior officer named Edwards, Bliss is still firmly listed as a serving officer. However, a full year's sabbatical on half pay — a reward for services above and beyond the call of duty — has provided him with both the time and the means to complete his great historical work, and it's no coincidence that he has chosen the faded Mediterranean resort of St-Juan-sur-Mer as his *pied-à-terre*.

From his Provençal apartment's balcony, David Bliss looks across the beautiful azure bay to the fortress on the island of Ste. Marguerite, the one-time residence of Louis XIV's legendary prisoner *l'homme au masque de fer* — the Man in the Iron Mask — and wraps himself in the ambience of the Mediterranean as he attempts to recreate the intriguing world of the French aristocracy at the end of the seventeenth century.

Three months, and Bliss's first draft of the true account of the legendary masked man, *The Truth Behind the Mask*, is already half complete. However, he is growing concerned that his schedule is slipping, and bubbly real estate agent Daisy Leblanc isn't helping, though he doesn't complain as he hears her key in the apartment's door.

"I 'ave brought you zhe dinner, Daavid," Daisy calls in her Gallicized English as the door closes behind her, and Bliss is drawn from the balcony to a sight more pleasing than the vermillion sun setting over the aquamarine bay and verdant islands.

"What would I do without you?" he says as he takes the tray, wraps Daisy in his arms, and kisses her.

"You would starve to death, I zhink." She laughs, putting a picnic basket and a bottle of local wine on the table, then she pulls back to give him a serious look. "Zhat is why I zhink I should come and live here with you."

"Daisy," starts Bliss without knowing where he is going, "I don't think … I mean … I'm not sure …"

"It is all right, Daavid," she says, picking up the laughter again and playfully slipping a hand down his shorts. "You zhink zhat perhaps you would not be able to write if I was here all zhe time."

"I *know* I wouldn't be able to write," he says forcefully as he removes her hand.

The day has started to wear thin for Trina in Vancouver by mid-afternoon. Every visit to the basement suite has left her more frustrated. Rick is anticipating a guest-free dinner in a couple of hours, and Trina is beginning to panic as she sits at her computer compiling a profile of Janet Thurgood, if that is her name, attempting to follow the investigative procedures laid out in a manual for private investigators she bought when she first dreamed of becoming a detective. However, the relevant chapter assumes the reader wishes to trace someone reported as missing and not the opposite. Trina has already tried all the hospitals and hostels without success. Mike Phillips phoned back at midday to say that no one matching Janet's description seems to be missing or on the run, though he again warned Trina to be wary.

"Motive for disappearance," she types once she has listed Janet's physical features, and she finds herself immediately stumped.

"Motive," she begins again, pauses blankly, then seeks guidance from the manual. "There are numerous possible motives for voluntary disappearance," it reads, "but most fall into just three categories: indebtedness, criminal conduct of some type, and domestic relationships."

"Useless," she mutters, realizing that she has no knowledge of Janet's past, then she perks up with an idea and types.

"Motive for disappearance ... In search of salvation."

"There," says Trina, satisfied that she is on the right track, and she is headed back to the basement for another try when Raven calls.

"Sorry. I would have called earlier but I only just got your message," says the professed seer and channel, and Trina can't help taking a shot.

"You're supposed to be psychic. I thought you would have known I needed you," she complains, then goes on to explain her predicament before Raven has a chance to protest.

"We all live in boxes — spheres, really," suggests Raven once she's had a moment's consideration. "We're surrounded by people and things that are familiar to us. Sometimes we're forced to move into a new box but we don't want to leave the security of the old one. Maybe she's just slipped back into her old box, the last time she really felt secure, and she's sort of trapped in the past."

"Could you bring her back to the present?"

Raven laughs. "When I say the past, Trina, I mean … like … a past life. With all this religious stuff she could be a fifteenth-century monk or a —"

"Or an angel?" cuts in Trina, remembering Janet insisting that she be called Daena.

"Daena!" exclaims Raven at the name. "Is that what she calls herself?"

"Daena XV to be precise."

"Wow!"

"What?"

"Trina. Don't do anything, OK? I've got to do some research. Talk to people. Wow! This is exciting."

"What is it?"

"Call you later. Wow! Daena."

"Hey, Mum," calls Rob as he flings open the kitchen door, "is the stick insect still in the basement? I wanna watch *The Simpsons*."

"Raven!" calls Trina into the phone, but she's gone, so she turns to her son and puts on a worried look.

"Actually. I think the stick insect, as you call her, has barfed all over the carpet, so you might not …"

"Oh, Christ!" spits Rob as he spins. "I'm goin' to Merv's."

"Good idea. Be home by ten —" she starts, but is cut off by the slammed door.

OK, says Trina to herself, and she returns to the computer in search of Daena.

By 4:00 p.m., Pacific Standard Time, Trina Button is no nearer discovering the true identity of her houseguest and is starting to worry about Rick's reaction when he returns. He's called several times during the day, but she let the answering machine take the brunt of his testiness. "Just let me know when she's gone," he said, firmly and finally, and Trina quickly wiped off the recording with the intention of swearing, "Blasted teenagers!" if he should demand to know why she didn't reply.

One more try, she says to herself as she heads to the basement suite with a pot of tea and a packet of Oreos.

"Can I go home now?" Janet demands as Trina opens the door.

"Of course," says the homecare nurse. "You're not a prisoner. But where is your home?"

"255 Arundel Crescent …" begins Janet robotically, but Trina puts up a hand.

"No. Start again. Your name is Janet Thurgood …"

Janet immediately jumps to her feet and holds her crucifix high, incanting, "I am Daena XV, queen of the angels … I am Daena XV, queen —"

"All right," soothes Trina, and she takes the agitated woman's hand, saying, "How long have you been Daena?"

Janet gives Trina a quizzical look, but she calms, as if sensing that she is being taken seriously, and says, "This is my fifteenth incarnation. I told you. I'm Daena XV. I'm Daena XV."

Trina grips the bony hand tightly, fearing that the woman is readying to run again. "All right," she says, "but what else do you know?"

There is a vagueness in her tone, as if she is mentally searching for more but isn't sure where to look for it as she replies, "Everything. I know everything."

"What about children, Daena. Did you have any?"

"We are all God's children."

"I know. But did you have any of your own?"

A smack on the head with a baseball bat might have caused a similar effect as Janet Thurgood's eyes pop and she stares rigidly into the past for a few seconds before slumping in a flood of tears.

That's interesting, Trina is thinking, with the sobbing woman bundled against her chest, when a loud knocking on the window stops the woman in mid-cry, and Trina, already startled by the outburst, leaps.

"Trina. Are you there?" calls a familiar voice, and Trina breathes a sigh of relief as she opens the curtains to find Inspector Mike Phillips and Sergeant Dave Brougham.

"I tried the front doorbell," explains the senior officer as she lets both of them in.

"I was just talking to Janet ..." she begins.

"It's Daena," yells an agitated voice from behind her. "I keep telling you. It's Daena ... Daena ... Daena XV."

"I know," says Trina softly and she reaches out in an attempt to placate the woman.

"Don't touch me ... don't touch me," yells Janet, and Trina backs off.

Mike Phillips steps in and guides Trina to the door leading to the main floor. "A word please, Trina," he starts. "She just fits the description of a woman the dead constable was inquiring about before he died, that's all," says Phillips once the basement door is closed on Janet.

"And you think she had something to do with it?" asks Trina worriedly.

Sergeant Brougham steps in officiously. "Someone or something scratched his hand. The guys at the morgue reckon it could have been long fingernails. Does she have long fingernails, Mrs. Button?"

"Yes. And so do I," spits Trina, waving hers in his face. "But that doesn't make me a killer."

"We're not saying she's a killer, Trina," tries Phillips with a friendly hand on her shoulder. "It's just routine inquiries. That's all."

"So. You could ask her now. She'll be scared if you take her to the police station."

"Trina. You're out of your depth as usual," suggests Phillips. "We'll just take her in for a few questions and then we'll get her some proper help."

"OK," agrees Trina after a momentary pause, then she spins on Sergeant Brougham and stabs him with a finger, saying, "No barbecues, all right?"

"What?"

"You know what I mean," she is saying as she opens the basement door, then she stops as she takes in the sight of an open window. "Oh. Damn. She's gone again."

A kind of peace has settled over the Button household by the time that Rick arrives and peers through the basement window on his way from the garage.

"It's all right. The crazy lady's gone," calls Trina as she spots her husband's shadow, and he enters to find her sitting in front of a blank television, toying with Janet's spiritual figurine.

"I told you she was a nut," says Rick in relief, but Trina's expression suggests that she has a different view.

"She's scared of something, Rick. Really scared."

chapter three

It's barely a twenty-minute run from Westchester to Dewminster on the bypass, but the aging bus driver steers with his knees and casually combs his hair with both hands as he takes the scenic route, meandering the wooded lanes and village roads like a Sunday excursionist, pausing to help passengers with loaded shopping carts and stopping for a "quick bite" at Moulton-Didsley's village store. "Best sausage rolls in Wessex," he loudly announces as he switches off the engine, and a couple other passengers take him at his word. Then it's on to Lower Mansfield, where he gives his face a once-over in the mirror and detours for Molly Jenkins. "It won't take a sec," he calls as he trundles the thirty-seater up a rugged cart track to a thatched cottage. "Only the poor old soul's going to the doc's in Dewminster."

Daphne eyes Mrs. Jenkins cynically as the elderly, though apparently agile, woman boards without assistance, whispering to the driver, "Thanks ever so, Bert," as she lays a friendly hand on his arm.

That's interesting, thinks Daphne, noticing that neither fare nor ticket changes hands, and her skepticism deepens as the new passenger makes a space for herself in the front seat by squeezing a toddler onto her mother's lap.

"There's plenty of room at the back," mutters the young woman angrily, but Mrs. Jenkins knows her place and is determined to fill it.

"I'll be all right here, luv," she insists as she removes her hat to signify that she is settled, and she gets a nod of approval from Bert.

I wonder if there's a Mr. Jenkins, thinks Daphne as she watches the couple chit-chatting like a pair of teenagers all the way to her destination.

"Dewminster Market Place," sings out Bert, and Daphne dawdles for few seconds until the driver and his lady friend lightly link hands and slink together into the Market Café.

"I ought to be a private eye," laughs Daphne under her breath, then she stops herself, asserting, "That's exactly what I am."

"You might want to start with the church," Trina suggested earlier, as if there might only be one in the small medieval market town, but Daphne has no other clues so she asks a traffic warden for directions to the nearest.

A bas-relief signboard atop the thatched lych-gate welcomes all to the parish church of St. Stephen's in the Vale, while inside the wooden structure the parish notice board announces that the Rev. Rollie Rowlands will conduct all manner of ecclesiastical services.

Daphne is momentarily fascinated by the conglomeration of swallows' nests hanging from the rafters before her eyes are drawn down the tunnel of ancient yew trees to the squat Norman tower of the centuries-old church, but she finds her view blocked by a man laboriously pushing his bicycle along the grave-lined path towards her.

"Sacrilegious to ride through the graveyard," explains the wheezy man as he stops to get his breath at the gate.

"The kids do it," he carries on between breaths. "No respect — no respect."

Daphne sizes him up, a man with a paunch like a ten-month pregnancy, and realizes that although his numerous chins conceal his collar he is probably the vicar.

"Rollie Rowlands, rector," he announces with an outstretched hand, dispelling any doubts as he rests his bicycle against the lych-gate. "Can I help you?"

"I'm inquiring about Janet Thurgood," says Daphne once she's introduced herself, but the big man takes off his trilby to shake his head, and Daphne has a hard job keeping her face straight as his combed-over coiffeur falls in disarray, leaving a monkish tonsure that is clearly more an act of God than Mr. Gillette.

"Sorry. Never heard of her," explains Rowlands as he tries to flatten the wispy grey strands across his pate. "But I've only been here a few years. Mrs. Drinkwater who does the flowers will know."

"You seem very sure," replies Daphne, and the reverence in Rowlands' voice borders on fear as he explains.

"Mrs. Drinkwater knows everything there is to know about this parish."

I guess that he and the flower lady have had more than a few words about the way he runs the church, Daphne is thinking and is on the point of asking where she can find the august woman when Rowlands stuffs his wayward hair under his hat and hurriedly grabs his bicycle.

"She'll be arriving in five minutes to fix up the church for a funeral," he continues, nervously checking his watch. "And if you'll excuse me, I have to leave now. Have to visit one of the parishioners — bit of an accident, sprained ankle, needs ministration. Mrs. Drinkwater will know about your woman I'm sure."

"Just one or two questions ..." starts Daphne, but Rowlands has swung a leg over his bicycle and is forcing the reluctant machine towards the roadway.

"Sorry … must dash."

"Well, I'm damned …" mutters Daphne to herself as Rowlands stands on the pedals of the old sit-up-and-beg machine, a jumble sale donation, and hauls himself away.

Daphne spends the next few minutes reading the parish magazine and bracing herself for the arrival of Mrs. Drinkwater, whom she imagines to be a big-boned matron with a booming voice. By the time the woman arrives, precisely five minutes later, she is still large in Daphne's mind, and her stature is not diminished by the fact that she is driven to the gate in a stately black Rolls-Royce.

However, despite the precision of the flower lady's arrival, Daphne is temporarily nonplussed by the appearance of a childlike figure from the front passenger seat. It is only when the wizened curmudgeon opens her mouth and yells to the uniformed chauffer, "Stop dawdling Maurice. Get those flowers into the church before they wilt," that Daphne steps forward.

"Mrs. Drinkwater?" she queries, and she's grateful that she chose a suitably serious grey tweed suit and one of her least ostentatious hats as she feels the weight of the diminutive woman's scrutiny.

"And you are?" demands the crone in an accent that totally refutes the supposed demise of the class system.

But Daphne can play that game and polishes her tone to reply. "I am Ms. Daphne Lovelace, OBE, at your service, ma'am."

"Oh!" replies the woman snottily. "That's rather pretentious of you." But she knows that she is outranked and concedes. "What exactly can I do for you, Ms. Lovelace?"

"Just call me Daphne," she suggests and waits momentarily for reciprocation.

Mrs. Drinkwater was born with a Christian name, but she rose above such familiarities when she married into money and became a lay magistrate. Even her long-deceased husband, a local brewery magnate inappropriately named

Cecil Drinkwater, only ever called her "Dear" or "My wife." And for most of her life Amelia Drinkwater has steadfastly resisted every attempt by family or friends to soften her.

"What can I do for you, Ms. Lovelace?" the flower lady reiterates coldly, and Daphne has no choice but to explain the purpose of her visit.

The name "Janet Thurgood" brings a cloud to Mrs. Drinkwater's face, and she quickly hustles Daphne under the lych-gate, as if sheltering from an expected thunderbolt, while darkly muttering, "She was an evil woman. Do you hear me? Evil."

"Evil?" echoes Daphne questioningly.

"I don't speak ill of anyone," says Mrs. Drinkwater. "But if I were ever to change my mind she'd be the first on the end of my tongue."

"Oh my goodness," breathes Daphne. "What on earth did she do?"

The tiny woman catches hold of Daphne's sleeve and draws her down with a conspiratorial whisper. "They say she murdered her children."

"Intriguing," says Daphne, her tone asking for more, but Amelia immediately backs off, crosses herself reverently, and recants. "But you never heard that from me. Everyone knows that I never speak ill of anyone."

"Naturally," replies Daphne and is tempted to push for more details, though she wonders if it's worth the risk, especially as she knows that she has a more accommodating ally in her camp.

"So, if that's all?" queries the ancient-looking woman as if daring Daphne to ask.

"Yes. Thank you very much," says Daphne realizing that she has little prospect of gaining further information. But, as Maurice the chauffeur labours past with his arms wilting under the weight of a floral display, she seizes a final opportunity. "Can I help?" she offers, hoping to penetrate

Amelia Drinkwater's barricades under a camouflage of cut arum lilies, but the funereal arranger steps in.

"No, thank you. Maurice is quite capable. Now, if you'll excuse us."

Plan B then, thinks Daphne as she heads back to the bus stop, and is not at all surprised to find Mrs. Jenkins taking the return trip.

"Everything all right at the doctor's?" she queries mischievously and smiles at the confused look on the other woman's face.

It's nearly five by the time that Daphne opens a can of Purr for Missie Rouge, puts the kettle on for a pot of her favourite tea, and picks up the phone.

Eight hours' time difference, she mentally calculates before dialling, but she's forced to leave a message. Normality has returned to Trina's world, and she's on her daily round of bringing cheer to the elderly residents of North Vancouver.

"I see the old pecker is looking up this morning," the homecare nurse jests as she showers Mr. Howlins.

The eighty-five-year-old beams toothlessly. "Not my fault, Trina. You could straighten a corkscrew with that smile of yours."

"Yeah, right." She laughs, giving his appendage a friendly tap. "I bet you say that to all the girls."

"Once upon a time," he replies. "Once upon a time." And ten minutes later, with the old man tucked under a blanket in front of a warm fire, she's on her way to clean up Mrs. Stewart.

"Sorry, had a bit of an accident in the bed," says the septuagenarian without getting out of her chair.

"What a surprise," mutters Trina *sotto voce*, saying aloud, "Never mind, accidents happen."

"Do they, dear?"

"Every day apparently," mumbles Trina as she pulls on rubber gloves and heads for the bedroom.

Back in Westchester, Daphne Lovelace pours herself a cup of Keemun tea musing, "It's the Queen's favourite," and tries another phone call with Plan B in mind.

"Allo," answers a foreign-voiced female, once Daphne has been connected to the apartment of David Bliss in St-Juan-sur-Mer on the French Côte d'Azur.

"Is that you, Daisy?" queries the Englishwoman, recognizing Bliss's Gallic companion, and within seconds she is talking to the man himself: Chief Inspector David Bliss, Scotland Yard detective turned author.

"David. How's the old novel coming along?"

"It's not easy, Daphne," he says, but is too polite to add, Especially when people keep interrupting me. Instead he asks, "So, what can I do for you?"

"Janet Thurgood …" begins Daphne, then she gives a brief account of her meeting with Amelia Drinkwater.

"Just this once," Bliss warns, once he's taken a few notes. "Try bugging Superintendent Donaldson at Westchester police station if you want anything else. I'm trying to work."

"David. You sound cross with me."

He softens with a laugh. "Not really. It's just that I didn't realize how difficult it was to write a book. And the commissioner has only given me a year off."

"Sorry."

"Don't worry. I'll make some inquiries and get back to you."

RCMP Inspector Mike Phillips in Vancouver is also making inquiries. Janet's hasty departure from Trina's basement suite can mean only thing, especially in Sergeant Brougham's mind. "Why else would she have run?" he demands, spreading his hands wide to invite suggestions, but while most ten-year-olds might easily come up with a dozen possible reasons for a person not wishing to be interviewed by the police, Sergeant Brougham has one and doesn't await contradiction. "She shoved him over the top, bet my pension."

"It was a heart attack," reminds Phillips, but that doesn't stop Brougham.

"Yeah, well, anyone would have a heart attack if they're chucked down a basement into a fish tank."

Phillips lays a cautionary hand on Brougham's shoulder. "Dave, think about it. Roddy Montgomery was twice — correction, three times — the size of this woman. You saw her, for Chrissakes, she'd have a job pushing a few grams of pot. How the hell could she have pushed him over those railings?"

"You just wait till the DNA results come back," continues Brougham, unfazed. "I'd bet my old granny that she was the one who attacked him. She certainly fits his description."

"So do half the hookers and druggies of Vancouver, Dave. Anyway, the DNA will take at least a week, perhaps two. We'd better find her before that."

The finding of Janet Thurgood has been on Trina's mind all morning, and with her daily doses of diarrhea and vomit behind her, the homecare nurse flipped through the section on disguises in her private eye's manual and prepared for a sortie into Vancouver's underworld.

Now she makes a final check of herself in the mirror, as suggested, and smiles at the result. A Yankees baseball cap, a pair of shades, and black lipstick top off her eye-popping luminous orange T-shirt, and a black leather miniskirt decorated with a rhinestone heart over the left buttock tops off a pair of fishnet stockings. The ensemble, confiscated from Kylie's closet, would be fine for a June evening, and she almost makes it to the front door before it dawns on her that it's late November, so she slings on an enormous faux mink that not only conceals most of her costume but makes the baseball cap and shades look ridiculous.

While Chief Inspector David Bliss might grumble about interruptions to his work, he is not at all ungrateful. In fact, he is quickly discovering that, in common with most authors, he will do absolutely anything other than write. After nearly three months of counting lemons on the tree beneath his balcony, luring gulls with tidbits, and staring for hour upon hour at the undulating sea, he is grateful for a valid excuse to put down his pen and get his teeth into an investigation.

"So what have you got?" asks Daphne excitedly when Bliss calls back in less than half an hour.

"Does the name Joseph Crispin Creston mean anything to you?"

"You mean the Creston chocolate guy?"

"That's the one," says Bliss, then puts on a deep tone to emulate a fifties TV commercial and adds, "We make the best chocolates in the universe. Just ask J.C. himself."

"That takes me back a bit," laughs Daphne.

"Well, I think that was actually Creston Sr. His son is the big boy now when it comes to worldwide chocolate trading. And I mean big. Though it seems he's been switching stock to diet products since the flab-fighters took over the world."

"He can't lose then, can he?" laughs Daphne. "But what's his connection to Trina's lost woman?"

"Janet Thurgood," muses Bliss aloud. "And I have no way of knowing if it's the same Janet Thurgood for sure, but Joseph C. Creston Jr. married someone of that name in the late fifties, early sixties. I could probably get someone to dig up the marriage records. Get Trina to find out the date of birth or parents' name of the woman in Vancouver —"

"Too late, David," cuts in Daphne. "The woman's on the run again."

"That's it then."

"But what about the dead babies?"

"Oh yeah. Well, that's the clue. Creston Jr. and his wife had three children in four years and they all died of cot deaths."

"Cot deaths?" breathes Daphne.

"Sudden Infant Death Syndrome, it's called now, and doctors are pretty hot at trying to establish the cause, but back in the fifties and sixties it was just accepted that babies sometimes died for no apparent reason."

Daphne feels a shiver up her spine as the words of Amelia Drinkwater come back to her. "I was told that she murdered them," she says with a suitably sinister tone, but Bliss has no knowledge.

"There's no record either of them were ever charged with any offence," he says. "But you could ask Superintendent Donaldson to dig up the files locally — if they haven't been destroyed."

"So, what happened to her? Creston's wife," Daphne wants to know.

"You'd have to ask him."

"I might just do that," Daphne replies, her mind beginning to whirl with possibilities as she puts down the phone and searches for Trina's number again.

David Bliss's number is on the radar screen in London. A criminal record search originating from a foreign source has raised a flag in the criminal intelligence section at Scotland Yard, and he gets a call from the duty commander, Chief Superintendent Michael Edwards.

"I thought you were supposed to be on a leave of absence," snorts the senior officer.

"That's correct, sir, working on my novel."

"Writing a book!" It could be a question, but it's not. It's a sneer, an unspoken disparagement that Bliss catches onto immediately: *Whatever next? We're supposed to be running a f'kin police force not a cultural establishment.*

"New trend, sir, police intelligence," explains Bliss, knowing the other man will steam at the implied oxymoron.

"How come you're doing criminal record checks then?" snaps the chief superintendent, and Bliss waffles for a few minutes about the possibility of the Creston family being somehow involved in his plot before cutting the call short.

"Sorry. Must get on," he says as he starts to put down the phone. "Anyway, I was wrong. It had nothing to do with Joseph Creston."

"Joseph Crispin Creston Jr. Now that's a name destined for greatness," the chocolate magnate's father trumpeted at his son's christening party, apparently ignorant of the fact that he bore the identical moniker. "It's powerful, memorable, suggestive of aristocracy," the suave executive pompously declared at London's Grosvenor Hotel in the run-up to war with Hitler. Shortly thereafter, with Londoners frantically digging Anderson shelters and preparing to hunker down in the Blitz, most men of Jospeh Creston Sr.'s age strapped on Sam Browne belts and officer's pistols. But the cocoa tycoon, together with his family and entourage, slipped aboard a two-hundred-foot private yacht registered in Casablanca and slunk off to his estates on the west coast of Africa.

"Chocolate is essential for the morale of our troops," he declared in a letter of justification mailed to the *Times* as they put into Lisbon for refuelling en route, though, as records later showed, it was never completely clear in Creston's mind as to which side's troops needed boosting most.

But Creston's empire wasn't the only one that profited even-handedly from the global hostilities. He was even able to justify it in his own mind. "Should the sins of the fathers be visited on their sons?" he questioned of anyone in the know. "Why shouldn't poor little German kids have a treat? And what of the thousands of workers in the plantations who can't read and have no radio? What do the crazy politics of a feudal Europe have to do with them? They just want to make enough money to feed their families."

Little has changed in more than fifty years; chocolate is chocolate, as alluring and addictive as ever, though penny for penny it is cheaper than it's ever been.

"It's all a question of supply and demand," the younger Mr. Creston will happily tell anyone interested today, and he is proud of the fact that his empire controls both. He might also concede, with a beam of self-satisfaction, that the Creston empire is richer and more powerful than it has ever been, though he may be more reticent in admitting that the policies of his company have broken the backs, and the dreams, of the West African farmers who labour alongside their children to provide his factories with their raw material.

"Two dollars a day may not seem a lot to some people," insists Joseph Creston as he addresses his weekly board meeting atop his glass tower in the centre of London. "But if only these people would stop warring, we'd probably be able to pay more."

It's a lie, and Creston knows it; he knows that constant conflicts prevent the subsistence farmers from ever forming any kind of stable collective.

"They'd only waste it on the demon drink if they had more," sneers Robert Dawes, Creston's company accountant, oblivious to the fact that he has supped his way through half a bottle of single malt in the past twelve hours.

It's 10:00 a.m. in one of the richest square miles of real estate in the world: the City of London. The British Empire may have crumbled, but echoes of its power still reverberate around the world, and in the boardroom of Creston Enterprises, a boardroom where "morning prayers" actually means morning prayers and where the teachings of the Bible take precedence over the balance sheet — but never over the bottom line — Joseph and his congregants discuss current business trends.

However, one contemporary movement has never, and will never, be discussed: "Just how many of the Disciples were women?" The Crestons, both senior and junior, might challenge anyone who suggested such apparent sacrilege, as the staid portraits around the boardroom walls show. The most recent — Joseph Crispin Creston Jr., the man of the moment — depicts a face that falls somewhere between the dour sagacity of Prince Charles and the virginal boyishness of Richard Branson: a man of the past trying to look into the future.

But Creston Jr. is struggling with the future as he sits at one end of the table that his father cut from a single West African mahogany. "It was the biggest damn tree in the world," Creston Sr. proudly insisted as he added the enormous hardwood to his trophy collection, alongside tigers and elephants.

"Organics and Fair Trade," advocate the research papers on the giant table in front of the board members, and Creston immediately scoffs.

"Fair … we are fair. Let's face it, who's going to pay five dollars for a bar of chocolate so some Ivory Coast cocoa farmer can hammer around his fields in a Hummer?"

"It's definitely a growing fad," observes John Mason, Creston's second-in-command and company lawyer. But the man at the head of the table is unimpressed.

"Yes. And we will remain fair within the context of the average wage. Anyway, like Robert says, they'd only drink it. Surely it's better for us to use the profits to fund the development of churches than to let them piss it down the drain."

"Steal from the poor and give to the rich," could be Creston's motto; after all it's the rich who need the money to buy his products. "In any case," he continues to preach, "how will it benefit them if we fail to make a profit?"

The poor may inherit the earth in the freely distributed Creston Bibles, but with the world's raw cocoa market concentrated in the hands of just a few powerful manufacturers, Creston and his fellow moguls will dine on the fat.

The cream of Joseph C. Creston's personal holdings includes Creston Hall, his mansion in Dewminster, and Daphne Lovelace, armed with the scant information obtained from David Bliss, has taken the bus back to the town and peeps through the wrought iron gates like a Dickensian waif peering wistfully at the grand Victorian house, wondering what great treasures and what dreadful secrets may lie therein.

The estate was built at the turn of the century by Joseph's father on the backs of peasant cocoa farmers, and has been supported similarly ever since. Creston Sr., a man who, to listen to him, tamed the tropics of Africa to bring chocolate to the masses, was, he claimed, a compassionate, God-fearing man, but whether a slave is subjugated by a whip or a Bible the result is much the same.

Janet Thurgood's family estate at 255 Arundel Crescent bears no comparison to Creston Hall, though Daphne gets a friendly reception at the front door of the modest house in the twitchy-curtained neighbourhood. The butter-coloured sandstone houses, solidly constructed just before the Great Depression, were built in a pastoral landscape that soon turned to Tarmac. Skylarks and nightingales were silenced by the roar of Spitfires and Lancasters, and despite assurances to the contrary, no sheep would ever peacefully graze again. Once the wartime debris was cleared, concrete council houses and towering flats blocked the surrounding sky.

"Long before my time," Jean Bentwhistle, the present owner, claims as she bounces one baby while a toddler clings to her legs. "I wasn't even born till sixty-one, dear. But you're welcome to come in and look around."

With little to be gained from an inspection, Daphne decides to try the neighbours and hits an elderly couple at number 259.

"The Thurgoods?" questions Mrs. Jones loudly as she shouts the name to her husband.

"I'm not sure ..." starts the man as he tries ineffectually to hold up his sagging trousers, but the tone suggests a tacit awareness and Daphne pushes on.

"Janet Thurgood. She lived at 255 until she married Mr. Creston."

"Oh ... her," sneers Mrs. Jones. "The so-called religious one." And Daphne doesn't need to ask more.

Now David Bliss is back on Daphne's target list.

"Do you know how difficult it is to write a book?" he asks angrily when she wants him to find out more about Janet.

"You had a perfectly good job in the police," she reminds him.

"And I'll have to go back to it if you don't stop pestering me. Although I doubt they'll take me if I keep getting caught doing unauthorized searches."

"Oh, David ..." she begs sweetly.

"I'll see what I can do," he says, and secretly he's delighted to shelve his manuscript. It has been more than a week since he's written anything of note. The true identity of the Man in the Iron Mask still evades him. He is even beginning to lose faith in his hypothesis that the prisoner was a seventeenth-century aristocrat who had his head encased in iron just to prove how much he loved a woman. Surely it's too far-fetched for a man to declare, "I will build you a dream château and I will sit in this cell for eternity if necessary, but no one will ever speak to me or look upon my face until you agree to be mine."

It is bizarre, Bliss admits to himself, but he can't get away from the fact that literature and histories are full of parallels: I'll climb the highest mountain, swim the widest ocean, throw myself to the waves, build you the Taj Mahal.

It was the exuberant era of Louis XIV when the lovestruck man locked his heart away and turned his back on all temptations; a time when, for those rich enough or corrupt enough, anything was possible. It was a period of grandiose architecture and lavish design, clothes and footwear so elaborate and ostentatious women couldn't move in them, outrageous food like lark's tongue pie and roast peacock. Above all, it was a time of great romanticism. *My theory is still valid*, Bliss tells himself, despite the fact that it has some major holes. The Château Roger was certainly built in 1687, according to the inscription on the gate pillar, the same year as the masked man's incarceration, and the geographic location puts it directly across the strait from the fortress. The size of the famous prisoner's cell suggests that he was not an ordinary inmate, and the murals on the wall, presumably penned by him, depict a joyous gathering, like a wedding.

But with more than half of the manuscript piled on to his desk, Bliss has hit a sold wall: why wasn't the seventeenth-century romantic successful? Who was the woman and where was she?

A similar question is being asked of Janet Thurgood in Vancouver, where the missing woman still tops the wanted person's list.

"Where the hell could she be?" demands Dave Brougham as he sits down with Mike Phillips and Constable Paul Zelke, and all eyes turn northwards to the mountains and the distant community of Beautiful.

"It's a bit of a hangover from the sixties," explains Zelke, the force's expert on religious cults and sects. "It was originally set up by a bunch of American anti-war existentialists more interested in staying high than avoiding the draft. They really worshipped Dylan, Che Guevara, and Castro, but they somehow wrapped it up in a sort of revolutionary religiosity; let's face it, almost anyone can see God through a haze of blue smoke."

"Yeah," laughs Brougham. "The only real difference between Mother Theresa and Marilyn Monroe is a bottle of rye and a couple of joints."

"Franz Kafka was their hero really," continues Zelke more seriously as he flicks through his notes. "David and Goliath; small men taking on the world. But there's no overall logic as far as I can see. Shit, Nietzsche was an atheist and they even twisted his ideas into it somehow."

"How do they get away with it?" asks Inspector Phillips as he tries to understand.

"Charismatic leader; usually the long-haired one with a guitar and a line on a regular supply of coke or other shit. Wayne Browning, a low-life from the southern United States, quickly took over, and most of the other men either grew up or blew out their brains, leaving him with all the women."

"And they never caught on?"

"You'll believe anything if you want to, Mike. It's like sending money to those nuts on television 'cuz God wants you to."

"So, what happens there now?"

"We've kinda given up, to be honest. Mr. and Mrs. Taxpayer wouldn't be too happy about us spending a bunch of money infiltrating a place like that. We've got a tap on his phones; we hear the odd rumours about kiddie abuse. It's odds-on that Browning has his pick of the young virgins as they leave the nest —"

"That's gotta be illegal," breaks in Brougham, but Zelke has heard it before.

"No different from any of the other communes, Dave. We'd take them on, but the world doesn't need another Waco or Jonestown."

Janet Thurgood knows nothing of the apocalyptic disasters in Guyana and Texas nor anything else that happened in the world beyond Beautiful for the forty years she was there — Wayne Browning made sure of that. And now, as she scavenges in the shadowy lanes of Vancouver's Chinatown, she is more than ever convinced that she has somehow slipped through a galactic wormhole. It should be 1953; in Janet's mind it is 1953. She is an eleven-year-old crying for her mother and crying over the loss of her precious Jesus.

"Our father who art in heaven, hallowed be thy name," she mumbles as she squirrels into a garbage bin behind a restaurant, and then she mentally runs a list of childhood facts as she seeks security.

"Once two is two; two twos are ... Twelve pennies in a shilling; twenty shillings in a pound ... Ring a ring o' roses ... The Queen is Elizabeth the second. Her official birthday is ... Her real birthday is ...

"Why can't I have two birthdays, Mummy?"

"That would be greedy, Janet."

"Is the Queen greedy, Mummy?"

"Get to your knees and pray that God didn't hear you."

"Our father ..."

The vivid memories and rambling mutterings continue as she searches for her past, for food, and for her crucifix. The loss of her precious icon worries her most. It's the crutch she has carried with her from childhood. Without it, she knows that she is forever lost.

chapter four

The West African rainy season is the subject of jubilation around the boardroom table at Creston headquarters in London.

"Looks like the crop from Ivory will be above expectations," croons Dawes, surveying the latest data from the man on the ground.

Joseph Creston is less optimistic. "Assuming the Muslims don't invade and destroy it."

"Why worry," retorts Dawes, ever the accountant. "It'll just push up the price of our Ghanaian and Nigerian output."

November in the coastal rainforests of southern Côte d'Ivoire may mean constant downpours, but along the southerly coast of mainland Europe, where the French Alps stumble heavily into the Mediterranean, brilliant sunshine still turns the beaches to gold and the clear cobalt sea mirrors the sky.

Detective Chief Inspector David Bliss is walking — hour after hour, mile after mile — seeking inspiration to complete his novel.

"Well, just how hard can it be?" he chastised Samantha, his lawyer daughter, when she questioned both his ability and his sanity. But now, as he wanders home along the deserted promenade in St-Juan-sur-Mer, he peers across the bay to the island of Ste. Marguerite and wonders whether or not he will ever be able to convince skeptical readers that he really has discovered the secret of the island's most notorious prisoner — the Man in the Iron Mask.

Despite the touch of warmth in the limpid afternoon air, the quays and beaches are silent, apart from the occasional screech of a hungry gull; the restaurants and beach-side bars are padlocked and boarded up. The transient workers of summer have been drawn north into the alpine ski resorts by the scent of money, and only a few arthritic and bronchitic Brits, desperate to escape the lugubrious English winter, wander in search of a fish and chip shop and a recent copy of the *Daily Mirror*.

Most of the apartments in Bliss's building in St-Juan-sur-Mer are as vacant as the beaches, and since his arrival at the beginning of September he has only twice spied another occupant. The whirring of the elevator usually signals the arrival of Daisy, the bubbly Provençale real estate agent whose company and bed he has been sharing for a while. *Isn't this what you wanted?* he has asked himself a dozen times. *Somewhere where you won't be disturbed.*

"I 'ave just zhe place for you," Daisy enthused with a glint in her eye. "No one will know you are here — except for me," she added, and at first the arrangement seemed perfect.

The sound of the elevator signals Daisy's approach — the third time today — and Bliss can't help thinking that he would have had more privacy had he stayed in London. But this is where it happened; this is where Louis XIV's legendary prisoner spent eleven years of his life locked in solitary confinement with his guards forbidden to see him or speak to him on pain of death.

"Maybe he was trying to write a book," muses Bliss wryly while he waits for Daisy's cheerful greeting as she lets herself in, although he knows that was not the case; he knows that the wretched man was consumed day and night by one thing alone: the love of the woman who owned his heart. He was waiting, day after day, month after month — waiting and praying that she would come to set him free.

"Hello, Daavid," Daisy calls in her heavily accented English. "I 'ave brought you zhe dinner."

"In here," he calls from the airy room that leads onto the balcony, the room where he has set up his writing station and where he can keep in view the masked prisoner's island fortress across the bay.

"*Terrine de volaille*," Daisy announces triumphantly as she places the dish of chicken on the table. Then she drapes herself around his neck, asking, "How iz zhe book today? Good, no?"

"No … yes … I don't know," answers Bliss despondently. "I'm beginning to think this was a huge mistake."

"Never mind," Daisy trills with a suggestive kiss. "Maybe we can do somezhing else."

Distractions, distractions, distractions, he muses to himself as he picks at the food, but at least he's grateful that he has escaped the television. "You must have satellite," Daisy insisted when he complained that more than ten minutes of translating the quickly spoken French on the local stations gave him a headache. "You can have maybe two hundred American channels."

"Terrific," he replied, but came to his senses within the hour.

"What is zhe matter, Daavid?" queries Daisy, sensing tension, and Bliss wishes he had a sensible answer; he wishes he knew why his enthusiasm is draining, why he has lost his drive.

"I don't know ..." starts the English detective, then he scuttles to the balcony and peers at the distant verdant islands. The fortress — the Fort Royal on the island of Ste. Marguerite — stands out sharply and appears strikingly forbidding as the wintry sun slips behind the island and heads for the depths of the Mediterranean. The wind is shifting to the north, kicking up whitecaps and darkening the sea from warm azure to bleak indigo, and goosebumps suddenly pepper his thighs as the chill hits.

The sound of Daisy's breath spins him. "What is wrong, Daavid?"

"It's getting cold," he says, though knows that is not the real reason for the goosebumps. "He is still there," he adds after a moment's thought as pulses of energy make a *whooshing* sound in his brain and raise his hackles.

"Who?"

"The Man in the Iron Mask — *l'homme au masque de fer*."

"Daavid, zhat was three hundred years ago."

"This is really weird," he carries on as he focuses on the fortress. "If I told anyone in the force about this they'd have me in front of a shrink and out on mental disability in a week."

"Daavid, zhere is nothing zhere," says Daisy, pointing across the bay to the island. "It is just a museum now."

Bliss knows different, though he still can't explain the powerful feeling that washed over him the first time he entered the cell that housed the famous prisoner. "It was like he was talking to me ... guiding me ... begging me to write his story," he explains, as he has explained many times before. "But now I've lost it. I don't what I'm doing anymore ... don't know how it ends."

"It will be all right —" she starts, but he cuts her off, shaking his head.

"No ... no ... no," he says, and then he spots the lemon tree in the garden below. "Watch," he commands, dragging Daisy to the edge of the balcony and pointing to the loaded tree.

"What?"

"Nothing happened, did it?"

She peers intently, thinking, *I missed somezhing.* "What is it, Daavid?"

"The first time I looked a lemon dropped off."

"They drop all the time."

"No, they don't. That's my point. I've been watching it for weeks now and I've never seen another, not while I was actually watching. But the first time, at the instant I looked, a lemon fell."

"But what does zhat mean?"

"It was like a signal, the start: a green flag, a cannon shot, a whistle."

"Start what?"

"The race — my race — to discover the identity of the Man in the Iron Mask. Everything here has been guiding me ..." he pauses as he loses direction and searches across the bay for his bearings.

"Are you all right, Daavid?"

"See, even you think I'm going mad now."

"No," she says, but her concerned mien tells him something else as he turns away from the island to look into her eyes.

"I have to go," he says quietly. "I have to go now."

"But, zhe dinner ..."

"I'm sorry ... " he says as the apartment's door closes behind him, and Daisy wipes a tear from her cheek before turning back to the island with a sinking feeling.

chapter five

Superintendent Ted Donaldson is doing his best to support the world's beleaguered carb producers as he battles his way through the dinner buffet at the Mitre Hotel in Westchester. "To be honest, Daphne," he tells his old friend between the linguine and the shepherd's pie, "I'd retire tomorrow, but the little lady has been cooking up a to-do list since the day we were wed."

"That's why I always avoided marriage," lies Daphne. "No lists for me; no expectations, no disappointments, never having to say sorry."

"Never understood that myself," confesses Donaldson with a laugh. "I love Mrs. Donaldson, but I've spent my whole damn life apologizing for something or other. Anyway, what did you want?"

"What makes you think I want something …" she begins, and then stops as he raises his eyebrows.

"First clue: you're a woman."

"All right," she admits, then briefly outlines the supposedly shady past of Janet Thurgood.

"Way before my time," he says as he picks at his shepherd's pie.

"I asked David Bliss, but he's too wrapped up in that book he's writing."

"And his little French chambermaid," suggests Donaldson with a wink.

Bliss isn't wrapped up with Daisy at all. Moonbeams may be sparkling off the Mediterranean, but the light is cold as he wanders the deserted promenade of St-Juan-sur-Mer. The island fortress is just a shadowy smudge on the horizon, and he turns his back on it as he peers up at the promontory and tries to find the Château Roger through the eucalyptus and palms. The dilapidated building is there, he knows, but even in daylight he would struggle. But he doesn't need to see it. He feels it and questions himself, *Do you honestly believe in past lives?*

Lots of people do, sensible, sane people who may try to deny it even to themselves, but why this compunction to reveal the identity of the masked man unless he's there, inside you, saying, "You must tell my story to the world; the greatest love story ever told. It is time."

Maybe it's just my excuse. Maybe I'm just trying to escape from the police.

You want to escape? Get a job; be a plumber or an electrician. Do something creative.

Oh yeah. Have tools will travel. That's really exciting. Anyway, writing is creative.

Five hours slip by like a long night's drive as he wanders the darkened boulevards and quays, and when he eventually wakes up his mind he searches in vain for memories of the road. It's nearing two in the morning when he opens his apartment's door and breathes in relief at the empty bed. He checks the garden from the balcony — no lemons. But would he spot one in the moonlight?

What do you want? What are you looking for?

"I want answers," he says as he peers across the promontory for signs of the dark château that dragged him into the mystery in the first place.

Greg Grimes, a potter with piercing blue eyes and bushy blonde hair who threw little pots on a wheel every evening on the promenade, was the trigger. He was scruffy and unshaved, but he had a certain magnetism that drove women wild. Bliss would stand most summer evenings in the balmy air, watching in wonder as the English artisan moulded ceramic white elephants — midget ashtrays, egg cups, vases, and candle holders — for a google-eyed audience of women.

"It is free, *gratuit*," the charismatic potter would say as he offered each freshly minted gem to a different young woman, but his begging bowl always overflowed, until someone roughly amputated his hand one night and left him to the rats in the Château Roger's basement.

That was more than a year ago, and although the stores are filled with pots from Picasso's town of Vallauris, high on the hill above St-Juan-sur-Mer, none carry with them the love that Grimes infused into his tiny master-pieces. However, the lustre on a floppy wet clay pot quickly wears off, and most of the little treasures that warmed a heart one evening would be flushed down the hotel toilet by the next morning. And with much of the plumbing dating back almost to Napoleon, the entire system would be gummed up in no time.

Bliss's suggestion that the hoteliers should affix a notice to each toilet was dismissed with typical Gallic disdain as "*autant pisser dans un violon*," or as much use as pissing into a violin, and irate members of L'ssociation des hôteliers de St-Juan were the prime suspects in the potter's mutilation. However, as Bliss was to discover, a much more sinister organization took the man's hand.

I have to go back in there, Bliss tells himself with little enthusiasm as he stares in the direction of the building. He knows that it won't be easy; since his previous incursion more than a year ago in search of the wounded potter, the custodians have redoubled their efforts to keep trespassers out. But inwardly, he knows that it isn't the security guards bothering him. He knows he can walk the twisted hills surrounding the château and expect only polite nods from the muscled men in dark suits while they whisper, "Zhat is the famous Scotland Yard detective who is writing a book."

Bothering him are the thousands of tortured souls that he stumbled over in the dungeons beneath the derelict building: souls of resistance fighters, Jews, gypsies, and anyone else who stepped on Adolf Hitler's toes. Even inconvenient husbands, ex-lovers, or business rivals, denounced as "traitors to the fatherland" with poison pens, were whisked out of their beds at dawn with a one-way ticket to Auschwitz or Buchenwald — if they survived the first stop in the château's notorious torture chambers.

The château hides itself in the darkness as Bliss questions, *What am I trying to prove? The widows and orphans of the victims don't want me prying into their cellars; they don't want an invasion of neo-nazi relic hunters digging up their past.*

"*Ce château et un panier des crabes*, a basket of crabs," Daisy claimed, and none of his discoveries changed that. But now, as he flounders in search of an ending for his novel, he can't help thinking that the ruined château holds the key.

Vancouver, British Columbia, has its share of derelict buildings, though none whose age or black history comes close to the Château Roger. However, no more than a salmon's leap from the waterfront hotels and glitzy restaurants that line the Fraser River is an abandoned warehouse that attracts the losers in life's lottery. Potheads, hookers, mainliners, pimps, and alcoholics all seek shelter from a harsh world under its leaking iron roof, while a shanty city of those still holding out hope grows outside its walls.

"Let's try down there," suggests Trina, dragging her husband into a tight alleyway littered with boxes and bags, the homes of the homeless, behind the warehouse.

Rick hangs back, "I don't —"

"Come on. They're only people," she calls as she surges ahead with a five-dollar bill in hand.

"I'm looking for a woman," says Trina as she squats by the side of an aging Jesus look-alike.

"So am I," he replies as the embers in his eyes briefly ignite, and he begins to reach out for her face.

Trina nudges him, laughing. "Cheeky." Then she gives him a brief description of Janet.

"Maybe," he says at the mention of Janet's head scarf, and Trina catches on.

"How much?" she begins, exchanging her five for a twenty, but Rick is quickly on her shoulder.

"Don't," he hisses. "Not until he tells you."

"OK," she says. She rips the bill in half, thrusts the Queen's head into the dropout's face, and puts on a mobster's tone. "The rest when I find her, awl'right?"

"Brilliant," complains Rick five minutes later when all the leads have fizzled and the bum has taken off.

"So? He hasn't got the dough."

"Neither have we," Rick is moaning when Trina spots a pile of cardboard boxes against a brick outhouse and senses a presence.

"Shh ..." she whispers, pulls Janet's crucifix from her bag, and gingerly advances like a vampire hunter. "Janet?" she coos. "Janet?" A brown head scarf appears.

The chase is short. Janet is too weak to struggle, and as Trina escorts her towards the car she says soothingly, "Don't worry. We won't tell the police where you are."

Behind her, playing backstop, Rick mutters under his breath, "You could get us five years for this."

Rick Button's warning seems likely to come to fruition the moment they take Janet into their house and Kylie sings out, "Mum, Dad, police on the phone."

"Let me," says Trina, grabbing it from her husband, but she instantly relaxes. "It's only Mike Phillips," she says with her hand over the mouthpiece as the inspector explains that he's been in touch with an officer who specializes in cults and sects.

"You know the sort of thing," he elucidates. "Twenty-year-old heiress runs off and gives everything to God, who turns out to be some freaky-haired junkie with a Bible."

"I don't think Janet has anything —" Trina begins, but he cuts her off.

"Not now she doesn't. That's my point. But she may have done. Anyway, Officer Zelke wants to talk to you."

"Hey," shouts Rob from the basement as he turns up the volume on the television. "It sounds like the stick insect."

"The RCMP and Vancouver police are searching for a woman wanted in the death of one of their own ..."

"Turn it off," shouts Rick, but Janet seems oblivious as she caresses her crucifix and rocks herself comfortingly on a kitchen chair.

"What makes you think she's from a cult?" Trina questions Paul Zelke from the quiet of her bedroom a few minutes later.

"Daena," he asks succinctly. "Is that what she calls herself?"

"Yeah. Daena XV."

"Thought so. There's a whole bunch of women in a joint they call Beautiful and they all reckon they're Daena. It's a religious freak show, usual stuff: polygamy, incest, child abuse. All ordained from on high, all in the Bible. But so is stoning gays and adulteresses to death, though we kinda frown on that today."

"Why do you think Janet is from there?"

"We got a call a couple of days ago from the jerk who runs the place. His name's Wayne Browning, though he calls himself The Saviour. Anyway, he gave a false ID, but we know it was him, and he seemed pretty keen to find her."

Wayne Browning isn't keen on finding Janet, he's desperate, and so is Janet's husband, the man who originally sent her there.

"I pay you," shouts Joseph Creston into the phone. "Keep her there, keep her quiet. Is that such a problem?"

"Forty years," Browning shoots back.

"Yes. And what I've paid you would keep her for another forty. I've funded that place."

"Yeah, but you've not done so badly out of it."

"That's not the point. Find her. Get her back."

"It may not be that easy," Browning admits before revealing that Creston is not the only one who wants his wife. "She's supposed to have killed a cop."

The international line goes dead as Creston analyzes the new data and crunches the numbers.

"All right. This may not be bad," he is saying as he thinks of the very last time that he saw her: a snivelling wretch on the edge of life following the death of her third child. "I love you. I'll always do the best for you," he said before she was whisked away to be put aboard the company jet. "You'll get help where you are going."

"Maybe she needs more than you can give her," he tells Browning. "Maybe they'll help her."

"She was OK when she wuz here," complains Browning, seeing Creston's funding slipping away.

"And so she ran away?"

"She's confused, she doesn't know what she's doing or saying, she's kinda lost her mind."

"Perhaps she needs a psychiatrist?" suggests Creston, then questions himself, *What if she recalls too much?* "What does she remember?" he asks guardedly.

"Hard to tell; all she does is pray."

"So, the chances are they would think that she is a little unstable?"

"Sir, your wife's a nut. You know that."

"She's still my wife," Creston insists sharply, then comes to a decision. "Hire someone ... a private detective, a pro, money's no object. I want her kept out of jail. Do you understand?"

"Yep."

"And I want her found."

Bliss is still searching, still seeking direction as he prowls the quays and streets of St-Juan-sur-Mer. His manuscript is shrinking daily as he pares off one implausible scene after another while trying to find a point of historical solidity from which to build his ending. His sticking point is that the fortress on the island of Ste. Marguerite, the Fort Royal, wasn't the first prison to house Louis XIV's famous masked prisoner, and neither was it the last.

The sight of the majestic cliff-top building rising out of the Mediterranean stops Bliss as dawn arrives with a crimson slash across the horizon and the sea shifts from cobalt to azure. "That's what I call impressive," he muses as if the show has been orchestrated just for him.

The smell of hot bread and croissants draws him from the scene to his favourite boulangerie just off the promenade, and as he sidles through the narrow doorway of the ancient bakery, he's salivating. A blonde-haired woman with her mind on her breakfast nearly butts him as she meets him headfirst in the doorway.

"*Pardonnez-moi,*" he mumbles, stepping back.

She glances up momentarily to reply, "*Merci.*"

If their eyes meet for a nanosecond neither notices, and Bliss is already at the counter silently practising his order, *Deux croissants, s'il vous plait*, before he feels a tingle of unease.

"*Bonjour, monsieur,*" calls Marie, the baker's little wife, her beaming grin barely making it over the mounds of warm bread and pastries.

"*Bonjour …*" he begins, though stops abruptly when he finds his gaze locked onto the spiralling coils of a *pain aux raisins*, his mind spinning as he thinks of the woman.

"*Monsieur?*" queries the rotund woman with a smile, but he's stuck in the swirling coils of the sticky pastry, trying to fathom who she was.

"And how is zhe writing, *monsieur?*"

Around and around goes his mind — she must be a local, just a familiar face. Then he stops and catches up to Marie. Disastrous; terrible; feel like giving up. The words are there but they won't take shape amid his confusion, then a prod from behind jump-starts him.

"Sorry. Very good, thanks, coming along nicely."

Marie smiles in relief as she takes his order and adds a complementary shortbread in celebration of his apparent success. "It must be very nice to be famous, is it not?" she continues chattily, happy to practise her English.

"I am not famous," he protests, but she stops him with a floury hand.

"Here, everyone, they say to me, 'How is zhe famous number one English writer today?' And I say, 'He is very good.'" The she leans in closely to add. "But I know zhat you are also zhe detective who finds zhe secret of *l'homme au masque de fer.*"

"The Man in the Iron Mask," murmurs Bliss as he sits on the quay wall eating breakfast, but his mind is still on the woman in the baker's doorway as he looks ahead at the infamous island through a forest of yacht masts.

The flotilla of million-dollar boats, neglected since September, bobs idly in the lazy water of the harbour. It is

a nautical ghost town. Most of the crews have switched uniforms and now serve the same well-heeled masters, this time
as lift operators and chalet girls in the alpine ski resorts,
although many of the flashier yachts and their owners have
followed the sun to the Caribbean or Seychelles.

Thoughts of the woman burn like a slow fuse as Bliss
wanders the deserted quays once he's finished eating. "For
Sale" signs occasionally pull him up and he muses on the
possibility of buying something modest and escaping
completely, but he knows that even modesty comes at a
premium here. And he's well aware that most of the owners
are simply trying to rid themselves of an expensive toy
before they are drawn back by the arrival of spring.

"Just one more year, get our money's worth," they'll
convince themselves as they begrudgingly pay for a refit
and paint job before hiring a crew.

Bliss scans the boats hoping to glimpse the woman,
thinking she could be a crew member, but there are no
blondes today. Blondes are the creatures of summer: northern
European crew members and ditzy starlets on the make.

It is winter and the olive-skinned locals have taken
back their town, though Bliss sees few of them working.
Most of the dark-haired, dark-eyed men and women sit
around in the few bars that still bother to open and wait for
spring. Their euphoria following the departure of the
summer vacationers has waned since the realization that
the visitors took off with the money. And with most of the
restaurants and clubs closed for the season, and stores cut
back to a minimum, there won't be a lot of joy until the
conferences and festivals begin. Then, by the end of May,
when the International Film Festival in Cannes lights up the
whole coast, everyone will paint on smiles, ready for the
sun. Christmas comes in August on the Côte d'Azur, when
the stores will be laden with glitz and trash and filled with
wallet-happy holidaymakers determined to wear the lustre
off their credit cards.

Sleep finally catches up with Bliss on a quayside bench. Daisy finds him two hours later.

"Where you been?" she demands, angrily poking him awake. "I look everywhere."

"Sorry, Daisy."

"Why you no love me?"

How many times has she asked? How many times has he wanted to say, I do, in a way, but there is someone burnt so indelibly in my heart that I can't escape.

"Because she's dead ..." he begins angrily, then stops himself and softens as he explains. "There's someone else, Daisy, but she died. I tried to save her, but I couldn't, and she took my heart with her to her grave."

The news hits Daisy harshly and she stands with a deeply furrowed brow as she tries to process the information.

"Someone else?" she questions vaguely after a few moments.

"But she's dead," he reminds her, though knows that won't be enough, that it isn't enough for him either.

"Oh, Daavid. Zhat is terrible," says Daisy, sitting beside him. "But why you not tell me?"

Bliss shrugs. He knows how unfair it would be to say to a woman, As much as I want to be with you, it is only because my one true love is not here.

"I've tried counselling, therapy, self-talk ..." Welling tears stop him as he replays memories neither coloured nor faded by time, perfect memories of a perfect relationship — just a few weeks of sheer ecstasy, a wonderful, magical time when two foreigners in a foreign land found pure love in each other's minds and bodies.

"She was everything a man could ever ask for," he says quietly, willing himself not to look at Daisy, knowing she has a right to be offended by the insinuation that she is less.

But Daisy is not blind to his words or his sudden coolness. "What happened?" she asks, though she would rather not.

"Long story," he says, finally relieved that he no longer has to pretend, either to her or himself. "Maybe I'll tell you one day."

But where does zhat leave me? questions Daisy silently, with a look of pleading, and Bliss sees what is going through her mind and tries to soften the blow. "Daisy," he says, gently taking her right hand. "I look into your eyes and I see a beautiful, warm woman and, in a way, I love you."

"But —"

"There is no magic, Daisy. There never was. We became friends before we were lovers and I ... well, I thought I would get over her."

"But you didn't."

"No. I could lie. I could marry you and tell you that you are the one I truly love, but that wouldn't be fair. I know, deep down, that I would always wish that you were her."

Tears are streaming down Daisy's face — tears for herself. "But she is dead," she reminds him, as if he needs reminding.

"I know. That's the worst thing. I have no way of ever getting my heart back. She took it with her."

"What about her grave — you could visit," begins Daisy hopefully. "You could kneel at her grave and say —"

"Cremated, I think," says Bliss, lightly putting a hand on her arm to stop her. "No grave. I never even saw her body. I was wounded ... we crashed ... I crashed."

"A car?"

"A plane."

"You were flying?"

"Yes ... no ... not really ... I don't know," he says, and then he stares out over the sea and relives the terrifying moments in a rusty Illushyn cargo plane when he grappled with the controls at the side of a dying woman — the woman who ran off to heaven with his heart and left him in hell.

"I did not hear," says Daisy once he has given her a sanitized version of the incident when he and Yolanda rescued a group of Western computer experts from Saddam Hussein's clutches before the Americans slung the dictator in jail.

"No one heard, Daisy. In fact, officially, I think I'm supposed to kill you now that I've told you." The Frenchwoman shrinks back in concern, but Bliss cracks a wan smile. "Just joking. Although you probably shouldn't tell anyone. We shouldn't have been there."

"What is her name?"

He wants to correct the tense but doesn't, and he knows why; he knows that she is still alive in his mind, that she will always be alive, that she will outlive him. "Her name is Yolanda … Yolanda Pieters," he says, and finds himself going off into the distance again searching for an image. It's an easy search. Her face, sheer unadorned beauty — the most beautiful face he ever set eyes on, with just a single imperfection that he found intriguing — is dreamlike today, though it isn't always that way. Sometimes, when he's feeling the loss most, it's nightmarishly marred by the agony of her death throes.

"Daavid. You must move on," Daisy tells him as she sits beside him and tries to comfort him.

"I've tried. God, how I've tried."

She reaches out to stroke his cheek. "Now I understand," she says, as tears stream down her face.

"I wish I understood," mutters Bliss. "It's been more than three years. How long will it last?"

"Forever, Daavid," she says, knowing that her tears are not only for him and his lost love, they are for those who took a piece of her heart when they departed. And she turns to the Château Roger, where, along with memories of her grandfather and several other relatives who were swept up by the Nazis during the war, she too can find an image.

Roland was his name, and Daisy closes her eyes as she reruns the painful image of the young Parisian boy — a city sophisticate with a Beatles haircut and Daddy's souped-up

British Mini — who was the first to sample her tender young flesh. She was a pretty fifteen-year-old schoolgirl at the time, in the mid-sixties, and was diving after a shoal of sardines in the bay one sunny summer's day. Roland was diving nearby with an entirely different kind of fish on his mind. He struck, and landed his virginal catch in a little hidden cove where the tunnel from the château's basement comes out onto a golden beach. Forty-five seconds later Roland hit his stride, and with a triumphant yelp and a premature ejaculation he left Daisy in the sand while he shot off up the château's tunnel in search of another adventure.

"It is *très dangereux*. You cannot go zhere," Daisy yelled after him, but his motor was running so fast he didn't care if he was coming or going.

Daisy shudders at the memory of Roland's dead body being washed ashore a couple of days later — minus his *zizi* — but at that time she was still scared of the château's legendary ghosts and kept silent about their tryst, worried that a vengeful resistance fighter in the basement mistook him for a Nazi storm trooper.

She shakes off the unhappy memories of her loss, realizing that she is facing another, and asks, "But why you in Iraq?"

"They did have weapons of mass destruction," replies Bliss. "Cyber-weapons. That's why the inspectors never found them."

"Cyber-weapons."

"A computer virus to attack our systems."

"What will happen?"

"Maybe nothing," he says, not wishing to alarm her with the prospect of a super-virus kicking in and screwing up the world. "Although I think we've seen the signs: major power outages in America; bank computers on the blink for a week; the internet crashing." He pauses, knowing that the big one is still out there, that everything to date has been small fry. But he knows that it is like waiting for the earthquake that will one day kill Los Angeles. "It's coming … it's coming," everyone warns, then *bang*, the bottom falls out of the Indian Ocean and swallows a quarter of a million people in Asia. *And all you have to do is constantly worry about one dead woman*, he chastises himself, but then admits that it's not constant, only when it's triggered — similar hair, voice, colour, eyes, shape.

Stop it … stop it … she's been dead for years, he tries telling himself, but the more that time has gone on, the worse it has become. *You need closure*, says the voice in his mind, but he disagrees. *I need Yolanda. Need to know that I didn't kill her.*

You didn't kill her. You would have died for her — you wanted to die for her.

And still she left me.

She didn't want to. It wasn't her choice.

"Daavid," breaks in Daisy from outside.

"I thought I'd got over her," he says, but he can't help comparing her to the château's victims as he sits looking towards the old building. Sixty years on and many of the town's widows still dream that their lovers were sent to a remote concentration camp and will one day march home, strapping young men.

Daisy's grandmother was amongst those who stayed awake night after night when the war ended, but the pain was always still there the following morning: the gnawing, insidious pain of hope, watching the door for hour upon hour, begging, praying, screaming, pleading. "Come back. Please come back. I love you — I love you more than you can possibly know."

"Daavid. You have to move on," Daisy tells him, and he wants to say he'll try, but he finally gives up.

"So do you, Daisy," he says as her tears continue to stream. "I'm sorry, but I can never take a chance with you or anyone else. I can never look into your eyes and say with honesty, 'You are the only one for me.'"

chapter six

Daphne Lovelace has dug out a serious-grey pillbox hat for her lunch meeting with Superintendent Ted Donaldson at the Hole-in-the-wall.

"The buffet looks good," starts Donaldson with his eyes in that direction, but Daphne is all business as she flips open a notebook on the table and readies a pen.

"The files are missing — well, not exactly missing," Donaldson admits as soon as he has stacked his first plate.

"Where are they then?"

"There never were any."

"Three dead babies and no files?" questions Daphne skeptically, wondering if her old friend is just being diplomatic about sensitive documents.

"All natural causes — death certificates duly signed by two doctors — so no police investigation or inquest. The coroner seemed satisfied; just a coincidence."

"Three is one more than a coincidence," says Daphne sharply. "Two is a coincidence, Ted. Not three."

"Daphne. If we investigated every natural death we'd never do anything important."

"And three deaths in one family isn't important?"

"Suspicious," he confesses. "But it was before my time."

"You're not hiding anything, are you?"

Donaldson's seat is a little uncomfortable as he admits that his predecessor wasn't always as straight as he should have been. "Old Bob Hinkey could bend the rules a bit at times."

"So who bought him off?"

"I'm not saying that," protests Donaldson, though knows that Daphne well understands the local politics. "Put yourself in Bob's place. He probably spent his weekends shooting and fishing over at Creston's estate. Have you seen the place? Bigger than Buckingham Palace, choppers flying in and out, more security than the padlock on the prisoner's pee bucket down at the station."

"So what's he scared of?" questions Daphne.

"Nothing ticks off a villain more than the prospect of being done over by another one," suggests Donaldson.

Daphne queries, "Creston — a crook?"

Donaldson shrugs. "I've got no proof, but that's how most of these bigwigs make it — either them or their ancestors. It ticks me off that we waste time nicking some unemployed jerk for pinching a bar of chocolate when people like Creston are siphoning millions out of their companies."

"If Creston is as pious as he claims he'll have to get off his camel sooner or later or he'll be going downstairs with the rest of us."

"Nice idea," laughs Donaldson. "But he's already working on that. According to someone — let's say a friend of mine — Creston shovels money into religious organizations all over the place. Mind, I take a less charitable view. I reckon he does it for the PR and the tax write-off."

"Trina said they think Janet was involved in a religious group," begins Daphne, then questions, "I don't suppose you could find out from your friend if any of Creston's largesse reaches Canada."

"You'll get me shot ... aiding the enemy."

"What enemy?"

"David told me that you and Trina had cooked up some crazy notion about being private eyes."

"And PIs are the enemy?"

"Competition ... definitely not privy to classified information."

By the time Ted Donaldson has persuaded himself that a second helping of bread and butter pudding would round him off nicely, Daphne figures that he is sufficiently softened to try another tack.

"D'ye know anything about Amelia Drinkwater?" she asks with blank-faced innocence.

Donaldson puts down his spoon. "You mean the venerable Mrs. Drinkwater, Chairman of Dewminster Magistrates ..." he begins, then lowers his tone. "I didn't know she qualified for a Christian name. I could tell you one or two things ..."

Daphne leans across the table. "Just one good one will do."

"Well, to start with she strikes more terror into my officers than she does the villains."

"Really?"

Donaldson checks around before saying, "Bloody old battleaxe. Her husband died young and her son committed suicide, and I can't say I blame either of them."

"I've met her," agrees Daphne. "What happened to her boy?"

"Abuse," mouths Donaldson. "She totally smothered him. He was still living at home in his thirties for God's sake; Peter Pan syndrome, couldn't grow up ... you know the type."

"Why suicide?"

Donaldson shrugs. "The only way out I suppose."

Janet Thurgood hasn't been trying to escape from Trina's again, but with the possibility that Mike Phillips or Dave Brougham might show up at any time, Rob has been turned out to make room for her in the main part of the house. However, Trina is convinced that a police visit is imminent so she checks the basement suite.

Wearing dark shades and Kylie's Nike runners, she slips from room to room, keeping low. She flips open each door and jerks back as if expecting a shot, then she launches herself into the room and dives for cover.

"I've seen them do this in the movies," she hisses over her shoulder to her daughter, who is standing at the bottom of the stairs pretending to stick her fingers down her throat.

Trina inches her way across the room on the floor and closes the curtains before turning back to Kylie. "Shh," she hisses with her fingers to her lips. "The place may be bugged."

Telephone, paintings, lamps, and a four-foot-high plastic flamingo all get inspected, though Trina has little idea of what to search for.

"Here's a bug," calls Kylie, picking a dead spider from behind the television, and she gets a tart look from her mother.

"There's a police car up the hill," calls Rick as he comes home from the office and catches Trina in the act.

"I know. They're after Janet."

Rick laughs — he can't help it. "April fool."

"That is not funny," screeches Trina, almost convinced that there is a SWAT team hovering in the neighbourhood, then Rick spots that Kylie is wearing Janet's brown head scarf.

"What are you doing?"

"Getting Janet away from here," explains Trina, and then she reveals the plan that she has inveigled her daughter into by lifting all embargos. "Kylie is going to run down the street and around the block to draw fire."

"No way," says Rick, grabbing his daughter.

"Don't worry, Dad. Mum's paranoid as usual. There aren't any cops. Anyway, they wouldn't fire on an unarmed woman."

"That lot would fire on their grannies if ..." sneers Trina before realizing that her words are self-defeating. "But Ky'll be fine."

The plan to move Janet to the home of Trina's enema-loving patient, Clive Sampson, was welcomed by the elderly man when Trina asked him.

"I wouldn't mind the company," the septuagenarian readily admitted, and the fact that Janet was wanted by the police didn't faze him at all.

"I've done a few things in my time —" he started, but Trina stopped him.

"I'm sure we all have, Clive. But Janet is innocent, OK?"

Janet sits on Rob's bed caressing her crucifix as Trina outlines her plan. The homecare nurse looks into her charge's face as she speaks and notices that some changes have occurred since the first time she saw the terrified woman. Gradual awareness of her surroundings and some decent food seem to be softening her, although at the mention of the police the muscles of her cheeks harden and her eyes glaze as she focuses intently on the face of Jesus.

"Don't worry," soothes Trina. "You'll be safe with Clive. He's a very nice man."

Janet relaxes, although the transition seems to leave her in a deeper fog. However, a moment later, something in her questing eyes tells Trina that she is trying to look forward.

"We'll just wait until it's dark," Trina is telling her when Daphne phones with an update on her meeting with Donaldson.

"I've got a plan," Trina tells the Englishwoman excitedly as she picks up the phone in her bedroom.

"I remember the last one," replies Daphne sourly, recalling the other woman's hare-brained scheme to raise money for kidney transplants by pedalling a kidney-shaped quadricycle from Vancouver to New York. "It's downhill all the way," the zany Canadian announced as they set off together on a practice run, only to end up imprisoned in a secret government establishment in the mountains of Washington State.

"No. This is a good one," Trina carries on, undaunted, before explaining her intent to secrete Janet in a safe house and then infiltrate the sect.

The drive to Sampson's house is, as Trina explains to her passenger, in accordance with the tactics she has learned from her private investigator's manual: it is peppered with sudden U-turns, last-minute lane changes, and several close calls with red lights.

"If you so much as touch her or even breathe heavily on her I'll never give you another enema, understand?" Trina whispers harshly to the old man as soon as they arrive, then she turns to Janet with a smile. "You'll be safe here. But don't go outside, all right? Now, any medication. Do you take any tablets?"

"I stopped —" starts Janet, and Clive Sampson jumps in as he rummages into the pocket of his housecoat.

"I've got some you can have."

"No tablets," spits Trina, wrenching the package of Aspirins from the old man's fingers. "No tablets, no touching, or no enema. Got it?"

"Sorry, Trina."

"How long?" asks Janet as she looks vacantly around the large room stuffed with overblown 1960s furniture that will never make it to Sotheby's or Christies.

"Just a few days, until I find out what's going on."

Ten minutes later, with twenty blocks between herself and her patients, Trina phones Mike Phillips.

"What's going down, Mike?"

"Don't give me that innocent PI crap," snarls Phillips. "What have you done with her?"

"Who?"

"The crazy lady ... you know who. Look, this is getting serious. The DNA we got from the saliva on her crucifix matches."

"That was only three days. I thought it took weeks."

"Emergency ... murder of a cop."

"She didn't do it, Mike."

"Says you."

"She hasn't got the strength. He was probably a fat, beer-soaked, donut-challenged —"

"It doesn't alter the fact that she was the last one to see him alive," Phillips cuts in before she goes too far. "We need to talk to her."

"I'll let you know if I find her," says Trina, then switches off her phone before he has a chance to reply.

Any residual warmth from the Mediterranean has been swept away by the mistral, and Bliss feels the cold as he sits at his desk culling more and more from his manuscript. Daisy hasn't shown up in days, and, despite what he told her, he is feeling a sense of loss.

The despairing neophyte author doesn't know it, but the heartbroken Frenchwoman has been slowly collecting things from around her house that are tied to him — cards, letters, sapphire earrings, a Tiffany necklace — and has put them in a shoebox. Now she knocks, holding the box in front of her, though whether she wants to ward him off or get dragged in she doesn't know.

She gets dragged in.

"I'm really, really sorry," he says, but can't help adding that he has seen the woman again — just a glimpse, just the hair, the same familiarity, same vibes.

"Who?" asks Daisy, as if she doesn't care.

"The woman ... the one who reminded me of Yolanda," he says, but his voice fades as he realizes that he is digging the knife deeper. Then he looks away, embarrassed by the fact that he cannot escape from a dead person. But was she dead? He saw her after the crash, bloodied and broken; he begged the doctor to help her, begged the medics for oxygen. He blotted out the carnage surrounding the crashed plane as he desperately focused on saving her life. But she was gone. He was given the news by Chief Superintendent Edwards himself.

Thoughts of Edwards further sour him as he pictures the poisonous little officer who stomped his way up the career ladder carrying a black book bursting with his colleagues' petty indiscretions. "Bloody Edwards," Bliss muses under his breath as he recalls the way the man informed him that everything would be taken care of: Yolanda's funeral, her personal possessions, the plane, her aging father, her son. "All taken care of," the snotty chief superintendent claimed, but no one ever considered Bliss's heart. Who would take care of that?

"Maybe you should look for her family," suggests Daisy, still hoping that he will find a way to move on, to move back. "You must bring zhis to an end."

"Closure," he mutters, but he doesn't want closure. Yolanda is still there, still alive in his mind, as hot and vital as the first time they made love, jammed together in an airplane's toilet where they reached incredible heights as Bliss penetrated her with every inch of his passion and she thrust her pelvis into his groin with heart-thumping power.

"Sometimes I think it's better this way," he confesses. "At least I can imagine that she is happy somewhere … that's all I want, Daisy. I just want her to be happy."

Daisy gives a knowing nod. "Like *Grandmère*. Sometimes she thinks that *Grandpère* found someone else in Poland or East Germany. But she still waits. Nearly sixty years and she still waits."

"Till death do us part …" he murmurs, regretting that he never had the opportunity to say those words to

Yolanda in front of a priest — but would it have made a difference? It may ease the pain a little to imagine Yolanda still alive and vibrant, but the pain won't end until his death. Or, if he is right about the tortured soul of the Man in the Iron Mask, the torment of his lost love will haunt him eternally.

Janet Thurgood still has some memories, worn thin by a regimen of tranquilizers and constant repentance. "You killed your baby," she repeatedly tells herself as she paces her bedroom in Sampson's house while caressing her crucifix, but those were her husband's words, not hers.

"You smothered him: hiding him in cupboards, in the cellar, in the attic," Joseph accused, then shook her, screaming "Why? ... Why? ... Why?" into her face. "You're an evil woman. You'll go to Hell. You'll go to prison," he yelled at her, and weeks ran into months as she shrank away from the front door at every knock. Then, when he'd broken her, Joseph finally explained that everything had been taken care of.

"Thank you. Thank you," she cried, throwing herself at his feet, but there was something missing. "Where is he?" she wanted to know. "Where is my baby?"

"He's dead, Janet. Don't you remember? You killed him," Creston snarled, knocking her down again, and no matter how much she begged and pleaded, she never found her son's ashes or grave.

"It's better that way. I'm protecting you, helping you," he claimed, implying, Because I love you so much, without saying so.

Janet's next pregnancy followed closely on the death of John. "I'll be more careful this time," she assured her husband. "This one is yours."

Bliss is staring at the lemon tree. His manuscript is now in ruins. He's lost his will and his way. *I need a new start*, he tells himself, willing one of the lemons to drop. Nothing happens, and he questions whether he needs to start a new book or a new life.

"I thought I was escaping," he mumbles, then tells himself that no one escapes from life alive. Escaping from love should be easier, he thought, but it has become harder and harder. And he thinks of Daisy, trying so enthusiastically to win his heart when it was never there to be won.

Poor Daisy, he thinks, then chastises himself for not foreseeing what might happen during the first few months when there was no magic, no fireworks, just a slow smoulder, then months of emails and long-distance telephone calls. The only fireworks were at the Liberation Day festival when the sky over the island of Ste. Marguerite was ablaze. But afterwards, Bliss fizzled as quickly as the last mortar. Memories of Yolanda put the fire out, although he didn't explain to Daisy, and he still has difficulty saying, even to himself, "I'm in love with a dead person."

Is that unusual? he questions, but he is living in a town full of grieving widows, women who, despite more than six decades in black weeds, are unable or unwilling to risk another relationship.

Why is that? he wonders briefly, though he well knows that it's not just that they are waiting for the return of their lover; it is fear that they might find a greater love and dishonour the one they lost.

Would I want a greater love than what I had with Yolanda? But he knows that road will drive him in circles.

Samantha Bliss is a London lawyer in her mid-twenties who has been tied to the legal profession since the day of her birth, when her father, Constable David Bliss, paced the delivery room at St. Thomas's Hospital in full uniform, making the staff as nervous as he.

"Get over it, Dad," says Samantha when her father phones from the South of France to say that he's broken up with Daisy over his longing for Yolanda.

"Easy for you to say. You've got Peter," he replies, speaking of his son-in-law and ex-boss, Chief Inspector Peter Bryan.

"What d'ye want, Dad?" she asks, suggesting, I'm real busy.

I want the fireworks back. I want to look into her wide open eyes while we kiss and know that our minds are in unison — that she loves me just as much as I love her. I want to feel our hearts syncopating in harmony.

"I want her back," is all he says, though Samantha is unsympathetic.

"It's been more than three years. I thought you were moving on. What about Daisy? What started this again?"

The blonde woman at the boulangerie, he knows, but he doesn't bother to explain. "A woman with Yolanda's eyes," he says, and then realizes that he didn't actually register her eyes at all, that he doesn't even know what colour they are.

"Just get on with the book, Dad," says Samantha. "It'll take your mind off her. Or take a trip," she continues. "Get away for a bit. Go somewhere exotic."

"Exotic," he mutters as he scans the palm trees, the snow-capped mountains, and the cerulean sea. "Where, Hawaii?"

"Yeah. And take Daisy."

Poor Daisy, he thinks as he puts down the phone, and he's tempted to call her. But where are the fireworks? The ones he has seen only once in his life — in a briefing room at a police station in the port city of Hoek van Holland, when he and Yolanda looked into each other's eyes and both knew instinctively that there could never be anyone else. They may have danced around each other for a few days, but they ended up in each other's arms as surely as day turns to night.

The wintry sun reflects brightly off the coastal mountains surrounding Vancouver as Trina prepares for her trip north by scavenging her and Kylie's closet for something flowing. She doesn't want tight, doesn't want to show off lumps and bumps that might be considered irreligious. *I could go for the burka look*, she thinks as she discards outfit after outfit, and considers running something up on her sewing machine. In the end she goes with a couple of printed cotton full-length skirts and several demure polo-neck sweaters. Janet's head scarf tops off the ensemble as she checks herself in the mirror, then she hurriedly wipes off all her lipstick and mascara.

"There," she says, "plain as a pimple. God should be happy with that — but will Rick?"

The sun is sinking over the island of Ste. Marguerite yet again, and Bliss sees his novel sinking with it. "God, why is it so hard to write?" he questions, still looking for the masked man to give him renewed inspiration as he watches the famous prisoner's home fade into the twilight. "It was easier winkling confessions out of diehard rapists and murderers."

A ruffle of cool breeze ripples across the bay and makes him shiver momentarily. He pulls his coat around him and is readying to return to his apartment when a feeling of presence bores into the back of his head. But he has been here before; has felt the vibes of love — always love, and always at sunset — and he knows that it is a trick. Yolanda's spirit is still alive in his mind, refusing to leave him, refusing to let him live: "Still thinking of you; still loving you."

It could be the Man in The Iron Mask, he tries convincing himself, but knows it's not, knows he's been abandoned as much by his three-hundred-year-old mentor as he has by his great love.

The creepy feelings continue to wash over him, and he is tempted to turn but doesn't want to risk disillusionment. *I'm going mad*, he tells himself as he stares at the prison that is slowly evaporating into the gloom, then a cough so slight it might be in his mind spins him. But he can't look at the blonde-haired woman who is already turning away.

"Sorry," she mumbles in embarrassment, and she keeps walking. "Sorry ... very rude."

"I saw that woman again," he tells Daisy when he meets her at the bar L'Escale for an evening drink, but she's heard enough of Yolanda.

"Just imagination, Daavid," she says dismissively. "It is like a parent wiz a lost child who spends their life running after strangers because of zhe hair."

"I know," agrees Bliss. "But it's not just her hair ..." He pauses, realizing that, in truth, it is only her hair; he hasn't consciously examined any other features. "Maybe you are right."

Marie, the floury baker's wife, adds to Bliss's consternation the following morning as she greets him on his way into the boulangerie. "Ah. *Bonjour, monsieur*," she cries as she rushes to the door to peer up and down the street. "You have just missed someone." Then she drops her voice conspiratorially. "I zhink you have a fan."

"Not yet," he replies with a chuckle. "But who knows. One day when my book is published."

"And zhe writing. It is good, no?"

Now what? How long will you keep up the pretence? "It's all right," he says with a shrug as he orders his usual, and he is halfway out of the door before Marie calls after him.

"But zhe woman who asks for you."

He turns. "Woman?"

"Your admirer. She ask what you do. I say, 'He is most famous number one English writer.'"

"Thanks," he says, laughing.

"And she say, 'OK.'"

"Just OK?" he queries, irrationally deflated.

"No, I zhink she say 'Okey-dokey' like no-good damn Americans."

"Yolanda always said ..." he begins, then drops his bag and takes off.

She's gone, whoever she was, and as he races around the tight, twisted, medieval lanes that were built in the time of donkey carts, he easily convinces himself that he is being utterly stupid. But it doesn't stop him, and he pushes on through the bustling market in the heart of the town, scattering customers in his path and knocking over a basket of olives.

"*Va te faire foutre!*" screeches the stallholder, but Bliss tunes out the offensive insult as he dashes on.

"It's obviously a coincidence," he tells Samantha by phone ten minutes later, seized by a compunction to confide in someone and not wishing to further upset Daisy. "I mean, lots of people must say, 'Okey ...'" he is adding as he leans over the balcony, gazing down at the garden. "Oh shit!"

"What is it, Dad?"

"A lemon."

"A lemon?"

"It just dropped off the tree."

"Sorry, Dad. You've lost me."

Bliss tries explaining about the woman, but Samantha finally loses it. "Dad, for fuck's sake, will you just put her out of you mind and get on with the damn book."

"Language!"

"Well, it's bloody ridiculous. You've got to move on."

"Is that you, David?" inquires Daphne Lovelace a few minutes later, after Samantha has threatened to block all further calls and have him arrested as a dangerous lunatic.

"Yes," he replies, though his mind is somewhere else as his elderly English friend gabbles excitedly about her plan to take up writing.

"I was hoping for a few pointers," she says.

"That's all I need — competition."

"No. Nothing major like yours. Not a global bestseller. Just a history of Dewminster's important families."

Bliss catches on. "And you really think that the chocolate guy will fall for that?"

"One of the advantages of age, David," she titters. "I'll just dress like a dowdy old fogy and pretend to be a bit slow."

"You don't need me, Daphne Lovelace," he tells her, then, with his mind totally absorbed by the strange woman, he quickly ends the call and focuses on the newly fallen lemon as he tries to picture Yolanda. The slightly bulbous nose and the single deep dimple come easily to mind, as do her perfectly formed teeth, then her smile, shaped by a pair of sweet rosy lips that most men would kill for, and finally her body, one that most women would die for.

With the image formed he tries to cross-match with the woman he'd glimpsed on the promenade in St-Juan. He draws a blank; he'd barely taken any notice beyond the hair.

What the hell am I doing? he asks himself, realizing that Samantha is right. *I should be locked up. She's dead you fool. Get over it. Get back to your novel.*

But writing is far from Bliss's mind. It's as if the masked man has stopped communicating, so the only thing to do is to get back into the Château Roger to try to pick up the trail from the woman that the château was originally built to impress in 1687. An hour later, armed with pad, pen, and flashlight, he walks the twisty hill that winds around the Château Roger's perimeter fence, looking for a spot where he can pry apart the rusty iron railings.

The Château Roger, eaten by time and swallowed by the encroaching undergrowth, is like a decayed maharajah's palace in the Punjabi jungle. The edifice was built by a man of great passion, much like the Taj Mahal was, but it has slipped ignominiously through the historical records because of the builder's failure.

How different things may have been if he succeeded, Bliss thinks as he surveys the cracked marble steps leading up to the enormous canopied front door, and he can't help but reflect on the fact that history is always recorded by the victor and no one writes about the losers with any relish.

But was it the man's fault, or was it the château that blighted his chances? Bliss doesn't need his manuscript to recall the plaint he has attributed to the island's most famous inhabitant: *Every day, ma chère amour, I watch my most magnificent château, Le Château Roger, rise on the promontory across the bay from the Isle Ste. Marguerite. Soon it will be ready, and then, my sweet heart, it will be my gift to you as a symbol of my great love. Reject me not, I beg of you, for I have asked the king to have me incarcerated incognito in the island fortress until you accept my endowment and release me by your love.*

Eleven years he waited. Day after day peering hopefully across the bay to the prize that awaited his dream woman, yet he was to be not just disappointed but totally destroyed by her rejection. He pined to death.

"Ah. The agony of true love," muses Bliss with total empathy, and then a feeling of presence sharpens his senses.

He felt it before, on a previous visit, and knows that it isn't just the tormented ghost of the owner still waiting, still hoping, still praying. It's the ghosts of the thousands of prisoners, resistance fighters and others, who succumbed in the building's torture chambers. When the Château Roger was commandeered by the Nazis it became the first stop on the pipeline that led to the gas chambers, though many never made it beyond the evil edifice's basement.

"Here goes," he says to himself as he slips through the aediculated doorway into a cavernous hall from which a couple of giant staircases curl off into the upper floors.

The three-hundred-year-old building has been abandoned for the past six decades; one more year has had little effect. Nothing has changed since his previous visit, but the hackles on the back of his neck still prickle.

"This is crazy," he tells himself. "It's broad daylight." Although he knows that beneath him, in the basement, it is permanent night. Looking upwards, he steels himself to try one of the rotten staircases, but a flustered pigeon takes off in an explosion of wingbeats and startles him.

"Pull yourself together," he tells himself, then decides to head down to the basement, where he is already prepared for the rats and lizards.

One day this will be a shrine like the extermination camps, he thinks as he plays his flashlight ahead of him down the flagstone steps. *One day, when my novel is finished and the truth about the Man in the Iron Mask is finally revealed.*

Murderous shackles and chains still festoon the walls in the torture chambers. It could be the setting for a Halloween dance, but Bliss knows it's not.

"What was that?" he questions at the sound of a soft footfall and he holds his breath. "This place could drive you mad," he muses, then seriously questions whether he is thinking of himself or another jilted lover — the Man in the Iron Mask. "I wasn't jilted. She died," he protests, but what of all the other ghosts that surround him, all the men who died here. Is there a difference?

It's one thing to have a flaming row and to have a lover walk away saying, "I hate you. I never ever want to see you again," he reasons as he fingers the rusted shackles. But what of the man who looks into the eyes of his lover as he is being dragged away on the end of a rifle, still yelling, "I love you. I love you. I'll love you forever." And what of those who still see the love burning brightly in their partners' eyes, wanting to yell, "Tell me you don't love me. Please tell me you don't love me. I can live with that. How can I live knowing you still love me as much as I love you?"

Bliss stops at the thought, realizing that he is no different from the widows of St-Juan; he is completely stuck, unable to move forward and unable to go back, in limbo for the rest of his life, knowing that he can never love another.

Think about it: one look into each other's eyes and you were both hooked — then she left you.

She didn't leave. She died.

Is there a difference?

The creak of a door opening sharpens him again. But this time he's sure. It's the door above him — into the basement.

"Shit!" he mutters under his breath as he flicks off his flashlight and flattens himself behind a brick pillar. Footfalls slowly clatter down the stone steps.

Bliss balances the cheap torch in his hand as a potential weapon, although it's plastic — useless — and he tries to control his breathing as the steps slowly descend.

Just walk out and confront him, he tells himself, guessing that the guard will be as scared as he, but he hangs back knowing that he is the intruder, and a jumpy sentry might be trigger happy. But the château itself holds him back. The building seems to love death, has revelled in death. In addition to the thousands of wartime victims it has already killed Daisy's one-time lover, Roland, and its builder, the Man in the Iron Mask.

"Hello, anyone here?"

Bliss steels himself to run, then stops. It's a woman's voice — a female guard — and he is readying to raise his hands and shout, "Don't shoot," when he has another thought. *English? Why is she speaking English?* He waits, holding his breath, sweat pouring down his forehead, his fingers taut around the flashlight.

"Hello," the woman tries again into the darkness.

"Hello," responds Bliss, stepping out and snapping on the light.

"Agh!" she screams, then stands her ground, demanding, "Who are you?"

"Chief Inspector Bliss, Scotland Yard," he says, hoping his voice sounds even. "Who are you?"

Her gasp of amazement hits him.

"I asked, who ..." he begins to reiterate as he raises the beam, but her hands fly to her face.

"No, no, no," she cries. "Who are you? Why are you doing this to me? You're dead."

"Yolanda?"

The few moments it takes them to escape from the gloom of the basement are fear-filled for Bliss as he worries that the beautiful spectre will evaporate in the brilliant light of day; suspicious that she is as ethereal as the rest of the ghosts in the château's basement, he keeps up a nervous banter as they climb the stone steps, his voice cracked by laughter and tears.

"They said you were dead; I love you; what happened; I never stopped thinking of you ..."

Yolanda stops at the top, suddenly aware that in the confusion they have missed a vital step, and she turns to silence him with a kiss.

"Oh my God," breathes Bliss as a million sweet memories flood back, and they dance, lips locked, through the expansive hallway until they are standing, crushed together, on the tiled patio in the warm sunshine.

Three difficult and pain-filled years take the resurrected couple twenty minutes to stitch together in between bouts of kissing and fondling, then, as they break for breath, Bliss wants to know, "What brought you here?"

"I really don't know —" she starts, but he stops her with a suspicious look at the masked man's island across the serene bay.

"It was the Man in the Iron Mask — his spirit."

Yolanda's puzzled frown is expected, and he briefly explains the legend.

"He wanted me to write his story," he continues. "I knew it the moment I walked into his cell. But I got it wrong. I believed the records, believed that he had been transferred to the Bastille in 1698."

"And he hadn't?"

"I'm beginning to think that someone, probably a common thief, was taken in his place so that he could be free."

"But what about the woman of his dreams; the one he built this château for?" asks Yolanda as she sweeps her eyes over the seemingly malevolent monolith.

"I don't know," admits Bliss. "Maybe she found someone else. Maybe she didn't love him."

"So after all this, he didn't get her. There was no happy ending."

"Life doesn't always end happily, Yolanda," says Bliss, then he breaks into an enormously grateful smile and grasps her tightly to his chest. "But maybe he's happy now." Then he kisses her tenderly and whispers, "I love you with all my heart. I am overjoyed that I have found you."

chapter seven

Raven is a sleek-bodied, black-haired channel who has a benevolent guide in the spirit world — Serethusa, a voice from beyond, who, as far as the young psychic knows, has never led her astray.

"Serethusa says you have to be slain in the spirit of God in order to be resurrected on the dawn following the third night of death," Raven explains seriously to Trina, once the wannabe private eye has expressed her interest in angels as she tries to fathom out Janet and prepare for her infiltration of Beautiful.

"You see," carries on Raven, "Spenta Armaita is the feminine angel of the earth who is the mother of Daena — the astral body of each of us which manifests herself to the soul."

"I think I've got it."

"While the six Zoroastrian archangels, three male and three female, who surround Ormazd, the light of God and Wisdom …" Raven stops at the total confusion on Trina's face. "You haven't a clue, have you?"

"Not really," admits the other woman, so Raven cuts to the end.

"Daena, your Daena, isn't a real angel."

"Thank God for that," says Trina, tongue in cheek.

"There's a bunch of freaks who've got a place in the boonies they call Beautiful. All the women are called Daena. And the chief freak has got about thirty wives, although most of them are probably his own kids. Apparently he treats them like his personal slaves, but they're dead loyal."

"I don't understand what it is with some women," admits Trina. "So desperate they just keep going back for more."

"Psychological abuse," agrees Raven. "Some jerk dumps me and I'm out the door. I'm damned if I'll beg. But some women, the more they're pushed away the harder they try to get back."

"It's the mothering instinct," suggests Trina. "The bigger the kid, the more some women will try to straighten him out — just like his mummy should have done."

"Hey. We all like to feel needed. Don't knock it."

"I'd rather have a real man like my Rick than a wimp any day."

"Read the books, Trina. Some women just can't handle good guys. Anyway, don't ask me what it is with Browning; maybe it's what he's packing under his cassock."

Amelia Drinkwater is someone who never felt the need to read books on psychological abuse or its effects.

"She managed to suppress it," Ted Donaldson confides in Daphne Lovelace, talking of the suicide of the magistrate's son, Simon. "The coroner was quite obliging. It wouldn't have reflected well on the judiciary in general — loss of faith if it got out that the chief magistrate had abused her son."

"Abused?"

"Oh, I doubt she hit him, but she knocked him about in other ways, kept him a boy instead of turfing him out and making him grow up."

Simon Drinkwater caught on eventually, when he found that his immaturity and insecurity turned most women off, so he tied himself a noose.

"Peter Pan," says Daphne knowingly. "But how did they cover it up?"

"Claimed he was painting the hall ceiling, slipped, rope caught in banister on the way down — could have happened."

"If not for this," she says as she scans Simon Drinkwater's suicide note, which Donaldson excavated from a sealed envelope in the bottom of the file.

"You'll get me shot one of these days, Daphne Lovelace," Donaldson says and laughs.

Amelia Drinkwater isn't in such a jovial mood an hour later. Daphne has splurged on a taxi, but the flower lady isn't anxious to see her. It's only Daphne's Order of the British Empire holding the front door open.

"I suppose you'd better come in," says Mrs. Drinkwater. "I've just made tea. Although if you've come about Janet you're wasting your breath. I told you, I don't gossip."

"No," says Daphne before pinning the woman down with the information gleaned from Donaldson with the skill of a welterweight: dancing lightly, jabbing and prodding.

Amelia gets the point and flares. "My son's accident has nothing to do with you."

Daphne takes a sip and screws up her face. "You should try Keemun. It's the Queen's favourite." Then she pauses to fix the woman with a stare. "I'm writing a book about Dewminster's characters, so, in a way, it could be my business."

"That's a threat."

"Yes. I believe it is."

Amelia sizes up Daphne and decides to give a little. "Stay there," she orders. "I might have something about Janet."

"Edwards!" Bliss screeches into the phone as soon as the senior officer answers his phone.

"Chief Super —" he begins, but Bliss cuts him off.

"Don't pull rank on me, you nasty little turd."

"Who the hell?"

"Bliss. David Bliss. Remember me? Remember that Iraq job: crashed aircraft, escaped hostages? Of course you do, you lying bastard. Well, it turns out that Ms. Pieters — the Dutchwoman you gave me crap for bonking — is very much alive."

"Exigencies of the service, old boy," claims Edwards, immediately catching on.

"What? What are you talking about?"

"Not my decision. The higher-ups thought it better that way."

"Better for who?"

"If I told you that I'd have to kill you."

"And if you don't, I'll kill you."

"OK. Let's grow up. It's probably best if you don't see her."

"Are you crazy," spits Bliss, wanting to say, Have you the faintest idea what it's like to find true love — the stuff of movies and songs? "Not only will I see her, I will get to the bottom of this. You lied to her as well."

"Not me, her people."

"And you never thought we'd find out?"

"It was a chance."

"Well, if you're worried that we might go public with what we know about the computer super-virus, worry away."

"Don't even think about it. The Americans will shut you down in a flash."

"So that's who was yanking your chain."

"I didn't —"

"You didn't need to."

Amelia Drinkwater is taking her time. Whether she is stalling or simply having difficulty locating whatever she has in mind regarding Janet, Daphne Lovelace has no way of knowing, so she takes off her black veiled hat and carefully arranges it on the Sheraton sideboard as an indication of her determination to stay until she has some answers.

The majestic room in the vine-covered mock-Tudor mansion is gracefully furnished with unostentatious antiques, and while she waits Daphne sizes up the owner as being a woman who never let her husband's fortune get in the way of good taste.

"Oh. There you are," says Amelia on her return, as if she inwardly wishes that Daphne may have vanished in the interim, and she takes a scratched photograph from an old album and places it on the tea table. "That's me and Joe," she continues as she points to two teenagers in front of a group of youths. "Brighton Beach, 1958," she adds, and Daphne puts on her glasses to look at the smiling youngsters holding hands under a grey sky.

"Joe?" questions Daphne.

"Joseph Crispin Creston Jr. That's a mouthful isn't it?"

"Janet Thurgood's husband?"

"The garden is such a mess at this time of the year, don't you find," says Amelia quickly as she looks for a way out of a tight spot.

Daphne stares at the picture and it takes her a few seconds to come to terms with the fact that the withered crone in front of her is barely in her sixties. *That's what a lifetime of summers does to you*, Daphne is thinking as the other woman sits staring into the picture, reliving her past. Then she looks at Daphne and spits angrily, "He loved me. He loved me. Not her. Do you know what that does to you?"

Daphne knows; she's taken that bus before.

"I was just sixteen. He was a bit older. We'd planned everything: wedding, honeymoon. We had the family fortune. We were meant for each other. We had class."

So, why did he marry Janet? is the question on Daphne's lips, but she doesn't need to ask as the other woman continues acidly, "She was a trollop. Got herself knocked up by some lout working on the travelling fair; didn't even know his name. Her father chucked her out and quite rightly. But Joe was a soft touch — not like his father. He used to watch her in church. I saw him. He didn't know. But I saw him ogling her. She was a tart: tight skirts, more cleavage than a plumber's mate. He married her just to annoy his father, I think. Just jilted me and eloped with her."

Amelia stares out of the window at the manicured lawn that slopes past a ha-ha to the willows overhanging a lazy stream, but it is more than the swirling mist in her eyes as she continues, "It scarred me for life. I never got over it. He loved me."

"So why didn't he come back to you after she left?"

Because he still loved her, and always loved her in a way, would be the correct answer, but Amelia can never bring herself to that admission. "I married Drinkwater," she says, skipping the intervening years when she lay awake night after night waiting for Joseph's call following Janet's departure. "I didn't really love Cecil, but I guess he loved me. He bought me things — had money. In any case, Joe never divorced her. He's too bloody religious for that."

The Creston empire was also a factor, and with Janet out of the way, Joseph Creston Sr. had wasted no time in inculcating his son into every aspect of the business.

"Money," continues Amelia snootily, as if it is a dirty word. "That's all he thinks about. I see him on TV smiling, giving millions to charity, everyone clapping, and I think, 'He's still got my heart.' More than forty years and he's still got it. But he doesn't care."

Daphne allows the emotion to subside for a few seconds as she sips her tea, then she digs. "You said Janet killed the children."

"Did I?" queries Amelia absently, her mind still on her ex-lover. "Probably just the jealousy talking. He was mine and she ... Well, never mind. It was a long time ago."

But Amelia Drinkwater does mind. Daphne can see that in the pain on her host's face as the other woman continues. "I read somewhere that everyone is entitled to one great love. I suppose he was mine."

"But the children?" pushes Daphne. "What happened?"

Amelia takes a final look at the photo before putting it back into the old album, and then she explains. "My father was a magistrate; long line of magistrates. It's like the family business, although you don't get paid — not directly."

"Then how?"

"Fringe benefits: a brace of pheasants from the lord of the manor, double measures at the bar, that sort of thing — connections. And my father was well connected."

"With the Crestons?"

"He didn't say much about any of the deaths," Amelia carries on with a nod, "not to me anyway. But after he died I went through his stuff and found that he'd been getting money from Joe's father."

"Hush money?"

"Scandal wouldn't be good for business," suggests Amelia. "Especially in the chocolate business. I mean, it always has such innocent connotations. 'Give her chocolates if you love her,' they say."

"Then make her fat and give her diabetes," adds Daphne somewhat caustically.

"Chocolate people are really touchy about that," warns Amelia. "Plus the Creston family are pillars of the church."

"I was listening to a program about that," admits Daphne. "Apparently all the big chocolate companies were founded by churchy people."

"Quakers mainly," agrees Amelia. "Although the Crestons have always been Church of England. Anyway, there was never any evidence that she killed the kids."

"Just rumour," muses Daphne, knowing that rumour can be much more insidious than hard evidence. And that, in small-town England in the 1960s, any hint of scandal in the manor house would stir up the old wives.

"I thought he might leave her after the first one," continues Amelia, knowing that Daphne will understand her reference.

"He didn't?"

"Couldn't. 'Till death do us part,' he'd said, and he was stuck with it. She fell for another almost straight away, and his family were thrilled, especially when it was a boy."

"Then he died."

"Only a few months," nods Amelia her face darkening again. "'Tragic,' my father said when the old vicar called, but it wasn't so unusual in those days."

"And that was an accident too?" Asks Daphne incredulously.

"Natural causes — suffocated on a feather pillow."

Too much luxury can kill, thinks Daphne as she goes on to ask about the third child — Johannes.

"More tea?" starts Amelia leaping up, and then she realizes that an answer is called for. "Same kinda thing I suppose," she adds as she takes the pot to the kitchen for a refill.

The old brown album containing the photo sits temptingly on a piecrust table by Amelia's chair, and with a quick check to make sure that her host isn't returning, Daphne ferrets through it until she discovers a newspaper clipping.

"Suspicious death…" runs the headline, and she quickly slips it into her bag and begins to put the album back.

"Would you like a chocolate biscuit?" asks Amelia poking her head around the door.

Daphne freezes with her back to the woman, but the album is still in her hand. "Lovely view," she says, pretending to peer out of the window.

"Foggy," complains Amelia, but she doesn't catch on. "Biscuit?" she asks again.

"Yes, please," says Daphne without turning. "I'm partial to a chocky bicky now and again." *Don't look, don't look*, she pleads as she waits for Amelia to leave, then she drops the album and hustles back to her chair.

"There," says Amelia returning with as pleasant a face as she can muster. "Now tell me more about yourself, dear. I'd love to know how you got the OBE."

The heat of the Mediterranean sun has returned for Bliss and has brought unbridled joy: three perfect days and nights, full of wonderful food, conversation, adventures, and passionate lovemaking. As he and Yolanda lie naked on his bed listening to Billie Holiday — one of their favourites — singing, "Let's do it. Let's fall in love," the air is scented with the sweet aftermath of sex as he pensively traces the scars across her breasts, saying, "I did that."

She clamps her hand over his mouth. "You did not," she says, talking of the moment that Bliss took over the controls of a crashing plane following their escape from Iraq. "You saved my life — the scars are a small price."

But the marks, like brands in her flesh, sear him as much as they have marred her, and he is close to tears as he mumbles, "I'm so sorry."

"Why did they lie to us, David?" she asks as she strokes his face.

"They were worried we might go public," he answers simply, knowing that hundreds of infected computers are still out there, ticking time bombs. Knowing that with a single command every major system in the world could come down: banks, navigation, power, communication, security, water … But now is not the time, and he raises himself on his elbows to look at Yolanda. "I never thought that love — real love — existed until I met you," he tells her.

"I know," she agrees. "I was the same. The others, all the others, were just practice, just a kind of extended foreplay leading to ecstasy."

"One night with you was better than all my other nights combined."

"You are a master, David. Do you know that? The first time we met I looked into your eyes and I knew it instantly. You are a master at everything you do."

"I'm not sure about the writing —" he begins, but she gently plants a kiss and stops him.

"A master," she breathes into his mouth.

"I remember I was trying to talk but I kept getting confused," he says, thinking of their first moments together. "I kept walking into pillars and things. And when you took my hand …"

"Your elbows are sore," she says and gently massages one as a cloud comes over her face. "David," she begins seriously, but he doesn't pick up the clue.

"Yes?" he queries lightly.

"There is something I have to tell you," she continues darkly.

Bliss freezes. Now he hears.

She waits, deliberating, her face full of anguish. He senses the pain, feels the pain as her brow furrows and he reaches out to try to smooth out the creases.

"It's OK," he says. "You can tell me anything. I want us to be completely honest with each other."

Ten seconds later he desperately wants to bite back his words.

"There's someone else in my life, David."

"Someone …"

"A man — Klaus. We've been together for a while."

The ground falls from under him. It's like a notification of sudden death, the worst job in the police — advising someone that their mother, son, or father is dead. And suddenly he is that person. "But I don't understand. Where is he? What ... why didn't you tell ..."

Yolanda has tears in her eyes. "David, I didn't know what to say. I love you."

Bliss is struggling into his trousers. His life is falling apart. *Is that it? Is that all I'm allowed — three days? I wait half a lifetime and all I get is three days. I want the rest of my life.*

"David. Wait. Look, I love you."

"You told me that. But now you say there's someone else."

"I thought you were dead. Klaus was very kind. I needed someone. I needed you, but you were dead."

"I wasn't."

"They said you were."

Bliss sits with his head in his hands fighting back the tears. "Are you married?"

"No, no, it's not ... He wants me, but first he wants me to change."

"You mustn't change to please a man. That doesn't work. I love you just the way you are."

She smiles. "That's a song."

"Don't smile, Yolanda. Please don't smile. I'm dying. You're killing me. Please don't smile."

"He was supposed to be here with me, but he had more important things."

Bliss perks up. "More important? He loves you, but he has more important things than to be with you?"

"I know. It doesn't sound good."

"It stinks. What kind of man would do that? And what kind of man would love you only if you change?"

"David. He's been kind to me. I was in hospital. I couldn't move. He came every day ..."

"And I didn't? How could I? I would have been there."
Then he stops. "What are you trying to say?"

"I have to go back to him."

"No. This isn't right. You've always been mine. The
moment I saw you I knew straight away — *we* knew
straight away. You said so."

"But he needs me."

"And I don't. Is that what you're saying? Do you think
I haven't thought of you every day? Poor Daisy has been
chucking herself at me for nearly two years and I always had
an excuse — got to work; got to write. And all the time it
was you. Knowing you were dead but refusing to believe.
Trapped, just as much as the widows here. Unable to move
on with my life, unwilling to give anyone else a chance,
knowing you were the only one."

Yolanda winds the bed sheet around her as if she is
suddenly embarrassed by her nakedness, saying, "David —
I must call Klaus."

"And tell him what?"

"I will tell him the truth."

"That you love me more than you love him."

"I cannot hurt him that much. You don't understand.
He is a kind man."

"Look at me. Do you love him more than me?"

"I must go, David."

"No."

"I'm sorry."

"When will I see you again?"

"I'm sorry, David. I just can't do this."

She gathers up her clothes and closes the door behind
her. Bliss hears a slam, and he sits fighting back the tears for
a few minutes before opening up. "Edwards, you bastard,"
he yells at the top of his voice. "Now I really do owe you."

If you love her, let her go, isn't that what they say, he
tells himself. *But why me? If he loves her shouldn't he let
her go? What if she loves me as much as she says? What if*

she just feels pity for him? He was kind to her. I would have been kind to her. I just didn't get the chance.

A deep hole opens and he's falling. There is only blackness beneath him for a few seconds before he tries to grab something. *Maybe she'll come back.*

She says she loves him.

But she said she loved me.

If I loved her that much I would have married her, he tries persuading himself, then he perks up. *Why didn't Klaus, or whatever his name is, marry her? She said they weren't married.*

Then he falls again. *Perhaps they are; perhaps she lied.*

Slow down, wait, maybe she'll come to her senses. True love conquers all. Think of the movies, the songs, the books. Doesn't true love always win out in the end?

Yes. But this isn't a movie.

It could be a book, though. Just write. Get back to work. Put her out of your mind.

Are you crazy?

Daphne calls. "You sound as though someone's nicked your bike," she says when she hears the despair in his greeting.

"She pinched my heart, Daphne, pinched my heart and trampled it into the ground. I can't talk."

She said she'd always loved me, he reminds himself. *That she had my image in her mind even before she was born, that she always knew I was the one. Was she lying? Why would she do that?*

A sharp knock on the apartment door jerks Bliss from his nightmare. *She's back*, he thinks. *She's changed her mind. She knows it has to be me.*

Not too fast, he warns himself. *Play it cool. Don't scare her off.* He opens the door on the second knock.

"Daisy?"

"I saw your friend. She was crying," says the Frenchwoman as she tries to enter. "I come to give you back your key."

Bless stands mute, his heart sinking lower as he blocks the door.

"Can I come in?"

"Um … I don't think …"

She nudges him aside. "You had a fight, no?" she says as she closes the door behind her.

"No. No fight," he says, and quickly reruns the entire movie of his time with Yolanda and is unable to find the slightest hint of discord; he cannot point to a single moment or subject in which they were not in total harmony. "No," he reiterates sadly. "We had absolutely nothing to fight about. We were made for each other."

"And now she cries?"

chapter eight

Neither Janet Thurgood nor Clive Sampson shows any signs of unhappiness when Trina checks on her clients following her daily rounds.

"Hey. I'll have to watch you two," she says, finding them holding hands, then she pulls Clive to one side. "Treat her nice or no more enemas," she warns, although his smile suggests he is now being satisfied in other ways. "Anyway, the heat's off," she adds, having confirmed with Mike Phillips that the dead constable's heart was already on its last legs.

"She may have done him a favour," Phillips suggested. "At least it was quick."

"She didn't do it, Mike," yelled Trina, but the inspector laughed. "The jails would be empty if you were a cop."

"Anyway," she added. "I'm gonna find out more about that place where she was."

"Careful ..." Phillips warned, but Trina closed her ears, and as she leaves her lovebirds' nest to drive home, she checks her watch for the time in England.

"Hi, Daphne," she says, driving with one knee as she switches between a banana sandwich, a coffee, and her cellphone, then she explains she is planning on going undercover for a few days.

"Are you sure that's a good idea?" questions Daphne.

"God. They're Christians," she says. "What are they gonna do — bore me to death with sermons? According to Janet all they do is pray."

Bliss is praying as he phones and re-phones Yolanda. Her recorded invitation to leave a message doesn't appeal to him, and he persists until she finally picks up.

"Hello," he starts, and then his world comes apart completely as she tells him that she cannot speak. "I have debts. I am not available," she says coolly and tries to end it, but he persists.

"You had money," he says, recalling the fact that she inherited a lucrative business from her father, but it takes her only a few moments to detail how, following their unauthorized escapade and plane crash in the mideast, she gradually lost control of the business and was forced to leave the police.

"It doesn't matter," says Bliss. "If I quit tomorrow I'd still have a guaranteed pension, plus royalties from my book and public appearances."

"Book?" she queries.

Bliss reminds her, adding, "We could have a wonderful life together and you'd never have to worry about the bills." Then he realizes that his rival may be similarly set up. "Does Klaus have money?" he inquires concernedly.

"No. None," she says and laughs. "But he cares for me."

"I love you, Yolanda. I don't just care for you. I've always loved you."

"I must go. Klaus would not like me talking to you."

"What are you saying? Does he own you?"

"He does not like me talking to other men."

"So he decides who you can speak to and who you can't?"

"I should not have followed you. I should never see you again."

"Did Klaus tell you that as well?"

"I have to go."

"Tell me you don't love me," he shouts as she prepares to cut him off. "At least do that for me."

"I can't," she says, and he hears a click that ricochets around his mind like a pistol shot.

"Give me back my heart," he cries, knowing his words are going nowhere, and he puts a Billie Holiday disc in his player and listens to "Lover Come Back to Me" as he turns back to his manuscript with a clear knowledge of where he has gone wrong.

There's no redemption, no benefit to my protagonist, the masked man, he tells himself, realizing that the incarcerated man's lifetime quest for true love was finally trashed; his story — so full of optimism and inspiration — ends in disaster and offers absolutely no hope for people who already think their lives are shit. *I lift them up then chuck them onto the rocks*, he tells himself as he considers dumping the whole thing in the bin. *Life's supposed to be happy ever after; what am I supposed to do, change history to suit Hollywood?*

The community of Beautiful may appear exactly as its name implies from the outside, but inside is where Trina is hoping to find herself, and she buddies up to a couple of long-skirted giggly teenagers pushing a supermarket buggy in the nearby community of Mountain Falls.

"Hey. Like your scarves," chats Trina, eyeing the brown headwear similar to Janet's.

The young girls turn pink, titter, and scuttle away, so Trina heads them off in the dairy aisle. "Are you from

Beautiful?" she asks as innocently as possible, but it's immediately clear that they've been primed.

"Bye..." says one, and they spin the buggy back to fruits and veg.

Stronger measures, thinks Trina, and she digs Janet's scarf from the bottom of her bag and quickly ties it around her head.

The confused look on the teenagers' faces as they meet up with Trina again in frozen foods tells her that she's winning, so she hangs back and lets them come to her.

"Are you one of us?" asks one of the girls, being careful to keep her eyes in her buggy.

"Similar," admits Trina. "But I've been travelling a lot."

An hour later, once the Beautiful bus service (a clapped-out 1960s minivan covered in hand-painted warnings against the dangers of mortal sin) has collected them and half a dozen others and driven them, singing hymn after hymn, to the community, Trina watches the surrounding forest of Sitka spruce and pine open into a stockaded compound of rusted cars and farm machinery. As the roughly hewn wooden gates let the visitor into the Saviour's world, the smell of overburdened septic tanks and rotting garbage make her want to retch, and she recoils at the sight of ragged urchins scavenging in bins alongside squirrels and dogs.

The young women and girls who sang their way home in the bus melt away as a small group of older women in gumboots, head scarves, and mud-stained dresses gather around to eye the alien. Trina looks into the sunken listless eyes of the scrawny inhabitants, thinking that they fall somewhere between anorexics and drug abusers, until the silence is broken by a bark from a bearded old man with hair flowing to his waist.

"Who is this?" he demands, and the women dissolve like phantoms at his approach.

"Mary," answers Trina, while Wayne Browning examines her with the eye of a cattle-buyer.

"Were you at Waco?" he asks from behind, fingering her head scarf, and she spins to confront him.

"No. I just want to ... I want to be part of Beautiful," she says, but he dodges her gaze and uses a hand to sweep around the grungy compound with an air of pride.

"You cannot be part of Beautiful. You have to be beautiful, feel beautiful, see beautiful. Everything here is beautiful. The Lord God has provided us with more beauty than anywhere else on earth. That's why no one ever leaves here."

"I see," says Trina, although she is having difficulty controlling herself at the spectacle of the dump surrounding her.

"Come," he says, walking away, knowing she will follow, and a few moments later she stands in an office that is only slightly less of a pigsty.

"Are you a beautiful person, Mary?" asks Browning as he roughly takes hold of her chin and forces her head up to a bare light bulb.

"I think so," replies Trina, but as she tries to look into his eyes he turns away, spitting, "Don't look at me. Have you no respect, woman? Would you look into the eyes of God?"

"Um ..." begins Trina, confusedly, but he cuts her off and rounds on her.

"Keep your eyes averted at all times unless I tell you, all right?"

"OK."

"Not 'OK,' Mary. 'OK' is trash talk. Say, 'Yes, Our Lord Saviour.' Do you understand?"

Trina hesitates a fraction longer than permitted.

"Yes, Our Lord Saviour," yells Browning into her face. "Say it. Say it."

"Yes, Our Lord Saviour."

Then his features melt. It's a game and he's a master — now for the reward. "There," he says sweetly, gently stroking her cheek. "You're learning already."

Punishment and reward — just like his mother taught him. Do something wrong, get punished. Do something right — but what is right? That is always a matter of conjecture. Only God is infallible.

It was a strategy well-learned as a child, and it has served him ever since. Keep everyone off balance; make rules that are illogical and then contort the Bible to validate them; cherry-pick the testaments, old and new, to justify anything. Isn't that what all theologians do? And Wayne Browning is a Jesus figure all the way, although he has done considerably better than his predecessor, who never made it to the biblical three score and ten. As Trina keeps her head down, she sizes up the scrawny, though firmly muscled, man and isn't at all surprised at his athletic build, considering that, according to Constable Zelke, he is servicing more than twenty wives.

"You are welcome in our community," says Browning amiably, the nice guy again, and Trina risks a peep. The old proselytizer turns away from her, so she stares at the back of his head, realizing that he is, if anything, shorter than she is. His waist-length brown hair, wispier than spider silk, is too thin to cover the stains of hair dye on his scalp, and his bushy beard has no trace of grey despite his age.

What a fake, Trina is telling herself when Browning places his hands together in a sign of prayer and spins to face her.

Trina's eyes drop as he begins, sermon-like, "Mary. We are surrounded by filth and evil," and she realizes that his power is in his voice as he continues. "Fornication, the wanton spilling of seed on the ground, greed, lust, and debauchery are destroying the world. We have to guard against those evils, Mary."

The illogicalness of the rant, considering his polygamous and incestuous relationships, is as blatant to Browning as it is to Trina, but God has provided him with an answer. "The Lord has chosen me," he claims quickly, before she has a chance to work out a more negative response. "He has protected me against sin. I am like Adam who ate the apple of knowledge and brought learning to the world; like Jesus who was crucified for our sins. Now I permit my earthly body to be a vessel, to absorb the sins of mankind and to beautify them. That is why here you will see that everything is beautiful."

"Really?" questions Trina under her breath.

"I am completely unselfish in my dealings with the Lord. I have given my body to Him for his great works. Believe me, Mary. Selfishness and greed are destroying the world. And this world *is* being destroyed. But here, everyone shares equally. There is no jealousy. Everyone gets the same measure."

Although you obviously get far more then most, Trina is thinking as she asks, "Where are all the men, Our Lord Saviour?"

"They leave," he says starkly, inviting no questions, but then he realizes that an explanation is called for. "We are very much like a convent in a way, Mary," he says taking a gentler tone. "And just as all nuns become Brides of the Lord, here most — well maybe all — of the beautiful woman give themselves to the Lord through me." Browning's voice cracks with emotion, and he wipes away an imaginary tear as he continues, "It's a very beautiful thing, Mary."

Especially for you, dirty old bastard, thinks Trina, wanting to throw up.

But Browning isn't finished. "Of course it's not that simple," he explains, as he sits at the desk and thrums his fingers impatiently. "If all God needed was for you to give yourself to him through me, we could do that right now."

Get ready with the kick-boxing, thinks Trina, but Browning is ahead of her.

"No. There are many stages of enlightenment necessary before you can be purified and become one of God's true servants through a visitation." He pauses and leaves space for Trina to lure herself into his net.

"What would I have to do?" she asks on cue, so now he backs off.

"Enough for today, Mary. You must rest now."

"But —"

"I said enough!" he yells — back to the punishment.

"Yes, Our Lord Saviour," answers Trina demurely, and then wants to know if she can join the other women.

"One day, Mary. One day," he says, then he escorts her down a brown corridor to a room and closes the door on her.

"It's two in the morning," complains Joseph Creston from his Zurich apartment when Browning phones a few minutes later.

"It's started," says Browning succinctly. "Undercover cop. She's pretty good. They tried the same at Waco."

"What does she know?"

"She was well briefed, and she's wearing Janet's scarf, so they must have her."

"I'll have to think about this. What are you planning for her?"

"I'll just shake her up a bit, be even loonier than usual. Give her twenty-four hours and she'll run back to Vancouver in bare feet."

Constable Paul Zelke's cellphone rings a few minutes later.

"Browning reckons we've got a plant in his joint," says a voice without needing or offering identification. "He called a guy in England."

"Not us," replies Zelke. "Maybe the Mounties."

"Maybe."

"I'll ask Mike Phillips in the morning."

Trina's room is a cell and she knows it. It's windowless, and the unpainted metal door is clearly not meant as an invitation to leave. The only furnishings are a canvas camp bed, a folding metal chair, and a battered pee bucket in one corner. It's 4:00 a.m. She hasn't slept — just dozed — when a key turning in the lock jumps her wide awake.

"It's time for your first lesson, Mary," says Browning in a sultry, mesmerizing tone.

"What ..." she starts, but then, as her eyes accustom to the faint blue moonlight through the open door, she sees that he is naked. "Ah ... um ..."

"Oh, don't worry," soothes Wayne, knowing what's going through her mind as he slides into the room. "You have many, many trials to pass through before you are worthy enough to be accepted into the Lord's body through me. But the first lesson — tonight's lesson — is that we are beautiful as we are. That is why we will begin as the Good Lord made us — without adornment."

"I don't ..." she mumbles nervously, but he piles on the pressure as he stands over her, building tension, waiting.

"You may take off your clothes now," he says, opening his hands and arms wide to demonstrate his own nudity as he adds reassuringly, "I get no pleasure from the flesh. I am above such things."

Yeah right, thinks Trina, but she's cornered. "I'm ... I'm not sure I'm ready ..." she stammers, and Wayne takes a long thoughtful breath, holds the moment, and then lets her off.

"OK," he says lightly. "We can start tomorrow." And he locks the door behind him.

"OK," sighs Trina in relief, recalling that according to Browning it is trash talk.

Outside the door, Wayne inwardly laughs at his performance before skipping back into his room, where Daena XXIII and Daena XXII, both fourteen-year-olds who bear a striking resemblance to their spiritual leader, sleep naked in his bed.

"Now get out of this," Trina says to herself, once she has checked that her tape recorder is working and has added a short commentary. But a windowless room with a locked metal door is too much for her. The cellphone in her purse offers a way out, although in her cloistered quarters, the signal is barely registering. Emergency only she decides, putting the phone back, knowing that, as part of her amnesty deal with her daughter, Kylie will put her father in the picture if she isn't home in seventy-two hours.

"I'm going to a religious retreat centre for a few days," she told Rick, not entirely untruthfully, but he eyed her suspiciously.

"Just a few days," she carried on quickly. "Just to get over the trauma of Janet."

"What trauma? What about me and the kids? You bring a raving loonie into the house, someone wanted for murder, and you need a break."

"Post-traumatic stress …" suggested Trina, ratchetting up the odds. "I nearly lost the guinea pig."

"You left him in the car."

"OK," she finally admitted. "The fact is that I'd really like to believe in God. It would make my life much easier and I wouldn't have to lie so much."

"Trina, who do you lie to?" he asked, confused.

"My patients of course," she explained as if he should have guessed. "I usually get ones who are on their way out, and I always tell them they'll go to heaven — but I don't believe it."

Trina has tried believing. She even goes to church occasionally. But she's too curious and too cynical to accept that her patient's sufferings are intended to ready them for their next great adventure.

"Why would a good and merciful God do that?" she has questioned many times as she sat at the bedside of tormented patients while they endured the agonies of a journey that has only one possible end.

However, Trina Button is not the only person with concerns about the immediate future. Her intrusion into the Canadian community has rippled across the Atlantic and sent Joseph Creston flying back to his London headquarters.

"I warned you this would happen," spits John Mason, but Creston stops him with a hand.

"Browning can handle it. The important thing at the moment is to divert resources to other sectors and make sure all the books are straight."

"And what about Janet?"

"The Canadian police must have her. The cop's wearing her scarf."

"And Janet's talking?"

"She doesn't even know what bloody year it is."

"Then what's the problem?"

"I hope there's none. Browning reckons he'll scare the cop off in a day or so. We'll re-evaluate the situation in a few weeks."

Trina tests the door to her room for the ninth time. Her watch and her stomach tell her that it is morning — nearing 10:30 a.m. — and she is beginning to panic. Browning hears the handle, looks up from his computer to check the clock, and decides to give her another half an hour.

In St-Juan-sur-Mer, David Bliss paces his apartment with leaden shoes as he constantly turns over the situation in his mind and tries to convince himself that it is just a nightmare. He's even written a poem in the margin of his manuscript:

> *If this be a nightmare*
> *Wake me soon*
> *That I may not suffer*
> *This intolerable torment.*

But as the sun sets on a black day, he momentarily brightens with thoughts that Klaus may not want Yolanda back. *Didn't she say I was the best lover she'd ever had, far better than him?*

What has that got to do with it? She must have loved him — she stayed with him for nearly three years.

A knock on the door tries to shake him from the depths. Probably Daisy, he thinks — still tear-filled, still trying — and he's tempted to ignore it, but the caller persists.

"Yolanda!"

She falls into his arms and he drags her inside.

"He didn't care," she blubbers.

"What?"

"Klaus. He just said 'Okey-dokey' when I told him."

Don't rush, don't overact. She's fragile, be careful. "I love you," he whispers in her ear.

"I know, and I love you too, David."

"So, Mary," says Browning when he eventually opens Trina's door. "Are you ready to begin your journey in search of the Lord?"

"Actually ... not today," she says as she pulls herself up to her full height and tries to march past him. He grabs her upper arm with powerful bony fingers and whispers menacingly in her ear.

"Hand over the tape recorder."

"What?"

He squeezes hard. "Either hand it over or I'll have you strip-searched."

"How did you ...?" she begins, but notices that a posse of four of his wives are standing fierce-faced ready to carry out his merest wish.

"That's theft," she protests as Browning snatches the recorder from her, but he just laughs.

"No, Mary. This is Beautiful. Everything here belongs to the Lord."

Two minutes later Trina is walking the logging road back to Mountain Falls with Browning's warning, "And tell whoever sent you to use a professional next time," ringing in her ears.

It's ten miles to Mountain Falls and her car, along a road that leads nowhere but Beautiful. She could try calling Rick on her cellphone but figures that it's better if he doesn't know so, as she slogs dejectedly through the silent forest, she sorts through what she has learned about Janet.

"Brainwashed," she muses aloud, realizing how easy it could be for an insecure woman with low self-esteem to fall under the old charlatan's spell. "Men are so lucky as they get older," she complains loudly as she scuffs at the loose gravel. "They just get wiser, more mature, and more women. Hah! Look at me: barely forty with stretch marks, wrinkles, and cellulite. I just get more flab and more stupid. International investigator, pah! International idiot. Browning wasn't fooled for a minute. Now what? Give up. 'Never give up,' the PI manual says. 'No matter how great the odds against you, never give up. There's always another way.'"

The rattle of an approaching vehicle turns her head.

"Our Lord Saviour thought you might want a ride back to town," says the driver of the compound's mini-bus, a girl in a brown head scarf who doesn't look old enough for school let alone a driver's licence.

Trina hesitates.

"Come on," calls the girl cheerfully. "He's a good man. He's just like God. He only wants us to do the right things so that we will be saved."

"Have you been saved?" asks Trina as she squeezes into the rear seat alongside two skeletonized supplicants.

"Oh yes. We've been saved," calls the driver over her shoulder, and they set off singing, "Jesus wants me for a sunbeam …"

"We're cleaning up the records for Beautiful," Mason tells Joseph Creston at lunchtime, but the company chairman seems unconcerned.

"Browning called back," he replies. "He's got it in hand. The cop ran. Just don't use him for a while."

"OK, J.C."

"Any news of where they're holding Janet?"

Mason shakes his head. "Early days. I've got the guy in Vancouver that Browning found working on it."

"Good man."

Mason's "guy" in Vancouver, Jody Craddock, is an ex-cop turned private eye who is having no more luck at tracking Janet than the two RCMP officers assigned by Mike Phillips.

Neither Janet nor her host has any reason to venture into the street, and as Trina is the old man's only regular visitor it seems unlikely that she'll ever be discovered.

Clive Sampson may be fifteen years older and somewhat frailer than his guest, but company is company, and since the loss of his wife to cancer he has become addicted to solitaire and staring: the television, the floor, the walls, the ceiling — the depressing view has been much the same wherever he looked. Trina's visits always perked him up, but now, as Janet slowly comes to life, he bubbles with excitement over checkers and Scrabble, and he fusses over her like a new puppy.

Janet still meditates over her crucifix and chants religious incantations, but only when she's alone, and now that her eyesight has improved she is even starting to read.

"Trina should be back in a day or so," explains Clive as he fishes a couple of ready-to-eat meals from the small freezer and pops them in the microwave. "She's a lovely woman."

"I know," says Janet, risking God's wrath by using the kitchen window as a mirror.

Without the head scarf she is less austere, although her pinched features, scraped-back hair, and glasses still give her the appearance of a girl's school headmistress. The ebony-rimmed reading spectacles, part of Trina's PI disguise kit, have brought the world into much sharper focus.

"When did you last have your eyes tested?" Trina asked, aware that Janet was suddenly more alert to her surroundings.

"Our Lord Saviour doesn't approve of adornment," she replied and was tempted to give them back — but only for a second.

The newspaper cutting from Amelia Drinkwater's photo album has finally drawn Daphne Lovelace back to Dewminster and she sits in a corner booth of a High Street tearoom rereading the headline.

"Suspicious death at Creston Hall," it states, but she knows that the line is a small-town editor's attention-gaining trick.

"What at first appeared to be the suspicious death of 6-month-old Johannes Creston, heir to the Creston Empire," the article continues contradictorily, "has been ruled natural causes by Dewminster police and the Coroner."

That tells me a lot, thinks Daphne as she skims ahead.

"The child's father was in Zurich at the time ..."

That rules him out then.

"The mother, Janet Creston, (22 yrs. née Thurgood), put the baby into his cot as usual ..."

Fair enough.

"Doctor Symmonds of Dewminster, the family's physician, reports that cot deaths are not uncommon and suggests parents regularly check on their young during the night."

I wonder if he's still alive, Daphne is questioning as she orders a pot of Earl Grey from the waitress, then she inquires.

"Oh yeah, luv," replies the women cheerily. "He comes in here some days. He only lives 'round the corner."

"Actually," says Daphne quickly getting up and slipping on her hat. "I think I've changed my mind."

"Dr. Symmonds?" Daphne asks ten minutes later, having located his Victorian townhouse by the rectangle of wood that used to hold his brass nameplate on the wall adjacent to the black lacquered door.

"Yes?" he acknowledges and invites her in.

The aroma of cigar smoke commingled with mentholated liniment momentarily takes Daphne back to her youth and her father slouched in his Sunday evening chair after a day in the garden, and she hesitates while she imbibes the atmosphere.

"I guess this was your surgery," she says, taking stock of the room with its old leather couch and wheeled fabric screen and recalling the days when she undressed and shivered in similar rooms.

"Before they opened the new clinic and replaced stethoscopes with a million quids' worth of gadgets that can't tell a tumour from a pimple on your ass," he says sourly as he ushers her to his living quarters.

"In here," he carries on, holding a door open, and she joins him in a high-ceilinged day room where he has been playing chess. "Do you?" he asks hopefully, but she shakes her head.

"Not for years. Although I used to."

"Never mind. What can I do for you?"

Peter Symmonds screws up his face in thought and spends half a minute relighting a cigar when Daphne inquires about the Creston family's loss of baby Johannes.

"Sounds like Sudden Infant Death Syndrome," he says as he vigorously shakes out his match. "Though to be frank, I don't remember the case."

"It was a long time ago," agrees Daphne.

"Quite."

"Apparently they lost three."

"Did they?" he asks while casually continuing with his game.

"You don't recall?"

"Three ... no ... as I say, it was a long time ago."

"True," admits Daphne, but can't avoid noticing that he's made an illegal move. "Should that go there?" she asks, pointing to the misplaced pawn.

Symmonds looks confused for a second as if trying to straighten his mind. "Oh, silly me; no wonder I never win," he says, forcing a laugh as he rearranges the piece.

"So you don't remember then?" Daphne pushes one more time.

"Sorry," he says and rises to let her out.

chapter nine

The sun has returned to Bliss's Mediterranean world, but he cannot stop himself checking and rechecking the figure in his bed, fearful that the beautiful mirage will vanish with the dawn.

If this be a dream
Wake me never
That I may not suffer
the pain of disillusionment.

He scribbles in the margin of his manuscript, telling himself that this is how his novel should end, realizing that it hasn't been only historical facts that have prevented him from finishing his book about the lovestruck man who incarcerated himself on an arid island to prove his love. He has been held back knowing that, in a way, he was that man; since Yolanda's apparent death, he has been wearing a mask. He has been hiding himself away, protecting his heart in the forlorn hope that one day she might somehow be resurrected. And now she is here, in his apartment, in his bed.

"David," calls Yolanda softly from the pillow.

"I thought you were still asleep," he whispers, lying beside her and stroking her face.

"I could you feel you watching me."

"I can't take my eyes off you."

"Are you real?" she asks, opening her eyes and peering deeply into his. "Are you real?"

"Of course."

"I still can't believe it; I still can't believe they lied to us."

"I know," he says, slipping out of his dressing gown and sliding under the bedclothes, "but we're together now and no one's ever going to separate us again."

"Promise, David," she says exploring his body with her hands.

"I promise, Yolanda."

"Will you marry me?"

"Of course. Today if I could."

Instant marriage may not be in the air, but love is, as the happy couple stroll the promenade hand in hand. However, Angeline at L'Escale has heard Daisy's side and is less than welcoming as Bliss and Yolanda stop for a coffee and croissant.

"Hah! So now I suppose you stop zhe writing," the waitress accuses acerbically without acknowledging Yolanda, and Bliss is forced to defend himself.

"Just for a few weeks, Angeline."

But Yolanda picks up on the slight and barely waits till Angeline is out of hearing before asking, "What is the problem?"

"Nothing," says Bliss and changes the topic. "So, why did you come here to St-Juan?"

"I have an apartment," she replies, waving vaguely towards several harbour-side blocks. "I didn't lose everything after the crash." But she makes no attempt to be more specific. He would like to see the place, but fears that, in a way, Klaus is still there, unlike Daisy, who was never more than a visitor in his bedroom.

The distant look in Yolanda's eyes warn him that her mind is somewhere else — still with Klaus, he assumes — as she peers across the harbour. Time is suspended as memories hold her gaze, and Bliss wants to break the link, but he knows it will take time for her to adjust to the fact that she has been abandoned by one lover even if she has discovered another.

"Yolanda," he calls softly after a minute, and she comes back slowly.

"Sorry," she says, as her blue eyes gradually find his, but there is no focus. "I was thinking of the time we were in Istanbul together."

"OK," he says, with no intent to challenge her.

"Coffee," says Angeline slamming down the cup and breaking the tension.

"Tell me about Klaus," suggests Bliss once Angeline has gone, and Yolanda's eyes wander again.

"I thought he loved me. He obviously doesn't."

"But he took care of you?"

"Let's not talk about it," she replies picking up her coffee cup and using it to block him out.

The following two weeks in the warmth of the Mediterranean tinges their world pink. Satchmo plays "*La Vie en Rose*" more than once on the stereo, and, as in everything else, the lovers find harmony in music, natural and composed: waves on the sand; breakers on the rocks; the gentle breaths of a contentedly sleeping partner; the timbre of each others' voices and the slight exoticism of their respective accents.

They may have been conceived in different countries and different cultures but they conjoin physically and mentally with such perfection that they could be womb-mates.

"I adore the earthy scent of rain on parched ground," Bliss admits one night as the sky darkens from the north.

Yolanda laughs. "It is my favourite smell."

With Christmas coming fast, the days and nights pass in complete unison: music, art, movies, books, food, sex — almost daring to find something on which they disagree, anything at all — cooking and sharing meals, walking sandy beaches, watching sunrise, sunset, and moonrise one day, then sleeping through all three the next.

Nothing has been heard of Klaus. "He will not come," Yolanda assures Bliss on several occasions. "He will never accept what I have done."

Daisy, on the other hand, has been more persistent, and when a Christmas parcel arrives, Yolanda is by Bliss's side as he walks from the past into the future by sending it back unopened.

"I'm sorry," he says, but neither blames Daisy.

"I think she loved you," Yolanda says, and Bliss nods agreement before explaining that, although he tried, he was never able to love her completely in return.

"I even took her to Las Vegas," he admits. "Even flew her family there. They all thought I was going to marry her."

"Were you?"

That's a good question, he thinks and digs deeply for an answer. "Possibly. But I lost the engagement ring and realized that it was an omen."

"Omens are important, David."

"I know," he says, amazed at his admission, but since his encounter with the Man in the Iron Mask and the numerous ghosts of the Château Roger he's dropped his skepticism of all things metaphysical. "It was like you being here without Klaus," he tells her. "It was planned that way to stop you making a huge mistake."

"He is a good man," she says again, and Bliss doesn't argue.

"I know. But where is he? Two weeks ago you told him about us. Did he phone, send flowers, email, write, beg, plead? Did he show up to beat my brains out and drag you back?"

"No," she admits sheepishly.

"I would have."

"Really?"

"Of course. I would have done anything to get you back."

"Anything?"

"Absolutely anything," he replies looking firmly into her eyes. "I would have done anything to get you back."

It's also been more than two weeks since Trina's abortive attempt to infiltrate Beautiful.

"You're damn lucky Browning let you go," Mike Phillips lectured her when she tried to lodge a formal complaint.

"What are you going to do about him?" she wanted to know, but Phillips was at a loss.

"Asking someone to take off their clothes isn't a crime, Trina."

"But he's screwing schoolgirls in the name of God."

"George Bush bombed Iraq in the name of God and we can't nail him either," Phillips reminded her, then seized a chance to catch her off guard. "I suppose that if we spoke to your friend Janet, or Daena, or whatever her name is, we might be able to do something."

Trina spotted the ploy and shied off. "Sorry, Mike, can't help."

Daphne Lovelace, on the other hand, has been more fruitful with her search for answers thanks to her persistence with Superintendent Donaldson.

"You'll get me shot," he said as they pored over sepia-edged folders in a damp corner of the basement of

Westchester Police Station. "It's lucky that this is the Divisional HQ, otherwise they wouldn't be stored here."

But they were not in luck. "Nothing," he said, once he went through every year's incident files from 1955 to 1965. "Nothing at all in the name of Creston."

"Is that odd?" inquired Daphne, peering over his shoulder.

Donaldson weighed one of the folders in his hand meditatively. "Yes, Daphne. I mean, three sudden deaths with the same name. I'd expect some record ..." then he paused with an idea. "Central Records. I bet the files were forwarded there."

A phone call later they had an answer.

"No records there either."

"What does that mean?" Daphne wanted to know.

Ted Donaldson gave her a sideways glance. "I guess that we were never involved. The doctor must have been satisfied."

Daphne still had the newspaper clipping in her handbag. She knew the police were called. "Doctors can do that?" she queried.

"Yeah," nodded Donaldson. "Two qualified, competent doctors are all that's required."

A trip to the public records' office in London has netted Daphne copies of the Creston children's death certificates, but the information is sparse: name, date of birth, date of death, cause of death. Three deceased siblings within as many years — the eldest only six months — may have rung alarm bells in Daphne's mind, but the registrar of births, deaths, and marriages seemingly had no problem accepting that each succumbed to prolonged bouts of pulmonary infirmity.

Maybe it was natural causes, Daphne is thinking, until she finally uncovers the names of the certifying doctors from the local registrar in Westchester: Dr. Symmonds in every case. Not just Peter Symmonds the chess player, but also Dr. Roger Symmonds.

"His father, I presume," she is telling Ted Donaldson by phone a few minutes later, and the superintendent agrees.

"It's quite common, Daphne. Especially in country practices. Just like the police."

The late December days on the Côte d'Azur still hold a memory of the autumn warmth, and a few hardy bathers still take to the crystal waters each morning. Avid sun worshippers, as brown and wrinkled as ripe passion fruit, still raise their faces to squeeze every last ray from the low-hanging sun.

The ardour between Yolanda and David Bliss has grown stronger each day, and they need nothing to keep them warm as they saunter hand in hand along the shore. All Bliss sees in their future is sunshine.

"We could go to Hawaii after Christmas," he suggests, determined to make up for all the time they have missed in romantic places.

"Maybe," she replies, just a little less enthusiastically than he anticipated.

"We don't have to…" he starts then feels the chill of a cloud on the horizon. "What is it now?" he asks, easing her to a stop and trying to look into her eyes.

She hesitates for a long moment as she looks over his shoulder at the sea then turns to look northward beyond the Alps.

"It is Klaus," she says eventually.

"What?"

"David, I don't know …"

"What are you saying?"

"It's just …"

"What? What?"

"David. Today is the day that Klaus was going to come here to me."

"But he didn't come."

"Because I told him not to."

"That's all right then," says Bliss with a sigh of relief as he takes her hand and tries to move on. But she stands rigid — everything is not all right.

"David. I have to go."

"What?"

"I am sorry, but I can't do this to Klaus. He has been so good to me."

The beach crumbles beneath Bliss's feet; hammers beat into his brain; sweat pours from his forehead. "We've been through this. He doesn't love you."

"David …"

"No. You can't do this again. This isn't fair. I love you. I've always loved you."

"I know, but —"

"You said you loved me."

"I have to go right now."

Bliss reaches out desperately. "No … Yolanda … please don't. Please don't leave me again."

"I'm sorry, David. I should never have followed you into the château. I should have let you go on thinking I was dead."

"Then tell me you don't love me."

"I can't."

Bliss's heartbeats crash against his ribs as he watches her walk away. "He doesn't love you, Yolanda," he yells after her. "He doesn't love you or he would have come." Then he slumps to the sand and buries his head in his hands. "Call me. Please call me," he pleads, but she doesn't hear.

The sun has sunk into the sea by the time Bliss pulls himself to his feet. He stands for a while seriously considering whether anyone would really care if he walked into the darkening ocean with his pockets filled with rocks, but he slouches back to his apartment.

"I should have known," he tells Samantha as soon as he gets through.

"Oh, Dad. Why? I thought she loved you."

"She does. She just feels guilty because this guy has done so much for her."

"But that's not fair. You love her."

"I know."

"Anyway, why did you say you should have known?"

"Because of the Man in the Iron Mask," he explains. "He lost the only woman he ever really loved. That's what's been holding me back, stopping me from finishing my novel. I wanted a happy ending. But there isn't one."

"Dad. You are not the man in the mask."

"Are you sure?"

"Oh wake up, Dad. She'll come to her senses. True love always wins out. Don't you read books and watch movies?"

"She says she loves him."

"She pities him, Dad. She just feels sorry for him."

"And she doesn't pity me?"

"She won't sacrifice herself and her future if she has any intelligence."

"She might."

"Then they'll both be miserable for the rest of their lives. Look at it from his point of view: imagine living with someone who you always know, deep down, would rather be with someone else."

"Maybe she lied to me. Maybe she really does love him."

"In which case, she could never have made love to you, not the way she did."

The apartment is empty. Not only has Yolanda gone, she has taken her spirit with her. Bliss wanders dejectedly picking at bits of clothing she's left behind. A dozen red roses, just one day old, bring back memories that are suddenly torturous and he's tempted to fling them over the balcony. The fallen lemon is still on the grass — if that was an omen, it was an ill one.

Bliss picks up the phone and puts it down twenty times. *She'll call. Don't call her. She won't answer. You'll make a fool of yourself on the answering machine. Worse — it'll be busy. She'll be talking to Klaus, whispering sweet nothings, saying, "I'm really sorry. Hurry, come to me. I love you."*

Stop tormenting yourself. He won't come. Keep thinking that; keep praying that he won't come. He won't come.

Maybe she'll go back to Holland to see him.

No, that's worse. I'll never find her.

The phone rings. He leaps for it. It's Daisy, coldly. "Zhe rent is due on your apartment, sir."

"Sir!" What is this "sir"? But he doesn't complain. He's tempted to tell her about Yolanda, but common sense prevails.

"I want her back," he yells to the walls.

After what she just did?

"Yes. I want her back," he shouts. "I love her. I love her."

The Man in the Iron Mask loved his woman and remember what happened to him.

Daphne phones. He lunges for it, praying for Yolanda.

"Glad I caught you —" starts the elderly Englishwoman.

"Not now, Daphne."

"David!"

"Sorry, Daphne. Expecting an important call," he says as he puts it down, then he sits by the phone all evening waiting for a knock on the door.

It's a mistake — come back please. He doesn't deserve you; what man would leave you like that? Not phoning, no flowers, nothing.

It is three in the morning, but the Land of Nod is way over the horizon as Bliss lies in the silent vacuum left by Yolanda's departure. He would walk the deserted quays in the cold moonlight but won't risk leaving the phone, so he stares at the ceiling, his mind full of her: her luscious kisses, her sweet scent, her heavenly body. He wills himself not to let her spirit go even for an instant. *You're the only woman I've ever truly loved, and you love me, I know you do. I would have died for you.*

The following morning comes an hour earlier to the offices of Creston Enterprises in frosty London as John Mason claps his hand over the mouthpiece of his phone. "It's the Canadian private eye," he explains to J.C. Creston. "He's finally found Janet."

"She's shacked up with some old guy in a big house in North Vancouver," Craddock continues in a Bronx accent he reserves for foreign clients.

"Are you sure it's her?" asks Mason, flicking the PI onto the speakerphone.

"Yup. Followed the broad who first found her. Tina somebody or other; been following her for a week. Christ. She drives like a freakin' —"

"No profanity please, Mr. ..."

"Craddock — just Craddock."

"So, Craddock," says Creston, leaning in to the speakerphone. "If we wanted her moved, would you be able ..."

"You mean like — heavies?"

"Well. She may not be co-operative. They may be protecting her."

"Hey, we're talking big bucks."

"Yes. But could you do it?"

"Mebbe. I'd have to bring in the whole team. It could cost —"

"We'll get back to you, Mr. Craddock," cuts in Mason.

"Just Craddock."

"What do you think, John?" asks Creston once the speakerphone is off.

Mason sits back and rubs his chin thoughtfully. "If she disappears now, first place they'll look is Browning's dump."

"She's obviously not said anything?"

"About what?"

"Anything," says Creston.

Janet is talking — mainly religion, but Peter Sampson doesn't care. A woman's voice in his home has taken ten years off the old-timer.

"I won't be needing anymore enemies," he whispers to Trina and she sniggers briefly at her patient's malapropism before looking worriedly in Janet's direction.

"You two aren't —?" she starts, but Sampson angrily cuts her off.

"No. Of course not. Daena's an angel. Angels don't do things like that." Then he bends to whisper in Trina's ear. "And God watches everything we do so I have to be careful."

"Oh, no," mutters Trina under her breath. "She's roped you in, has she?" But she puts on a smile as she says, "I'm very pleased for you both."

Bliss's mind is in such turmoil that he finally picks up the phone. She answers. "Yolanda — I have to see you."

"I don't think that is a good idea."

He hears the coldness. *She is shutting me out. Quick, I need an excuse.*

"I have some of your clothes."

The silence as she seeks a rebuff is deafening.

"You really should have them," he says to fill the void.

"I …" she starts then pauses. He senses her reluctance to relent, but he waits.

"Okey-dokey," she concedes eventually. "On the seafront — L'Escale in half an hour."

The phone goes dead. She won't talk. She can't talk. *She loves me and she knows it. If you love her let he go, but why should I let her go. She loves me. She always loved me. Klaus should let her go, not me.*

The bar L'Escale is as deserted as the rest of the jaded resort, but at least it's open. Bliss wants to grab her; shake some sense into her — *You're mine, Yolanda. You're mine* — but all he manages is a weak, "Hello."

"I'm sorry, David, Klaus is coming. I have no choice."

"Yes, you do."

The meeting lasts an hour, but it's over in the first minute. He begs and pleads, but Yolanda is unshakeable. "I am really sorry. I'm just not available at the moment. I'm promised to someone else."

"At the moment?" Bliss questions. "What do you mean?"

Yolanda shrugs. "Just give me a little time, David."

"And you'll come back?"

"Perhaps. Maybe things won't work out with Klaus."

"Maybe they will," he says, and he knows he's lost her as he walks away with his eyes on the ground.

At least I don't have to try to change history, he tells himself in consolation as he spies the fortress on the island. The Man in the Iron Mask really did die of a broken heart.

Bliss's phone is ringing as he opens the door to his apartment. His heart leaps — she's changed her mind again — but it is Daphne.

"David. Are you all right?"

Some woman just run me over with a steamroller, he wants to say, but he doesn't want to explain, so he snaps, "Yes. What did you want?"

"I think I'm onto something, David," she says conspiratorially, but Yolanda is the only thing on his mind, and he doesn't keep up as she explains her theory that the three Creston children were all murdered and Doctor Symmonds is hiding something.

"That's why they sent her to Canada," she is saying by the time he gets his focus.

"Sent who to Canada?"

"Have you been listening?"

"Yes … no. Sorry, what do you want?"

"I want to know if you have anyone who could do a bit of break and enter for me?"

"What?"

"I'd do it myself, but I'm not quite as slim as I used to be."

"Daphne, all you'll need is a lawyer if you do things like that."

Aha! A lawyer, she thinks. "Great, David," she says. "I knew you'd have an answer." Then, armed with an excuse, she phones Samantha, his daughter.

"I'm really worried about your father," she claims.

"Don't worry. He's in love," says Samantha, catching on immediately.

"I thought he was ill."

"It's the same thing, Daphne. At least it is when it hurts."

"The old unrequited love kick."

"No, not exactly," says Samantha, but she's not sufficiently sure of the facts to explain. "Anyway, what can I do for you?"

"I need to get a hold of some medical files," explains Daphne, then fills in the young lawyer with details of the Creston deaths before outlining her suspicions about Symmonds. "The funny thing is that the police paperwork's missing and the doc who signed the records and death certificates reckons he doesn't remember them."

Doctor Peter Symmonds has concerned himself with nothing other than the deaths of the young children since Daphne's visit, and he is finally driven to call Creston.

"Symmonds," he announces himself when he's put through to Joseph's private line.

"Peter —" starts Creston cordially.

"Someone's making inquiries."

"About?"

Joseph Creston is well aware of the subject of the doctor's call, as is Trina Button when Daphne phones her.

"Three kids in four years and the doc doesn't remember," Daphne complains, her voice full of incredulity. "The Crestons are the biggest family around here. You know, Creston chocolates?"

"Yeah. We get those here."

"Anyway, Amelia Drinkwater remembers all right, and it was nothing to do with her. Well, not directly."

"Indirectly?"

"She claims that Joseph Creston dumped her and went off with Janet. She called her a trollop, but she's a sour old witch."

"So would I be if I was in love with an heir to a fortune and he dumped me and pushed off with someone else."

"Anyway," says Daphne, "the only place I can think that there might be something incriminating about the deaths would be at the doctor's place. I've spoken to David's daughter; she reckons there's no chance of persuading a court to give me a search warrant."

"PIs don't use warrants," says Trina, laughing. "PIs use stealth."

"I'm getting just a little bit past —"

"Don't worry. I'm coming over."

"What?"

"Janet's safe now. I can't get back into that Beautiful dump. I'll get an overnight flight."

"Oh, to have that kind of money," sighs Daphne as she puts down the phone.

"England!" exclaims Rick when he arrives home from work and walks into a heavy suitcase in the hallway.

"It's Daphne," explains Trina with a pained expression. "She needs me."

"But you've only just got back from that retreat centre."

"That was weeks ago," she claims. "Anyway this isn't for my health, it's for Daphne's."

"How long?"

"Thanks ever so," she says breaking into a smile and kissing him. Then she turns as she heads out of the door with her suitcase. "There's banana curry in the fridge ... make sure you take the guinea pig for a walk."

chapter ten

By the time Trina's 747 gently kisses the Tarmac at Heathrow the following morning David Bliss has crashed in the South of France. He's worked his way through a litre of wine and enough brandy to pickle a dozen peaches, but the pain in his heart is so severe that he's considering a bottle of Aspirin.

"She will call ... She will call," he repeats like a mantra, but by midday the silence gets to him and he's forced out to walk the lonely quays again.

Trina has studied her manual for PIs during the flight and found the section on mobile surveillance particularly riveting.

"This is great," she breathes as she practises trailing unsuspecting drivers as she leaves London for Daphne's Hampshire home.

The narrow roads and zippier cars of England are seen as a bonus to Trina as she whizzes the rented car in and out of traffic with the alacrity of a rally driver. "Got ya," she yells time and again as she sticks to the tail of vehicles when they switch lanes to avoid her.

"Move over, I'm coming through. Oh shit!" she shouts to the air as she battles her way into an impossible gap. Private eyes ought to be allowed to have sirens like police, she tells herself as she races a set of changing lights. She loses, but it doesn't stop her, and she gives a friendly wave to the driver of skidding truck. She's out of earshot before his shouted insult catches up to her.

"Right," says Trina as she hits a roundabout at double the posted speed, then she panics. "Or is it left?" The stream takes her, but she's on her third circuit when the truck she cut off at the traffic lights catches up.

"Hey. Yer a crazy freakin' lady," yells the driver as he uses his forty tons of gravel to squeeze her onto the wrong exit.

"Rats," says Trina, realizing she is headed back to London, so she makes a U-turn into the path of a taxi.

"God, the drivers here are real aggressive," she complains to Daphne an hour later when she arrives. "Always on their horns and swearing."

"I hadn't noticed," admits Daphne.

"No wonder they have so many accidents," continues Trina as she sips a cup of tea in Daphne's living room. "I saw at least three near misses."

"Well. You'll have to be very careful," warns Daphne, but she is anxious to move ahead with her plan to infiltrate Peter Symmonds' archives so she pulls out her carved soapstone chess set to help explain her strategy.

Vancouver's ace private investigator, or so he would like to believe, also has a plan in mind when he phones Creston.

"Craddock, Vancouver," says the PI with as much weight as he can put into the two words. "The target's minder is on the lam."

"In English please, Mr. Craddock."

"Just Craddock. The crazy woman who's been minding your wife has taken off. One of my associates picked her up on a B.A. flight to the U.K. last night."

Craddock has no associates, just a client working at Vancouver airport who happens to owe him a favour — several favours.

"Only, I was thinking," continues Craddock, seeing his future bank balance ballooning, "if you were looking to get your wife out, now might be a good time."

Creston puts his hand over the mouthpiece and sits back in thought.

"Sir?" asks Craddock after a few seconds.

"Call back tomorrow," spits the executive gruffly. "I'm thinking."

Dr. Peter Symmonds eyes Daphne coldly as she stands at his front door.

"I was wondering about that chess game," she prattles on, careful to avoid his gaze. "Only you looked as though you might be grateful for someone to give you a game."

Symmonds hesitates long enough for her to add a little pressure. "Of course, I'd quite understand ... only I'm on my own as well. And I just thought you might like a bit of company."

"I was having an afternoon nap," Symmonds lies as an explanation for his apparent reticence.

"Daphne ... Daphne Lovelace," she says, smiling while holding out her hand. In her other hand is a confectioner's box tied with a red ribbon. "I brought a couple of éclairs ... fresh cream ... naughty but nice," she adds as a peace offering.

"All right," he says, relenting and opening the door, and, as he guides her through the disused consulting room to his private quarters, she asks, "Do you still see patients?"

"Not really. Just a few old friends who don't trust the kids who practice today."

"Bunch of cowboys," scoffs Daphne, as if she has frightful experiences to share.

"Quite."

Symmonds was a good chess player in his time but he's been playing solitaire so long he's lost his edge. The disquiet caused by Daphne's presence, and some apparently wacky plays, keep him off balance, and no one is more surprised than Daphne when she wins the first game.

"Checkmate," she shrieks triumphantly, but the look of dismay in the old doctor's face suggests that she's more likely to win if she loses.

"How about a cup of tea and a chocolate éclair?" she proposes, leaving him no alternative, and she starts to rise with the kitchen in mind.

"I'll make it," he says patting her back down, but she gets up anyway, explaining, "Old bones ... need to stretch." Then, as he heads into the adjacent room, Daphne saunters to the rear window.

"I'll bet this is very pretty in the summer," she calls out as she surveys the overgrown rubbish heap that was at one time a back garden.

"It used to be. It's got away from me since the wife died."

Daphne peers deeply into the undergrowth, but it's nearly four and in the wintry twilight she sees no sign of Trina amid the brambles and lilacs that have rampaged since Symmonds' wife's sécateurs ceased to cut.

"Maud used to spend most of her time out there," Symmonds carries on nostalgically, making Daphne jump by his nearness, and she spins to find him peering over her shoulder.

"Oh!" she exclaims. "I thought you were making the tea."

"Almost ready," he says, skipping back to the kitchen. "Kettle's almost boiled."

"Where are you? Where are you?" mutters Daphne under her breath as she returns to the garden and searches for Trina. Then she spots movement in a neighbour's oak tree.

"Oh no! Wrong garden," she murmurs between clenched teeth as she wills Trina to look her way.

"Do you take milk?"

"Yes, please."

Trina. Trina, she mentally yells, and after a quick check over her shoulder she frantically signals to the woman below.

"Sugar?"

"No thanks," she calls, then spots a table lamp.

"It's getting dark," she carries on as she picks up the lamp and waves it back and forth across the window.

"Are you all right?" questions Symmonds entering with a tray.

"Oh yes," says Daphne, holding the porcelain-bodied lamp high and peering at the base. "I was just wondering if it was Meisson."

"Royal Albert," says Symmonds, carefully placing it back on the table. "I was a G.P. not a brain surgeon."

"Right," says Daphne, still unsure if Trina got the message.

David Bliss, on the other hand, is getting the message. Two dozen unanswered phone calls leave him in no doubt that his chance of getting back his lost love is rapidly slipping away.

"She's even moved," he tells Samantha as he holds back the tears. "I made some inquiries and found her place. It's empty. She's gone, Sam. She's gone."

"Well don't just mope, Dad. If you love her that much get her back."

"But how? She won't talk to me. I don't even know where she is."

"Have you ever heard of scripting?"

"What?"

"Scripting. You write down what you want to happen. You centre on exactly the kind of future you want, and who you want to share it with, and you carefully script it."

"Sounds like hocus-pocus ..." he begins, then reminds himself that he didn't believe in the possibility of past lives and spirits until he felt the masked man's presence on the island of Ste. Marguerite.

"Look. You're writing a book anyway," she explains.

"Not anymore," he says dejectedly.

"Why?"

"Because it has a sad ending."

"And you want a happy ending?"

"Everyone does, Sam. Everyone does."

"Well it's your book, Dad. Write it the way you want your life to turn out."

"But my book is about what happened three hundred years ago. I can't change history just because I've been jilted."

"So you were there were you?"

"No."

"Then how do you know for certain what happened?"

"But I'd have to rewrite the whole book. I'd have to change the story. It will take months."

"Dad, do you want Yolanda back or not?"

"Of course I do."

"Then start writing. Script the story of the Man in the Iron Mask the way you want your life to turn out."

"With a happy ending ... with Yolanda."

"Unless you prefer to die a miserable old bachelor."

"So there I was behind the Germans' lines," Daphne is rabbiting on as she pours herself a third cup. But her wartime experiences, and her visit, are wearing on her host and she senses it. Peter Symmonds has checked his watch half a dozen times. The tea is cold and he's made no offer of warming it.

"I really must tell you about the time I saved my life with a packet of chocolate digestive biscuits," she continues enthusiastically, trying to spice up the conversation, but Symmonds has heard enough.

"Some other time, Daphne," he says, rising and pointing at the mantelpiece clock. "I'm afraid I have to get ready for an engagement."

"Oh, silly me," she says, but as she stands a muffled crash makes them jump.

"What the hell was that?" demands Symmonds.

"Probably my chair," Daphne replies quickly and tries to reproduce the noise, but Symmonds isn't fooled.

"Stay there," he commands and runs for the stairs to his basement.

"Trespass; burglary; aiding and abetting; conspiracy ..." Superintendent Donaldson reels off a list of charges that add up to a life sentence as the two women stand in front of him in the charge room at Dewminster police station. "What the hell were you doing breaking into his basement?"

"I am a Canadian private investigator," states Trina loftily, but Daphne digs her in the ribs and puts on a smile for Donaldson.

"Ted ..."

"It's Superintendent at the moment, Ms. Lovelace."

"Right," she says sheepishly. "The thing is that I — we — suspect that the Creston children were murdered."

"Stop right there, Daphne," says Donaldson, shaking his head in despair. "We've been through this. Natural causes, remember?"

"But there are no records."

"Because there was nothing to record."

Daphne still has the newspaper clipping in her handbag that gives lie to Donaldson's assertion, but she decides to leave it there for now.

"Anyway," continues Donaldson, "you're lucky that the good doctor doesn't want to press charges."

"Does that mean we can go?" asks Trina already inching towards the door.

Donaldson pulls her up sharply. "No. Not until I've formally warned you. You may be a foreign visitor, Ms. Button, but if you or Ms. Lovelace try another stunt like this you'll get a guided tour of a British prison. Understood?"

"Understood."

"Hah! Private investigators," he scoffs as he shows them the street.

"Did you get anything?" asks Daphne excitedly as soon as they are out of range.

"Think so," replies Trina as she ferrets down the front of her pants. "Good job they didn't strip-search us."

"What happened?"

"Stupid book," she moans, complaining of her investigator's manual, which suggested that professional burglars open a cabinet's bottom drawer first and work their way up so they don't have to close one before opening the next, adding that closing drawers takes time and makes noise.

"That makes sense," admits Daphne.

"No it doesn't," bleats Trina. "'Cuz when all the drawers are open the weight tips the whole thing on top of you."

"Oh dear," titters Daphne.

"Plus," continues Trina, "Creston starts with C and was in the top drawer anyway."

The file is thin — too thin to properly record the lives and deaths of three children, according to Daphne. "There should be more than this," she says as she surveys the scant pages pulled from Trina's pants: copies of the death certificates and a few handwritten pages of notes.

"All there was," says Trina with a quick check.

"That's interesting," says the elderly woman, scanning the forty-year-old handwriting. "I can never be sure if my doctor's prescribed Aspirin or hemorrhoid cream, but I can read this without glasses. Weak lungs; bronchitis and asthma attacks; coughs; colds; pneumonia-like symptoms …" She looks up. "All three had weak chests according to this."

"Let me see," says Trina taking a couple of the pages, then she pumps a fist in the air. "Yes!"

"What?"

"OK," she explains. "This one is John Creston."

"That was Janet's first son, the one with the other guy."

"Correct. Well his notes are all signed by Roger, the old doctor, Peter Symmonds' father, and they are in blue ink."

"Yes," says Daphne peering over her shoulder.

"And this is Giuseppe's file, the second son, and all the entries are signed by Peter Symmonds in black ink."

"Yes."

"And the third one, Johannes, is back to the father. But look at the handwriting."

"It's different from the first one."

"Yes," says Trina, "and you're not even an expert like me. I've studied this in my manual. It says that people who forge documents disguise the size and shape of their letters but can't change the slope or spacing. I'd have to put them under a magnifying glass, but I'm pretty sure the second and third ones were both written by the same person."

"That interesting …" begins Daphne, still unsure, but then she has a revelation. "Wait a minute," she shouts. "Why did Symmonds let us get away with them?"

"What do you mean?"

"Look, he knew that I was inquiring about the Creston deaths. So when he found you in the basement with an upended filing cabinet, why didn't he check to see if they were missing?"

"They were all over the floor."

"So he calls the police. We get arrested and then what?"

"Then he had time to check."

"And to tell Donaldson that the Creston papers were missing."

"And he didn't."

"Why not? That's what I'd like to know."

Doctor Peter Symmonds knows the answer. So does Joseph Creston Jr.

"Shit, Peter, this is a bloody mess," fumes Creston as he sits opposite the old doctor in the study of Creston Hall a couple of hours later. "Are you sure she's got them?"

"I've been through the whole lot."

"Why the hell did you keep them?"

Symmonds gives the irate man a quizzical look. "Because it might have seemed a tad suspicious if anyone came calling from the ministry and I couldn't produce them."

"All right, all right," says Creston as he pours himself a very large single malt from a crystal decanter.

Symmonds doesn't have a drink, and although his troubled expression suggests that he could use something to bolster him, the local laird isn't offering.

"So what's the damage?" asks Creston, slumping into a buttoned leather chair and slugging back most of his drink. "What can they find out?"

"I don't really know. It was forty-odd years ago. I'll stick with my story and my old father isn't around to contradict me."

"So. Do we have a problem?"

"We may," says Symmonds guardedly. "The Lovelace woman has been talking to Amelia."

"Oh."

"She still loves you. You know that."

"Yes. Don't remind me. But she's not going to say anything, is she?"

"Probably not," agrees Symmonds. "But what about Janet?"

"Leave her to me," says Creston, draining his glass, and minutes later Craddock is woken by his cellphone as he daydreams in his car a few hundred yards from Clive Sampson's house in leafy North Vancouver.

Despite Trina's warning to Clive Sampson to keep his hands to himself he smiles warmly as he strokes Janet's cheek while they snuggle in front of a movie.

Three weeks ago she would have recoiled at the touch; she would have flayed herself at the feet of Wayne Browning, begging forgiveness for her wanton ways, begging absolution for craving both a man and a movie. And she would have suffered, as God intended. But isn't that what women are supposed to do? Doesn't the Bible ordain that women should suffer? Shouldn't a woman kneel at her master's feet? Shouldn't an adulteress be stoned to death?

But Janet is not an adulteress — not with Sampson, anyway. And if she ever worried that being penetrated by Browning violated the vows she made to her husband, the cult leader was quick to point out that it wasn't his penis inside her, it was merely an instrument of God, and that sex for him was no more exciting than the administration of a priestly sacrament.

"I have sacrificed all worldly pleasures for my God," the preacher sermonized as he pumped furiously with a smile on his face. "I am doing this for your sake, Daena."

"Do you think you could love me?" whispers Sampson tentatively, but Janet isn't sure she's allowed.

"I'm still married ..." she starts, then takes stock. Clive is older — at least fifteen years — though his eyes still sparkle and his brain is alive. "Maybe," she admits. "But I've nothing to offer you. Even these clothes are from Trina and her daughter."

"We'd manage," Sampson is saying as the doorbell interrupts. "Who could that be at this time?" he wonders aloud, and is on the point of answering when he looks at Janet. "You'd better hide."

"Why?"

"I don't know," he admits, "but Trina said we ought to be careful."

The bell rings again with seeming urgency and draws the elderly man to the spyhole. "Who is it?" he questions loudly and puts an ear to the door.

Another ring, and Clive Sampson is readying to quiz the unrecognized visitor again when a shoulder bursts through the panelling and he is thrown to the floor.

Another dawn in St-Juan-sur-Mer comes without sunshine for Bliss. "Klaus is probably here by now," he tells himself dejectedly, with Billie Holiday crooning "That's Life I Guess" in the background, as he scans the town roofs from his balcony.

St-Juan-sur-Mer is not a big town, not like nearby Cannes or Nice, and it lacks the pizzazz and ritz of Monte Carlo further along the coast. It's just a neglected backwater famous only for a brief, though triumphant, visit by Napoleon in the early 1800s after he escaped from exile on the island of Elba. But amongst the tight seventeenth-century lanes and crowded twentieth-century apartments, there are a thousand places that Yolanda could be. Bliss is tempted to search for her, but what if he finds her hand in hand with Klaus? At least he can still preserve her image unsullied by the presence of another; he can still picture her naked in his arms.

He picks up the phone — Samantha again.

"Oh God, Dad. I'm trying to work," she complains from her office in drizzly London. "Just do what I told you. Write the damn book and make it come out the way you want it."

"But what if she doesn't come back, Sam?"

"That'll be her loss. Anyway, you'll have the book. And think of the publicity. I can see the headlines in the *Times Literary Review* now: 'Heartbroken detective writes novel to win back his lost love.' You might even make international headlines with a story like that. Christ, Dad, I wish someone would write a novel for me."

"Aren't you happy with your Peter?"

"Of course. But he's not exactly Casanova. Anyway, my point is that publishers and the media will love it. Just do it."

"Rewrite the whole thing?"

"Yes, if that's what it takes. Yes."

As Bliss is putting down the phone in his Côte d'Azur apartment, J.C. Creston is getting an update from his man in Vancouver.

"We had to give her a sedative," explains Craddock, adopting a partner to boost his credibility and his final invoice. "But she'll be OK."

"And what happens now?"

"Well, my people on the inside will let me know when the heat's off. As soon as everything's cool we'll move her."

"Not back to Beautiful."

"Shit, man. That's the first place they'll hit. In fact you'd better warn your man there to expect a visit."

However, neither Wayne Browning nor Joseph Creston need worry yet. Clive Sampson is telling no one of Janet's abduction and won't be talking at all unless a neighbour, or the mailman, investigates his smashed door and unties him from his bed. In any case, Janet doesn't officially exist. In fact, officially Janet Creston, née Thurgood, has never existed in Canada. She was shipped into the country over forty years ago by private jet, and not a single government official has ever recorded her name. She's not alone.

Beautiful is not the kind of place where record keeping is encouraged, although since Janet's disappearance, Wayne and a couple of his most trusted angels have been quietly shredding everything that could be linked in any way to the Creston foundation.

"So where have you got her?" asks Creston thoughtlessly and Craddock explodes.

"Christ, man. Are you shittin' me?"

"Mr. Craddock —"

"Craddock."

"Craddock. Will you please stop taking the Lord's name in vain."

"Sorry, man, but this is an open line for Christ ... Jeez ... What in hell am I supposed to say? Hey. She's safe, OK? That's all you need."

"All right. Keep her that way. I'll have to decide what to do."

Janet's safety is not at stake. Being bound and gagged in the back of a van parked inside Craddock's garage may not be comfortable but, in many ways, it is no worse than the privations of Beautiful.

Trina Button's confidence in her private investigator's manual, and her own abilities, may be unswerving, but Daphne Lovelace would rather consult a professional over the handwriting on the doctors' records, and she stands in front of the mirror in the tight hallway of her Westchester home and works her way through her hat rack as she prepares to visit one in London. Flouncy, lacy, and white are out, and she finally settles on a staid bowler with its serious edge taken off by a slender pink ribbon and a silk rose, then she shrinks at her partner's millinery choice.

"We are going to the City, you know," she reminds Trina a touch acerbically at the sight of the other woman's Yankees baseball cap, but the Canadian shrugs it off with a laugh.

"Oh, Daphne. Sometimes you can be so ... Miss Marple, so Agatha Christie. Me, I'm more of an Ian Fleming."

Mark Benson is an ex-MI5 operative who never came close to anyone resembling James Bond during his service. He's a spindly, pencil-sharp figure with Coke-bottle glasses and a taut mouth who spent his time as a spy in a back room poring over ciphers, until he discovered that there was more capital and less politics in private practice.

Daphne and Trina find the document examiner's garret office from the brass plaque beside a door in a narrow backstreet behind the Central Criminal Court — the venerable Old Bailey — from where he caters to the hurried needs of defence lawyers.

"In my opinion, based on a cursory examination," Benson advises them over the top of his bi-focals, once they've laboured up four flights, "at least one of these documents may not be precisely what it seems."

"A definite maybe," suggests Daphne under her breath, but Trina is less pessimistic.

"I knew it —" she starts, but Benson cuts her off with a warning hand.

"Ms. Button. Document examination is an art, not a science. There is always an element of subjectivity." Then he eyes the papers critically. "An ink analysis will show that two different types were used, but we can see that by the colour. As to whose hands were holding the pens at the time, that will always be open to a degree of speculation."

"We'd be happy to accept whatever you can give us," says Daphne, while Trina wanders the room, nosing at various pieces of equipment as if she is conversant with their uses.

"It'll take me a day or so ..." Benson starts, and then he firmly removes a calibrated magnifier from Trina's hand and gently replaces it on his workbench. "Very delicate," he warns as Trina pulls out a chequebook.

"We only have a couple of hours," she says with pen poised. "How much would that be? Say, five hundred dollars?"

"I thought he was going to faint," laughs Daphne a few minutes later as they wait in a nearby coffee house from where they can see the scales of justice atop the renowned court's dome.

"I'm sure it's the same writing," says Trina. "And I'm pretty sure that our Doc Symmonds knows more than he's letting on."

"But how we will get him to talk? You won't buy him off with a few hundred quid. Fixing death certificates has got to be a serious crime."

"So why would he have risked it?"

"Money," suggests Daphne.

"There you go," says Trina with a hint of triumph. "Everyone has their price."

Janet Thurgood is paying the price for her escape from the nightmare of Beautiful as she lies, bound and gagged, on an old mattress in the back of a broken-down Ford van in Craddock's garage. The taste of the duct tape across her mouth makes her retch, and her bony wrists ache from being immobilized, but she is no stranger to isolation.

I don't deserve this, she tells herself, and then admits that she probably does; for the past forty years, judgment day has always been just around the corner. But hasn't she been punished enough? Four decades in a prison administered by a lunatic; forty years of beatings and sexual slavery; forty years of pseudo love — love used as a weapon to be withheld or given on a whim: one word out of place, one wrong move, and a week's isolation.

"Our Lord Saviour must be obeyed," Browning would declare. "You will only find salvation with God through me. I am punishing you for your own good. You must change your ways Daena … change your ways to please your master."

"Yes, Our Lord Saviour."

"You must change before I will speak to you again."

One week, two weeks — the agony of rejection, the withdrawal of affection, even the twisted affection of a control freak.

"Chastise me. Tell me I must change to please you. Tell me what a terrible person I am. Tell me anything. Brand me, mark me, just don't ignore more. Please don't abandon me, I need you."

And then, eventually, when he is ready and not before, "See, I've forgiven you, Daena. Our Lord Saviour is pleased with you. You can rejoin the fold."

"Thank you, Our Lord Saviour. Thank you."

chapter eleven

---

*T*he Truth Behind the Mask *by David Anthony Bliss*, writes Bliss on a clean pad of paper as he prepares to start his novel for the third time. But now he has a mission; now he knows the conclusion and knows the direction he must take; now he knows the passion felt by Louis XIV's most notorious prisoner as he endured eleven years in the island fortress across the bay from the fishing village of St-Juan-sur-Mer in the late 1600s; now he knows of the heartbreak of a man whose stolen love took him to the edge of sanity; now he knows that he will do all in his power to reclaim Yolanda.

It is the month of May, sixteen hundred and eighty-seven, Bliss continues writing, his pen flowing easily across the virgin page. *Orange blossoms, jasmines, and mimosas scent the air of Provence, but only the stink of hot coals and sweat pervades the forge in the Fort Royal on the Isle Ste. Marguerite. In a hell's kitchen of fires and furnaces, legionnaires wrestle to hold screaming men down as blacksmiths forge shackles around their ankles and wrists. However, in one corner, two flambouyantly attired Musketeers anchor a man whose head is being sheathed in an iron mask. Unlike the shackled prisoners in the their rags, this man holds himself aloof, and as the final rivet is hammered in place, he has a smile on his face as he is helped to his feet; though no one sees it. Indeed, no one will see his face again — ever — should his great plan fail.*

Mark Benson turns up trumps with the documents. "Good news, ladies," he says with a smirk of satisfaction as he welcomes Trina and Daphne back into his office.

"Hold on a minute," wheezes Daphne. "Those stairs …"

"Here," he says, offering a chair, then he carries on. "I would say that there is a ninety-nine-percent chance that the second and third documents — those pertaining to Giuseppe and Johannes Creston — were written by the same person, despite the fact that they purport to have different signatures."

"Really. How can you be so sure?" Daphne wants to know, though Trina is beaming as she silently pumps the air with a fist.

"Similar characteristics," he explains, then he pulls up a greatly enlarged computer image from a comparison microscope. "Fortunately these were written when most pens still had nibs," the expert carries on as he indicates consistencies between the two magnified samples that sit side by side on the screen. "Also," he adds, "judging by the wear pattern on the nib I would say that the all the entries relating to the third child — Johannes — seem to have been made at roughly the same time, even though it was supposedly written over a six-month period, from birth to death."

"When was it written?" asks Daphne as she critically eyes both the screen and the original medical record.

"That's another interesting thing," says Benson becoming more animated as a second digital picture from the microscope pops onto the screen. "I've enhanced this area," he says as he points to a corner where a faint impression of "August 17ᵗʰ, 1963" can be seen like a spectre in the paper.

"But Johannes died on August 15," Daphne reminds herself as she picks Amelia Drinkwater's newspaper clipping from her bag and shows it to Benson.

"What does that mean?" asks Trina, peering inquisitively over his shoulder.

"It means that when this document was written, the previous one on the pad was dated two days later," says the examiner sagely over the top of his bifocals. "It appears that someone rewrote these records after the child's death."

"Wow," says Trina, then her cellphone interrupts. "Rick?" she asks, hearing her husband's voice. "What time is it there?"

"About nine. Look, your office called in a panic about one of your patients, a Mr. Sampson."

Clive Sampson is nursing a smashed face and a bruised ego as he sits by the phone, refusing to go with the paramedics until he's spoken with Trina.

"They took her," he shrieks as soon as Trina gets through.

The angered woman spits, "I bet it's Browning and his freaks," as soon as she's heard his tale. Then she spins around to include Daphne in her plans. "OK. We've got everything we need here. We're on our way back."

"We?" questions Daphne jauntily.

"Of course," says Trina, lacing her arm through her partner's and leading her out of Benson's office. "If anyone knows the truth it's Janet."

"And Doc Symmonds," adds Daphne.

"Yes. Well he ain't talking to us is he?"

"But …" protests Daphne, so Trina puts on a frown.

"You don't want another trip to Vancouver?"

Daphne bends. "I'll have to get someone to look after Missie Rouge."

"It's a deal, then," laughs Trina, and she whips her baseball cap back to front to signify success.

Coppersmiths beat the final pieces of sheathing into place atop the Château Roger while beneath them a legion of workers decorate the expansive rooms with Chinese silks, Persian tapestries, and Venetian chandeliers from the island of Murano, writes Bliss as he views the now decrepit building from his balcony and imagines the original owner taking a similar view.

"My great testament to my lost love nears completion," said the lovelorn man, watching from his cell across the bay as the edifice's state rooms were filled with the most sumptuous furnishings from around the world: opulent gold and silver ormolu furniture, emulating the style set by Louis himself in Versailles; the finest porcelain and silverware from the king's own factories in Gobelins; beds made of the softest Norwegian down. Servants by the score, all decked out in uniforms of finest Egyptian cotton, walked the halls …

"Thirty pages," muses Bliss with satisfaction as he sits back and puts down his pen at the end of his first day's serious writing. It's amazingly easy when you know the whole story, he thinks, although he knows that is not true; while he wants a happy ending to his story he has a huge stumbling block in his path — historical fact. No matter how he contorts his plot he cannot alter the authenticated records of the day that show Louis XIV's unnamed and unknown prisoner was destined to die miserably in the Bastille in 1703. *However*, Bliss tells himself, *would I get onto a plane if I knew it was going to crash?* So, knowing that somehow he will find a way to avert disaster, he falls onto his bed, exhausted, eager to start early tomorrow and the next day, and next, *ad infinitum,* until his script is complete and, just like his rejected predecessor, he can wrest his true love from another and begin the remainder of his days in her arms.

Maybe I really am a reincarnation of the Man in The Iron Mask, he considers as he falls asleep no more than a couple of leagues from the place where the famed prisoner slept three hundred years before.

Clive Sampson, septuagenarian widower, a man trapped inside his front door since the death of his wife five years ago, has forced himself out and anxiously paces the arrivals concourse of Vancouver airport the following afternoon. "I'm so sorry, Trina," he cries, rushing up to the homecare nurse as she emerges with Daphne in tow. "He just broke down the door and grabbed her."

"Oh look at your poor face," says Trina as she puts an arm around the distraught man's shoulders, but Sampson isn't bothered about the scars on his nose or his black eye.

"They took her, Trina."

"I know."

"But I love her."

"I didn't know that," she admits as she uses a Kleenex to gently wipe his swollen eyes. "Never mind," she adds. "I've got contacts. I'll get her back for you."

"I want her back, Trina," he snivels and Daphne steps up to sandwich him.

"Don't worry, Clive," the visitor says kindly. "Trina knows what to do."

Trina has no idea where Janet is or how to release her. Neither has Mike Phillips an hour later when he pays an official visit.

"I'm very cross with you," says the RCMP inspector, putting on his police voice and a stern face as he corners Trina in her kitchen. "You were hiding her."

"Mike," coos Trina with a warm smile as she straightens his tie. "Remember when everyone thought your wife had murdered her first husband?"

"Of course."

"Who believed in her? Who said she didn't do it?"

"You did."

"Right. So if I say Janet didn't kill your cop friend —"

"I know," he butts in. "We don't think she did either."

"Good," says Trina. "Although," she adds *sotto voce*, "she might have killed her kids."

Janet Thurgood accepts that she killed her children; accepts the forty-year sentence her husband imposed on her; accepts that she is an evil woman who deserves the punishment meted out to her; accepts that, even now, after a lifetime of prayer and supplication, she may still fry in the fires of hell. And she lies quietly on the dirty mattress in the back of the old truck reliving the time before her transgressions.

Amelia Sawbridge, as the curmudgeonly magistrate was in those far-off days before she latched onto Cecil Drinkwater, occupied a private family box at the front of the nave in St. Stephen's in the Vale, while Janet and her relatives were forced to shoulder their way into the hard wooden pews with everyone else. Joseph Creston in his choirboy's cassock and surplice, an angelic figure with straight white teeth and soft blonde curls, looked over Amelia's head to find the one he truly lusted after. Amelia spun around to glower. Money might land you a front row seat in life but sometimes the view is better from the back, Janet recalls thinking as she relives the scene and smiles discreetly at her young admirer.

And afterwards, amongst the bluebells in the churchyard, Amelia in her Sunday best satin draped herself over

Joseph while all the time his eyes never left the one he really wanted beside him.

Amelia's parents — financially and socially secure, although nowhere near the same stratum as the Crestons — attempted to catapult themselves into the aristocracy on their daughter's back. "Our Amelia's pretty soft on your boy, J.C.," her father said as he offered a Churchillian-sized cigar from a monogrammed silver case, but Joseph Creston Sr. shrugged it off.

"They're only children. Joseph needs a few years in the city before he's ready for that."

But Joseph Creston Jr. was ready "for that," though Amelia wasn't. "It's a sin. We'll both die," she insisted when he finally got down to her underwear on the back seat of one of his father's Jaguars after a church youth group meeting.

Janet was more accommodating — much more accommodating. "I love you," she whispered in his ear the very first time they consummated their relationship, and he loved her back instantly. But he already knew he loved her. He knew he loved her the very first time their eyes met, and he continued loving her despite the knowledge that another man's fetus was growing inside her.

Janet wasn't the only one escaping when she eloped with Joseph; she wasn't the only one rebelling against an overpowering and over-religious father. But once the knot was tied over the Bible, neither they nor their families were willing to risk the vengeance of God by untying it.

"Janet," a voice calls softly as the back door of the old van creaks open. Inwardly, she wants to yell, "It's Daena XV," but knows that time has passed; she has finally moved on.

"I've brought you something to eat," says Craddock as he carefully removes the tape.

"Thank you," she mutters, though she is aware that the words are blurred by the numbness of her lips.

"Drink this," he says, putting a straw into her mouth, and she does as she is commanded, as she has been programmed to do all her life.

Her only escape was with Joseph, but that was short-lived. Her baby got in the way. It wasn't his and he knew it, and when it died — and to him it was an "it" — he was happy enough to announce that the next one would be theirs.

Giuseppe Crispin Creston was his baby, just like he had been to his father, and he doted on the blue-eyed little boy who even had his blonde curls.

"It's chicken," says Craddock, feeding Janet some pieces from a KFC carton.

"Thank you," mumbles Janet, though her mind is still on the sickly baby who never went a night without a fit of coughing until, one night, he simply stopped.

"It wasn't your fault, Janet," young Doctor Symmonds assured her as he certified the death. "It happens," he said, as if it happened every day.

But the loss of a child, like the loss of a true love, leaves the heart irreparably torn, and Janet's third pregnancy brought more apprehension than joy.

"Bathroom," pleads Janet as Craddock prepares to leave her, and he helps her out, half carrying her to a stinky toilet at the back of the garage. Janet doesn't retch at the ammoniacal smell. It's no more putrid than the ones at Beautiful. The only thing missing are the religious quotations reminding users that wherever they are, whatever they are doing, God is watching.

"Thank you," she says again as Craddock helps her back into the van.

The PI shakes his head, laughing. "You sure are a crazy lady."

"I know," she says as he reties her wrists, reattaches the tape, and closes the door.

In the darkness, Janet returns to her thoughts of earlier times, when she and Joseph danced around each other at a distance, kept apart by the pain of the death of her second child, their child — kept apart rather than drawn together by the loss. Then the third pregnancy, a pregnancy forced upon them by Creston Sr., who demanded that his son produce an heir.

"It'll help you get over the loss," the vicar from St. Stephen's in the Vale counselled after he was brought in by the godfather of the family. But what did the bachelor cleric know of loss? His losses in life were usually other people's. He could always go back to the vicarage, take off his collar, and cheer himself with a few glasses of sacramental wine at the end of the day. He didn't have to live with the pain around the clock, as Janet did.

The third and final death — baby Johannes, nicknamed from birth as Joe-Joe — was the final straw, and Janet had no choice but to accept the blame. Joseph, her husband, was away in Zurich taking over some of the business reins, and Margaret, the nanny, was off for the weekend. Only Janet and the baby were at home in their modest thatched cottage in the grounds of Creston Hall.

A few days later, once Peter Symmonds straightened everything out, the executive jet that had rushed her husband back from Zurich slipped her across the Atlantic and on to Beautiful.

"You need treatment," the doctor told her as he shot a sedative into her arm, and he flew with her all the way to an abandoned air strip carved out of the British Columbian forest.

Wayne Browning, barely thirty years old at the time, was a brash white Alabaman who used and abused his Bible with as much skill as he controlled the people who sought his ministry. He absorbed his biblical knowledge from his mother as other children absorb milk. His father was a broken-down alcoholic who could barely read and rarely worked, but his mother prayed loudly night and day that things might improve. They never did, and Charlotte

Browning often ended up flat on her back with a bar drunk to pay the rent. The abuse never stopped her praying or her belief that she was headed for a better world, but if she did end up in heaven it was on the end of a carving knife that Wayne's father plunged into her heart one night when he was too far gone to know or care.

Browning was sixteen and barely schooled when he packed his bag and headed north for a new life in a new country. But he knew all the best bits in the Bible: the really powerful bits, the bits that sensible theologians waltz around in chamois pumps. He knew Samuel: "Obedience is better than sacrifice; Defiance is a sin against God." Leviticus: "Homosexuals shall be stoned to death." Deuteronomy: "If a man's son is disobedient, the elders shall destroy him at the city gates."

He could recite every damnation and every self-serving text, but whether he understood was another thing, and it didn't matter to him or his flock. His words alone would control as he played good cop/bad cop with the religious texts. And women — usually with low self-esteem — were always anxious to please, anxious to do his bidding, anxious to be branded by him, anxious to go to heaven.

Janet had, in her mind, many sins to atone for, and, like a prison lifer, she quickly learned that obedience was all that was required to survive and prayer was all that necessary for her salvation; prayer, and the pleasuring of God's representative on earth, Wayne Browning.

It has been three days since Janet's disappearance, but this time the police have pulled out all the stops. Forcible abduction from a house in the ritzier end of town is less easy to ignore than a crazy woman who wanders away from a commune, even if she is witness to a fellow officer's death. In any case, with Daphne and Trina both putting the bite on him, Inspector Mike Phillips wants her found. The press have been pulled in and Craddock is getting worried.

"I gotta get her outta here," the private eye tells Creston once he's scanned the headlines in the Vancouver dailies, but he assumed that he would eventually take Janet back to Browning's commune and now has no plan since Beautiful is out of the question. According to the *Vancouver Sun* an entire police division is camped out near the community.

"You should have made better arrangements," fumes Creston, although he's convinced in the back of his mind that Janet poses no real threat. "Is she still mentally disturbed?" he asks.

"A real fruitcake," says Craddock. "No one would believe a word she says."

Creston wavers. "I don't know."

"Well, I can't keep her forever," protests Craddock.

"I'm aware of that," shouts Creston, slamming down the phone.

David Bliss is someone else whose ordeal is far from over. The writing is progressing, but after an initial burst in which he managed to keep Yolanda in the back of his mind for a couple of days, he's come unglued again.

"Why did she do it, Sam?" he wants to know, calling his daughter for support.

"Just keep writing your script, Dad."

"You're humouring me."

"Someone has to. But like I said, if she doesn't come back you'll have a mega-bestseller on your hands."

"Really."

"Of course. Everyone loves a great romance, and yours rivals *Romeo and Juliet*. You could be the next Shakespeare."

"Now you are joking. Anyway, I wonder if it isn't more like *Taming of the Shrew*, with me as the shrew."

"Stop worrying. I can just imagine you on the radio," she says, primping up her voice to sound like a BBC announcer. "So — just how far would you go to get back the love of your life? A few soppy poems, a couple of dozen roses perhaps. Well, that might be enough for some women, but on today's show we have a lovestruck man who wrote, and got published, an entire novel. Please welcome … Yeah!"

"I'd rather be with Yolanda, thank you," Bliss moans dryly.

"Then do it properly. Have faith."

Trina's son, Rob, wakes Daphne when he barges into the basement suite at seven in the morning looking for his skates.

"Mum," he protests, when he tracks her down in the kitchen. "This place is like a friggin' hotel when you're here."

"I know," says Trina, mixing banana pancakes. "And I'm thinking of letting out your room as well."

"Very funny."

"It's only Daphne from England," she explains. "You remember her?"

"Is she the old lady you nearly killed last year?"

"It was an accident."

"Yeah right. I remember, anyone can get lost in the Cascade Mountains in a bathtub."

Daphne pops her head around the door looking for a cup of tea. "Good morning."

"Hi, Daphne," chorus the family.

"According to Amelia Drinkwater the kids were murdered," Daphne succinctly sums up over the breakfast table as soon as Trina's husband and children have left. "Doc Symmonds is covering for someone, the police files have been dumped, and Janet is round the bend. I'm not sure what we're trying to prove."

"Think about it," says Trina excitedly. "What if we cracked three forty-year-old murder cases?"

"And what if we discover that Janet really did kill all her kids?"

"She didn't. She's too religious," suggests Trina.

"Oh, come on," protests Daphne. "Half the murders in the world are committed by religious zealots."

Trina is stumped for a second. "All right, let's say she did; then we can switch sides, put on blinders, and prove she didn't. Lawyers do that all the time."

"Don't let Samantha Bliss hear you say that," laughs Daphne.

"Anyway, I'd like to do something about that freak up at that Beautiful joint. Those women are all like zombies," Trina continues, putting on a monotone. "'Yes, our Lord Saviour,' 'No, our Lord Saviour,' 'Three bags full …'"

"Maybe Janet will be able to help if we find her."

"I doubt it. She believes she's a reincarnated angel."

David Bliss is still lost in a deep hole, and Daisy seizes an opportunity to slip in to fill the void.

"It wouldn't be fair to you," insists Bliss when she shows up at his apartment with a bottle of Côtes du Rhône and a couple of dozen oysters.

"But, Daavid. She might never come back to you," says the Frenchwoman as she tries to muscle her way into the kitchen.

"That's true," he admits, blocking her. "Then I'll just have to be on my own for the rest of my life."

"Zhat is crazy."

"No, Daisy. That's love," he says, knowing that the masked prisoner faced a similar quandary; despite the lovesick man's outrageously romantic gesture he risked permanent incarceration if he failed in his mission. "I feel terrible about letting you down," he carries on as he gently turns her around. "But the truth is that I've always been in love with Yolanda."

"Not always," protests Daisy, but Bliss shakes his head and edges her back out.

"Always, Daisy. And she said the same about me. She told me that the moment she saw me she realized my image had always been in her mind. That she had spent her life looking for me."

"And now she leaves," scoffs Daisy.

"She'll come back Daisy … she'll come back," he assures her as he slowly closes the door.

But will she? he questions, as Daisy wipes a tear and turns away, and then he walks through to the balcony and looks across the town to the promontory where the Château Roger hides its shame amid the giant eucalyptus trees.

And if she does, will it take eleven years? he asks himself, knowing that, despite the masked man's grandiose gesture of offering the magnificent building as the prize to his dream woman, she apparently rebuffed him.

And if Yolanda rebuffs you? he asks, but he stops the dark thoughts with the realization that his novel offers an opportunity to salve more than one sore. *If Samantha's scripting thing really works*, he reasons, *and I do write Yolanda back into my life, then why not get revenge on Chief Superintendent bloody Edwards while I'm at it. He's the gerrymandering villain who claimed she was dead and trashed my dreams.*

"So," he questions aloud, seeking a character to imbue with Edwards' malevolent traits. "If the Man in the Iron Mask was the good guy, who was the rogue of his day?"

Louis Quatorze, Duke of Normandy and King of France — Louis *le Grand* as he insisted on being known — springs readily to Bliss's mind, and he hunts through his stack of research papers for information.

"Gambling was the main entertainment at the court of Louis XIV," he reads from a piece culled from a biography of the sovereign. "It was well known that the king was not only good at the table, but that he was a quick-witted intriguer who could adjust the odds in his favour," the paper explains, and Bliss hits on a way to incorporate his nemesis in his scripting.

If his own situation was orchestrated by the machinations of Edwards, he reasons as he flips his notepad onto a clean page, why shouldn't the masked prisoner have been goaded into his romantic ploy by his Machiavellian master? *"Sacrifice is what all women desire,"* the sovereign opined to the young Ferdinand, a handsome Hungarian prince who sought his advice in the art of seduction, he scribbles quickly as King Louis' devious plot takes shape. *"In everything women enjoy abundance. From the size of one's house to the dimensions of one's organ. The only way to win favour is to spend extravagantly on the table, on clothes, carriages, houses. But it is never sufficient for the fair maidens to use their wiles and their loins to take your heart, usurp your power, and spend your money — they want sacrifice. 'Why wouldst thou not fight a dual for me? Risk thine life for me in battle? Joust until dawn for me?'"*

"But I am neither a dueller nor jouster, not of any repute," protested the love-sick man. *"Though I am esteemed for my grace in the minuet and gavotte."*

"Few women would consider the sacrifice of a pair of dancing shoes to be sufficiently noble to win their affection," suggested the king, an expert in heart matters. *"And you are but a poor fool if you cannot conspire to lay your neck upon the block without risking your head."*

"Very clever," muses Bliss, seeing the deviousness in the king's design to inveigle the heartsick young man into building a great château on the very edge of his kingdom — a château that, if the scheming ruler gets his way, will end up belonging to him.

No wonder Louis was detested by associates and enemies alike, admits Bliss with a certain chief superintendent in mind, although the French king was shrewd enough to outlive most of them. But was he happy?

Who is happy?

I was.

Don't start that again. Keep writing — write her back into your life. It's not over till it's over.

You mean it's not over until she marries Klaus.

No. I mean it's not over until you die.

But now, with his story progressing, death is definitely not an option. Absolute victory is now Bliss's only aspiration, so he calls Samantha with the good news and discovers that Daphne is in Canada with Trina.

"Oh God," he moans. "Not another hare-brained charity fundraising scheme?"

"Not this time — no crazy marathons, just something to do with murdered babies."

"Those two will get into serious trouble one of these days."

"Right," says Trina flopping a large notepad and her PI manual onto the table in front of Daphne. "Strategy session."

"First we have to find Janet," suggests Daphne.

"And then?"

But beyond that neither of them has any notion.

"OK," says Trina a few moments later as she writes "Find Janet Thurgood" across the top of the first page. "Let's work on that first. We'll figure out the rest as we go along."

"Find Janet," echoes Daphne, and she peers out of the window across the haze covered city of Vancouver towards the surrounding mountains as if seeking clues.

"Newspaper," cries Trina and excitedly grabs the day's copy of the *Vancouver Sun*. "I flushed out a friend's husband once with a photo on the front page."

"Really?" gushes Daphne.

"Actually, I was a bit naughty," admits Trina with a girlish giggle. "I bared my titties on the Lions Gate Bridge and stopped the traffic."

"Oh, Trina!"

"I know … but it worked. Anyway don't go all la-di-dah on me Ms. Daphne Lovelace, OBE," she carries on, giving the elderly woman a cheeky nudge. "I've heard stories about you."

Daphne's inner smile gives nothing away, although in the back of her mind she sees flashes of times long ago when, as a wartime agent, the exposure of her breasts in public would have seemed childishly innocent. "We could try the papers…" she begins, but her tone suggests that there are alternatives, "but why don't we put ourselves in the minds of her kidnappers first?"

"Kidnapper," corrects Trina. "According to Clive Sampson, there was only one."

"If only he'd got a look at him," muses Daphne, then she leaps up with an idea. "Come on. Grab your hat," she says. "We've got some legwork to do."

"Legwork?"

"Yes. If we're supposed to be detectives, let's act like real detectives."

Trina glances at the clock. "The bars don't open till eleven," she says mischievously. "Though we could get a coffee and donut."

The winter hours of the bar L'Escale in St-Juan-sur-Mer are as laissez-faire as Angeline, the waitress. During the ten tourist-filled weeks of summer the dusky-skinned local dashes back and forth across the racetrack of a road to her customers seeking shade under giant parasols on the promenade overlooking the harbour. Balancing heavily laden trays, she plays chicken with fast-footed stallions at the wheels of gaudy chick-magnets, and generally causes enough fender-benders to keep the local repair shop owner happy all year.

But the heat of summer is now only a memory, and David Bliss is the only remnant as Angeline brings him yet another glass of red wine.

"So how is zhis book about *l'homme au masque de fer*?" she asks as she peers over his shoulder.

Bliss looks at the blank page — the same page he's been looking at for six hours — and shakes his head. Then he picks up the glass and studies the red liquid seeking inspiration.

Come on, he tells himself. *You can do it. Remember what Sam said. Have faith. Write it properly and she'll come back.*

"Do you believe in love, Angeline?" he questions, looking into the dark Latino eyes of the pretty waitress.

She shrugs. "*Bof! Mais oui* ... Of course, monsieur. But I am half Italian and half French. I have no choice but to believe."

Do I have a choice? Bliss wonders as Angeline needlessly dusts off a nearby table, and he watches her for a few minutes questioning why he could not fall in love with her. What's so special, so different about Yolanda? "Magic," he tells himself and springs his mind back to the moment their eyes first met, when his brain fell out as he attempted to brief her and her fellow officers about the disappearance of an English computer agent aboard a ship bound for Holland. It was a moment of total, overwhelming magic, he decides, and finally picks up his pen knowing that his legendary character must have felt the same in order to have been so smitten.

"*I was instantly captivated by your opal eyes,*" he begins, giving a voice to the lovelorn Prince Ferdinand while using the pretty dark waitress as a model. "*I dissolved at the soft tenor of your melodious voice. I recognized the sincerity and honesty in your smile. I felt the wisdom and intelligence emanating from your mind. I quivered at the perfect form of your body.*

"Your flowing nigrescent hair, your delicate fingers, and your slender legs, completed a portrait of such perfection that a heavenly lyre player strummed my heart and the voice of a sweet trumpet sang in the air.

"Rippling wavelets on the Mediterranean shore continued the perfect rhythm of the universe, while, for me, time stopped. Then the lyre player took over — plucking my heart until my whole being vibrated, and the sound of my rushing blood pulsated in my ears."

Daphne and Trina's quest may have not have the same significance, or passion, as Bliss's search for the truth behind the fabled masked man and his own destiny, but it has, nevertheless, borne fruit.

"I can't believe the police didn't find this," muses Daphne as she pores over the handful of evidence that she and her friend found in the street not far from Clive Sampson's house.

"I can," sneers Trina. "That lot couldn't find a johnny in a condom factory. All they do is hound innocent motorists like me."

"It was fairly obvious that he didn't just turn up and burst in," says Daphne, agreeing by implication. "He would've been shadowing the place for hours ... maybe even days. He'd need to know the odds. Who was at home?"

"He had to suss the place out," suggests Trina. "For all he knew the fuzz might have had the place under surveillance."

"Oh, that's very English," says Daphne.

"I've been watching Inspector Morse," admits Trina. "Your cops always seem a lot cleverer than ours."

"You've gotta be good if you are not carrying," drawls Daphne in a New York twang, and she catches the look of surprise on Trina's face.

"*NYPD Blue*," says the older woman, laughing, then she goes back to the items scattered across Trina's dining table and lists them. "Twenty-four cigarette ends — all the same brand, smoked to the filter — from three separate locations in sight of Clive Sampson's house; one receipt — Pizza-Pizza, $15.27 — the day before Janet was snatched; a Creston chocolate wrapper; and several lumps of spearmint gum."

"Wait a minute," says Trina flicking through her private investigator's manual for the section on tracing people. "How did he know where to find her? She didn't register a phone, a TV, or a car; she didn't buy anything; she had no mail; she didn't tell anyone — she didn't even know where she was."

"What about Clive, your patient? Would he have told anyone?"

"You are kidding. He thought he'd died and gone to heaven. He wouldn't have done anything to risk losing her."

"Oh! What love will do to a man," mutters Daphne wistfully.

"So — hang on," says Trina. "The only people who knew she was with me were Mike Phillips and that creepy sergeant who's always trying to nail me."

"Maybe they followed you when you smuggled her out."

"Hold on a minute," says Trina as her face lights up, than she grabs her baseball cap and makes for the door. "Won't be long."

Three minutes later she's back, smiling, and with her baseball cap reversed. "Look," she says, popping open a closed fist like a magician to reveal half a dozen cigarette butts that match those on the table. "He must've been watching me; must've followed me to Clive's place."

"So how did he know she was here?" Daphne wants to know.

Trina spits, "I bet that little snot Brougham grassed on me."

"Grassed?" queries Daphne with a smile.

"More Inspector Morse," admits Trina while picking up the phone to call Mike Phillips.

"Be careful what you say," warns Daphne. "Maybe it was Mike who told someone."

"Not Mike," replies Trina, shaking her head with absolute certainty, but she slowly puts the phone down. "Hey, let's do this ourselves. Who needs the police?"

chapter twelve

Joseph Crispin Creston Jr., son of the great man himself, sits on his throne at the head of his boardroom table under the heraldic crest bearing a motto that translates loosely as, "We are one family under one God," and he tries to focus on Dawes' weekly financial update.

"American chocolates are down again," reports the accountant. "But our Californian division has a new low-carb drink coming out next week."

"And Europe ... Southeast Asia ... Australia ..." quizzes Creston one after another as he assimilates the state of his holdings and the health of his bank balance.

"The Muslims have snatched another bunch of farmers in Ivory," adds Mason, once Dawes has closed his ledger and left.

"Anything more about Janet?" asks Creston.

"Nothing, J.C.," replies the lawyer with a shake of his head. "Look, according to our man in Abidjan they're asking ten thousand a head."

"Pounds or dollars?"

"Dollars — but I reckon they'd settle for a thousand."

"Forget it. You'll just encourage them."

"But we ought to do something. If they keep this up we'll lose half this year's crop."

"So? Pull out. Start somewhere else."

"But these are our people …"

"No, John," says Creston, turning on his right-hand man. "They are not our people. They're just damn lucky we buy their crops or they'd starve. Look, get hold of Craddock again. From what Peter Symmonds says that crazy Canadian woman seems pretty determined. Tell Craddock I want a one hundred percent guarantee that she won't find Janet."

"But Janet won't talk. Not after all this time."

"I'm beginning to wonder if I can take that risk."

"Can you believe it," shrieks Trina with her cap on backwards again as she emerges from a pizza parlour a couple of blocks from Clive Sampson's house. "He even gave them his phone number."

"Amateur," smiles Daphne.

"They won't take the order without a home phone number," continues Trina, then she stops, asking, "You know what this means?"

"That we can find out who he is," guesses Daphne, but Trina is already ahead of her English associate.

"Of course we can," she says as she pulls out her cellphone and calls directory inquiries. "But it also means he's working alone. If he had a partner he wouldn't have ordered. One of them would have just rushed in and paid cash."

"Unless he is very stupid …" Daphne is musing, when Trina shouts, "Rats!" and clicks off her cellphone.

"Maybe he's not so stupid," she says, spitting, "Unlisted," as she mentally rattles through her manual to the chapter on accessing discreet sources. "I've got it," she trills after a few seconds and calls her homecare dispatcher. "Margaret," she asks sweetly, "does your sister still work for the telephone people?"

"I told you the police were useless," says Trina five minutes later as they slowly cruise past Craddock's tree-ringed suburban house.

"True," admits Daphne as she tries to peer beyond the greenery to see through the curtained windows. "But maybe we should call them now and tell them what we've got."

"You're kidding, Daph," says Trina, the smell of success lifting her voice. "I'm pretty sure they tipped this jerk off in the first place."

The sincerity of Craddock's guarantee to Janet's husband may have comforted the English executive, but it rang hollowly in Craddock's own ears. The fact he pulled a major favour with his ex-colleague, Sergeant Dave Brougham, to find out where she was when she was at Trina's house didn't seem a big deal at the time, but now, with half the Vancouver Police on alert for the missing woman, he is coming to terms with the possibility that he has backed himself and his police informant into a corner, and what if Brougham decides to jump?

"I bet that's his car," says Trina excitedly, eyeing Craddock's dated Chevrolet Impala in the driveway. "I saw it parked down the road a couple of times near my place."

"Well, he wouldn't be stupid enough to keep Janet here," suggests Daphne without considering the fact that they traced him so easily. "Let's turn the tables and follow him."

"Great," yelps Trina, pulling out her manual and looking up covert surveillance techniques. However, a few minutes later she is less enthusiastic. "It says here that we need to set up a static observation post and we need at least two cars."

"Look out," says Daphne, spying Craddock's bald head through the winterized foliage as he emerges from his front door, and Trina quickly hides her face under her manual.

"Not that," screeches Daphne snatching the book away. "We don't want to give him ideas."

Craddock has no idea he's under surveillance although it is certainly on his mind as he carefully checks the street. Then he spots Trina's black Jetta parked a few hundred feet away in a no parking zone. "Oh fuck," he mutters and ducks back into the house.

"That's torn it," says Trina.

"True," says Daphne, "but he's got a lot more to lose than us. He's a wanted man."

Craddock picks up the phone and puts it down a dozen times as he races to come up with a plan to spirit Janet out of his garage, but with Trina and Daphne on his tail he's out of his depth.

"Trina," says Daphne with her eyes on Craddock's front door. "Maybe we should cover the back in case he does a runner."

"Can you drive?"

"Sure," says Daphne, stretching, ignoring the fact that she has never actually bothered with the formalities of a test as she slips behind the wheel. Ten minutes later she sighs in relief at the younger woman's reappearance.

"No back entrance," Trina declares breathlessly as she slides back in. "He's well and truly trapped."

"So are we," points out Daphne, crossing her legs meaningfully.

"'round the corner," says Trina. "There's a bunch of rhododendron bushes. I just went."

Time passes like a day on death row for Craddock as he checks and rechecks Trina's car from behind his bedroom curtains, and he is not cheered by the knowledge that even a relatively short jail stretch can turn into a lengthy, or even terminal, nightmare for someone who has ever worn a police badge.

The hours pass slower, much slower, for Janet, who, abandoned by her fretful captor, is sinking both physically and mentally as she lays motionless in the back of his van. But she has been here before: same situation, same silence, same isolation, same abuse — different abuser.

"You have displeased the Lord," Browning, her self-appointed saviour, said whenever she balked at participating in perverted and painful rituals apparently ordained by his version of the Bible. And while he and some of his devotees might be spiritually uplifted by sexual acts too taboo even for the Kama Sutra, Janet more often than not took isolation and meditation as a penance for her disobedience: a day, three days, a week — the punishment as arbitrary as Browning's biblical interpretations.

Possible punishment is also uppermost in Craddock's thoughts as he sneaks another peek at the persistent duo camped out on his doorstep. Losing his PI licence is a certainty, though not the end of his world, whereas a conviction for abduction, bodily assault, and forcible confinement are not even on the same planet. "How the hell did I get into this?" he questions himself, but knows it was the money.

Money is also on Joseph Creston's mind as he and his cabal of cronies meet to discuss the growing crisis in Côte d'Ivoire's cocoa fields.

"We could step up security," suggests Mason. "Hire some heavyweight mercenaries from South Africa. They're a dime a dozen now."

But Creston is shaking his head. "Big picture, gentlemen," he says. "Let's look at the big picture. Chocolates have been declining per capita in relation to other commodities for almost a decade and relative prices have slid in response."

"Oversupply," mutters Mason unnecessarily.

"Quite. So let's redress the balance. We don't need more security. We need less."

"There could be all-out religious conflict, us against the Muslims," warns Mason, but Creston shrugs it off.

"Not us," he says. "Anyway, it's been happening for years, and most of these people aren't really Christian. Shit, if I lived in a mud hut and scavenged for peanuts all my life, I'd believe the tooth fairy was God if you paid me."

"But the church gives them hope, J.C.," says Dawes, surprised at Creston's unusual irreverence. "We offer them a brighter future."

"Grow up. You spend more on shit-paper a day than most of them earn."

"It's the market price, J.C. You said so yourself."

"Yes. And who sets the market? If the price gets too high we'll pull out. No one else is going to buy it, and it's not as though they can live on the stuff."

"Couldn't we start paying a fair price?"

"We could if the Americans did the same," Creston explodes. "And that's just about as likely as them giving Iraq back to Saddam."

Creston's uncharacteristic flare-up scatters his pink-faced deputies, but Mason holds back.

"This Janet thing is really getting to you isn't it, J.C.," the lawyer says tactfully once the room has cleared.

"I never stopped loving her, you know. I just couldn't trust her after what happened."

"And you couldn't turn her in now? Get her some proper counselling?"

Creston comes back to the boil. "I told you, I love her," he snaps as he pours himself a scotch. "Any news from Canada?"

"Nothing more from Craddock; I guess he has everything under control. Browning called just to confirm that he's wiped all records of transactions —"

Creston stops him with a wave of his glass. "It won't make any difference, John. We've funnelled millions through that place over the years. If anyone digs deep enough they'll find it. Somebody will catch on eventually."

"I'm amazed no one's ever audited him," agrees Mason, although he is well aware of Beautiful's remoteness, both geographically and politically. "But we're pretty fireproof: private company, no wussy-assed shareholders bleating about poor performances at the A.G.M. Plus, you happen to have a very good lawyer."

"Yes. Thanks," replies Creston as the fiery drink mollifies him. "I'd say I owe you, but I happen to know what you charge."

Bliss has sunk and is forlornly wandering the darkened medieval laneways and deserted quays of St-Juan-sur-Mer in the hope of spotting Yolanda. His apartment walls keep crowding in on him, and his bed is as cold and uncomforting as a prison bench.

The verdigris stained roofs of the Château Roger glint dully in the moonlight, reminding the neophyte historian and jilted lover of his task.

"Eleven years," he muses as he tries to find the masked prisoner's island across the gloomy strait and seeks to infiltrate the masked man's psyche while questioning whether he has as much stamina. But that was three hundred years ago, he reminds himself, wondering if in a less frenetic era such a gesture might have been easier to bear. "At least I'm free …" he begins, and then stops himself with an ironic chuckle. "I'm not free. I'll never be free if she doesn't come back. I'll be wearing a mask for the rest of my life; shuffling through life like a prisoner. There has been a miscarriage of justice," he cries across the dark abyss. "Yolanda is mine. I love her. I've always loved her. She loves me."

A warm light from the windows of L'Escale draws Bliss across the road from the promenade with the promise of a good night's sleep, and as he orders the first of a long line of cognacs he pulls out his pad with both Louis XIV and Chief Superintendent Edwards in mind.

Prince Ferdinand of Hungary listlessly haunted the hallways of Louis' great palace at Versailles with a wan face as he contemplated a lonely future without his great love. How can I do as the king suggests? *he asked himself repeatedly.* How can I prove my love without need of the sword or lance?

The king, at cards with the Marquis de Dangeau in the Salon de la Guerre *at the north end of the great gallery, spied the lovestruck prince and leaned conspiratorially into his opponent with sport in mind.*

"You are noted for your deftness of hand at the tables, Dangeau," said the wily king. "What odds would you give that I can outwit that sad-faced fellow?"

"Outwitting may be of little consequence if it has no profit in it," replied the marquis.

"Then I shall profit by it," announced the king joyously. "A thousand livres *says that I may persuade this downhearted petit prince to build me the great château that I desire in Provençe — a château of elegance and grandeur befitting my state, a château which I have oft desired but which, I lament, my chancellor forbids for lack of riches."*

"Then, should you win, you will have both the château and a thousand livres," *said Dangeau. "But what if you lose?"*

"You forget yourself, Dangeau," said His Majesty leaning across the table with fire in his eyes. "It is not my practice to lose."

"Perhaps another cognac, monsieur?" inquires Angeline, seeing an empty glass.

Bliss momentarily forgets that the waitress is not privy to his concerns as he adamantly replies, "I will not lose, Angeline. I will not lose."

Joseph Creston professes a love for his wife equal to Bliss's love for Yolanda, despite the fact that the company chairman hasn't seen Janet for more than forty years, and once Mason and the rest of the staff have left the office high above London's Liverpool Station in the heart of the city he paces the deeply carpeted executive suite thinking how different life could have been.

"I did everything for that damn woman," he might fume bitterly, but what he did for Janet was provide for her as long as it suited his business, care for her as long as it fitted his timetable, and think of her when time permitted. And if questioned as to why he never divorced her or sought out another, he could always fall back on the Church. "Whosoever God joins together in holy matrimony," he would recite haughtily, "let no man put asunder."

Trina and Daphne have no intention of waiting another forty years to rescue Janet Thurgood, although as the evening drags by without any sign of movement in Craddock's dark house, they are beginning to wonder if they might not already have missed their chance.

"Perhaps he climbed over the back," suggests Daphne for the *n*th time, but Trina is skeptical.

"No. He's scared. I bet he's creeping around like a cockroach hoping no one turns on the light. We could bust in and stomp him into the woodwork."

"You've been watching too many movies," laughs Daphne, but Trina seems to have a plan.

"OK," she continues positively. "Let's just flush him out."

"How?"

"I don't know. I was hoping you'd have some idea. Didn't you train for this kind of thing?"

"Not exactly," says Daphne, although her cogs are spinning as she whips back through her wartime training days trying to come up with a similar scenario. After a few minutes recalling lectures about sabotage, explosives, and escape manoeuvres, she spends several more replaying a series of real-life incidences before shaking her head negatively. "The problem is that we need him to lead us to Janet. He won't risk that as long as he thinks we're following him."

"But if we don't follow him we won't know where she is," explains Trina unnecessarily. "He'll never go to her as long as we're here. He'll be checking every car, pulling U-turns, racing. We'll never keep up and chances are he'll just drive in a circle."

"Wait," says Daphne with a remembrance from the past. "'Always keep the enemy guessing,' they said. 'Never do the expected.' We've got to out-think him, Trina, not out-race him. We know he's stupid, so let's give him some rope and wait for him to tie a granny knot."

"You're the boss," says Trina, starting the engine.

"Oh ... Oh!" exclaims Craddock seeing the Jetta's lights flare. "What the hell are they playing at now?"

"Home," declares Daphne. "There's more than one way to skin a rabbit."

"I was hoping for a nice piece of steak," says Trina as they drive slowly past Craddock's house, both staring fixedly ahead.

"That'll get to him," says Daphne, laughing, as they reach the end of the road and Trina steps on the gas.

"I've got to get out of here," Bliss says to himself when he finally wakes, fuzzy-headed, and realizes that even his alcohol-driven dreams have solely featured Yolanda, and he phones Samantha.

"I'm going to Paris for a while," he tells his daughter. "I need to do some research in Versailles and the Louvre."

"You're not running away are you?" she questions.

"No," he insists, thought he knows he is partially lying. "Look," he protests vociferously, "you told me to script into my novel all the things I want in my life. Well I am. But this isn't just about Yolanda anymore."

"You don't have to convince me, Dad."

"I know what you're thinking," he carries on without listening. "But I really do need to spend time in Paris. Don't worry, I'll be back here in a couple of weeks."

Will I ever return? Bliss deliberates a couple of hours later as the speedy SNCF electric train, the luxurious *Train Grand Vitesse,* accelerates almost silently out of St-Juan's station while he stands at a window scanning the narrow streets as they whip past, still hoping for a glimpse of blonde hair, still wondering if the entire episode has been either a dream or a nightmare, still thinking that he might simply wake at his destination and find himself at Waterloo railway station on his way to a normal day at Scotland Yard.

But nothing has been normal since Yolanda's hurried departure and he questions his true intentions, knowing that his suitcase is straining with all his clothes and personal possessions. As the speeding streets begin to blur and the train smoothly gathers speed along the coastal track, he catches glances of the Château Roger, then the austere cliff-top fortress on the island of Ste. Marguerite across the tranquil azure bay, and he knows the answer.

"Yes," he says to himself *sotto voce,* knowing that he has an obligation to a man who surrendered his liberty and his voice in the name of love. "I will come back to finish the novel. I will tell your story. And I will get Yolanda back, however long it takes."

"Janet," calls Craddock softly in the early hours, once he's satisfied that the coast is clear, but as he opens the old van's door he's knocked back by the stench of stale vomit.

"Janet," he calls louder, shining a flashlight into her face, but her eyes won't open and she lays as listless as a dropped doll.

"Shit!" exclaims the ex-cop, blaming Daphne and Trina in his mind as he desperately searches for a pulse. "Wake up. C'mon, wake up," he mutters frantically as his mind whirls with dark thoughts. Then he drags the limp body from the van and hacks at her wrist bindings with a blunt craft knife.

"Wake up. Wake up," he calls frantically, seeing his own life rapidly drifting into darkness as he massages her dead hands. Then she lets out an exhausted gasp and he almost faints in relief.

"We could always tip off the police," Daphne suggests over the supper table at Trina's, but the other woman isn't easily convinced.

"I tipped them off about Osama Bin Laden once and they threatened to arrest me for being a public nuisance."

"Osama Bin Laden in Vancouver?" queries Daphne incredulously.

"Well it could have been," replies Trina shortly. "He looked like him. He had a beard and everything. Anyway, what I'm saying is that I wouldn't trust that lot to pick up a two-bit hooker let alone a wanted kidnapper."

"In that case we have to come up with a plan," says Daphne, then she yawns and checks her watch. "Goodness, I must be getting past it. It's only ten o'clock."

"We'll start first thing tomorrow," agrees Trina as she clears away the plates.

Craddock watches his clock and waits for midnight to roll around before picking up the phone to call England.

"Mr. Creston isn't in yet," the early shift receptionist at Creston Enterprises tells him, but she's wrong. The company president hasn't left the building all night. Concern over Janet kept him up until three when a security guard spotted a light and poked his head around the door to make sure there were no intruders.

"Only me," Creston assured the watchman as he waved him away, and an hour later he finally fell asleep on a deeply cushioned settee. Mason wakes him at eight-thirty, just as Craddock is phoning back.

"I'll check," the receptionist tells the anxious Canadian caller, "though I haven't seen him come in yet."

"It's for you J.C.," says Mason, taking the call, and Creston signals for his henchman to leave as soon as he recognizes Craddock's voice.

"We're a bit worried about your wife," says the Vancouver private eye, temporarily forgetting his hard man act while trying to share some of the responsibility with a non-existent partner.

"What are you saying, Craddock?"

"We think she should maybe see a doctor."

"Well do it, then."

"But — they'll ask questions."

"Oh, for Lord's sake," spits Creston. "I thought you were supposed to know what you were doing."

"I do."

"Then tell 'em not to ask questions, you idiot," Creston screeches.

"Everything all right, J.C.?" queries Mason sliding back into the room.

Creston slams down his phone. "Not it's not," he seethes. "You told me he was a professional; professional what — babysitter?"

"Sorry, J.C. He's an ex-cop. Came recommended by Browning."

"And what the hell does that freak know? Find someone else."

"Yes, J.C."

"And while you're at it get me a flight. Shit. Do I have to do everything myself?"

"Flight, J.C.?"

"To Canada."

"You could take the Lear."

"Oh, right. Wake up, man. Do you think I want everyone knowing my business? Clear my schedule for three days and book me business class; and don't use Creston. What was that passport you got me?"

"Smythe."

"Yes — Smythe. And call Craddock. Tell him to get one of his people to meet me at the airport."

"Yes," says Mason, half out of the door.

"And tell him that Janet better be in one piece when I arrive or I'll break his fucking neck."

"Right, J.C."

"Oh. One more thing. You've got a good contact in the police haven't you?"

"Mike Edwards, chief superintendent at the Yard," Mason nods. "We were at school together."

"Right. Get onto him. I want someone to make sure that everything to do with the children's deaths is destroyed — every note, every record, every scrap of paper."

"Um. He might not …"

"John. I'm not asking, OK. I don't give a monkey's fart what it costs — and don't give me any crap about duty. He's got his price the same as anyone else."

"I'll try."

"No. You will," spits Creston nastily. "I might have to bring her back here and I can't risk anything going wrong — understand?"

"Yes, J.C."

"Good."

The news of Creston's visit hits Craddock with the force of a fly ball in the forehead. "Oh Christ, that's all I need," he says as he puts down the phone and looks at the frail woman asleep in his bed. Then he stares at his watch as he tries to calculate out how much time he has to work a miracle.

Bliss has more time to achieve success than Craddock, much more time, and as he begins a tour of Louis XIV's great palace on the outskirts of Paris, he is beginning to wonder if it might not take him as long as his predecessor to entice back his lost love.

"The Palace of Versailles was originally a royal hunting lodge," explains the cropped-haired student guide in perfect English as Bliss tries to takes notes, but he is now a long way from the Mediterranean and he can't stop shivering.

"King Louis XIV, who was later known as the Sun King, always said that the mark of a man was his fortitude to all things — heat, cold, hunger, and thirst," explains the young woman, pointing out the paucity of fireplaces and the draughtiness of the doors and windows in the *Salon de la Guerre*, the monarch's oft used war room, before continuing into the great gallery, the magnificent Hall of Mirrors, which stretches seventy-five metres across the west end of the building.

"The ceiling was painted by Le Brun," she continues, sweeping a hand the length of the great room. "And the mural pays tribute to of the king's valiant defeat of the Dutch …"

I can see where the designer of the Château Roger got his ideas, thinks Bliss, tuning out the young woman as he surveys the ornately decorated stateroom with its giant windows that overlook the sculpted gardens and the ornamental canals and fountains.

"Approximately ten thousand people lived in the palace during the height of the Sun King's reign ..." the guide continues to the little knot of tourists as she leads them into the king's private rooms. Bliss hangs back in the mirrored gallery for a few seconds, on the spot where the devious monarch's throne sat on a raised dais, imagining the scene as hundreds of bewigged and outlandishly costumed courtiers milled at Louis' feet, desperate to catch his eye. It was all about control, Bliss knows from his research, and he has no difficulty combining the malevolent psyche of the French king with his present-day adversary.

"Keep your friends close, but your enemies even closer," may be Chief Superintendent Edwards' maxim, but he is not the first dictator to understand the dictum's importance, and Bliss can't keep Klaus out of the equation either. He didn't really want Yolanda, he tells himself as he pictures Louis carefully noting the absence of any nobles from his audience. He just couldn't stand the thought of someone else having her.

Maybe that's not fair.

Of course it's not fair, but what she did to me wasn't fair either. Now I'm the one in the cage while she is free? Or is every moment with Klaus torture as she tries to focus on him when all she sees is me? Does she close her eyes in bed and imagine that it is me inside her?

"*Monsieur* ..." calls the young shepherdess, realizing that she has lost one of her sheep, and Bliss quickly closes his pad to catch up, but now he knows how easily the besotted man suckered himself into being masked and shackled while his sovereign sat on his throne laughing at his dupe's misfortune.

"*Remember — sacrifice!*" exclaimed the king to Prince Ferdinand, writes Bliss, finding a quiet corner in Louis' bedroom while the guide tells of the king's legendary sexual appetite. "*Even the plainest, ugliest old crow — one who*

*should rightly be on her knees pleading and begging —
expects you to lay down your life in order to get between
her sheets. How would she know that you would not hide
in the closet were a burglar come to visit if you have not
proved yourself on the field?"*

*"Then I fear that I will be a lonely bachelor," said the
lovelorn man, but the king offered a smile. "Come, come,
my young prince. Do not give up so easily. I have a
scheme that may enable you to woo this noble woman
without risk to your limbs."*

*"A scheme, my liege?" queried the prince with light in
his eyes.*

*"Indeed," said the king, taking the young man aside.
"But first you must promise that you will keep it a great secret
until you are ready to spring the trap. For, assuming that the
woman of your dreams has the cunning of her gender, if she
were to scent an intrigue then she would immediately wish to
take it over and make it her own. Believe me, there is nothing
more dangerous to the plans of a man than permitting a
woman to peek into the architect's drawing house."*

"The water gardens and the Grotto of Thetis were
designed by the Sun King himself," the cicerone continues
as she points out of a window to the landscaped grounds,
and Bliss is happy to escape from the group as he goes in
search of material to bolster his manuscript.

"The Grotto of Thetis, an ornamental cavern filled
with mythological allusions, signifies the place where
Apollo takes his rest at the end of a busy day flying across
the heavens," Bliss's guidebook tells him as he stands alone
in the marble chamber, imagining it as it was when water
cascaded from gilded fountains and chandeliers of solid
gold lyres set with pearls cast a romantic glow. *I wonder
how many of his concubines Louis managed to mount in
here*, ponders Bliss, thinking that this has to be the ultimate
love nest on a warm July night. But now, on a wintry
December day, there is no warmth, and mental images of

heated sexual encounters merely drag him down.

"I might have killed myself for all she cares and knows," he says aloud, hearing his words echo hollowly around the deserted stone room. "'I love you more than I've ever loved anyone else in my life,' you told me," he carries on nostalgically. "'And I know that you love me in every possible way.'"

"I do," he replied, not needing to ask what Yolanda meant, knowing that at times he was a lover, while at others he was a father, a brother, and a son.

"I was everything to you, Yolanda, and you know it," he says to the walls. "And you were everything to me ... you *are* everything to me."

chapter thirteen

"It could be a long day," warns Trina as she crams lunch into a wicker hamper for herself and her English counterpart. "I did creamed banana sandwiches," she adds, but Daphne has experienced enough of Trina's experimental cuisine not to inquire what other ingredients might be included in the mix.

"I was thinking of wearing this," the visitor says, modelling a deerstalker she bought as a joke when the idea of being a private detective first came up. Trina turns up her nose. "It's a bit obvious," she says and quickly switches it for a neon green baseball cap.

"So, let's go through this again," says Daphne a little nervously as they head off in Trina's car.

"It's called overt surveillance. I read it in the manual," explains the animated woman. "First we hire another car. Something really honky that he can't possibly miss — a snazzy big red number. You can drive that one."

"Umm," murmurs Daphne, indicating a problem. "I don't think I brought my licence with me."

"No sweat," says Trina. "I'll hire it in my name. You just follow me to Craddock's place, but I'll park round the corner and we'll drive up in the rental. Then I'll slip back to mine."

"Then?" asks Daphne, still somewhat uncomfortable.

"Then I'll phone him and pretend I'm a friend of friend who's tipping him off about a police raid."

"And he runs."

"Yeah — and you take off after him."

"But I lose him after the first couple of blocks."

"And he goes, 'Great, I've shaken them off.' But I'll be right there on his ass. It's textbook."

Trina's plan may be according to the text, but Craddock hasn't read the book. With Creston on his tail he's already flown, together with his charge, and booked himself into one of the cookie-cutter tourist hotels clustered around the airport.

"You'll be all right here," he told Janet as he carried her into the threadbare room under cover of darkness, but she was too weak to reply.

"Oh drat. His flipping car's gone," says Daphne with a sigh of relief as she and Trina roll around the corner in their souped up Mustang, but Trina isn't fazed.

"Great," she says, already half out of the car. "Let's break in and see what we can find."

"Trina, we might get caught," complains Daphne, sitting tight, but Trina is unsympathetic as she forges up Craddock's driveway with his garage in sight

"Hey. You got me arrested at the doctor's place."

A few minutes later, once they have pried open the garage door and found the mattress in the back of the van, Trina exclaims, "Oh my God, she was here! Look," she carries on, holding up the roughly cut lengths of duct tape as evidence, "he tied her up."

"We don't know that," cautions Daphne, but five minutes later, when Trina spots a familiar sweater on the floor of Craddock's bedroom, there is no doubt.

"Now what?" asks Daphne, and Trina's study of the private investigator's manual comes in handy again.

"Redial," she says, hitting the button on the bedroom phone, and is not totally surprised when an English voice answers, "Creston Enterprises. How may I direct your call?"

"Sorry, wrong number," says Trina as she puts down the phone, then she turns to Daphne and quotes from the manual. "Golden rule," she explains. "Never just cut off a pretext phone call. That's too suspicious."

"Very interesting," says Daphne, "but what do we do now?"

"Put ourselves in the mind of the villain of course," replies Trina without the faintest idea of what she's talking about.

Bliss on the other hand has no difficulty imagining the world of his villain — King Louis XIV, Duke of Normandy and King of France from 1643 to 1715 — as he wanders the regimented gardens of the great palace at Versailles and spins his mind back nearly three hundred and fifty years to the time when Louis *le Grand* delighted in showing off his designs to visitors. "The fountains, waterfalls, and canals were the king's personal favourites," the guidebook tells Bliss, but the waters have turned to ice and even the statues that surround the ornamental ponds seem particularly lifeless in the frosty northern air.

"The King's insatiable appetite for all things ostentatious is symbolized in the grand design of his great palace and the statuary in the surrounding grounds," the guidebook continues as Bliss eyes a marble nude who leaves nothing to his imagination.

"I bet the old lecher loved this one," says Bliss as he runs his hand over a silky smooth thigh, but he recoils at the snake-like coldness of the damp stone and can't help lumping the women currently in his mind, if not actually in his life, into a slippery heap. "Yolanda had no right to do this to me," he fumes under his breath. "I was happier thinking she was dead." And what of Prince Ferdinand's reluctant paramour? How callous or careless was she of her suitor's heart?

"I give up," admits Trina after she and Daphne have watched Craddock's house for a couple of hours without success. "I guess we'd better tell Mike Phillips what we've got. Maybe they can track him with dogs. Although I suppose I could try Raven and ask her to use her psychic powers."

"I think Mike Phillips would be the answer," suggests Daphne, having been somewhat leery of the scheme to beset Craddock in the first place.

"OK," says Trina leaping out of the sports car and heading for her own. "Race you back to the rental place."

"No!" yells Daphne.

"Spoilsport."

RCMP Inspector Mike Phillips listens attentively to their story, though he pretends to clamp his hands over his ears when Trina admits breaking into the private investigator's house. "You're gonna end up in jail one of these days." He laughs as he shakes his head in disbelief, and then he spends a few seconds mulling over the name. "Craddock, Craddock ..." he muses. "I'm sure I've heard that name before. Hold on," he adds and he phones Dave Brougham of Vancouver's City Police.

"Craddock, PI," repeats Brougham vaguely, apparently deep in deliberation, then he questions guardedly, "Who wants to know, Mike?"

Phillips hesitates for a thoughtful second before answering. "Friend of mine. He just wants to know if he's on the level ... thinking of hiring him for a job."

"Oh yeah," says Brougham, seemingly at ease. "Good guy, used to be on the force — reliable."

"Ex-cop," explains Phillips putting down the phone. "Are you sure he's the man?"

"How else did Kylie's sweater get in his bedroom?" snaps Trina, stuffing her daughter's garment into his nose. "She gave Janet this to wear."

"I get the point," he says, brushing it off. "But these are serious allegations. He could do time, big time, for this if you're right."

"I'm right ..." she starts, then turns to include her partner. "We are right."

Craddock's cellphone makes him jump as he sits worriedly by the side of Janet's bed gently massaging her hand.

"It's me," whispers Brougham. "What the fuck have you done?"

"What?"

"The RCMP are asking questions. Phillips didn't let on but I reckon that stupid Button woman has figured out who you are."

"Shit."

"So what have you done?"

"Nothing, Dave."

"Don't try snowing me. I was the one who put you onto the woman. I'm in this as well. So what did you do with her?"

Craddock hesitates long enough to annoy his ex-partner.

"I said —"

"OK, Dave. Look, I'm in a bit of a bind. She needs a doctor."

"What?"

"It was that crazy broad Button and her sidekick. They staked my place out. Look, I never meant to hurt her."

"All right. Where are you?"

Mike Phillips has also been on the phone, assembling a small team, and fifteen minutes later he briefs half a dozen men in his office and assigns tasks.

"His name is Craddock," he says pointing to one of the sergeants. "Ex–City detective — friend of Dave Brougham. Get everything you can on him. He's supposedly a PI, but he sounds like a shit one."

Phillips turns to the next officer. "Brougham, sergeant, Vancouver City — get me the works. You two," he says, moving around the room. "Get a search warrant on Craddock's joint and take a forensic team. If my info is right he's had a hostage there for at least a couple of days."

"Name?" asks one of the team.

"Thurgood — Janet Thurgood. The woman linked to Constable Montgomery's death a few weeks ago."

"Evidence for the warrant?" queries one of the men as he furiously takes notes.

"This sweatshirt," says Phillips passing around the bagged item while covering for his informant. "It was found on the driveway of the house by one Mrs. Trina Button, a friend of the missing woman."

"And she can positively ID it?"

"She can," continues Phillips, "and I'll have a statement to that effect for you in about ten minutes."

"Sounds good enough."

"Right," continues Phillips, pointing to the two unassigned officers. "You two start asking questions on the street. I want him found fast."

"OK, boss."

"And put out an APB on a vehicle as soon as we know what he's driving."

Finding Craddock's car will be little help to the officers. Now that the ex-cop has finally woken up to the enormity of his actions he's tucked the vehicle away in a dusty corner of the airport's parking garage and rented a replacement from Avis.

Dave Brougham pulls alongside the hired car in the hotel parking lot half an hour later with a friendly doctor in tow. Then he pulls his ex-colleague into the bathroom, slams him against the shower cubicle, and shuts the door.

"What the fuck have you done to her?"

"Nothing, Dave. She just passed out on me."

"You weren't screwing her."

"No way. I'm a pro, Dave. Everything was cool till that freaking Button woman set up camp on the street. She's the one who needs screwing."

"Leave her to me. I owe her anyway."

A gentle rapping on the door signals that the doctor has finished.

"That was quick ..." starts Brougham, putting on a smile as he opens the door, but the doctor isn't smiling.

"We gotta get her to a hospital stat."

"I'm not sure ..."

"She's in a bad way. Dehydration, malnutrition — for some time I'd say. Could be anorexia, but look at her. I bet she doesn't weigh a hundred pounds. Her blood pressure is on the floor and her reflexes are slower than a city bus. She has to go to a hospital."

"OK," says Brougham backing Craddock into the bathroom again. "Give us a minute, will you?" Then he turns on his ex-colleague. "You're out of this all right. You'd gone before I arrived."

"But ..."

"No buts. You're out. Just get your ass out of here damn quick. Pack yourself a big bag and take off. Get some distance until it blows over."

"What if she croaks?"

"You'd better hope no one ever finds you 'cuz your name is all over this — understand? And nothing I say can change that."

"But, Dave …" Craddock is still protesting as Brougham opens the door and heads for the bedside phone for an ambulance while telling the doctor to grab a cab. "I'll take it from here, Doc," he says. "You might as well get going."

Craddock's mind whirls in indecision as he drives back to the airport garage. His own car will mark him wherever he goes, but if he sticks with the rental for any length of time his Visa bill will arrive by truck. In any case, he has no idea where to lay low.

"Maybe I should get some sun," he says checking out the leaden Vancouver sky and trying to cheer himself as he reaches the terminal buildings and hears the roar of a jet taking off. Then he brightens. "Why not?"

The RCMP forensic identification team are already taping off the sidewalk and garden of Craddock's house by the time the search warrant arrives. A knot of spectators have been drawn down their leafy driveways by the multitude of flashing lights to huddle under umbrellas on the sidewalk. "I think there's been a break-in," Kathy Anderson, the next door neighbour, is explaining, pointing to the damaged garage door, when one of the uniformed officers approaches.

"Would any of you ladies happen to know where Mr. Craddock is?" he asks as if he's not particularly concerned.

"He was here yesterday," offers Kathy. "But his car was gone this morning."

"Does he live alone?"

"Oh yeah."

"What's going on, officer?" asks another of the neighbours, but the constable blanks her out and turns back to the house.

"I'm gonna call the papers," the woman whispers to the group. "I bet there's a body in there. I always said he was weird. Coming and going at all times of the night."

"Oh my God!" exclaims Kathy Anderson. "Maybe he's a mass murderer. What if the place is full of bodies?"

Craddock's house is devoid of dead bodies, but by the time the forensic team have pulled in all their equipment and began taking photographs the first pressmen have arrived intent on finding some.

"Who tipped them off?" fumes the sergeant in charge as he peers from Craddock's window, but he knew it was only a matter of time.

"No comment," he announces a few minutes later when a couple of microphones are stuck under his nose, so the reporters turn to the rapidly expanding cluster of neighbours for information.

"He used to be a policeman," Kathy Anderson explains, but beyond that little is known of the occupant.

"He seemed like a nice man," says another, leaving the reporter muttering into his recorder, "They always say that."

The arrival of a television unit complete with satellite dish adds to the weight of the situation, but the camera team are fishing just like everyone else.

"I think our bird has flown," Mike Phillips explains to Trina and Daphne an hour later as they stand at a receptionist's desk at Vancouver's General Hospital waiting for news of Janet.

"How did you find out she was here?" asks Daphne.

"Whoever booked her in had no documents for her: no health card, no passport, no driver's licence, no credit card — nothing. I'm guessing it was Craddock but we should be able to ID him when we take a look at the security tapes."

"But they took her in?" questions Trina.

"Apparently she's pretty far gone," says Phillips. "They weren't going to turn her away over a technicality. They were suspicious and gave us a call."

"So, where's Craddock flown to?" Daphne wants to know, but Mike Phillips shrugs.

"We've circulated his licence plate. My guess is that he'll head south for the U.S. We've tipped off the border crossings."

Craddock is heading south, way south, though he's not driving.

"You're in luck, Mr. Davies," says the cheerful desk clerk at Aloha Airways. "We can get you to Honolulu by seven this evening, allowing for the time difference."

"Great," he says, handing over the dodgy driver's licence and credit card that he obtained when he set himself up as a PI.

It is late in Paris, the City of Lights, and, spurred by his visit to Versailles, Bliss sits on the balcony of his hotel across the mist-covered Seine from the Champs-Elysées and the Place de Concord with ten handwritten pages under his belt. "The Louvre, Bastille, and Notre Dame in the morning," he resolves as he prepares to close his journal for the day, and his eyes follow the riverbank lights along the Seine to the distant buildings. But he's not interested in old masters, Egyptology, or religious relics. He wants historical colour to bolster the credibility of his historical saga. He wants to view the buildings as they were in the time of Louis XIV when Paris was the centre of the world. He wants to walk the streets and corridors where French aristocrats walked long before the Revolution, absorbing the ambience of the ancient city. Above all, he wants to know how Prince Ferdinand might have felt as he tasted the heights of Parisian life before his self-incarceration in Ste. Marguerite's fortress, and he spends a few minutes in the mind of his hoodwinked romantic as the prince offers thanks to his false god.

"'My liege," writes Prince Ferdinand to his king,
Louis XIV, "soon my great château will be finished and I
will send a courier to my heart's desire expressing my love
for her and asking for her hand for eternity. I will send her
the key to the château, a key that will in turn open my cell
door. I will say to her, 'This mask will keep me from all
eyes and a prisoner's cell will keep me from all temptation.
My body shall remain as pure and unsullied as my heart,
and only my true love will ever look upon me again. I will
be imprisoned unto eternity unless the one whom I desire
accepts my solicitation and raises her flag over the
château to signal an end to my torment.'"

Back at Vancouver General Hospital Trina pulls Daphne
away from Mike Phillips on the pretext of visiting the
bathroom.

"There's no point in sticking around here; we need to
get after Craddock."

"Where —" starts Daphne, but Trina cuts her off.

"According to the manual, when looking for a missing
person you always start from the last place they are
known to have been."

"Here, probably," suggests Daphne, implicating the
emergency department's reception desk

"Possibly. But the ambulance driver said they picked
her up from a hotel near the airport and the guy followed
in his car."

"The airport would certainly be a good place to fly
from," admits Daphne.

"Quite."

One quick drive around the hotel parking lot tells Trina that
Craddock is no longer in residence, and a twenty-dollar bill
gets her no further. "He probably paid cash and gave a false

name," she tells Daphne once the desk clerk has pocketed the cash and conveniently turned his back on the register.

"Let's try the airport then," suggests Daphne with nowhere else to go.

The international departure area bustles with early afternoon travellers hoping to escape the midwinter blahs, and the two women quickly realize that they have little hope of finding Craddock based only on the distant glimpse that they had at his front door.

"Let's try the parking," suggests Trina after a few minutes, and Daphne rides shotgun with her head out of the window as they race around the multi-storey garage scanning the blur of licence plates for Craddock's Impala.

"Stop," yells Daphne more than once, but each time the numbers are off.

Then Trina spots the wanted vehicle, spins her baseball cap, slams on the brakes, and yelps, "Gotcha."

The tires of a British Airways' jumbo from Heathrow puff smoke as they heavily hit the runway on the other side of the airfield, and as the monster taxies towards the terminal, Joseph Creston fidgets impatiently, waiting for the moment when he can switch on his cellphone and connect with Craddock. But it won't happen today. The Aloha Airways Boeing 757 carrying the PI is already revving up for takeoff at the other end of the same runway.

"I've seen this in the movies," says Trina as she bends the end of a wire coat hanger into a hook and rams it down the side window of Craddock's car. Five minutes and three coat hangers later she gives up, pulls a heavy metal jack from the trunk of her car, and slams it through the glass.

"Oh my goodness, Trina," shrieks Daphne, but the elderly woman is inside the car in seconds rummaging through the glove compartment. "Look at this," she cries triumphantly as she pulls out an expired driver's licence bearing Craddock's photograph.

"OK. Let's get outta here," yells Trina grabbing the licence, and a few minutes later, as Joseph Creston is fighting his way to the front of the line at the immigration desks downstairs at the international terminal, the two women are racing from airline booth to airline booth upstairs in the departure area, asking, "Have you seen this man?"

Twenty minutes later Creston emerges through the arrivals gate to an anxiously smiling wall of people, but he wouldn't recognize Craddock's face even it were there. Upstairs, the detective duo have much more success with Craddock's image, and Trina has a pleading tone as she calls her husband, Rick, on her cellphone, saying, "I know it's short notice, dear, but Daphne's looking very pale. I just think she needs a few days in the sun, that's all."

"But …" protests Rick, then he gives up.

"You and the kids can manage," she carries on without a breath. "It's only Hawaii for goodness' sake. It's not like the end of the Earth."

"I don't know why that man puts up with you," laughs Daphne as Trina closes her phone and turns to give her credit card to the Aloha Airways clerk.

"'Cuz he loves me, Daphne," replies the Vancouverite. "'Cuz he loves me."

David Bliss is singing a similar song in Paris as he phones his daughter to tell her that his book is progressing. "I really do love her, Sam," he bleats, and she sighs in exasperation.

"I know, Dad. You've told me a million times. Now get on and finish that damn book. The sooner it's done the quicker you can get her back."

"Do you really think she'll come back, Sam. Honestly?" he questions, as he has questioned himself a thousand times a day since Yolanda left.

"If she has any sense she will."

"But what if she doesn't?"

"Bestseller, Dad. Just remember that: bestseller. You'll be so famous you'll have women tripping over themselves to get to you."

"I don't want that," he shouts vehemently. "I just want my Yolanda."

"Then keep writing."

"Mason," yells Creston into his cellphone as he wanders the near deserted arrivals concourse. "Have you heard from Craddock?"

"I thought he was meeting you."

"He's not here and his phone's not answering."

"I don't know —"

"What's happening there? Did you get hold of your man at the Yard?"

"He wants four thousand. He says it's risky but he'll do it."

"Give it to him. Cash. Nothing traceable, and let me know when it's clear. I want a cast-iron guarantee, all right?"

"All right."

"Make sure you tell him that: cast iron. I don't want any more foul-ups, no more surprises. I don't want Symmonds or anyone else ever popping out of the woodwork."

"OK, J.C. But how are you going to get hold of Craddock?"

"He gave me an address. I'll take a cab if he doesn't show up soon."

Craddock's face is also the subject of discussion at the news desk of Vancouver's local television station. "Does anyone have a picture of this guy?" yells the red-faced news producer trying to put the evening's broadcast together. "Do we know anything about activity at the scene? What the bejesus is going on? Will someone please tell me."

"They're keeping tight-lipped," says the reporter, turning his back on the crowd outside Craddock's house and whispering into his microphone.

"One of their own," suggests the producer knowingly. "Nothing closes ranks faster than a cop off the rails."

"Apparently he's been off the job a couple of years," continues the reporter.

"Is there a story there? Booted off for being happy-handed with a prisoner perhaps?"

"Tight-lipped," reiterates the reporter. "No one's talking here. Only speculation."

"We need something," spits the producer into his microphone as he flicks switches to bring up a picture on his monitor. "Camera two, pan the crowd again, pull up a few nervy faces — mother clutching a kid, that sort of thing." Then he flicks back to the reporter. "Graham, give us a voice-over. Something about worried neighbours fearing the worst as teams of heavily armed men surround this innocent looking house in their upscale suburban neighbourhood … you know the routine."

"Gotcha, Paul," says the reporter as the camera begins its pan.

The tropical sun has just dipped over the horizon into the Pacific Ocean when Craddock emerges as Paul Davies from the immigration hall at Honolulu International.

"Aloha," welcomes the smiling face of a young Polynesian girl as Craddock, together with a couple hundred other sun-seekers dragging suitcases of winter woollens into summer, walks into a wall of humidity.

"No thanks," mutters Craddock gruffly as he sidesteps the young woman when she tries to throw a plastic lei around his neck.

"Aloha," she calls to the next in line and gets a smile in return.

"I want a hotel," he says to the plump-faced Chinese woman at the wheel of a cab and she turns, confused.

"Which hotel?"

"Something cheap."

"This is Hawaii, mister. Not cheap. You want cheap you go to China. China cheap."

"Fine," he says. "Just not too expensive."

"Waikiki," she says setting off at a quick pace. "All of Waikiki is hotels. Plenty hotels. You find cheap."

"Where will we stay?" questions Daphne as she and Trina race back to the airport with hastily packed suitcases.

"The Sheraton on the beach at Waikiki is very nice," says Trina from experience. "Although I bet Craddock will be slumming in a backpacker's hovel."

"Are you sure you can afford this?" queries Daphne suddenly aware that Trina has footed the bill for everything, including her flight from England.

"Not me," laughs Trina. "This is Rick's treat."

"That poor man," laughs Daphne.

"Like I said, he loves me."

"The RCMP and Vancouver Police are keeping mum about a major incident in the city today ..." says the newscaster on the citywide evening news as the camera pans the crowd outside Craddock's house. "So let's go live to the scene for an update."

"As you can see," says Graham Jarvis the reporter, doing his best to sound enthusiastic, even excited, "a very large crowd of anxious neighbours have gathered outside this rather ordinary looking suburban house where teams of tight-lipped forensic experts have been furiously working since lunchtime today."

The camera continues to sweep the crowd, now held behind police tapes that cordon off an entire section of the street, as a taxi pulls into view. The cameraman cuts back to the house, but heads in the crowd turn as one to view the new arrival.

Joseph Creston taps the driver on the shoulder, demanding, "What's going on?"

"No idea," says the driver with a nod to Craddock's house. "But I think that's the address you asked for."

"Wait here," orders Creston as he gets out and makes his way towards the crowd.

Two minutes later he's back, sitting in thoughtful silence for a few moments before pulling out his cellphone.

"J.C. It's three in the morning," complains Mason bitterly.

"I don't give a shit ..." starts Creston, and then he backs down. "Look. Something's happened to Craddock. The police are swarming all over his house and nobody's saying anything. Get a hold of your man at the Yard. Tell him I want to know what's happening."

"It's three in the morning," emphasizes Mason, but Creston isn't looking for any excuses.

"Double what you offered him," he screeches into the phone. "Whatever it takes. I want to know what's happening and now — all right?"

"You're the boss."

"You're damn right I am."

"Do you think we'll see the volcanoes?" Daphne wants to know as the 757 lifts through Vancouver's clouds into the star-filled sky over the Pacific Ocean.

"Wrong island," says Trina, shaking her head. "Although we might end up there. Anyway you'll like Honolulu. Lots of palm trees and sandy beaches. We can watch the surfers." Then she nudges the elderly woman playfully. "Hey, maybe you and me could catch a few waves."

"I don't think I packed my costume," murmurs Daphne. "Although this looks fun," she adds as she skips through the in-flight magazine and finds a picture of a catamaran sailing across a serene bay.

"You're on," says Trina, flipping her baseball cap back to front again. "Hawaii here we come."

The Ohana hotel sits a few blocks off the beach at Waikiki. It's not as cheap as Craddock would have liked, but it's cheerful enough with its high-rise towers looking over the green Koolau Mountains to the north and glimpses of the rolling surf hitting the reef off the beach to the south.

Craddock's room on the sixteenth floor has turned its back on the beach and faces into the perpetually cloud-shrouded mountains. But it suits his mood.

"Who knows, a few days, a week at the most," he told the quizzical receptionist with a note of exasperation when he booked in without luggage. "Just until they find my bags." But he knows that Davies' credit card will only stretch so far. What then? he questions gloomily as he unpacks his jacket pockets. Get a job perhaps. He's deluding himself and he knows it. In reality he's praying that Janet will recover sufficiently to be certified insane, and he'll be out of the woods.

"So," says Daphne, once their meal has arrived. "How are we going to find him?"

"No idea," admits Trina unconcernedly. "But we'll have fun trying."

Daphne pauses with a piece of chicken halfway to her mouth and gives Trina a confused look. "Why are we doing this?" she questions as if the illogic of their actions has just struck her.

"To help Janet," offers Trina between bites.

"I know that," says Daphne, "but I'm just hazy about why we need to find Craddock. After all, Janet's safe now."

"Look," says Trina waving her fork at Daphne to emphasize her point. "This isn't about Craddock or to save Janet's life. This is about us. You and me. Lovelace and Button, International Investigators Inc. Just remember, we've never lost a case yet."

"Trina," laughs Daphne at the younger woman's bouncy enthusiasm. "We've never had a case yet. How could we lose one?"

"That's not the point. Someone murdered those little kiddies; someone locked Janet away for most of her life with a whacko religious freak; someone covered up the deaths of her kids; and someone is doing his best to stop us finding out the truth."

"Therefore?"

"Therefore, we have no choice. I'm sure your friend David Bliss would understand. He knows all about determination. He nearly got himself killed to save us when we got lost in the States last year."

"I know that ..." starts Daphne.

"No more questions then," says Trina, giving a military salute. "We will be the Mounties. We will get our man."

David Bliss's determination to win Yolanda back has been unflagging in recent days and it takes a sharp upward turn when he realizes that his manuscript has grown to nearly thirty thousand words. It won't be long, he tells himself as he sits atop the Eiffel Tower watching the cruise boats ferrying a few hardy visitors past the Louvre and various other monumental buildings that served as palaces to the line of Bourbon kings.

"Your château should be the most magnificent château in the whole world," writes Bliss in the voice of King Louis as the con man coaches his willing prisoner, the besotted Prince Ferdinand of Hungary, and goes on to detail the architectural features that the devious monarch wants incorporated into his prize. *"Corinthian pillars with acanthus leaf capitals should support an enormous shell canopy over the entrance; soaring turrets surmounted by roofs of copper should pierce the Provençe sky; a flight of Carrara marble steps, purer than snow, will lead your loved one into a great hall befitting her status as your wife; and fountains ... fountains and waterfalls cascading all the way down to the beach will take her eye across the bay to your home on the island."*

I wonder if Yolanda would like a place like that, Bliss daydreams as he stares across the mist shrouded river to the Tuilerie gardens where another of Louis' great palaces once stood, then he pulls himself together. *I know, I know. Just keep writing. Don't think about her, it's too painful. Just have faith. She will come back. Just keep plodding on; you're almost halfway there.*

"Aloha," says the Polynesian greeter as Daphne and Trina emerge from their plane in Honolulu, and Daphne beams as she is lassoed by a vibrantly coloured lei.

"It's late," says Trina putting her watch back two hours to local time, and by the time they reach the Sheraton it's almost 2:00 a.m. in Vancouver.

"Janet's in hospital, J.C.," says Mason when he finally gets word from his old school chum. "Mike Edwards had to pull pretty hard to get the information. Apparently Craddock is an ex-cop and his buddies are covering for him."

"What the hell did he do to her?"

"I dunno. But according to Edwards there's a round-the-clock guard on her door and there's an all-ports warning out for him."

"You said he was a pro," seethes Creston. "What the hell were you thinking?"

"Sorry J.C."

"I should think so. Now which hospital?"

"Lets call it a night," says an exhausted Mike Phillips once he's debriefed his officers. "We know she was in his house, we know the hotel, we've got his car, and we've got her. I don't think we can do anything else tonight."

"All we haven't got is him," mutters one of the sergeants, and Phillips looks up.

"Give it time, Leonard."

"He could be anywhere by now," suggests the officer tiredly.

"Well, we've checked all flights leaving since lunchtime. His name didn't come up."

"What if he used an alias?"

"Then we might never know what happened to him."

Anxiety-induced insomnia and the need for a strong drink force Craddock out of his hotel in the early hours. The sidewalks and back alleyways of Waikiki are alive with music leaking from the late-night bars. Neon signs scream-ing "All Totally Nude" blaze appealingly from dozens of dark corners and are reflected off the tropical clouds that have drifted in from the mountains. The heavy sky is alight with the glow of the perennially partying city, but it will take more than flashy lights to lift Craddock. The sultry air drags him down further as he wanders the streets seeking a corner away from the spotlight.

Bogus hula dancers with fake coconut bras and fake grass skirts grind to raucous disco pumped through a sixties amplifier; a one-man band sings "On the Beach at Waikiki" in a distinctly Australian accent; and an army of flesh vendors yell, "Hey Joe. Come in. See the girls. All nude," as Craddock looks for a quiet spot. But he's a natural target for the pimps; single Caucasian male with a beer gut and a glum look.

"You want love?" asks a partly-dressed pretty Polynesian woman in her thirties.

"Don't we all, dear," he replies seriously. "Don't we all."

The bar he finally chooses is so far back off the beach that it's mainly filled with all-night cabbies and other diehards who are more interested in the prices than the paintwork.

"Rum — make it a triple," he orders, and the rotund barman gives him a knowing look.

"Hey, man. You look like you got woman trouble," says the dusky-skinned local as he pours the shots.

"Yeah," agrees Craddock. "Woman trouble."

The Canadian PI actually has women trouble, though he doesn't yet know it. Daphne and Trina are just a few blocks away in their room at the Sheraton. However, he'd never recognize them even if he bumped into them on the beach. The two women detectives, on the other hand, have a distinct advantage. In addition to his photograph they also know the alias he used to book his flight.

"First thing in the morning," Trina says as she and her friend prepare for bed. "We'll split up and do every hotel in town."

"And after that we could go sailing or even take a submarine ride," enthuses Daphne, picking through the glossy pamphlets by her bedside.

chapter fourteen

"Nothing would be more wearisome than ceaseless pleasure," King Louis XIV reportedly proclaimed to his court in the seventeenth century, but it is a truism that is yet to be grasped by many of the Sheraton Hotel's coddled visitors as they surface to another day of luxury in the warm, hibiscus-scented air of Hawaii.

The hotel's full name, the Sheraton Moana Surfrider, is as pretentious as the beachfront building itself: a building with half a dozen fluted columns supporting a soaring canopy over the front entrance that stands sentinel in the centre of Waikiki bay and fights the less fortunate off the golden sand beach with ropes and with signs declaring, "Registered Guests Only."

"Our hotel is known as the First Lady of Waikiki," says Tony, the morning maître d'hôtel, as he escorts Daphne and Trina through the colonnaded entrance hall to the Banyan Veranda where breakfast awaits.

The Sheraton, built more than a century ago to cater to colonialists, retains much of the Victorian elegance of a plantation house, although it is far larger than any that graced the tobacco or cotton fields of the Carolinas or Virginia.

"Breakfast under a banyan tree," exclaims Daphne in delight as she and Trina take their seats under a monster whose branches radiate like the arms of a cartoon octopus.

"This tree is just a few years older than the hotel," explains Tony with a toothy smile as he pulls out a chair for Daphne under the 115-year-old giant.

"Oh, look at the sea," exclaims Daphne in delight as she spies the early morning bathers riding the gentle rollers into the cerulean bay.

"Are you sure you wouldn't like to try surfing?"

"Maybe," jests Daphne. "Once we've found Craddock."

Joseph Creston would also like to find Craddock, but he's way off his mark as he returns to the private eye's last known place of abode in Vancouver. The police tape is still in place, though the crowds and media have melted away overnight, and a lone uniformed constable now patrols the perimeter.

"Can I help, sir?" asks the officer noting Creston's interest.

"I think I know him," suggests Creston with vague wave to the house, but the officer eyes him warily.

"Know who, sir?"

"Mr. Craddock," replies Creston with nothing to lose. "He's a private investigator, isn't he?"

"Is he?" questions the officer with a deadpan face.

"You didn't know?"

"I'm only a constable, sir. I'm not paid to know," the officer continues, still playing the Englishman, but the arrival of a cruiser takes his attention and he steps aside and lifts the tape to let it through. "That's the inspector," he carries on as Mike Phillips parks on Craddock's driveway. "He's the one who's paid to know."

"Inspector," calls out Creston. "Could I have a few words please?"

Mike Phillips wanders inquisitively towards the tape with "No comment" readied on his lips when his would-be inquisitor thrusts out a manicured hand.

"Joseph Creston."

Mike Phillips keeps his hands in his pockets. "And …?" he queries.

"Creston Enterprises — chocolates," continues the magnate.

"Oh," says Phillips, patting his gut. "Try to avoid them myself, but what can I do for you?"

Here goes, thinks Creston. "I just wondered if there was any news on my wife."

"Wife," queries Phillips, quickly putting two and two together. "Do you mean Janet?"

"Yes. That's right, Inspector. She is my wife."

"You'd better come in then," says Phillips, lifting the tape.

"Oh my sweet Jiminy Cricket. Just how many hotels can there be?" moans Trina two hours later as she and Daphne rest under a shade tree on the golden beach and massage their feet.

"I must have done twenty," complains Daphne. "But he might have another alias for all we know."

"I thought of that," admits Trina. "And what if he paid cash and just picked a name out of the air?"

"Or he could be somewhere else altogether. He might have flown on to one of the other islands," agrees Daphne. "What will we do then?"

"Well," says Trina, paddling in a puddle under a drinking fountain to cool her feet. "We'll do this one first and move on if we have to later in the week. You wanted to see volcanoes."

"Actually, I got an inquiry about your wife from someone at Scotland Yard late last night," Mike Phillips tells Creston as they enter Craddock's house, and Janet's husband has no problem confessing.

"Yes. I asked one of my staff to make some inquires. I was worried about her."

That's interesting, thinks Phillips, eyeing the sharply dressed executive cautiously as they sit at Craddock's kitchen table, realizing that he must have left England well before the alarm was raised. "So, when did you last hear from your wife?"

Creston fidgets momentarily, but quickly stops when he sees the inquisitiveness in Phillips face and feels the jaws of a trap. "There's no point in me lying to you, Inspector. The truth is that Janet and I have been separated for quite some time."

"But you still care."

"I still love her to be honest ... always have. But she had one or two problems." He puts his finger to his forehead expressively, adding, "Psychological problems."

"Well, she has other problems now," says Phillips, and is intrigued by Creston's apparent lack of curiosity as the man simply inquires, "Can I visit her?"

Phillips shrugs. "I don't see why not, if you're her husband."

"I'll do that then," says Creston rising and he's half out of the door before Phillips stops him.

"Don't you want to know which hospital?"

"Oh. Yes. Silly of me," says Creston, opening his pocket diary and using a monogrammed Waterman to take details. "Thanks," he says, turning back to the door, when Phillips hits him again.

"By the way, how did you know your wife had been here?"

Creston stops, asking, "In Vancouver?"

"No," questions Phillips pointedly. "In this particular house, Mr. Craddock's house."

Creston's mind is clearly spinning as he fights for a plausible reply, but his mumbled response about putting two and two together lacks both credibility and conviction, and as the Englishman walks down the driveway towards the street and his rented car, Phillips pulls out his cellphone and arranges for a surveillance team to be waiting at the hospital.

"And brief the guard on Janet's room," he adds. "I don't want him left alone with her for a second."

"Try Robert Davies," persists Trina as she begins checking hotels again. But this time she's at the Ohana on Kuhio Avenue.

"Robert Davies," repeats the female desk clerk loudly, and a man stops in his tracks as he passes. "That's right ... Robert Davies," reiterates Trina as Craddock takes in the scene and is in the elevator and on the way to his sixteenth floor room within seconds

"Shit! Shit! Shit!" mutters the cornered PI as he wills the elevator to speed up, and when a couple of Korean women try to get in on the twelfth floor, he roughly pushes them out and stabs the "close door" button.

Craddock is down the fire escape and out into the searing light of the mid-morning sun in less than a minute, while Trina is running in the opposite direction, intent on finding Daphne as quickly as possible.

It is early afternoon in Vancouver and still raining, though Joseph Creston doesn't seem to notice as he peers across the city from his wife's room with a hint of a tear in his eye.

"How did she get like this?" he questions, turning to the doctor who is checking Janet's pulse.

"Years of neglect probably," the doctor suggests, though he steps back, admitting that it could well be self-induced.

"Self-induced?" questions Creston.

"Eating disorders; depression; general mental problems; self-loathing," the white-coated medic suggests, running off a list of possibilities. "Anything ring a bell?"

"Probably," admits Creston. "I don't think she really thought she was good enough for me."

"And was she?"

The question seems to take forever to sink in. "Good enough?" repeats Creston eventually, and then finally answers, "Financially, we were miles apart. It didn't bother me, but I think she found my family a little daunting."

"Well," shrugs the doctor. "It's not unusual to find the in-laws overwhelming. Was there anything else?"

The death of the children seems to have slipped Creston's mind as he seriously ponders the question, leaving Mike Phillips, who has quietly sidled into the room behind the visitor's back, shaking his head perplexedly.

"Ah, Mr. Creston," says the officer seeming to arrive with his notepad in hand. "I was hoping to catch you."

"Is there something I can help you with, Inspector?"

"Yes. I just need a statement."

"But I don't know anything."

"Formality, sir. I'm sure you understand."

"In case she dies, Inspector," says Creston harshly. "Is that what you're saying?"

Phillips' cellphone saves him. "Excuse me a moment," he says, taking the call.

It's Trina, breathless. "Mike, he's in Hawaii," she shouts excitedly. "Craddock is in Hawaii using the name Robert Davies."

"Hang on," says Phillips with a wary eye on Creston, and then he excuses himself, saying, "I'll be back in a second, sir."

"You are brilliant, Trina Button," says Phillips once he's in the corridor. "Now go to the nearest police station, tell them what you know, and get them to call me, all right?"

"Right, sir. Roger, wilco, sir."

"It's Mike, Trina. Don't get carried away."

"OK, Mike."

"Now, sir," says Phillips returning to question Creston. "You were telling me how you knew that your wife had been at Mr. Craddock's house. Would you mind explaining that again — just for the record?"

While Inspector Phillips waits for Creston to try to worm his way out of that question, he is mentally preparing the next: "Are you psychic, or was it just a very lucky coincidence that you happened to arrive in Vancouver before we knew that Craddock had kidnapped her?"

It takes half an hour for Trina and Daphne to get through to the smartly dressed Polynesian officers that a wanted man is in their midst, thanks largely to Trina's over-excited inability to focus on one thing at a time. Beautiful, Craddock, guinea pigs, dead babies, banana sandwiches, and religious freaks all get confused in a gushing tale that runs the officers around in circles.

In the end, Daphne shuts Trina up with a scowl and starts from the beginning.

It take another hour for enough men to be rounded up to surround the inexpensive hotel, and by the time that a passkey opens the private eye's door, the fugitive is on a small plane bound for the volcanoes of Hawaii's Big Island.

"Now what?" questions Daphne, surveying the hastily abandoned room.

"We could always go catch some breakers," suggests Trina with a grin.

Almost half a world away, not far from the Eiffel Tower, David Bliss is dreaming of Yolanda as his mind prepares for his return to St-Juan-sur-Mer. But the anguished spectres of past centuries surrounding the beautiful, though seemingly malevolent, Château Roger become entangled with her image and drive him out of bed much earlier than his alarm clock planned.

"I don't really want to go back," he told Samantha the previous evening. "There's too many memories there."

"Warm memories?" queried his daughter.

"Very," he said.

"In that case go back; think of the good times, remember what you had. It'll spur you on to finish your book and get her back again."

"Thanks, Sam," he said, cheering, and he meant it.

Now, with his bags packed and — unlike Craddock — his hotel account settled, he still has two hours before the first southbound train. His suitcase drags heavily as he struggles along the deserted platform, tempting him to turn north and walk away from his ghouls — the masked man, the massacred resistance fighters, and even Yolanda — but he shakes off his fears, driven by the knowledge that their souls will be forever lost should he fail in his resolve.

As Bliss's day begins in France, another marathon is winding down for Mike Phillips in Vancouver.

"There is something very odd going on here," he confesses once he's gathered his team together for a late-night debrief. "This big-shot Creston knows a lot more than he's letting on."

"He hasn't left her room all day," pipes up one of the surveillance officers.

"I know," says Phillips. "But he's on the phone non-stop."

"Can we bug him?"

"Cellphone," says Phillips throwing his hands wide, knowing the difficulty of tapping into digital radio waves. "Anyway, we'd need a warrant and we've got nothing to go on."

"So," asks one of the sergeants, "what's his connection with that religious joint up in the mountains?"

"That's what I'd like to know. Get onto it in the morning will you? Have a word with Zelke, the cults and sects guy, see what he's managed to dig up."

Wayne Browning may have a vault full of skeletons, but unearthing them will take more than a lone specialist officer. Since Trina's visit to Beautiful the pharisaic religionist has been weeding out all reference to Creston and his enterprises and building a pyre.

"What about Craddock, boss?" pipes up another officer as the debriefing closes in on midnight.

"He's on the run again. Honolulu was the last sighting, but he could be anywhere by now."

"And the Thurgood woman?"

"I suppose she's technically the Creston woman now," explains Phillips. "She'll probably make it."

"Some good news then."

"Yeah. Although I've given orders that she's not to be left alone, even for a second, with her husband."

"You think he might pull the plug?"

"There's something fishy about him," admits Phillips, although he has nothing solid. However, the late-night call from a Scotland Yard chief superintendent, apparently acting on the executive's behalf, doesn't take away any of the smell. "This guy has got clout," Phillips continues to his crew. "Big clout, but I'm just not sure which side of the fence he's on."

Joseph Creston has lost steam and has finally fallen asleep, slumped into an armchair by his wife's bed in a luxury room. "I want her to have the very best at whatever cost," he told the hospital administrator earlier, but the man shook his head.

"This isn't America, Mr. Creston. Everyone gets the same treatment here regardless of ability to pay."

"Right, I understand," he replied, but the administrator coughed to indicate that he wasn't finished.

"The only problem is that, legally, it seems your wife is not registered as a Canadian resident."

"She's been here forty years."

"I'm aware of that, but she's never registered or made contributions."

"What are you saying?"

"Well, naturally we'll treat her, but there may be a question of payment."

"Oh," said Creston catching on. "Maybe I could make a small charitable donation."

"You could, but only if you want to."

"Say a quarter of a million dollars? How does that sound?"

"Qua ... qua ... quarter of a million?" the administrator stuttered.

"All right," Creston cut in and watched the man choke, "let's make it a half million. I'm sure there's some vital piece of equipment you could use in Janet's care."

Nothing has changed in Bliss's apartment on his return. The warm memories of Yolanda in his bed are instantly chilled by the knowledge that she is no longer here and may never be here again. "What if she marries him?" he worries as he peers over the balcony and finds the single lemon still on the grass, but then he pulls himself together. *She wouldn't do that*, he tells himself. *She admitted that he didn't really love her, not like me. But what if he insists, just to spite me, just to make sure I can't have her?*

"Keep writing," Samantha's voice in his mind tells him. "Keep writing and do it quickly. Get it done and send it to her before she makes the biggest mistake of her life."

Craddock, alias Robert Davies, has slipped under the radar of the Hawaiian police department and is working his way towards the very edge of Polynesia as Daphne and Trina take the evening off in Waikiki.

A grassy beachside stage, overhung with banyans and loaded coconut palms, hosts a ukulele band and a trio of hula dancers as the sun turns to a fireball and burns a hole in the Pacific. The fiery spectacle stops the musicians and they turn, together with the audience, to applaud the celestial show before picking up their swaying rhythm again.

"Who would like to hula?" cries the bandleader, and Daphne is not at all surprised when Trina is plucked out of the crowd to end up on stage in a grass skirt.

"Come on, Daph," shouts the exuberant Canadian as she takes the spotlight with a perversion of hula that somehow combines elements of breakdancing, the Twist, and kick-boxing. The audience goes wild, but the band-leader throws up his arms and his ukulele in despair.

"Boy, that was great," screeches Trina with her base-ball cap on backwards as she comes off stage, and the two women head to the international market where vendors switch back and forth between English, Cantonese, and the local pidgin as they push "local" souvenirs made almost entirely in China.

Fendi, Louis Vuitton, Christian Dior, and Armani all have glitzy stores backing on to the beach, but carbon copies of most of their products can be found on the market stalls just a pebble's throw away. Ten-dollar RayBans, twenty-dollar Rolexes, and a thousand other glassy knock-offs sit side by side with glossy fool's gold and tempt the wary and unwary alike.

The pearls are real, though mainly seeded, and buckets of live oysters wait to be sprung by gamblers willing to risk a few dollars to discover a little gem.

And after the market the two women share a pineapple-laced pizza before taking a late-night stroll along Kalla

Road where much of the entertainment is provided by the tourists themselves.

"Oh my God, look at this," Trina laughs, pointing Daphne towards a man welded into a metal straitjacket.

"It's fake," said Daphne with hardly a glance, but she acknowledges to herself that many of the freakily attired show-offs are just misguided people living in a fantasy land.

By midnight, scantily dressed hookers are out in full force along with the panhandlers and the drunks who are starting to fall out of the bars.

"Time to go home," Daphne says when she has side-stepped one too many inebriates, but they spend another hour laughing at their experiences over pina coladas in the bar of the Sheraton before finding their way to their room.

"We really ought to be looking for Craddock," Daphne suggests tiredly around 2:00 a.m. as she gets into bed, but Trina isn't concerned. "It's an island," she says. "He can't have gone far. The police will soon pick him up."

Joseph Creston is still asleep when Mike Phillips checks in at the hospital on his way to the office the following morning.

"He hasn't left the room all night," the guard on Janet's room whispers to Phillips when he inquires.

"Phone calls?"

"He switched it off."

"How's Janet doing?"

"Still the same, I think," replies the young woman officer. "She sort of drifts in and out."

"Saying anything?"

"She mumbles things about 'God' and 'Our Lord Saviour' and 'Sorry.' She says 'Sorry' a lot, but nothing else."

"Stick with it," Phillips is saying as Creston surfaces.

"Ah, Inspector. Glad I caught you," says the drowsy man. "I wanted your opinion. I was thinking of having my wife flown back to England."

"Nothing to do with me," says Phillips putting up his hands to block the man. "That will be up to the doctors."

"Only I could charter an air ambulance. She wouldn't suffer."

"Like I said, not my department." Then he checks his watch. "Sorry must dash ... meeting ... we've found Craddock."

Creston's face falls, but he quickly picks himself up. "Oh. Good show. Where?"

"State secret," says Phillips on his way out of the door. "State secret."

Now let's see what happens, muses the inspector as he heads for his car and the police station.

Chief Superintendent Edwards is clearing his desk for the day when Mason calls.

"I need something else, Mike," says Creston's right-hand man.

"Not at the office," spits the police commander, knowing that all lines in and out of the headquarters are recorded. "I'll call you back in thirty minutes."

"Make it ten."

Half an hour later Mike Phillips takes the call he's expecting from his English counterpart. "That didn't take long," he muses under his breath as he checks his watch and puts on a sweet voice. "Chief Superintendent Edwards," he trills. "Pleasure to hear from you again — and so soon. What can I do for you?"

"Just wondering how things were progressing?"

"Fine, thanks."

"Any developments?"

"Developments?" queries Phillips, playing the British officer along. "What did you have in mind?"

"Weren't you looking for a private dick?"

"Were we?"

"Look, Mike," says Edwards, suddenly aware that he's hitting concrete. "Mr. Creston is in the big league."

"So I've heard."

"Anyway. I just thought you should know that. So, if there's anything he should know ..."

"I'll be sure to tell him."

"Good. Good. And if I can help in any way."

"Actually, you can," says Phillips, pausing for a second before pushing a red button. "I'd like copies of the files relating to the deaths of his three children."

Edwards stalls, "Oh. I don't think ..."

"Well, you did ask."

"I ... I know, but I don't have access," continues Edwards trying to backtrack. "It was a different force ... long time ago. Doubt we could find them now."

"OK," says Phillips, seemingly letting the other man off the hook. "I'll call you if I need anything else."

Mike Phillips puts the phone down before Edwards has a chance to reply and mutters, "Sucker," before gathering his team around him for a briefing.

"OK," he says. "I may be wrong but it looks to me that Creston hired Craddock to snatch his wife."

"Because?" asks one of the officers, leaving Phillips in a mental vacuum.

"Still working on that," he says after a few seconds. "But I don't buy that he loves her so damn much that he rushed here to be by her side. I might have done forty years ago, but it's a bit lame now. Christ, I'm amazed he even remembers her name."

Phillips is wrong about Creston in some ways. The words "Till death do us part" have always held him locked to Janet, but so has the advice of a specialist lawyer hired by his father after the death of the third child.

"My suggestion would be to keep her as far away as possible," the white-haired family law expert opined. "But never divorce her. That way you'll always retain control."

"And that's important?" Joseph Creston the younger questioned.

"Yes it is, young man. Very important," the lawyer continued sagely. "Get her into a convent or similar sort of place where she'll be isolated from the rest of the world and from the temptation to talk."

The remote community of Beautiful was just as far from leafy Dewminster as the North Pole, and not a lot warmer, and it fitted the lawyer's criteria. "It's for the best," the elder Creston told his son's wife as he and Peter Symmonds ushered her aboard his executive jet while his son sat at home and wept.

"But it wasn't my fault," Janet cried as she was escorted up the plane's steps. "I loved him. I loved them all."

"I know," Creston Sr. soothed. "Maybe you loved them too much."

"No."

"Maybe you smothered them with love."

"No. No I didn't," she protested, but it made no difference. The sedative that Symmonds injected kicked in, and by the time she awoke, Wayne Browning was inculcating her into his sect, flagellating her into submission, and feeding her drugs and whacky notions in equal proportions until she no longer knew her own mind; she no longer knew for certain what happened to her children.

"Creston is anxious to get her out of the country," explains Phillips as he continues briefing his staff. "Now why would that be?"

"Worried about her," gets a young female officer nowhere.

"Worried she might talk now she's not under Browning's control," tries another.

"Could be," agrees Phillips pointing at the officer who made the suggestion, asking, "What have we got on that Beautiful place? Who was digging into it?"

"Me," says another officer putting up his hand. "It's early days but the finances of the place don't seem to stand up."

"In what way?"

"Off the record," says the officer, "but our man in Mountain Falls, the nearest town, reckons that Browning and his harem keep the whole town afloat."

"Big spenders?"

"Big laundry is more like it. Apparently the banks up there handle millions for him, but most of it doesn't stay long."

"Where does he get it?"

"Pot growing possibly," suggests the officer, "but I'm only guessing. We'd need a warrant to look at his records."

"And we don't have grounds," says Phillips knowingly. Then he has an idea. "What about the tax man. Look into it. See if they know what's happening."

"What about Craddock?" asks the woman officer.

"Still on the lam in Hawaii," admits Phillips and gets six volunteers to immediately go in search of him.

"Very funny," laughs Phillips "but actually I've already got two of my best men out there."

Phillips' "men" in Hawaii are sleeping in this morning. In fact there's a very good chance they'll sleep until lunchtime.

Craddock, on the other hand, is wide awake. *I could always live rough*, he tells himself as he saunters along a black volcanic beach lined with shady coconut palms under a tropical sky, thinking that life would be just peachy if there weren't a storm brewing over the horizon.

The wayward PI has gone as far as he can get without dropping off the Hawaiian archipelago into the Pacific, but the volcanoes and legendary sunsets of the Big Island hold no interest for him. His only concern is surviving for as long as possible without using either his own or Davies' credit card.

"I'll pay cash," he insisted the first night in a backstreet hotel in the capital, Hilo, but he knows that the money he hurriedly withdrew from a few ATMs before leaving Honolulu won't stretch more than a couple of weeks, and he knows he can never risk using the card again.

David Bliss is also walking a palm-fringed beach, but the only storm clouds on his horizon are quickly evaporating as he realizes that his manuscript is coming together faster and better than he could ever have anticipated

The Château Roger is now complete, the lovelorn Prince's passionate plea to the woman of his dreams is written and already in the hands of a courier, and the mask is fitted.

Will the plan work? Will he succeed?

Yes, Bliss adamantly decides as he sits on the promenade at St-Juan-sur-Mer with both the château and the fortress in view, preparing to write the final chapters of his novel. *Because if he fails so will I. And I have no intentions of failing. This is the biggest challenge of my life. I cannot let Yolanda go — I will succeed.*

"Good for you, Dad," he imagines Samantha saying, and he pens his own feelings in the words of the newly incarcerated prince.

"I will permit no other images but yours into my mind. Your spirit is forever conjoined with mine. The silence of my cell rings with your joyous laughter; the air is scented by your sweet breath; the softness of your voluptuous body washes in on the gentle Mediterranean breeze and soothes my troubled heart.

"The velvet-surfaced alabaster of these walls enfolds and protects me as if I am encased by your womb; your heat warms me; your inner glow lights my path. I am nourished by memories of you and encouraged by the certainty that, when I am reborn, it will be into your sweet bosom. Until that time I will countenance neither sunrise nor sunset, for here is but a single solitary night that will break into a

glorious dawn when you return to me. And I will not countenance failure."

"How is zhe writing?" questions Angeline as she strolls benignly across the deserted road from the bar L'Escale to peer over his shoulder.

"Good, Angeline," he says with a broad smile. "It is very, very good."

"And your friend ... zhe woman you love. She comes back, no?"

"Soon, Angeline," he replies with more conviction than he's had for a long time. "Very, very soon."

A message awaits Bliss on the answering machine at his apartment, and he's surprised to hear the Canadian voice of Mike Phillips.

"Daphne Lovelace gave me your number," says Phillips, once he's introduced himself. "Could you give me a call, Dave? I'm getting a bit of interference from someone in Scotland Yard and wonder if you have anything that I could use?"

"Michael Edwards," exclaims Bliss as soon as Phillips has put him in the picture. "Do you mean that scumbag chief superintendent who's made everyone's life a bloody misery for the last god knows how long?"

"I guess so," laughs Phillips.

"Oh, boy," says Bliss. "Have you come to the right person. In fact, I've just made him the main villain in my novel."

"Novel?" queries Phillips.

"Long story," admits Bliss, "but you've got big problems if Edwards is on your case. He's shittier than a cesspit — specializes in black book diplomacy."

"He's got nothing on me."

"Then you're about the only one," says Bliss. "Although he's never been able to pin anything on me either — though he's tried."

"I need something, anything," carries on Phillips, "especially if I can link him to Creston."

"I'm really busy, Mike," starts Bliss with his mind on his almost completed manuscript and Yolanda's anticipated return, but then he realizes that he has made the demolition of Edwards an important element of his script, and should he fail in that, his entire plan may crash. "I'll get hold of someone," he says, and five minutes later he's talking quietly to his son-in-law, Chief Inspector Peter Bryan.

"How's the book coming on, Dad?" asks Bryan and gets a rebuke.

"Cut out this 'Dad' stuff, Peter," he snaps, then softens. "Actually it was Sam's idea, but it's going to work. You've got a brilliant wife."

"I know that. But what can I do for you? Need a few tips in the bedroom department for when the lovely lady comes back?"

"Not from you, I don't," he bites, then lets it go. "Actually, Peter, I need your help to nail Edwards' bollocks to the floor once and for all."

"Breakfast under the banyan tree again," trills Daphne as she peers out over the ocean watching the early morning surfers catching breakers that have rolled across a thousand miles of open water.

"Minnie and I were going to come here on our world tour," she adds wistfully, recalling an old friend who threw herself under a train in a fit of depression.

Trina reaches across the table to gently stroke her elderly partner's hand. "I remember. That was a terrible thing. Are you OK now?"

"OK," repeats Daphne as if she is trying to work out what the expression means. Then a few tears dribbles down her cheeks. "Do you know, you never fully realize how much you really love someone until they're gone."

"Pave paradise and put up a parking lot," sings Trina and Daphne gives her a quizzical look. "From the sixties," explains Trina. "Joni Mitchell I think. You don't know what you've got till it's gone."

Daphne pauses in thought for a few seconds as she drinks some fresh local pineapple juice, and then she puts down the glass. "Actually that's not really true. Minnie may have been a bit of a silly old woman, and I could get pretty cross with her at times, but I think I did know what I had. I think you do know when, deep down, you really truly love someone."

Joseph Creston stopped shedding tears for Janet long ago, but now, as he sits by her bed in Vancouver, he still conjures images of the perky teenager he could never take his eyes off. Janet may be a hollow shadow, barely a ghost of the young woman he remembers, yet her spirit, her essence, has never left his mind.

"What do you think about me taking her to England, doctor?" he asks as the physician does his daily round. But Mike Phillips has already spiked that idea, and the medic shakes his head firmly. "Absolutely not possible. Not at the moment."

"But you said you would consider it," pushes Creston, seeing his plan unravelling.

"And I have, Mr. Creston. And I'm saying no."

"Maybe I should speak to the administrator?"

"You could call the Lord himself, sir, but it's my decision and I'm saying she's not fit to go anywhere."

Creston, unused to hearing "No" from anyone, rises quickly. "I could get a second opinion."

"Naturally."

Then he backs down and takes a different path. Putting on a smile he places a warm hand on the doctor's shoulder. "Maybe there's something I could do for you? I mean, how much do they pay you here? Not a lot if our National Health Service is anything to go on. What if I took you on to look after Janet? A couple of hundred thousand to start — we could call it a 'golden hello' and then —"

Doctor Jurgen shakes off Creston's hand and looks fiercely into the other man's eyes. "I said she is not fit to travel."

"I know, but —"

"Look … sir …" the doctor starts, then changes his mind and picks up Janet's wrist, searching for her pulse.

"So?" questions Creston hopefully.

"So," the doctor repeats glowering fiercely. "You decide what's more important, Mr. Creston: your wife's well-being or you getting your own way."

"I'll get another opinion," Creston yells after the doctor as he closes the door behind him.

chapter fifteen

"Time for prayers," says Mike Phillips as he rounds up several members of his gang a few days after Christmas, but it's a couple of weeks since Craddock slipped his noose and the entire investigation has stalled over the holidays. Trina and Daphne have returned from paradise to a drizzly Vancouver winter. Janet Thurgood is making a slow recovery, and Creston has been forced back to London by a flare-up of civil unrest in Côte d'Ivoire.

"We've got to get our people out of there," Mason told his chief in a panic. But in Creston's eyes "his people" include only the white traders and buyers. The indigenous farmers will have to fight for themselves.

"We've got the DNA back from the lab," reports one of Phillips' men as they sit around an untouched box of Christmas chocolates, but the positive results change nothing. They already know that Janet was confined in Craddock's van and bedroom, that he gagged her with duct tape, and that she was with him at the airport hotel. But the forensic evidence, though crucial in a criminal trial, will end up on the cutting room floor unless the villain of the piece can be found.

"Anything more on the money trail?' asks Phillips with a nod to the officer he asked to track down Beautiful's books.

"Have you ever tried to deal with Revenue Canada?" spits the constable. "More red tape than a Valentine's bouquet."

"Nothing at all?" queries Phillips.

"They're looking into it, boss," she says, but her tone suggests she knows different.

"Keep on them," says the inspector, then he looks around the room at the officers with the realization that the time is fast approaching when he'll be forced to stand them down and move on to more current matters. "Anything else … anyone?" he asks hopefully.

"Maybe the Thurgood woman will give us something when she's stronger," suggests one officer, but Phillips shakes his head. "Not if her husband is around. He's already hired that dick-shit lawyer Rudy Clayton to represent her, and he's warned me to expect a lawsuit if I even break wind within earshot of her without his permission."

"What's Creston scared of?"

Phillips is well aware of the allegations concerning Janet's dead children — Daphne and Trina have given him the full picture — but he sees no point in blackening the woman. Whatever happened in England forty years ago, Janet is today's victim in Canada. "I wish I knew," he says slowly. "I wish I knew."

Joseph Creston's fears over his wife are on his back burner with a high-priced lawyer standing guard over her bed. The inter-religious fighting in Abidjan and other cities of Côte d'Ivoire are playing havoc with cocoa supplies, though he's already shifting his staff and resources to neighbouring countries.

"The futures are up again," John Dawes tells him at the weekly progress meeting, but it doesn't bring the expected smile.

"And the good news?" queries Creston, knowing that higher prices at one end mean lower sales at the other.

The accountant is more bullish. "Overall we could still be up two or three percent on the year."

"What about financing? Have we covered the situation left by Canada?"

"Yes. We've got a place in Nicaragua offering a similar deal — fifteen percent."

"Still cheaper than Inland Revenue. Set it up," orders Creston, knowing that Dawes has probably already done so.

"Any news on Janet, J.C.?" asks Mason once Dawes has left.

"Yeah. I wanted to talk to you about that. I want to bring her back. That man of yours at the Yard has squared everything hasn't he?"

"As far as I know."

"Did we pay him?"

"Four big ones."

"Then let's assume it's done. Start making arrangements. She's going to need a passport and stuff."

Creston's four thousand pounds may have filled a hole in Michael Edwards' pocket, but he doesn't have a smile on his face as he sits, shuffling papers, in his office at Scotland Yard. A sense of unease has been gnawing at him for a while, thanks largely to the very guarded response he received from Ted Donaldson, Daphne's friend, at Westchester Police Station.

"Just cleaning up old files," Edwards told his opposite number when he asked for anything relating to the Creston deaths. "I've got a mandate from God," he carried on chattily, referring obliquely to the Home Secretary. "I'm supposed to feed the whiz-bang fact eater with every suspicious death case going back fifty years."

"That damn computer of yours is taking over every-thing," moaned Donaldson, complaining about the Police National Computer, then he joked, "I tried to do a wanted person check the other day and it asked me if I'd had my morning crap."

"Funny," Edwards said, forcing a laugh, then he pushed harder. "Anyway, Ted, these Creston cases. We don't seem to have anything recorded, and I don't want to have to send it upstairs on paper."

Donaldson shrugged off the threat, recalling his search through the records with Daphne. "You can send it to God herself if you like," replied Donaldson. "It won't make any difference. There's no paperwork. It was natural causes times three."

But Ted Donaldson has worn his superintendent's crown long enough to know when he is being taken for a ride and eventually calls David Bliss.

"It certainly sounds iffy to me," admits Bliss as he sits under the warm midwinter sun outside the bar L'Escale sipping a cappuccino while finishing his novel. "I'll find out and get back to you."

Knowing Edwards I bet it's something tricky, Bliss tells himself, then realizes that the chief superintendent's cunning antecedent, Louis XIV, was equally renowned for his deviousness. By the time he starts a second cappuccino, he has found a suitable anecdote to include as a vignette in an earlier chapter.

"Come, my dear marquis," said the king, writes Bliss, referring to the French monarch's gaming partner, the Marquis of Dangeau. *"I have word the Maréchal de Gramont intends to prostrate himself at my feet to seek a favour for one of his idiot nephews and I wish to groom you in the sport of diplomacy."* Then, with Dangeau at his back, Louis bustled out of his chamber as if in a great rage and burst upon Gramont, who pulled up short and made his obeisance.

"Ah. My dear Gramont," bellowed the king. "Just the man I seek." Then he thrust a paper at the maréchal, saying, "Take a look at that. 'Tis supposedly a sonnet. Though 'tis in my view one of the worst I have yet seen."

"I must agree," said Gramont scanning the few lines. "The absolute worst."

"'Tis utter rubbish," continued the king, snatching back the paper and tearing it to shreds.

"'Tis true, Sire," said the maréchal, sensing that he was on the winning side.

"Childish nonsense," carried on the king, still in high dudgeon as he threw it to the ground and stomped upon it.

"One of the most puerile poems yet devised," pressed Gramont, then he sensed that he might gain some leverage if he knew the author.

"The author!" exclaimed the king, upon Gramont's inquiry. "Why it was me of course. I wrote it ... Now what is it that you wished to ask of me?"

With a satisfied smirk and an eye on the clock, Bliss finally folds his manuscript and phones his son-in-law at home.

"Enemy action, Peter," he says, using code, despite the fact that the chief inspector is on his cellphone. "A certain chief super is trying to get his hands on documents relating to the Creston murders."

"Murders?" echoes Bryan. "That's only what Daphne reckons."

"I've never known her to be wrong," carries on Bliss. "Anyway, why would our man be interested?"

"Not him," agrees Peter Bryan. "But I bet his handler is."

"Anything on that front?" questions Bliss.

"Actually, Dave, yes. Quite a bit," says his son-in-law, before outlining how the officer assigned to tail Edwards, once internal affairs was alerted about the senior man's involvement with Creston, found him at lunch in a pricey restaurant with Mason.

"Apparently they didn't speak," Peter Bryan continues, "but Mason left his *Times* on the table and Edwards snatched it faster than a pigeon on a sandwich in Trafalgar Square."

"That's pretty old-fashioned stuff," scoffs Bliss. "Mind, he's not exactly James Bond. So, what was in the paper?"

"Maybe he just wanted something intellectual to read for a change," suggests Bryan sarcastically. "But the tail said he just rolled it up, paid his bill, and got out of there faster then a scorched rabbit."

Daphne Lovelace is also preparing to leave.

"I'd better get back to Missie Rouge," she explains to Trina as they sit over the breakfast table. "I've been here more than three weeks."

But the Canadian woman looks crestfallen. "You can't," she says. "Not yet. We still haven't finished the case."

Daphne smiles at her friend's enthusiasm. "I think we did all right."

"No," insists Trina grumpily. "We didn't get anywhere. Craddock is still on the run, that Beautiful joint is still as freaky as ever, and Creston's got Janet back — according to Mike Phillips, she'll be gone in a few days. We never did find out what happened to her kids ..."

Daphne lays a hand over Trina's. "At least we helped save Janet's life."

"Life," spits Trina. "That's not life. Not what she had. She was just a slave."

"I guess some women are happy being slaves," says Daphne despairingly. "Some women just like to serve men. They think it's their duty. For some women, the more they are disrespected the harder they try to please."

"Not me," says Trina.

"Me, neither," agrees Daphne. "But some just keep pleading for more."

"Reverse psychology," suggests Trina knowingly.

"Oh poor little me. What to do? My husband won't talk to me anymore," whines Daphne, smoothing back her hair, and Trina laughs as Daphne continues, "I shall have to pamper him — cook him nice dinners …"

"That would be nice for a change," says Rick Button as he slips in to give Trina a goodbye kiss. "So what adventures are you two cooking up today?"

"Actually, I'm going home," says Daphne.

"Oh," he replies with a look to his wife. "Does this mean you're going back to work?"

"Guess so," she says then she gives him a friendly poke. "Hey, we've been working."

"Hawaii," he sneers.

"Lovelace and Button, International Investigators," she reminds him as he makes for the door.

Last chapter, Bliss tells himself as he begins with a clean sheet and a glass of Côtes du Provençe at L'Escale. The chilled nor'westerly wind, the mistral, sweeping down the valley of the Rhone from the distant Alps has taken the last vestiges of the summer's heat and pushed it south to the savannahs and deserts of Africa. The wintry nip may have forced Bliss indoors, but through the misted window of the bar the masked man's island fortress stands out sharply against a cobalt background in the clean mountain air, and the remnants of his great testament, the Château Roger, are clearly visible through the windblown vegetation.

"Nearly finished," says Bliss as he sees Angeline approaching and guesses that she will inquire.

"Zhat is good, no?"

"Yes, Angeline. Zhat is very good."

"And your friend?"

"Yolanda," he reminds her. "Yes," he adds confidently, "she will soon come home."

"That is good also, no?"

"Yes, Angeline. Zhat is good, no," he parodies as he picks up his pen and begins:

"Today I view my magnificent château across the blue bay with a lightness of heart. Today, I know that my plan is working. Today I know that my lover is thinking fondly of me ..."

Bliss's cellphone interrupts his writing and he's tempted to ignore it, but he has Yolanda on his mind and is answering "Dave Bliss" before he has a chance to check the call display.

"Is that you, David?" queries Daphne from her home in Westchester.

"Oh. Hello, Daphne," he replies, trying to take out the note of disappointment. "What's happening?"

"I need your help," she begins, and he immediately tries to duck.

"I'm really busy."

"I know," she says, "but it will only take a day or so."

"Couldn't Ted or Peter do it?" he suggests, but she has made up her mind.

"No, David. Peter's too young and Ted's too old. You are the perfect man for the job. You could easily pass for forty any day."

"Thanks ..."

"Plus, you're not officially in the police at the moment."

"Oh. Oh," he says picking up the implication. "This sounds dodgy."

"Devious, David," she admits, "but not exactly dodgy," and he gives in.

Chief Superintendent Michael Edwards is dodgy and has always been dodgy. He didn't climb the career ladder on the backs of other officers; he stomped his way to the top one head at a time. If he spent as much time and effort getting the dirt on villains during his service as he does on blackening his colleagues he would probably be "top of the cops" in Police

Review. But playing by the rules and keeping the streets clean doesn't always lead to the top. Good guys come last as easily in the police as any other field, and Edwards was never inclined to risk taking the long route.

It has been a few weeks since Creston's grateful handout found its way into the chief superintendent's pocket, but the cash has burnt a hole. Crisp £50 notes take up surprisingly little space, but he knows that it will not take a genius to trace the consecutive numbers back to the issuing bank, so he's already shifted them four times around various nooks and crannies in his house and garage.

Don't flash it about. Don't spend it all in one place, he told himself repeatedly, but he's had his eye on a new car for some time now. *Why would anyone be suspicious?* he asks himself.

"Thinking of treating myself to a new motor," the schemer declares loudly, sowing a few seeds as he lines up for lunch in the cafeteria behind Bliss's son-in-law, Peter Bryan.

"Oh," asks Bryan as if cued. "Another beemer, sir?"

"I guess so," says Edwards, as if it's a punishment. "What are you scooting around in these days, Peter?"

"An old Jag."

"I should've thought you'd have gone more up-market with a lawyer for a wife."

"Well, the money's not everything."

"Damn right," says Edwards. "By the way, how's her dad? Have you heard from him?"

"He's OK."

"OK," sniggers Edwards as he grabs a chicken curry. "Silly bastard. Reckons he can write a fucking book."

"Well, he is."

"Yeah. But let's face it, Peter. There's no poxin' money in that is there? He'll never be driving a beemer that's for certain."

"I wouldn't be so sure, sir," says Bryan as he goes for the beef stew. "I actually think he's turning out a real blockbuster."

"Two days," warns Bliss as soon as Daphne answers the knock on her front door. "I've got a return ticket."

"All right, David." She laughs as she ushers him into the kitchen. "But what's your hurry?"

"I've got to finish my novel. I want it done by the end of January at the latest," he tells her, then goes on to explain his mission vis-à-vis Yolanda.

Daphne sits back in admiration. "My goodness, David," she sighs. "That is the most romantic thing I've ever heard. You have actually written an entire novel just to get back your lost love. That's absolutely brilliant."

"I just hope Yolanda sees it that way. Anyway don't blame me, it was Samantha's idea."

"I always said your daughter was a genius."

"That why she's a lawyer and I'm just a starving author."

"You're not starving," chuckles Daphne. "In any case you'll always have your police pension to fall back on."

"True," he admits, but his brow crinkles. "Although I'm beginning to worry she might hate me for doing it, for making our affair public."

"What if she doesn't read it?" queries Daphne putting up another block. "I mean, what's the chance of it being published in Dutch?"

"About as much chance as Urdu or Swahili," he replies. "But I've already thought of that. As soon as the manuscript is finished I'm going to track her down and send her a copy."

"And if she explodes?"

"She'll never come back to me," he acknowledges. "But I'll have the best damn love story ever written. Like Samantha said, every talk show and newspaper in the country will want me. Sam reckons it could make me a millionaire. 'Jilted detective writes award-winning novel,'" he adds as if reading a banner headline.

"She might sue," cautions Daphne.

"For what?" questions Bliss. "Telling the truth, saying, 'I love this woman so much I tried to script her back into my life'? Anyway, nothing pushes book sales higher than a rip-roaring public muckrake."

"You've thought of everything haven't you?" says Daphne with a broad grin.

"I hope so," replies Bliss. "You've no idea how much I love that woman."

"I think I do, David. I think I do," she says, seeing the passion in his sparkling blue eyes, and then she segues into her tale of Amelia Drinkwater and the crusty woman's romantic attachment to Joseph Creston. "One second she's all sanctimonious, telling me that she never has a bad word to say about anyone," continues Daphne, "and the next she's lynching her ex-boyfriend's wife."

"You mean Janet Thurgood?"

"Yes. Miss Holier-Than-Thou Drinkwater couldn't wait to put the boot in."

"Jealousy?" queries Bliss.

"That's what I suspected at first, but Trina is absolutely convinced of Janet's innocence."

"That's hardly a good start," scoffs Bliss, letting Daphne know where he stands on the subject of the zany Canadian. "If I remember rightly she wanted me to dress up as a giant condom to raise money for the Kidney Foundation —"

"Yes. All right," breaks in Daphne holding up a hand. "She gets carried away at times, but I actually think she may be right."

"Because?"

"Methinks Miss Goody-Goody Drinkwater doth protest too much."

"Mrs. Drinkwater?" queries Bliss tentatively, standing back from the door as if preparing for an explosion.

"And just who are you?" demands the woman, using her magisterial tone despite the fact that it is a little after nine in the morning and she is standing at her own front door in a pink flannelette housecoat, nylon toilet brush in hand.

Bliss has a confused, perhaps lost, expression that he practised in Daphne's bathroom mirror, and he fidgets with apparent unease as he stammers, "Um ... well ... um ... Actually, I'm no longer sure. I ... I was hoping you might be able to help me."

"What are you talking about?"

"Look," he carries on with downcast eyes. "This is quite awkward but, um ... may I come in?"

"Well, what do you want?" she demands, standing her ground.

Bliss pauses for a very long second while he focuses fiercely on his fingers, then he appears to make up his mind, and with a look suggesting he's close to tears he pleads, "I'm hoping that you might be able to tell me who I am."

Amelia Drinkwater stands back with a very suspicious eye, but her visitor's sharp suit, Hermes tie, and shiny shoes can't easily be dismissed, so she wordlessly sweeps him into her breakfast room and waves him to a chair.

"Carry on," she instructs and waits with raised eyebrows.

"You see," he says with due seriousness, "when my mother — my adoptive mother — passed away about six months ago ..." he pauses to correct himself, to add weight. "Actually it was in April. So it's nearly a year now. Anyway, I found this in her papers."

Putting his hand into the inside pocket of his jacket, Bliss pulls out a copy of the birth certificate relating to the third Creston child, Johannes, and hands it to her.

Amelia Drinkwater slowly pales as she reads, and then she shakes her head. "But Joe is dead ..."

"That's what they told me at the public records office."

"Then why are you asking me?"

"Well, I've always wondered about my natural parents, I think most adopted kids do, but my mum and dad, the people who brought me up, would never tell me."

"You're not listening to me," continues Amelia, clearly flustered. "I told you, Joe is dead. You cannot be Joe."

"I know, I know," he says apparently placating her. "And that's why I didn't come when I first found my ... when I found Johannes' birth certificate."

"Then why are you here now?"

"Well," he says, going for the other pocket and extracting the copy of the boy's death certificate. "August 15, 1963," he points out, jabbing his finger on the date of death.

"So?"

"Mrs. Drinkwater," he says solidly, forcing her gaze. "My adoption was commenced on August 16, 1963, and my birthdate is February 4 of that year." Then he raises an eyebrow as he directs her towards an apparently inescapable conclusion. "Exactly the same as Joe's."

Amelia Drinkwater's face drains, and she grasps her knees to stop them shaking. "But ... but ... but ..." she stutters like a cheap outboard motor. "But ...you're dead."

"So, where's my grave?" demands Bliss, piling on the pressure. "I've been to all the churches. There's no record of a grave."

"I ... I don't know ..." she starts angrily, but doesn't suggest the Creston estate. Instead, she decides it is time to escape. "I'll make some tea," she says, hurriedly rising. "Would you ... would you?"

"Yes, please," he says. "Milk. No sugar."

Fascinating, he thinks, watching the woman stagger to the door; something seems to have rattled Madam Drinkwater's cage. Although fifteen minutes later, when Amelia returns with a neatly laid tea tray, she has dressed in a grey suit, dabbed on some makeup, and seemingly pulled herself together.

"All right..." she starts strongly, then pauses, searching for his name.

"David," he offers. "David Jenkins ... that's my adopted name."

"Well, David. Why are you asking me about this?"

"Mr. Rowlands, the vicar of St. Stephen's," he replies as per Daphne's briefing. "I was searching the church records, looking for my … looking for Johannes' christening records and stuff, and he said you would be the best person. That you knew everything about the parish."

"I'm flattered," she starts with a wan smile, but then claims ignorance. "I'm sorry but I can't help. I only know what was rumoured around town at the time."

"I don't suppose you kept a copy of the local paper …"

"Good grief, no!" she exclaims. "Why on earth would I?"

"I thought you might."

"No."

"Are you sure?" he pushes, suggesting by his tone that he has inside information.

"I said no," she snaps and flies from her chair to peer out of the window.

"Well," says Bliss, trying to smooth her down. "It's just that the vicar said you were a very close friend of Mr. Creston, my … Joe's father."

Amelia turns and explodes. "Look. You are not Johannes Creston, all right. Just put it out of your silly head —"

"But the birth date —"

"I don't care about your birth date," she screeches as she stabs an angry finger in his direction. "You are not Joe. Joe is dead. Do you understand? Joe is dead."

"You seem very sure."

"I know all right," she shouts as she storms across the room and pointedly opens the door. "Now if you'll excuse me I have things to do."

"I'll leave my number," says Bliss as he hands over a card on his way out. "I live in France now."

"Daphne Lovelace, you are a wicked genius," Bliss tells his old friend ten minutes later as they sit over a cup of tea in the Olde Curiosity Tea Shoppe in Dewminster.

"I knew she was hiding something," chuckles Daphne with satisfaction, although she has to agree with her collaborator when he points out that they have no idea what bones Ms. Drinkwater may have concealed in her basement.

"We'll find out, David. Mark my words. We'll find out."

"So," he says, biting into a cream slice. "What do you think she's doing now?"

"Looking for this," says Daphne, slyly pulling out the sepia newspaper cutting that she liberated from the woman's photograph album.

Daphne is right. Amelia Drinkwater rushed to find the album as soon as she slammed the door on Bliss, and then she slumped into an armchair, mumbling, "How the hell did he know?"

"Where do we go from here, David?" asks Daphne as they drive back to her Westchester home.

"I don't know about you," he says tapping the dashboard clock. "But my flight leaves in six hours. I'm meeting Peter and Sam for dinner in London, and then I have a book to finish."

"All right, David," she says, laughing. "You're excused."

"Thank you."

Then she puts a kindly hand on his arm. "I really hope this works for you. I really hope Yolanda comes back."

"She will, Daphne," he says confidently. "I know she will."

chapter sixteen

The Taj Mahal Restaurant in Hatton Cross will never win a Michelin star or even a Lonely Planet rubber stamp, but it's close to the airport. Once he's dropped his rented car, Bliss munches his way through a pile of pappadums while waiting for his daughter and her husband to arrive and uses the time to weave a caricature of Amelia Drinkwater into his plot.

Queen Anne of Austria, he begins, finding a striking similarity between the magistrate's pious disposition and that of Louis XIV's mother, *was a woman whose knees, it was said, got far more practice than her more feminine parts. Indeed, according to the king's valet de chambre, Pierre La Porte, after many years of being rebuffed in his desire to produce a son and heir, His Majesty, Louis XIII, had turned his attention, and his weapon, to pink-bottomed footmen. So, one might imagine the incredulity in the royal household when, after a barren decade, it was suddenly claimed that the king had made a single lunge at his consort and not only found his mark, but had done so at the precise moment when the fruit was ripe.*

"Sorry we're late, Dad," gushes Samantha with a hurried peck on his cheek, exclaiming, "Traffic!"

"Hello, Peter," Bliss says, offering a hand while pointing to his manuscript. "I was just writing about the conception of a right royal bastard."

"Speaking of which," says Bryan. "Our man Edwards has apparently come into a regal fortune."

"Really," says Bliss. "What a surprise."

"New beemer — top of the line," carries on Bryan, but Bliss is cagey.

"I bet he's covered his ass. Proper receipts and stuff.

"Of course. He even bleated about the price."

"What are you saying? It was clean?"

"Dave. Does Edwards ever do anything clean?"

"But —"

"He chopped in his old motor, dropped a couple of grand on the counter, and took a six-month holiday on the balance," says Bryan, but the smug look on his face tells Bliss there's more and he waits.

"Forty newly minted fifty-pound notes," continues Bryan, slapping a photocopy of the bills under Bliss's nose. "And guess what? The very same folding stuff that one of Mr. J.C. Creston's maggots withdrew from Lloyd's Bank, Bond Street a few weeks ago."

"We've got him," breathes Bliss, but Peter Bryan is less certain.

"Hang on, Dave. This is Edwards we're talking about. He's more slippery than Bill Clinton. We're gonna need more than this."

"Yeah. You're right," admits Bliss and he sits back to study the menu for a few minutes while he gives some thought to this situation.

"Any news from Yolanda?" asks Samantha during the hiatus.

"Not yet," says Bliss. "Give her time."

"What about the book?"

"Last chapter, Sam."

"The fairytale ending?"

"That's the one. Every man's dream: the love of a perfect woman."

"And every woman's dream," she says reaching out to caress her husband's face. "The love of a perfect man."

"Well I don't know about perfect," protests Bliss, but Samantha cuts him off.

"You were perfect to Yolanda."

"Then why did she go back to Klaus?"

"Guilt, Dad. She just felt obligated to him. But that's not love. Love is what you two had together. You know that."

"But does she really love me?"

"Of course she does. She'll come to her senses. Mark my words."

Details of Bliss's afternoon encounter with Amelia Drinkwater fills the time while they nibble pita and wait for their food, but neither Samantha nor her husband have any concrete suggestions.

"She was obviously lying about something," explains Bliss. "I'm damned if I know why."

"What did Daphne think?"

"No idea," admits Bliss, "but knowing her she's got something up her sleeve."

"Sounds like the Drinkwater woman is covering for someone," says Peter Bryan after some thought. "Maybe Creston has bought her as well."

"Wouldn't be surprised," admits Bliss, "but what are you going to do about Edwards?"

"'We,' Dave," his son-in-law corrects him. "What are *we* going to do?"

"Not me," says Bliss. "I'm doing my part. He's just about to get his comeuppance in my novel. Real life is up to you."

The warmth has returned to the Côte d'Azur by the time that Bliss's flight touches down at Nice International Airport close to midnight, and he opens the cab window to inhale the scent of the Mediterranean as he returns to his apartment in St-Juan-sur-Mer. Then, despite the hour, he sits on his balcony and continues work on his literary revenge.

The sight of a thousand candles illuminating the windows of his great château caught the attention of Prince Ferdinand as he peered longingly across the strait from his island home. "Perhaps she is come," he told himself with excitement, imagining that festivities were being prepared for his triumphal unification, and his heart took flight. But across the bay, the multitude of aristocratic guests who danced and made merry in the beautiful building knew nothing of the poor man's desperate plight.

"So. My dear marquis," said the king, addressing the Marquis of Dangeau from his throne in the great hall of the Château Roger. "What do you say of my beautiful new palace?"

"I bow to your superiority, Sire. I would say that you are truly a worthy adversary."

"That is most true," agreed the king holding out his hand.

"However, I fear that you may one day be called to account by a higher power for the wrong you have worked upon that poor prince," continued Dangeau as he paid his dues.

"That is also true," said the king. "However, while it may be useful to die in God's grace, it is exceedingly boring to live in it."

Satisfied, Bliss puts down his pen and peers over the balcony in the bright clear moonlight. He looks down to the lemon tree, expecting to find the lone lemon on the ground, and then he breaks into a broad smile. In his absence, the warm southwesterly sirocco has swept up from the Sahara and now a hundred golden lemons dot the grass.

"If that's not an omen I don't know what is," he tells himself and decides it is finally time for revenge.

"*Louis XIV, the so-called king, is a bastard and a fraud and I can prove it,*" he writes in the voice of Prince Ferdinand. "*Louis XIV, the man who pretentiously calls himself Louis le Grand, is nothing but the son of a jumped-up commoner, and once my great love returns to be at my side for eternity, I will shout to the four corners of the French Empire, 'Louis, the man you call king, is a usurper and pretender. Depose him and right the terrible wrong that has been worked upon this proud nation of France.'*"

"That's better. Now we're getting there," muses Bliss, and he goes to bed confidently anticipating a night of pleasant dreams.

Chief Superintendent Michael Edwards is also dreaming as he drives his new BMW home from his regular Freemasonry meeting. The soft hum of a herd of horses under the hood and the smell of real leather and freshly polished wood transport him to a world of leisure that he could never have envisioned as he grew up the son of London dock worker. "You gotta be f'kin tough in this world," his father told him whenever he complained of being picked on at school. "Beat the f'kin crap out of them bastards, son," he often said, and Edwards beams at the knowledge that his father would be proud of him if he could see him now. "I beat the bastards, Dad," he is musing woozily to himself as the Volvo driver ahead of him spots a red light.

"Fuck," says Edwards, sharpening his brain, but his brake foot takes longer to catch on.

"I'm requesting that you blow into this machine," a hot-footed young constable says to Edwards ten minutes later, and the chief superintendent makes his second mistake of the evening.

"Don't be f'kin stupid son," he says knocking the Breathalyzer away. "I'm a f'kin chief super,"

"I don't care if you're the commissioner, sir. You've been involved in a road traffic —"

"C'mon, son," says Edwards. "Use your loaf, man. You can see I ain't been drinking."

"Actually, sir, I believe that you have."

"Just a couple," admits Edwards, and then he makes his third mistake. "But look. Let me just sort it out, OK. I'll just pay for the damages."

"Sir, I require you to blow —"

"Wait, wait, wait," says Edwards going for his wallet and extracting a crisp £50 note. "Let's just keep it between ourselves, shall we."

"Well, I suppose ..." starts the officer, giving Edwards more line, and he bites.

"OK, let's make it a round hundred," he says adding a second fifty. "And I'll square off the other driver."

"Thank you, sir," says the constable taking the proffered notes, then he hollers for his partner, who is taking the details from the other driver. "Get some backup, Jim. We've got a prisoner."

News of Edwards' arrest reaches Bliss the following morning, and he repeatedly rereads the last entry in his manuscript and shakes his head in disbelief. "Well I'm buggered," he says, and then he runs down four flights to the apartment garden, scoops up a handful of lemons, and makes himself a jug of lemonade for breakfast. "Now for Yolanda," he says as he sits on the balcony, opens his writing pad, and picks up his pen.

The arrest of a senior Metropolitan police commander for attempted bribery and drunken driving is enough to knock most other headlines off the front page of London's morning paper. The withholding of Edwards' name is only to be expected, especially as he is yet to be charged, but news of his arrest has been toasted with raised coffee cups throughout the force.

Peter Bryan smiles smugly as he studies the nightly incident log, and even the commissioner might admit a degree of satisfaction were it politically correct to do so.

"Nothing's proven yet," the deputy commissioner cautions the other commanders at morning prayers. "Chief Superintendent Edwards is entitled to the same presumption of innocence as everyone else."

"Just like every other villain," mutters one of the officers under his hand and gets a titter of agreement from his neighbours.

"Morale is the name of the game," the deputy continues. "Justice must be seen to be done."

"And about time," suggests another officer, and the deputy decides it might be prudent to move onto other matters.

Mike Phillips and his team in Vancouver moved on from the Janet Thurgood abduction case more than a week ago now. Craddock is still on the loose in Hawaii, though his options are narrowing as his wallet shrinks. Trina is back to wiping bottoms and washing dirty old men, and while the fresh snow may have brightened Wayne Browning's grubby compound in the mountains north of Vancouver, the old pretender is beginning to feel the pinch. Without Creston's largesse, and with the banks in Mountain Falls under pressure from Revenue Canada to open their books, his utopian world is rapidly coming adrift.

"We must be strong and vigilant in the face of those who would destroy us," he preaches to his devotees. "The devil is trying us ... tempting us ... testing our resolve. Do not let him into your hearts. Do not be tempted."

The woman and girls kneeling obediently at his feet have no idea of the trials that may await them, and as far as Browning is concerned, they need not know. "Just follow God's commands through me," he says, "and we will reach the Promised Land."

The arrest of Edwards doesn't land on Creston's desk until late in the day when Mason is tipped off by the chief superintendent's defence lawyer. The warning, shrouded in doublespeak, heavily hints that Edwards has no intention of admitting the source of the large bills that he used for his car, but neither he nor his lawyer have any idea that Peter Bryan and the internal investigation team are only too aware of the money's provenance.

"We'll keep that up our sleeves for now," Peter Bryan tells the select group of trusted officers he has been seconded to lead.

"You might as well do the footwork on this," the assistant commissioner in overall charge of the investigation told him. "It seems that you're already up to speed."

Keeping up with Edwards and his high-priced help is one thing, but Peter Bryan knows that getting ahead of him and his lawyers is the trick. It should be possible to make the charges of attempting to pervert the course of justice and refusing to take a breath test stick on the evidence at hand, but Bryan is not alone in wanting the big one — the acceptance of a bribe by a public official.

"Neither Creston nor Mason are likely to cough," Peter Bryan carries on to his four officers, "and the only link we have is flimsy. We know that Edwards tried to squeeze info out of the Canadian Mounties, but I'm sure we've all called in favours from other forces at times."

"How much was he paid?" asks one of the officers, but Bryan shrugs. "Creston's bank is being co-operative. They paid out twenty big ones — four thousand quid altogether — but we've no idea how much Edwards pocketed."

"What about a warrant? Do his place over looking for the rest."

"Difficult," admits Bryan. "His mouthpiece will scream harassment. He'll say, 'Show us the evidence,' and we don't have a lot."

Daphne Lovelace is looking for evidence at Creston Hall, and with the estate's laird tied up in London, she has persuaded the groundsman to take her on a guided tour.

"You picked the wrong bloomin' time of the year fer it, missus," Grainger, the old retainer, said when Daphne found him in the Black Swan and explained her upcoming book about local places of interest. "Everything's in such a bloomin' state at present."

"Don't worry. I'm not taking photos," she explained to the cheerful little man and sealed the arrangement with a beer and a slice of pork pie.

Now, with notebook in hand, Daphne shows interest in everything.

"Rhodeedendrums, wisteria, oaks, willows," he says, waving at various trees and bushes with his walking stick. "And over there is the walled garden."

"Is that a cemetery?" questions Daphne pointing out a row of small headstones.

"Pets," he spits, clearly unimpressed at the waste of fertile land. "Dogs, cats, parrots, even a bloomin' monkey."

"What about the family's graves?"

Grainger uses his stick as a pointer. "Over there in the chapel," he says, leading her to view a doll-sized church topped with an elaborate wooden spire surmounted by a gilded cross.

"Oh my!" exclaims Daphne, and she is already marching across the lawn when the gardener stops her.

"It's sorta private," he calls nervously, but Daphne spins with a comforting smile.

"Don't worry. I won't tell anyone."

Grainger scratches his nose with his stick for a second, and then capitulates. "Can't do no harm I s'pose," he says, catching up. "None of the family are here at present."

The walls of the tiny chapel are adorned with an array of religious paintings, but it is a genealogical chart cataloguing the growth of the Creston family since the mid-eighteenth century that immediately takes Daphne's eye.

"Oh," says Daphne in surprise as she runs her finger down the tree to the 1960s. "I thought Mr. Creston Jr. had three children."

"Nah. Just the two," says the gardener unconcernedly. "And they both died."

"Oh. You saw them then, did you?"

"Yeah. O'course I've been here nigh on fifty years; man and boy."

"So the babies were sickly?"

Grainger carefully checks over his shoulder then pulls Daphne to a number of stone tablets set into the adjacent wall.

"This one," he says pointing to a plaque bearing Giuseppe's name, "he was a runty-looking little thing. Nothing but trouble from the day he were calved."

"And this one?" questions Daphne, pointing to Johannes.

The old man's face warms in memory, and with a toothless smile he says, "He was a bonnie little lad. Chubby cheeks and arms like plump little vegetable marrows."

"But he died as well," says Daphne with her finger on the date.

"Yep. Same thing: cot death. That were a bloomin' shame. Bonnie little thing."

"Not sickly," Daphne continues, egging him on.

"Not him. Gawd knows how the missus kept him fed. He would a' been a bloomin' bigun if he'd lived — shame."

"Shame," agrees Daphne.

"Cot death," reiterates Grainger, his face saddening.

Michael Edwards' first court appearance is not one of his happiest moments. He and his legal mouthpiece are well aware that the knives are out.

"Anyone else would have been granted police bail to appear at a later date," complains Martin Shaw as they wait for the magistrate to be robed.

"Your point?" Bryan replies gleefully.

"In my client's opinion you are deliberately humiliating him."

"Really?"

"And he wishes me to make a formal complaint."

"Right," says Bryan firmly sitting and taking out his notebook with an air of determination. "Let me get this down Mr. Shaw and see if I've got it correct. Your client, who is charged with attempting to pervert the course of justice, wishes to complain about the justice system he was attempting to pervert." Bryan looks up mischievously. "Would you say that's an accurate assessment of the situation, sir?"

The lawyer throws up his hands in disgust, but in deference to the reputation of the force rather than his errant client, the corps of baying pressmen are led in a circle by a wild goose while the still defiant senior officer is paraded backstage in the magistrate's chamber.

"I am not guilty," he insists when the charges are read, but the magistrate, specially chosen because of his straightforwardness, looks Edwards in the face and says, "This is a bail hearing, Mr. Edwards, as a man in your position should know. You'll have plenty of opportunity to enter a plea in the appropriate court at the appropriate time."

"That took him down a few pegs," laughs Peter Bryan once Edwards has been released and told to hand in his warrant card.

"It just annoys me that the bastard is on full pay," spits one of Bryan's sergeants, but the chief inspector throws a celebratory arm around his colleague's shoulder, laughing, "Don't worry, Greg. His mouthpiece will get most of it."

By the time Edwards has cleaned out his desk under the watchful eye of the assistant commissioner, Daphne is back on the phone to Bliss.

"I knew it," she says excitedly. "There was nothing wrong with the third Creston kid."

"Daphne, luv," complains Bliss. "I'm trying to write."

"I know," she says, "but the doctor deliberately changed the records to show the kid was weak. And the first one isn't there at all."

"I'm not surprised," says Bliss. "He wasn't a Creston, was he? Janet got knocked up by someone else. Didn't you say that was why Amelia Drinkwater was so ticked off?"

"That's right," admits Daphne. "She lost her boyfriend to a shotgun wedding, and he wasn't the one who'd pulled the trigger."

"No wonder she wasn't happy with Janet."

"I guess it's a bit like the way you lost Yolanda."

"No it wasn't," replies Bliss fiercely. "Anyway, Yolanda's coming back to me. Amelia didn't go back to Creston."

While Amelia Drinkwater, née Sawbridge, may not have got back into Creston's life, or his bed, once Janet was shipped off to Canada, she certainly tried: joining the hunt club; buddying up to his friends; switching place cards at formal banquets; "accidentally" walking into him in the High Street; wheedling invites to the Creston estate for family events. Hardly a dinner, ball, or musical soiree passed without Amelia's smiling face, but Joseph Creston never smiled back.

"Why don't you leave me alone, you witch?" he finally spat at her in the middle of Dewminster High Street, and she cried for a week.

"Anyway," carries on Bliss to his elderly tormentor. "If you want me to do anything else you'll have to wait till I've finished the book — just another week or so."

"No, David," says Daphne. "You carry on. I just wanted to let you know that I have everything in hand."

There is a question hanging mid-air, but Bliss refuses to bite. "OK, Daphne," he replies. "Good luck."

"Now," he says to himself as he views the Château Roger from his balcony, listens to Billie Holiday singing "I've Got a Date with a Dream," and settles back to work. "The masked man's revenge and the return of his great and only true love."

The rising sun cuts sharply across the bay of Cannes towards the fortress ...

"Trina," says Daphne, putting the next stage of her plan into action.

"Oh, hi, Daphne," says the Canadian woman. "You were lucky to catch me. I'm just going to work. What's happening?"

"I'm still on the case," says the Englishwoman. "No sign of Craddock, I suppose."

"You're kidding? I said it was a waste of time calling in the police; we would have done better calling a cab. Mike's given up and Sergeant Brougham is so useless he couldn't even catch a cold."

RCMP Inspector Mike Phillips hasn't given up; he's hit a snag. The full forensic report concerning Janet's confinement is on his desk but he has been sitting on the results for a couple of days. The evidence concerning Craddock's involvement is overwhelming. Janet's DNA from hair, saliva, and other bodily fluids places her squarely in the ex-officer's hands, but several fingerprints lifted from the bedroom and bathroom at the airport motel point straight to Dave Brougham. And although the picture is grainy and the person kept his head down, the image of the man booking Janet into the emergency room at the General Hospital could certainly be the Vancouver City sergeant.

"So, Trina," says Daphne with a hint of impending triumph in her voice. "I guess we're going to have to solve this case ourselves."

"You've got a plan?"

"If you can impersonate Janet."

Trina thinks for a few seconds then darkens her voice and says, "Well I've lived in Canada for forty years, so I guess I sound kinda Canadian now."

"That's great," shrieks Daphne, "but don't overdo it."

"So who am I going to call? What am I supposed to say?"

"Dewminster 7497," answers Amelia Drinkwater an hour later, once Trina has convinced Daphne that she knows her lines.

"Is that Amelia?"

"Who's this?" demands the Englishwoman warily, still unnerved over Bliss's visit.

"You don't remember me?"

"Should I?"

"You probably don't recognize my voice. I've been in Canada for over forty years."

"Janet?" queries Ms. Drinkwater, but Trina admits nothing.

Instead she pauses for a second to let the tension build before saying menacingly, "I know what you did, Amelia." A sharp intake of breath at the other end tells Trina she's hit a nerve. "You thought you'd get rid of me, didn't you? You thought Joe would throw me out if I lost another baby —"

"No," cuts in Amelia, but Trina continues in the same threatening monotone.

"You thought he'd come back to you. But you were wrong. Little Joe-Joe didn't die."

"He did. He did."

"No, Amelia. You were wrong. And now I'm back ..."

"Shut up. Shut up."

"He's out there, Amelia. Joe-Joe's out there ..."

The sound of Amelia Drinkwater's phone hitting the cradle cuts Trina off and she immediately calls Daphne.

"Lets see what happens now," says the Englishwoman with her fingers crossed.

David Bliss is barely half a page into his final defining chapter when his phone rings. He already has "Yolanda" on his lips when he has to quickly adjust. "Mrs. Drinkwater?" he queries in amazement.

"I may have been a bit hasty," she says with apparent contrition. "Perhaps you could ... um ... maybe ... um ... maybe I do have something for you."

Daphne Lovelace I could throttle you, he is thinking as he agrees to return. "The day after tomorrow," he suggests.

"Is that the earliest?" she asks, suddenly anxious.

"Afraid so. Like I said, I live in France now."

"She wants to see me again," fumes Bliss to Daphne a few minutes later.

"I thought she might. That's very interesting."

"No it's not. It's bloody inconvenient. That's another three days wasted by the time I've flown up tomorrow and flown back again. I'll never get my book finished."

"Softly, softly, catchee monkey, David," says Daphne. "Don't be so impatient. She'll come back if she loves you enough."

"She'll come back if I ever get time to finish my script."

There may be a depression over Bliss as he packs an overnight bag in St-Juan-sur-Mer and prepares to lock his apartment again, but there is a definite lightness in the air over Scotland Yard the following morning. Canteen workers, cleaners, constables, and even the commissioner have an extra bounce as they go through their daily routines, and while most would be unable to finger the cause, Peter Bryan has no such problem.

"We've got him. We've got him," he repeats with a smile to everyone who questions hopefully. "Don't worry. We've finally put the skids under him."

However, by midday, as Bliss's flight lifts off with a roar over the cerulean Bay of Angels and begins its steep climb up the slopes of the Alps, Peter Bryan's euphoria is slipping. Paul Schwartzberg, the senior lawyer in the force prosecution's department, lifts his heavy spectacles to his forehead every time he looks up from the case papers on his desk then flicks them back down in order to read. His glasses go up. "You're going to have to do a lot better than this if it's going to stick." And down. "Look at this charge — accepting an unwarranted remuneration from Creston." And up. "You've got no proof as far as I can see." And down. "Not unless you've got something up your sleeve?"

"No. Not at the moment, Paul," replies Peter Bryan. "But it's a bit of a stretch for him to say that it's just a freaky coincidence."

The glasses go up as Schwartzberg gives Bryan an incredulous look.

"OK, Paul, I know," says the chief inspector. "We're working on getting more. But the attempt to pervert case is solid. That P.C. did a bang-up job."

The glasses hit the bridge of Schwartzberg's nose with an audible *pop*. "No corroboration," he says tapping the stack of statements. "His colleague was fifty feet away when it's alleged —"

"Alleged?"

"Yes — alleged," he says as his glasses go back up again and he gives Bryan a meaningful look as he repeats. "It is alleged that Edwards tried to slip him the cash. What if Edwards says, 'Liar, he took the money out of my wallet when he was looking for my licence and started waving it in the air shouting, "Bribe"'?"

"Oh, come on," yells Bryan. "Who's gonna believe that?"

"Twelve befuddled nincompoops called jurors who'll sit to attention every time his defence counsel says, 'So tell us, Chief Superintendent Edwards …'"

"Yes. I get the picture. We need more."

"You need a lot more, Peter. Of course he'll probably plead to the Breathalyzer refusal."

"Yes. And get fined a hundred quid, get a slap on the wrist from the beak, and be back at his desk in a week with an even longer list of people to crap on."

Including you, Chief Inspector, thinks Schwartzberg lifting his spectacles for the final time.

Bliss's cellphone rings as he walks out of the terminal at Heathrow with his eyes on the Hertz office.

"Dave, I need your help," says his son-in-law, wasting no time on pleasantries.

"You'll have to wait your turn," Bliss replies before explaining his mission on Daphne's behalf.

"Hey. She could be onto something," agrees Bryan, brightening momentarily before sinking again.

"Oh, Christ!" exclaims Bliss once he's heard the dismal prognosis. "What the hell do you expect me to do?"

"Just give me a few days, Dave," pleads Bryan.

"No. I've got to get back to my book. I'm down to the last forty or fifty pages."

"Please … Dad. It's for a good cause."

"This isn't bloody fair. And cut out the 'Dad' crap."

Amelia Drinkwater has visibly shrunk by the time that she opens her front door to Bliss the following morning. Three anxiety-filled days have weighed heavily on the sixty-something widow, and the state of her hair tells Bliss that she is losing her grip.

"Come in ..." she says, opening the door before he has a chance to knock.

"David," he reminds her.

"Yes, David ... Come in," she carries on and, as he follows her through the gloomy entrance hall towards the sitting room, Bliss realizes that most of the gloominess is emanating from the deflated woman herself.

"I've been thinking about what you told me," she says, waving him to a soft armchair. "And I just wanted to let you know that you're obviously confused."

You didn't bring me all this way just to tell me that, he thinks as he perches on the edge of a chair, but he knows that she will take her time.

"I'm not sure," he says, on safe ground. "Only I understand that there are only two children's coffins in the family vault, but my mother ... Janet lost three children."

"How do you know that?" she questions, rising quickly.

"Sources," he says.

Then she picks up a degree of defiance. "And what else do your sources tell you, David?"

Bliss has an ace in his pocket and he nearly draws it out, but his hand closes as he decides to play her a little further. "Do you think I look like my ... like Mr. Creston?" he asks, knowing that physically he is not far away from the tall, manicured executive whose permanent tan marks him as a well-travelled man.

Amelia Drinkwater looks deeply into his face, and he can tell from the softening of her eyes that she sees what he wants, but she holds back. "Not particularly," she lies, but the wobble in her voice gives her away.

Now for the coup de grace, he thinks as he rises with deliberation and peers out of the window into the garden.

"Actually, there is something else," he says slowly, building the moment, and then he draws the document examiner's report from his pocket together with Doctor Symmonds' bogus medical record and spins on her.

"This can't be true …This can't be true," she mutters repeatedly as she reads the report, but Bliss keeps prodding.

"You see — Doctor Symmonds just copied the symptoms from Giuseppe's death."

"But he was dead. He was dead."

"No."

"He was, I … I …"

"You what, Amelia?"

"I …"

"What?"

"It was in the paper."

"Was it? Are you sure? Do you have it?"

"Yes … No … You're confusing me."

"How do you know I was dead, Amelia? How can you be certain?"

Fifty years of guilt finally sink her and loosens her tongue. "Because I kill—"

"You killed me," he prods, and she realizes with a jolt that she's gone too far.

"Obviously not," she says, relaxing with a touch of a smile. "I obviously did not," she adds and a flush of colour rushes back to her cheeks as she believes that the burden she's carried most of her life has been lifted. "I couldn't have done, or you wouldn't be here would you?"

"Correct," says Bliss sitting back down and eyeing her critically. "But you thought you had, didn't you?"

The colour drains again as a dark memory drags her back more than forty years to the warm August night she crept past Creston Hall to Janet's house and slipped through an open window into the baby's room, but now, faced with apparent evidence of her failure, she has no choice but to question what happened.

"I think my father ... Joseph Creston ... knew that someone wanted to hurt me," answers Bliss without pointing at the woman in front of him. "So they got me out of the way and pretended I was dead."

chapter seventeen

Daphne Lovelace is wearing her flounciest hat a couple of hours later as she and Bliss meet Ted Donaldson for lunch at the Mitre Hotel in Westchester.

"Nice to see you again, old chap," cries the superintendent as he jubilantly claps the London officer on his back, and then he bends under Daphne's feathery creation to give her a peck on the cheek. "God, I'm starving," he carries on as he sits and picks up the menu. "So, what's this all about, you two? Daphne was so excited when she called I couldn't keep up with her."

"Revenge," suggests Daphne once Bliss has put the local superintendent in the picture, but Bliss goes deeper.

"I think Amelia was hoping that if Janet lost a third child, and a bouncy little baby at that, Creston Sr. would insist that his poncy son should turn his todger on someone with a bit more class."

"Not that Miss Airs-and-Graces Drinkwater has much of that," sneers Daphne. "Although I suppose she was a step up from Janet."

"I just think the old man wanted a grandson to keep the line going," suggests Bliss. "These aristocratic families are like that," he adds, realizing that he is also talking about the political pressure applied to Anne of Austria to produce a male protegé for the House of Bourbon, with or without the aid of her husband, Louis XIII.

"What about evidence, Dave?" asks Donaldson between the stuffed olives and the cream of mushroom soup, and Bliss shakes his head.

"Not good at the moment. She'll probably clam up if she gets herself good counsel, but I think the doctor is the one to go after."

"Peter Symmonds changed the records," explains Daphne pointing to the examiner's report. "He obviously knew that the sudden death of a healthy baby would raise a flag at the coroner's office so he rewrote his father's notes."

"But what was in it for him?" asks Donaldson, before realizing that he already knows the answer. "OK," he says. "Money talks. But why would Creston want to protect Madam Drinkwater?"

"He didn't," responds Daphne confidently. "He thought Janet had done it."

"And he loved his wife," chimes in Bliss.

"And still does, in a way," adds Daphne. "That's why she was smartly shipped abroad after the funeral and locked away with a lunatic so that she could spend the rest of her life in penitence."

"She would've been better off in jail," muses Donaldson as he starts on a second bowl of olives. "At least she would have been out in twenty-five. But," he wants to know between bites, "what happened to the first two kids?"

"I've got a feeling that Lovelace and Button, International Investigators, are going to crack that as well," says Bliss, raising his glass to toast Daphne.

"What are your plans now, Dave?" asks Donaldson in the parking lot after lunch. "I could always use a real detective. All I get is bloody carrot crunchers and God's gift to the fairer sex down here."

"Not me," laughs Bliss, "on either count. But I'm trying to get back to writing my novel. I've only got half a chapter left."

"Daphne tells me it's going to be a huge bestseller. She says you're going to be very successful."

"One way or another," he admits, although he knows that his idea of success may differ from Donaldson's. "Anyway, my son-in-law wants me in London for a few days, though God knows why he can't manage without me."

"Oh to be so popular," laughs Donaldson as he drives away.

D.C.I. Peter Bryan is not high on Bliss's popularity poll the following morning when they meet in London for breakfast.

"I could be sunning myself over an onion tart and a croissant in the Med," complains Bliss as he peers through the café's grimy window to the grey of a January day. Peter Bryan isn't particularly happy either. He is still frowning over the possibility that Edwards might already be planning a triumphant return.

"Just a few days," Bliss reminds his son-in-law as the waitress slaps a couple of cups of instant coffee on the table, asking brusquely, "Somefink to eat?"

Bliss looks around at the backstreet café, at the smoke-stained, grease-engrained walls and the finger-smeared display cabinet containing the remnants of yesterday's lunch, and thinks, *Eat — in here? Are you kidding?*

"No, that's all," he says without consulting his son-in-law.

"Three quid," says the plump woman with her hand out.

"Keep the change," he says, giving her exactly three pounds and watching her smile fade halfway to the cash register.

"Frickin' funny," she spits over her shoulder.

"Shoot," says Bliss trying to take away the coffee taste with several spoonfuls of sugar. "What have you got in mind for your dear old dad?"

"Hey, don't you start," says Bryan, laughing, then he pulls out a couple of legally signed warrants. "Wiretaps," he says flourishing under them Bliss's nose. "One for Edwards and one for Creston."

"How the hell —" starts Bliss, but Bryan cuts in.

"Friendly judge, hates bent cops more than he hates villains. 'At least villains are honest about what they do,' he says to me as he signs Edwards up."

"So what do you need me for? Just listen and learn."

"That might work," admits Bryan. "But I doubt if either of them will be stupid enough to sew themselves up without a little encouragement."

"And you expect me to encourage them?" questions Bliss.

Bryan nods in agreement, saying, "I'd use one of my crew, but I'm not sure who I can trust."

"Because," starts Bliss, but he doesn't push the point. He's well aware that few of his colleagues are completely fireproof; that no one can be certain that Edwards' lawyer won't spring out of the defendant's box with a trial-stopping revelation that will leave them without a pension while Edwards paints on a broad grin and walks free.

"The taps are going in as we speak," carries on Peter Bryan. "It's going to take all day — Edwards' place; Creston's home, apartment, and office."

"Cellphones?" queries Bliss.

"The works."

"So like I said, what do you need me for?"

"Hey, are you two finished?" yells the stubby waitress from the cash desk. "People are frickin' waiting you know."

"Couple of minutes, luv," replies Bryan, then he leans in to Bliss. "What I need is an undercover man in Creston's office."

"That could take weeks —" Bliss is starting when Peter Bryan stops him.

"No. I want a really clumsy one. Someone who'll be sussed in ten minutes flat, someone so dense that a ten-year-old would catch on."

"I'm sure we've got a few of them," laughs Bliss, but his son-in-law isn't laughing. "I want you in there, Dave, in Creston's face, bumbling around like a greenhorn, asking stupid questions, dropping hints, offering backhanders. He's already jumpy. He knows Edwards has been lifted. Plus, he's snowed under trying to keep his wife quiet, and he's got a war on his hands in West Africa."

"It doesn't sound as if he's having fun."

"Oy," shouts the waitress with a tone of finality. "I need that frickin' table for real customers."

"Nice lady," mutters Bliss, but he's got all the information he needs. "Give me a couple of hours to think it over," he says as they leave. "I really want to get back to my writing. I'm scared she'll think I've forgotten her."

"Not much chance of that, Dave," jests Peter Bryan as he throws an arm around his father-in-law's shoulders. "I'd never forget you and I've never even slept with you."

George McMahon, the manager of the janitorial company responsible for cleaning the Creston tower, is a pushover for Bliss two days later.

"Are you really sure you want this?" queries the softly spoken Liverpudlian, eyeing Bliss's bronze skin and sharp jeans. "Only you ain't the usual type."

"Need the bread," says Bliss pushing his cockney accent as far as it will go. "I got the trouble and strife on me bleedin' back to get off the dole."

"Well, sign here, then. Start at six Monday mornin'. Amy's the boss over there. She'll be right chuffed. She's always bendin' me ear about not having anyone to do the liftin'."

"I can do that all right, guv," says Bliss, flexing his biceps as he prints the name and social insurance number that Peter Bryan provided for him. "What about uniforms?"

"Blue overalls — pick 'em up from Amy. You wash 'em."

"Right-oh, guv."

"And make sure you do. Creston gets real foony about things like that."

"'kay."

"An' watch yer language. They're a bunch of bleedin' Bible punchers. No fookin' swearing, awl right?"

"Awl right," agrees Bliss.

"I should have brought my manuscript with me," grumbles Bliss to himself as he whiles away Sunday afternoon feeding ducks in St. James's Park after watching the guards at Buckingham Palace, and he's tempted to pick up a notebook and carry on. But he knows he'll be wasting his time. He knows that he needs a completely clear mind to focus on his writing. He knows that what he has to write is too crucial to his plot to be picked at between the Tower of London and Westminster Abbey like a backpacker's travelogue.

"Paul Mann," he says at ten minutes to six the following morning as he reports to an office stuffed with toilet paper and light bulbs in the basement of Creston tower, and Amy beams.

"Wow. I heard you wuz big," she says with more than just a friendly smile as she hands him his overalls. "You can start with the rubbish bins."

"Thanks," he replies screwing up his nose.

"Don't worry," she says. "They ain't mucky. It's just paper and stuff."

Joseph Creston is in his office by eight when Bliss and the rest of his co-workers are breakfasting in an equipment store twenty-seven floors below.

"So, what did'ye do before?" Amy wants to know, but Bliss isn't ready to start sharing.

"This and that," he mumbles and keeps his head down.

"Stairs and lifts," says Amy once the break is over and she points Bliss to a buggy loaded with mops and buckets. "And try not to get in any of the bigwigs' way or they moan like shit."

It is nearing ten before Bliss finally makes it to the twenty-seventh floor, and as the elevator whirrs smoothly to a stop, he readies his key to lock open the door while he cleans the surrounding area, but Creston's receptionist jumps on him.

"Do that later," orders Tracy, a tightly suited young woman with slicked down hair, from the safety of her mahogany framed counter.

"Sorry," says Bliss, continuing to turn the key. "Orders is orders."

"Well I'm ordering you not to do it now. Mr. Creston may want to use it."

"He can use the other one down the hall," suggests Bliss, but the gatekeeper has left her seat and is headed his way.

"Do it later," she is saying when the boardroom door opens and Creston storms out with Mason in his wake.

"Professionals," spits Creston over his shoulder. "Shit, Mason. For what I pay, I expect professionals." Then he turns on the receptionist. "What's this?" he demands and Bliss is unsure if he's talking about the cleaning cart or himself.

"I told him to come back later ..." the girl is trying apologetically when Creston pushes her out of the way, grabs Bliss's cart, and angrily yanks it aside, yelling, "Get out of my way." Then he turns to the girl and waves his cellphone at her. "Emergencies only."

"Well. I guess I might as well clean the offices, now," says Bliss once Creston and Mason have disappeared from view. Tracy scowls in reply and Bliss puts on an empathetic smile.

"Just get on with your job," she says going back to her computer.

"That was a waste of time," explains Bliss later when he meets to report to Peter Bryan. "Someone peed in Creston's morning coffee and he stormed out in a huff. I never got a chance."

"Oh," says Bryan sheepishly. "That was me doing the peeing. I gave him a call and asked him to come in for a chat about the money in Edwards' pocket."

"Oh great. What did he say?"

"What d'ye expect, Dave? 'No idea; never heard of him; not me, guv'nor; mistake …' All the usual rubbish. But at least I've got it in writing with his moniker on it, so if he tries singing a different tune when we stand his bank manager up in the witness box, he'll have some explaining to do."

The second and third days of Bliss's drudgery get him no nearer Creston, but cracks are starting to appear at the front desk.

"He's a bit of pusher," suggests Bliss to the snotty receptionist with a nod to the president's door, and at first she blanks him and sticks to her desk.

"Actually," she says eventually, when she's sure the executive's doors are all shut, "he's not usually like that. But his wife's ill."

"Wife?" queries Bliss. "I thought he was single."

"So did we," chuckles the woman, and then she whispers conspiratorially. "It seems he's been keeping her dark."

"Girlfriend trouble," suggests Bliss with a suggestive wink.

"No," laughs the woman. "It's Tracy by the way," she says pointing to the sign in front of her. "He's too churchy for that."

"I see," says Bliss as he reaches for the waste bin behind her counter, but she stops him with a hand. "That has to be shredded."

"No worries," he says with a helpful smile. "I'll do it for you. I'm going down to the shredding room right now."

By Thursday morning, with nothing to show for his clumsiness, not a hint that anyone suspects him, and the ending of his novel and the return of Yolanda receding into infinity, Bliss pushes buttons.

"What are you doing?" demands Mason, catching Bliss closing a desk drawer as he enters his office a little after eight.

"Just clearing up, guv."

Mason eyes him suspiciously. "Are you new here?"

"No, not me," lies Bliss as he fidgets uneasily with a bag of garbage. "Bin here ages, guv'nor."

"What's in the bag?"

"Bag?" questions Bliss, as if he's surprised to find it in his hand. "Oh this? Rubbish I expect."

"Let me look," says Mason advancing, but Bliss gives him the runaround.

"I don't think you're supposed —"

"I said show me what's in there," carries on Mason with his back to the door, but Bliss sees fear in the man's eyes and pumps up his torso menacingly.

Mason is out of the door, yelling, "Call security," before Bliss has a chance to move, but he's not far behind, dumping the garbage bag into his cleaning trolley while casually remarking, "I guess I'd better be off."

Joseph Creston hears the commotion and rushes out, demanding of his sidekick, "What's up, Mason?"

The company lawyer, now bolstered by his boss, advances on Bliss, who is struggling into the elevator with his haul, and sticks his foot between the doors. "You're not going anywhere," says the lawyer, getting into a tug of war with Bliss's cart, when a panting security guard emerges from the adjacent stairwell.

"He's a cop," the guard reports ten minutes later when Bliss has been stripped of his overalls, his security badge, and his cleaner's buggy.

"I bloody knew it," swears Mason as he studies Bliss's details in the guard's proffered notebook.

"Yeah," continues the uniformed man proudly. "He must think we're stupid or something. The silly bugger had his police ID in his wallet and he even —"

"That'll be all," says Mason shooing the man out, then he picks up the phone and calls Edwards.

Chief Inspector Peter Bryan can hardly control his voice when his father-in-law gets through to him ten minutes later.

"Brilliant piece of work, Dave," laughs Bryan, who has just been briefed by the surveillance officer listening in on the wiretaps. "Edwards nearly took Mason's head off. 'I told you never to f'kin call me here,' he yelled down the phone. Then Mason says, 'Don't worry Mick. Me and J.C. told 'em we didn't know anything about the money.' 'Don't be such f'kin pratt,' Edwards said. 'They know damn well you gave it to me. Anyway, why the fuck are you calling?' Then Mason gave him your name and I thought he'd had a heart attack. Edwards goes dead quiet for like twenty seconds then he says, 'Hang on a mo, Bliss ain't here, he's writing a f'kin book in France.' Then Mason says 'What?' and Edwards ... and this is really funny, Dave ... Edwards says 'It's a double f'kin bluff.' And Mason says 'Why would they do that?' And Edwards ... get ready to laugh, Dave ... Edwards says... 'Cos they've tapped your f'kin phone you pillock. They're prob'ly listening in right now ... Oh shit!"

Bliss and his son-in-law are still laughing an hour later when the digital recording is replayed by the surveillance officer.

"Well I'd better get back to France," says Bliss. "I wouldn't want to prove Edwards wrong."

Heathrow Airport. The Thursday evening commuters who at one time would have balked at driving home to far-off Oxford or Cambridge now stretch their weekends in Provence, Tuscany, on even the Algarve. Two hours in a business seat aboard an Airbus to Florence is less challenging than two hours behind the wheel in a smog-laden snarl up on the motorway, and the end result is certainly more rewarding.

David Bliss isn't travelling business, but it's only an hour and a half to Nice so he doesn't mind. And he's lucky. He has snagged a seat because of a last-minute cancellation, though it did not come cheap. "How much?" he exclaimed at the standby desk and promised himself that he will get it reimbursed through his son-in-law. "It's for business," he told the check-in clerk, and inwardly he is still laughing at the way that Edwards stuck his head in the noose as he heads towards his plane.

"Chief Inspector Bliss?" questions a uniformed sergeant tapping him on the shoulder as he shuffles towards the boarding gate with his ticket and passport in hand.

"Yep."

"Sorry, sir. But there's an urgent call for you in the police office."

"I'm just getting my flight ... who is it?"

"Sorry, sir," the sergeant continues with genuine apology. "But I've been told that you must take it."

Bliss dithers.

"I think that's an order, sir," says the sergeant.

"You've got time," says the girl taking the tickets. "Twenty minutes at least."

"OK," replies Bliss and he hurries the sergeant to the airport police station.

An hour later Bliss is still waiting. His flight is skirting Paris, but he's drinking cafeteria tea at Heathrow while a car is sent to collect him from Central London.

"Sorry, Dave," Peter Bryan told him in a downcast voice when he answered the phone. "Edwards has pulled a switcheroo. His lawyer and Creston's people have got together and they've filed a complaint of trespass and theft against you."

"Brilliant!" explodes Bliss as soon as he catches up with his son-in-law, but he quickly rationalizes. "Attack is the best form of defence, Peter."

"I think it's probably his only defence," agrees Bryan, with Edwards' admission on tape.

"So why the hell did you stop me? I would've been back home by now," starts Bliss, and then he thinks, *That's interesting, I just called St-Juan-sur-Mer home.*

"Sorry, Dave," says Bryan, "But the assistant commissioner thought it best if we fronted them, faced them down, saying, 'Yeah, OK. So what? So he trespassed, since when has that been a crime?'"

"But what about theft? What the hell am I supposed to have stolen?"

"Company documents, they claim."

"That's a load of bollocks."

"I know," says Bryan. "They're flying a kite. They think that you were there to pinch evidence, but they don't know what's missing. In any case, they know they won't get any mileage out of a civil trespass charge."

"So, what now?" asks Bliss as they arrive at Scotland Yard.

Peter Bryan checks his watch. "Well we've missed the assistant for the day. You'd better stay with Sam and me tonight, and we'll sort it out in the morning."

"We'd better," seethes Bliss. "I've lost another week on my book."

"Don't worry, Dave. She's coming back."

"Easy for you to say; your entire future isn't on the line."

"Dave, don't worry," says Peter Bryan. "They're not going to fire you over this."

"I was talking about Yolanda," Bliss says, pronouncing every word separately to make sure that it sinks in.

The depression that settled over Bliss in France on Friday morning is nothing compared to the storm brewing on the executive floor of Creston Enterprises. A half a dozen lawyers and their assistants from Barnes, Worstheim and Shuttlecock sit around the enormous table scratching their heads over the stupidity of the owner and his sidekick.

"We have to stay on the offensive," says Barnes, opening up as soon as the introductions have been made. "The way we see it at present ..." then he pauses to give Mason a fierce look, "... assuming we are in possession of all the facts, is that you received no information of any value from this ... what's-his-name ... Edwards. Is that so?"

"That's correct," answers Creston, while Mason mops his brow with a handkerchief.

"Therefore," continues Barnes, "could we assume that you, Mr. Mason, simply offered an old friend a small ... shall we say almost insignificant ... loan, so that he could purchase a new motor vehicle. Would I be right if I said that?"

Mason brightens a touch and grabs the outstretched hand. "Yes," he says. "Yes, I think that would be true."

"However," cuts in Jackson, one of the lesser lawyers whose name has yet to appear on the company's letterhead, "you did make a statement to the police saying that you had actually given Mr. Edwards no money whatsoever."

Mason returns to his handkerchief for a second, leaving Barnes to step back in.

"Perhaps Mr. Mason was confused," the senior lawyer carries on, talking to the table in general. "Perhaps Mr. Mason didn't consider a personal loan to an old friend to be any business of Her Majesty's Metropolitan Police Force. Perhaps Mr. Mason should revisit his statement, apologize profusely to the officer, and make the necessary amendments."

Mason, appearing more confused than ever, looks to Creston for guidance but is unable to read anything into his boss's expression, so he asks, "But how will that leave Mike Edwards?"

"Mr. Edwards is not our concern," replies Jackson, taking back the reins. "Accepting an unauthorized remuneration under any circumstances is a dangerous matter for a senior officer. He will have to explain that himself."

"And if he says it was a bribe?"

"Then he would be a very foolish man."

"This was a pretty stupid stunt, Dave," says the assistant commissioner as Bliss stands before him checking out the pattern in the carpet.

"Yes, sir."

Then the senior commander looks up with a wry smile. "It paid off though, didn't it?"

"Yes, sir"

"Relax, Dave," says the assistant. "Sit down and let's get our story straight."

"Straight, sir?" queries Bliss, unsure of the route this officer is talking.

"The way I see it," continues the assistant commissioner, "is that we recalled you to duty because we thought you were the best man for such a sensitive case."

Bliss laughs to himself. *Edwards obviously has something on you as well*, he is thinking as the commander continues. "A sensitive case which possibly ... and only possibly ... involved one of our most senior, and beloved, officers."

"Yes, sir," replies Bliss now seeing clearly the path that is being taken.

"And," the assistant continues, "you were merely acting under orders for the purpose of potentially clearing Mr. Edwards' name."

"That's absolutely true, sir," says Bliss, keeping his face as straight as he is able.

"Good. I'm glad we've got that sorted out."

"But what about the documents they claim I took?"

The assistant looks up sharply. "You didn't, did you?"

"No. I didn't"

"OK. Well. Just tell it the way it was. Say you didn't, and if they claim different they'll have to prove it."

"So. What happens now, sir?" asks Bliss, anxious to get moving.

"Well." The assistant commissioner checks the wall clock as if searching for the day. "It's Friday. Let's see if anything transpires over the weekend, and if not, Monday you're on your way again."

"I was hop—" is as far as Bliss gets.

"A couple of days won't hurt, and we'll have to reinstate you on full pay for the whole month, plus all your travel expenses: flights, hotels, meals, hire car, the works. Now that's not so painful is it?"

"No, sir," says Bliss as he rises.

"Monday morning at eleven then," orders the assistant commissioner opening the door to let Bliss out.

The prospect of a wet weekend in London isn't appealing to Bliss, especially with his mind stuck so determinedly on Yolanda and his unfinished book. But with little choice, the historic city of Westchester with its gaily decorated side streets and promise of a mid-winter festival or a pantomime in a local church hall has more appeal, and his daughter and son-in-law take no persuasion. "I'll stay at Daphne's," he tells them when they pick him up at the front entrance of Westminster Abbey an hour later. "And I'll treat you two to a romantic weekend getaway at the Mitre."

"That's very generous of you, Dad," says Samantha, and he turns with a mock snarl to his son-in-law.

"Yes it is. Especially considering the poop your husband dropped me in. But I can afford it now I am back on full pay plus expenses."

Peter Bryan catches on and laughs. "I guess the hotel receipt will be in your name."

"Well," says Bliss. "You can always stay at Daphne's if you prefer."

The slow drive out of London in the dusk is lightened by Peter Bryan, who sits in the backseat playing with Bliss over his scheme to win back his lost love.

"I can just picture you on television with Michael Parkinson or one of those Americans, Oprah probably," laughs Bryan. "'So Chief Inspector,' she says, 'If I've got this right, you wrote an entire novel just to impress a woman.' And you say, 'Yep. That's correct, Oprah,' and she says … and to be honest I think it probably would be Oprah … she says, 'So tell us, Dave, did it work? Did the lovely come back?'"

"Yeah, all right," sneers Bliss. "I know it sounds corny."

"No, no," says Bryan. "I've not finished, because, just before you give your reply, Oprah turns to the camera and says, 'OK, folks, let's go to commercials. And what do you think ladies? I mean he's a good-looking chunk of change. Did the lucky lady say 'Yes' or was she absolutely crazy and said 'No'? We'll have the answer when we come back.'"

"All right. Enough," says Bliss putting his foot down, but Bryan can't help one more dig.

"So the ads are over and the camera is back on you, and you go all silly and say, 'No. She bloody well didn't.' Then what? They get Yolanda on the phone and Oprah says to her, 'So are you totally crazy or …'"

"I said, that's enough," shouts Bliss, but Samantha can't help chiming in.

"The TV station's switchboard will light up like a firework," she says. "Limos loaded with rich widows will be lined up outside …"

"Yeah, yeah. All right," scoffs Bliss as he pooh-poohs the notion. "Look, I'm not interested in anyone but Yolanda; I don't care about being famous or about the money and I certainly don't want a widow, rich or otherwise. I've waited a long time for Yolanda and if she doesn't come back, I don't want anyone else — got it?"

"Yes, Dad," says, Samantha, affectionately stroking his hair. "I just hope she realizes how lucky she is. No one's ever written a novel for me."

"Or me," laughs Bryan.

Daphne Lovelace greets the trio at the front door of the Mitre Hotel in Westchester High Street. "Ted Donaldson is meeting us for dinner," explains the sprightly woman, wearing a pink taffeta hat in celebration. "And I've booked the room as requested," she adds. Then she tugs at Samantha's arm and whispers, "I got you the bridal suite with a Jacuzzi. Your dad can afford it."

"Thanks, Daph," says Samantha, giving her a con-spiratorial nudge.

"If the devil should cast his net ..." jests Donaldson as he sweeps the group towards the dining room. "I don't know about you lot but I'm famished."

"Nice to see you again, Ted," says Bliss, offering his hand, and Donaldson reciprocates.

"I knew you'd take up my offer. I told you I could use a good detective."

"You don't need me," laughs Bliss. "You've got young Daphne here."

"Now you're talking," says the superintendent, lacing his old friend's arm through his and leading the way. "Come on," he calls over his shoulder. "Friday night is steak night."

Amelia Drinkwater and the deaths of the three Creston children dominate the conversation as they wait for dinner, but as Donaldson points out, until forensic doc-ument examiners have done their job he doesn't have enough to arrest her.

The document examiners at the Home Office forensic science laboratory may be no better qualified than Mark Benson to give an opinion on the validity of the certificates and records, but their reputations stand or fall on their ability to persuade judges and juries in accordance with legal niceties.

"We'll need at least a couple of weeks for a prelim report," the receiving officer explained, despite the fact that Donaldson stressed that it was a murder case.

"It's basically your word against hers at the moment," Donaldson explains unnecessarily to Bliss, and then he turns the conversation to his favourite subject: the food.

Ted Donaldson excuses himself after dinner, leaning on his wife. "She'll have a bit of supper waiting for me," he says as he rises, patting his ample gut. "She knows how to keep a man satisfied."

"All right, Ted," says Daphne as he heads off, then she turns back to the others. "I didn't want to say anything in front of Ted, but I've been thinking about the Creston kiddies, and what confuses me is where they buried the first one, John."

"The town cemetery," suggests Peter Bryan, but Daphne shakes her head. "No, I checked all the graveyards in the entire parish. There is no record of a John Creston or Thurgood anywhere."

"And he is not in Creston Chapel?"

"No," she says. "I looked. And Grainger, the old gardener, just shrugged it off because the baby wasn't a legitimate Creston."

"That never stopped Louis XIV," says Bliss, explaining that the French monarch made a career of legitimizing his bastard children.

"I know," admits Daphne. "Kings have always done that; half the world's royalty are actually Smiths and Joneses. But I don't think Creston Sr. was overly chuffed about his precious son marrying Janet in the first place, let alone taking on her child."

"What about Amelia Drinkwater?" suggests Samantha, but her father shakes his head.

"No," says Bliss. "She didn't seem to know where any of them were buried."

"Doctor Symmonds might know," continues Daphne, "but I don't think he likes me."

"Or Trina," laughs Bliss. "But I don't know who else to turn to."

"Maybe we should take a snoop around Creston's manor in the morning," suggests Peter Bryan, half-jokingly. "I have a feeling that his lordship will be spending the day in bed with his lawyers in London."

"You've got me into enough trouble already ..." starts Bliss, but he doesn't rule out the plan entirely.

chapter eighteen

Saturday dawned with a festive glaze of frost on hedgerows and roofs, although the hoar is slowly dissipating in the watery winter sun by the time that Daphne pours David Bliss a cup of Keemun tea.

"Maybe we should pop over to Dewminster," says Bliss, eyeing the milky blue sky from Daphne's kitchen window and seeing the beginnings of a brighter day. "I wouldn't mind taking a peek at the scene of the crime."

"Locked," calls Peter Bryan without surprise a few hours later as he tests the ornate metal gate at the end of Creston's driveway and eyes the "No trespassing" sign on the adjacent stone pillar.

"We could try the back," suggests Daphne, and two minutes later they take the servant's route that she followed with Grainger.

"Imagine the headlines," says Samantha as they track through a small copse and emerge to spy the sprawling

Victorian hall surrounded by clipped lawns. "Two senior police officers, a lawyer, and a —"

"And a private detective," pipes up Daphne as they stroll through the grounds like Sunday picnickers.

"Yes," continues Samantha. "Two officers, a lawyer, and a private detective were apprehended in the act of …" She stops and points to a small grassy area cordoned off by a low box hedge. "There's some gravestones."

"Pet cemetery," explains Daphne. "Grainger showed me."

"Let's have a peep," suggests Peter Bryan. "It always amazes me that people go gaga over a mangy mongrel or a flea-infested moggy."

"Grainger said something about a monkey," Daphne is saying as they paddle across the wet grass and line up in front of a row of miniature headstones that are just as pretentious as any of the marble monuments in the town's graveyard.

"Bonzo, Prunella, Chi-chi …" reads Samantha as she reels off the names of lapdogs, cats, hounds, parrots, and a pet chicken. And at one end, with no more ceremony than the others, "Micky, the monkey."

"It doesn't surprise me," says Daphne brushing a hand over the inscribed tablet. "The family lived in Africa during the war and all the chocolate comes from there." And then she stops with a curious look. "That's a coincidence," she says, pointing. "I can't remember the actual date, but Janet's first kid died about the same time."

"The chapel's over here," calls Samantha, moving on, and Daphne hustles to catch up.

"I'll have to check his death certificate," the elderly woman is saying as they test the chapel door and slip inside.

"I knew it," exclaims Daphne two hours later, following a clotted cream tea in Dewminster and a joyride around the countryside, as she stabs her finger on her photocopy of John Creston's death certificate. "Just a week before the monkey," she says with an expression that invites only one conclusion.

"What are you saying, Daph …" starts Bliss, but he's already catching on.

"They wouldn't …" begins Bryan, but the events of the past few weeks suggest that nothing would be too devious for the Crestons and he changes his mind. "I suppose it's possible," he carries on, taking another look at the certificate. "Although I've no idea how we'd go about getting an exhumation warrant."

"We wouldn't need one," suggests his wife in a lawyerly tone. "It's not consecrated ground and it's not human remains … apparently."

Daphne lights up and grabs the key to her garden shed. "I've got a couple of spades …"

"Whoa," warns Bliss holding onto her. "It's just the sort of thing Creston's lawyers would love."

"Then Sam and I will do it. You two can stay in the car."

Darkness falls very early despite the star-scattered sky, but the rising moon lights a path for the two would-be grave robbers as they sneak back into the grounds of Creston Hall.

"It's getting nippy already," whispers Daphne as they slip from tree shadow to tree shadow but the work soon warms them.

The rotted wooden casket lies four feet down under a heavy stone slab, and by the time they've reached it, Daphne has gone too far. "You'll have to get the boys," she says, slumping onto the dewy grass and taking off her appropriately sombre black hat, and five minutes later the two chief inspectors slink back through the copse with a crumbling casket between them.

A large plastic bag from Daphne's garden shed shrouds the kitchen table while the four stand around warming themselves with brandy-laced tea. "Here goes," says Bliss, wearing a pair of Daphne's pink rubber kitchen gloves, and he picks away at the decayed box until a small skeleton lays exposed.

"I think it's a monkey,'" says Bryan taking a closer look, but Daphne is determined not to have been wrong.

"I don't know," she says. "Those arm bones don't look overly long."

"What other differences should there be?" asks Samantha with a handkerchief clamped over her nose.

"Hair ... tail ... lower forehead ... bigger teeth ..." comes from around the table but no one spots anything obvious.

"We need a pathologist," starts Bryan, but Daphne has another idea.

"What about a doctor?"

Peter Symmonds is both surprised and annoyed to find Daphne Lovelace on his doorstep again, especially as it is nearing midnight, but the elderly troublemaker is backed by a formidable posse so he puts on a polite face. "What do you want now?"

David Bliss steps forward. "Dr. Symmonds. We are police officers. Can we have a word?"

"I said I didn't want to press charges —" he is explaining when Bliss cuts him off.

"If we could just step inside, sir."

Peter Symmonds rattles the decanter against the rim of the glass as he pours himself a whisky, but he manages to hold his voice in check as he scans the quartet around his dining table and asks, "Are you sure won't join me?"

"Not for me, Doc," says Bryan, while the others shake their heads.

Symmonds sits and slaps his hands, palms down, on the table with forced bravado. "Well?" he questions. "What can I do for you?"

The doctor's denial over the missing documents precludes Daphne from referring to them, so she begins circumspectly, "You must have seen a lot of dead babies in your day —"

Symmonds stops her almost immediately. "Look, please stop dancing around. I'm well aware that you and your accomplice stole certain records —"

"Then why did you deny it?" steps in Bliss.

Symmonds eyes the group for a few seconds then takes a meditative drink before slowly lowering his glass. "My father was a good man," he begins, and then pauses to conjure up a mental image. "He was a caring man," he carries on with a fond picture. "A man committed to the welfare of his patients." Then he stops, realizes his glass is empty, and fetches the decanter from the sideboard while he brushes aside a nostalgic tear. All eyes follow the old doctor, watching in silence as painful memories appear to age him; slowly, perhaps reluctantly, he returns to the table and sits motionless for several long seconds before haltingly continuing. "Dad ... um ... Dad began practising before the war, before the National Health Service, when patients had to pay."

"When the rich got preferential treatment," suggests Daphne from personal experience.

"And the poor didn't even get an opinion unless Dad paid for it out of his own pocket or got some of the richer families to help out."

"Like the Crestons," suggests Bliss.

"Precisely," agrees Symmonds. "Half the oldies in this town probably owe their lives to the Crestons one way or another. They built the hospital, paid for the beds, stocked the pharmacy shelves ..." Then his voice trails off as his story heads into murkier waters.

"So," says Daphne, taking his hand and leading him in the direction she knows he's going. "If Mr. Creston needed a small favour in return it was only natural that your dad would oblige if he could."

Symmonds doesn't answer but his face says that he agrees as he drains his glass.

"Would that include looking the other way to avoid getting the family bad publicity?" tries Bryan, and Symmonds bends.

"It might," he agrees, shamefaced for his father.

Would he have gone so far as to cover up a murder, Bliss wants to ask, but he already knows the answer; knows that it is only a matter of time before Amelia Drinkwater has her day in the dock.

"We'd like your medical opinion on a delicate matter," says Peter Bryan, leaning on the doctor's vulnerability, and half an hour later they are all back at Daphne's.

"It's definitely human," pronounces Symmonds. "Young male I'd guess, though I can't be sure."

"And the cause of death?" insists Bliss.

Symmonds knows he's in a corner and dithers for a second as if trying to find an easy way out. "The skull is fractured," he says eventually. "Although you'd need a forensic pathologist to tell you conclusively whether that occurred pre- or post-mortem."

"Thank you, Doctor," says Bryan, stepping in as if the consultation is over, but Symmonds is now the one with questions.

"Is this official? I mean ... where did you get this body?"

"Just leave it with us, Doc," Bryan carries on. "We'll run you home now."

"I could call Superintendent Donaldson —" Symmonds begins, but Bliss cuts him off.

"And tell him what? That your dad covered up a couple of murders? That you falsified medical records and fixed death certificates?"

Symmonds freezes while his mind churns, then he looks questioningly into Bliss's eyes, asking, Just how much do you know?

"Maybe you'd like to come into the sitting room," suggests Daphne, breaking the moment.

A warm front sweeping in off the Atlantic has clouded the sky and brought back the mist by Sunday morning as Bliss and his son-in-law tamp down the mound of earth over the replaced coffin.

"We'll have to dump what's left," whispers Bliss, seeing that they still have a pile of earth as they stand back to check their handiwork.

"It'll be all right as long as it keeps raining all day," says Bryan, and then he goes back to poke at the turf while Bliss shovels the excess soil into the hedgerow.

"Let's just hope that Symmonds keeps his story straight," says Bryan as they stick Daphne's spade into the car's trunk and head to the doctor's house.

An hour later, Doctor Peter Symmonds sits in front of Ted Donaldson at the Friar Tuck restaurant — "The only place where you can get a breakfast worth a damn," according to the superintendent — and explains, "So, I've discovered that some of my papers ... actually my father's papers ... appear to be missing."

"Really," says Donaldson in mock surprise.

"And," carries on Symmonds with the script pre-pared for him by Daphne and the two London officers, "I suspect that the documents in question may contain false information regarding some medical examinations that my father carried out before his death."

If Symmonds' confession sounds rehearsed to Donaldson he doesn't mention it, nor does he let on that David Bliss has already put him in the picture.

"Just act dumb," Bliss told him by phone when he arranged the meeting with an early morning phone call.

"So," questions Donaldson, picking over his pile of pork sausages to get at the bacon, "these examinations. Did they perhaps relate to the deaths of certain people connected to the Creston family?"

"I knew it, I knew it," trills Daphne when the superintendent reports his findings an hour later, and Donaldson gives her a knowing look.

"The strange thing is," he says with a suspicious eye on the entire ensemble, "that the good doctor can't explain why he thinks we might find the child's body in a monkey's grave."

"The big question is, who did it — who smashed his skull?" suggests Bliss, moving quickly on, and Daphne immediately flies to Janet's side.

"According to Trina, Janet didn't do any of it."

"And you believe her?" queries Bliss. "The woman who nearly killed you in a mobile bathtub?"

"I know," agrees Daphne. "She seems a little crazy at times, but her heart's in the right place."

"Amelia could have done it," suggests Samantha, but her husband has other ideas.

"I bet it was old man Creston, ticked off that his son had been lumbered with a little bastard, worried that his empire would fall into the gutter."

"He wouldn't be the first," agrees Bliss, and he can't wait to get back to finishing his novel to expose the bastardly lineage of Chief Superintendent Edwards' cunning predecessor, the Sun King, Louis XIV of France.

Peter Bryan's cellphone rings as they crawl through the rush hour traffic into London on Monday morning with Samantha at the wheel. He grabs it, says, "Hello," then claps his hand over the mouthpiece and offers it to Bliss. "It's for you," he says with a straight face. "It's Oprah. She wants you on next week's show."

"Piss off," says, Bliss pushing it away.

Bryan laughs as he takes the call from his office. "Sorry," he says. "Just went through a tunnel."

"Good weekend?" greets the assistant commissioner at the eleven o'clock meeting, and Bliss shrugs nonchalantly.

"Quiet," he says. "Visiting old friends, digging up a few old skeletons." Then he asks hopefully, "Do you need me anymore, sir?"

"I'm not sure..." starts the senior officer scanning an email on his screen. "Creston's legal beavers were requesting a meeting, probably hoping for a deal. 'I'll show you mine if you show me yours' kind of thing, but now they've postponed — something about an urgent matter in Hampshire. You'd better stick around for a day or so."

Bliss's face drops, and the assistant commissioner holds up a couple of fingers. "Two at the most, Chief Inspector ... promise."

Now what? Bliss asks himself and is tempted to take off. It's been well over a month since Yolanda left, and despite the fact that her image and her smile are with him every moment, awake and asleep, he feels her slipping away. Then he thinks, *Perhaps I should speed things up a bit.*

Tracy, the president's personal receptionist, emerges from Creston tower's front entrance on her lunch break, and Bliss, with a newly purchased trilby hat over his eyes, sets off in pursuit.

"Remember me?" he says, sliding alongside her as she walks to a deli in the next street, and she stops with a quizzical look.

"Dave?" she queries when he lifts his hat. "What happened? They said you were a policeman."

"I am," he says taking out his police ID, adding, "This is very hush-hush, Tracy, but we're investigating a possible terrorist plot to kill your boss."

"Oh my goodness," she gasps. "He went to Hampshire this morning. Will he be all right?"

"The Hampshire police are keeping an eye on him today," continues Bliss entirely truthfully, wondering what arguments Creston and his legal team are using to convince the magistrate not to issue a warrant to send in a team of excavators. "We don't want to alarm him because we think it might involve someone close to him."

"Is this to do with the Ivory Coast?" asks Tracy in a conspiratorial whisper, well aware of the volatile situation in West Africa.

"We think so," says Bliss darkly. "But the trouble is we don't know where Mr. Creston's wife is."

"And you think they might get to her?"

"They just might," agrees Bliss with a deeply worried tone, "unless we can get to her first."

The duty sister at the nursing home in ritzy St. John's Wood checks Bliss's ID for the third time, saying, "I wish I could get hold of Mr. Creston. He specifically said that his wife was to have no visitors."

"Don't worry," replies Bliss with a disarming smile. "I promise not to tire her."

"How is Trina?" Janet wants to know as soon as Bliss has bitten his tongue and introduced himself as a friend of the zany homecare nurse.

"She's fine," he tells her; considering the reports he received from Daphne concerning Janet's mistreatment, he is pleasantly surprised at the woman's chirpiness.

"And Clive?"

Clive? he wants to question, but doesn't. "Oh yes. I think he is all right."

"I miss him," she admits.

Bliss has a rough idea of what's happening when he asks, "Are you happy here, Janet?" and her face pains before she simply nods obediently.

"Trina was asking about your children," he carries on with a note of sympathy, using the Canadian woman as a shield.

"They died."

"I know."

"It was my fault. I didn't look after them properly," Janet says as her face begins to drop. "I said sorry to God, but I don't think he was listening."

"Do you remember what happened to the children?"

"The doctor said I was a really bad mother," she starts, as tears begin to dribble down her cheeks, "but I loved my babies."

"Are you all right, Mrs. Creston?" asks the sister poking her head around the door, still concerned about her position.

Bliss waves her away. "Mrs. Creston's fine, thank you."

"Hit the bell if you need me, dear," she continues to her patient while making a point of ignoring Bliss.

"What happened to little John?" presses Bliss as the door begins to close, but then he notices that it has been left ajar so he stands to shut it.

"The doctor said he just died in his sleep," says Janet as Bliss finds the sister's foot jamming the door. He is momentarily tempted to trap it, but something is happening to Janet and he is drawn back to the bed by her inner cries as she relives the moment when she cradled her dead baby in her arms and realized that her life had forever changed.

"Did you go to John's funeral?" asks Bliss as he tries to get into her thoughts.

"They said I'd be upset," she says shaking her head as the tears flow. "I wanted to but they were afraid I'd be too upset."

"And the second one, Giuseppe?"

"He was always ill."

"But what about Joe-Joe, Janet? Mr. Grainger ... you remember the gardener ... he said Joe-Joe was a fine little lad."

Memories flood back, and seconds later Janet is loudly blubbering, "I didn't do it. I didn't do it. They said I did, but I didn't."

The sister barrels back in, red-faced, yelling, "You've upset her."

"Not me," says Bliss.

"Out," orders the sister, and Bliss starts to leave, but he turns back.

"Where was John buried, Janet?"

"I don't know," she cries. "They wouldn't tell me. I kept saying, 'Where's my baby? Where's my baby?' But they wouldn't tell me."

"Out," howls the sister again, and Bliss makes a feint for the door, then he tries a desperate final stab.

"Joseph killed your baby, Janet."

The moment stops, the sister freezes, then Janet grabs her bronze crucifix and clasps it to her chest, mumbling, "He said he'd kill me if I ever told."

The tense atmosphere deflates like a punctured balloon as Janet slumps back on the pillow with her taut face softening as if she has finally been exorcised.

"I'm getting security," says the sister, but Bliss roughly grabs her arm and hisses, "Stay." Then he turns back to Janet and speaks softly. "How, Janet? How did Joseph do it?"

"With my Jesus," she says clasping her icon tighter. "He hit him with my Jesus."

"Creston and his people are fighting the exhumation," Donaldson tells Bliss when he phones the superintendent ten minutes later to give him more ammunition. "Good lad," enthuses Donaldson. "Creston is beginning to look like that Dutch kid who tried plugging a leaky dyke."

Dermot Barnes, QC, the leading mouthpiece of Barnes, Worstheim and Shuttlecock, believes that the Magistrate's court in Dewminster is beneath his dignity, so Malcolm Jackson is trying to plug a leak on behalf of his client by badgering the Crown Prosecutor to reveal the name of the person or persons who trampled on Mr. Creston's rights and grounds.

But whatever the prosecution lawyer may suspect, he knows only what he's been told, and he shrugs to the justice of the peace. "Your worship, this application is based solely on the information contained in the statement of Dr. Peter Symmonds."

"Someone's been digging around ..." complains Jackson, but it gets him nowhere.

"I'm inclined to accept the doctor's word," says the lay magistrate who doubles as the town's soccer referee and finds a certain delight in red-carding a team of London barristers. "I hereby issue a search warrant."

"We could appeal," suggests Jackson as he and his team mill around Creston in the foyer. "But it might make it look as though we have something to hide and will only delay matters."

"Long enough to move the body?" questions Creston hopefully, and he gets an immediate reprimand.

"What body, sir?" asks Jackson. "I thought we agreed that we knew nothing about a body."

"Right, sorry," says the executive, but Donaldson was correct: he is a man trying to plug leaks and a deluge is heading his way.

"Mr. Joseph Crispin Creston?" queries a uniformed inspector from Dewminster police station.

"Yes."

"I'm arresting you on suspicion of murder," continues the officer, placing a hand on Creston's shoulder. "And I must warn —"

"Murder, what murder?" spits Creston, throwing off the hand. "You haven't even dug up the bloody body yet."

"And what body would that be?" queries the inspector.

"Shut up, Mr. Creston," Jackson hisses to his client through clenched teeth, but J.C. is under too much strain to listen.

"You can't prove it," he yells into the officer's face and lashes out with a fist as a constable tries to slap on handcuffs. "You can't prove a bloody thing."

"I'm just waiting for one of the local lads to show up with some statement forms," Bliss tells Donaldson from the nursing sister's office when he gets the news.

"Are you sure you don't want a job?" asks Donaldson, but Bliss already has his hands full.

"Sorry, but I've got a book to finish and two women to woo," says Bliss with both Yolanda and his prince's paramour in mind. "I'll check in at the Yard, fax you a copy of the statement, and see if I can get a flight out this evening, whether the assistant commissioner approves or not."

It is after one in the morning by the time that Bliss hails a cab outside Nice airport, and nearly two before he hits the pillow in his apartment. His manuscript of more than five hundred handwritten pages will wait until the morning, and so will the letter sitting in his mailbox in the concierge's office.

Daphne wakes him at nine. "Damn," he says, glancing at the clock as he reaches for the phone. "I wanted to be writing by seven."

"Trina's on her way over," Daphne explains, as if he should care. "She's bringing a visitor to see Janet."

"Clive?" he questions, and Daphne laughs.

"Apparently he's quite smitten with her."

"I don't know what her husband will say about that," says Bliss, but Daphne is unconcerned. "According to Ted he isn't going to be saying much at all for a very long time."

"I wouldn't be so sure ..." starts Bliss, but he doesn't know that Creston's dyke has finally ruptured now that Peter Symmonds has seen the light.

"His old dad must've been worried that the wheel would fall off the Creston charity bus one day," Daphne tells him. "So he kept two sets of notes."

"About John's murder?" Bliss questions.

"Yep, Peter found them in his dad's papers after he died. It's all there: smashed skull, blunt instrument, and — and this is the best bit — J.C. Creston Jr. so cut up about it that he had to shoot him full of a sedative."

"Doesn't prove he did it, though," cautions Bliss, although he admits that it will corroborate Janet's testimony.

"You're right, David. But he's going to have a job explaining why he was so upset about the death of another man's child."

"So where's Creston now?"

Joseph Creston is still in a cell at Westchester Police Station, despite his lawyers' attempt to get him bail, and is facing further charges of resisting arrest and assaulting a police officer.

"Life begins when you're in love," sings Billie Holiday as Bliss puts down the phone and looks across the azure bay to the island of the Man in the Iron Mask. "Time for you to finally get the woman you deserve," he says, speaking of both himself and the besotted prisoner, and he gaily plucks his pad and pen off the table with a croissant and café au lait in mind.

It's time the world woke up to the fact that true love always triumphs, he tells himself as he shuns the elevator and bounds down the stairs.

"Ah, monsieur. Bonjour, you have returned," sings out the concierge as he wafts a letter in Bliss's direction.

"Ms. Yolanda Pieters," Bliss reads from the return address, and it takes no more than a second for the information to sink in.

"Oh my God," he breathes. "It's worked. She's coming back."

Bliss rips open the letter with the enthusiasm of a birthday boy and starts, "Dear David ...," then he stops as his eyes scan the single sheet. The words *married*, *Klaus*, and *sorry* leap off the page, and he feels his knees buckle.

Daphne is first in the fining line. "It's your damn fault," he complains bitterly. "If you hadn't dragged me back to nail Amelia none of this would have happened."

"David ... I'm so sorry," she starts but he cuts her off and lashes out at his daughter instead.

"She's gone. Sam," he cries as tears well in his eyes. "I've lost her."

"Are you sure, Dad?" she asks as she dances outside an Old Bailey courtroom, knowing that if she doesn't take her seat in less than two minutes she'll get an earful from her leader.

"Of course I'm sure," he shouts. "She married him."

"But why?" asks Samantha. "She loves you. She told you. Didn't she?"

"A thousand times, Sam," he keens. "She told me a thousand times. She told me I was the only one for her and the best lover she had ever had. She looked into my eyes and told me that she'd had my face in her mind from the day she was born. Even before that."

"Then why would she marry him?"

"Bloody Klaus," he yells in desperation. "I bet he couldn't wait to get a ring on her finger."

"Dad, I've got to go —" she starts but Bliss holds onto her.

"No wait, Sam. You've got to help me. What can I do?"

Samantha checks her watch ... a minute late. "Dad, hurry up, what —"

"Why did she do that?" he carries on, but his voice breaks.

"Why did *he* do it?" asks Samantha more to herself than her father. "He must be crazy, Dad. Why would he marry someone he knows is in love with another man?"

"He doesn't love her, Sam," mumbles Bliss. "He just doesn't want me to have her."

"Wait, wait," says Samantha, slowing down, no longer concerned at the rebuke she'll get when she takes her seat on the defence bench. "Are you sure they're married?"

Bliss skims through the short letter again, feeling himself close to vomiting as he finds the word *married*, then he reads, "Klaus and I are getting married."

"There you are," yells Samantha. "It doesn't say 'we are married.' She might mean next month, next year, or even five years' time for all you know."

Bliss reads it over again. "True," he agrees.

"Well then stop her, Dad. How long will it take you to finish your novel?"

"Three, maybe four days if I work around the clock."

"Well work around the clock. Put everything you've got into it, every bit of passion, every bit of love. I'll track her down and as soon as you've finished you can get it to her."

"But what if she's already married?"

"Then Oprah will have one of the best shows ever, and you'll be writing bestsellers for the rest of your life. Now get on with it."

chapter nineteen

"*There is a small pinnace approaching the island,
Captain,*" writes Bliss, in the voice of a seventeenth-
century legionnaire as he sits across the road from
L'Escale on the promenade at St-Juan-sur-Mer with fifty
clean sheets of paper under his hand. Then he looks
across the calm waters of the bay to the masked man's
fortress and spins himself back to 1698.

"*I see a royal pennant flying from the mast, Captain,*"
sang the lookout. "I think it is a messenger from Versailles."

"*Very well," replied Captain Montelban, the captain
of the guard. "Bring him to my quarters the moment he
arrives and I will escort him directly to Maréchal Mars."*

"*As you command, Captain."*

*Prince Ferdinand, peering hopefully through the bars
of his cell window, also saw the courier skimming across
the bay and his heart momentarily leaped.* Perhaps today
is the day, *he told himself.* Perhaps the woman I crave has
finally consented ... *But eleven years of dashed expectations have weakened his resolve. The trickery of his mentor,
Louis XIV, has become more evident in his mind ...*

"Would you like another *café*?" interrupts Angeline, but Bliss shoos her away.

"Busy," he says, but then he looks up to see Daisy eyeing him from the next table.

"Are you all right, Daavid?" the sad-faced real estate agent asks, and he's tempted to tell her of his problems but doesn't see the point of adding to her woes.

"Fine ... just working, Daisy," he says, bending his head back to the page, but she's not fooled.

"I zhink you have been crying, no?" she says.

"No, Daisy. I'm fine. But I have to get my book finished."

"But where is your lady friend? I have not seen her ..."

Bliss stops, gives up, and gives in. "All right," he admits fiercely. "She's gone, Daisy. She left me ... she's marrying someone else."

"But, Daavid," Daisy protests. "She loves you."

"I know she loves me."

"And you love her."

"Yes, Daisy, I love her. I love her more than any man has ever loved a woman. I would happily die for her ..." then he pauses to correct his tense. "I would have died for her."

"Oh, Daavid," she says with a compassionate hand on his shoulder. "I am so sorry for you."

"Thank you, Daisy," he says forcing a brief smile. "But now I must get my book finished."

The bounce has gone from Daisy as she walks back to her office along the street from L'Escale and Bliss watches her for a second.

"She's still yours if you want her," a voice tells him deep in his mind, but he shakes his head. No spark ... no magic, he tells himself and continues writing.

"It is a message from someone in Paris," the governor of the fortress, Maréchal Mars, told the masked prisoner as he handed over the letter with its wax seal.

"She is coming, she is coming," mused the prisoner, and he broke the seal with impatience.

"*My dear Prince…*" Bliss begins, with the words *I regret to inform you* already formed in his mind, when he stops himself. "What the hell am I doing?" he questions aloud. "She has to come to him."

Bliss's cellphone shakes him back to the present, and he's amazed to discover he already has four pages written.

"Yes," he says no longer considering that it might be Yolanda.

"It's Trina," says a faraway voice. "Daphne told me what happened."

"Oh," he says.

"Don't worry David," she carries on. "We're all praying for you."

"It might take more than prayers. It might take a miracle."

"I've just called Raven in Vancouver," she carries on as if Bliss should know that the young woman is a seer. "She says she's been in touch with Serethusa on the other side and you will get your wish."

"Serethusa …?" he questions vaguely then changes his mind. "OK. Thanks," he says hurriedly, but he's forced to listen for a few more seconds while Trina bleats about the success of her subterfuge.

"We did it, Dave. Daphne and me; Lovelace and Button, International Investigators. We solved the Creston murders."

"With a little help from me," he mutters under his breath, but he doesn't want any credit. He just wants to finish his script.

Day two is simply an extension of day one for Bliss. He has cat-napped a few times during the night and has often been tempted to simply write, *and the masked man's great love returned to him,* but he knows that won't wash; knows that he has to finish the saga with as much passion as he began; knows the end of the book is what the readers will react to. And he knows that if he is too late to save Yolanda from making the biggest mistake of her life, he must offer publishers and the media the most compelling bittersweet love story of all time.

The days dragged more slowly than ever for the masked prisoner as he sat in his cell reading and rereading the letter, wondering if it was just another of the illegitimate king's callous deceptions ... Bliss is writing, when Samantha calls.

"I've found her, Dad," she enthuses, and for a few seconds he's scared to ask if he's missed his chance.

"I don't know," she replies honestly, when he's plucked up the courage. "But I've had a lawyer friend of mine in Holland track her down to a place on the outskirts of Amsterdam."

"I could just go to her, Sam ..." he starts, but she's less sure.

"Finish the book, Dad. A couple more days won't make any difference."

"You're just humouring me again," he accuses. "She's already married isn't she?"

"No, I told you I don't know."

"Then I should just jump a flight to Schipol today."

"Dad. Do the book," she says fiercely. "I've asked my friend to find out the score."

"OK," he says, though he yelps in pain as he picks up his pen. "Damn," he swears, seeing that he has a blister the size of a peanut on his middle finger.

By lunchtime, with the masked prince picturing his great love's carriage heading south from Lyons down the valley of the Rhône towards Avignon, Bliss has written himself to a standstill. He frantically fights off the drowsiness with several strong espressos, but he finally drops.

In London, Trina drags a petrified Clive Sampson onto a tube train, where he sits mesmerized by the flashing lights and the constant bustle as he admits that he's never previously been further than Saskatchewan.

"We'll do the town: St. Paul's, Buckingham Palace, The Tower, Big Ben," Trina tells him as she holds onto his hand. "But first we'll see Janet."

Janet Creston has put on ten pounds and lost twenty years since Clive last saw her, and there have been a number of other changes in her life that have yet to sink in.

"The thing is, Mrs. Creston," says Edith Milsom, a junior member of Creston's legal team specially chosen because of her soft voice and trustworthy face. "Your husband really loves you. I'm sure you are aware of that."

Janet's face suggests that she is unconvinced, so Edith sits on the edge of her bed and reassuringly strokes one of her hands as she carries on. "Joseph realizes that you may be a little confused."

"No, I'm not," Janet says firmly, snatching her hand away.

"Well. We think you might be …" Edith is trying when the door opens and a trio of visitors arrive.

"Samantha Bryan," says Bliss's daughter, summing up the situation at a glance and stepping in with an outstretched hand. "I'm Mrs. Creston's personal legal advisor."

Janet Thurgood looks more confused than Edith Milsom, although she keeps quiet as her husband's lawyer tries to bluff.

"Milsom — Barnes, Worstheim, and Shuttlecock," says the young woman, putting on her courtroom voice. "We represent Mr. Creston and his companies."

"Good," Samantha replies plunking herself down on Janet's bed in Ms. Milsom's place and offering her adversary a business card. "Then please advise your client that all future contact with his wife should be addressed through me. Good day."

"Her face was a picture," Samantha tells her father later when she calls to check on his progress. "I think she was about to get Janet to sign a waiver relinquishing her rights ..." she is saying when she pauses, sensing a deep melancholy on the other end. "Are you all right, Dad?" she asks.

"This is useless Sam," he says. "My fingers are bleeding. I'm still miles away from the end, and she's probably on her honeymoon in Taipei or Timbuktu by now."

"Dad, listen to me. Think positive. No more excuses. Get that fucking manuscript finished in forty-eight hours or I'll personally ram it down your throat."

"Language."

"Yeah and you'll get more if you don't get a move on. It's Wednesday today — Friday at the latest, and book a flight ... no ...," she pauses, "I will book a flight for you. Now get on with it."

"Roger, wilco," he says and picks up his pen.

"This mask weighs too heavily upon my shoulders," mused the prince in despair and was sorely tempted to abandon his quest ...

Bliss crashes again near midnight. "Sam," he bleats catching his daughter as she readies for bed. "This won't work; she'll never be able read my writing."

"Get it typed then."

"Typed," he echoes as if it is a foreign word.

"Yes, Dad. You're near Cannes and Nice. There must be loads of typing agencies."

"French ones."

"International ones if it's anything like London. Take everything you've got first thing in the morning —"

"It'll cost a bomb ..."

"And you care? I thought you loved her."

"I do, Sam, I really love her, OK. You're right."

"And if you have to finish the last chapter on the plane to Amsterdam then you can read it to her when you get there."

"Thanks, Sam," he says, wanting to ask if she has any news from her friend about Yolanda's marital status, but he chooses not to.

Billie Holiday is singing "What a Little Moonlight Can Do" as he picks up his pen, painfully popping a blister in the process, then writing, *Moonlight bouncing off the Mediterranean picked out the turrets of the Château Roger...*

"Joseph Crispin Creston. You are charged that you did, on or about the seventh day of December, 1961, wilfully and maliciously murder ..."

"Let's see him try to buy his way out of this one," whispers Donaldson to Peter Bryan as they listen to Creston's application for bail.

"He'd probably get it if he wasn't already on bail for bribing Edwards," suggests Bryan and Donaldson pats him on the back. "Smart move that, Peter."

"I thought so," says the London officer with a smile.

Bliss is right about the cost of transcribing his manuscript, but he doesn't care. "Whatever it takes," he says, handing over nearly six hundred pages. "But I must have it by lunchtime tomorrow — two copies."

The Englishwoman in charge of the agency in Cannes runs her eye over the first few pages. "It won't be perfect," she begins, but Bliss isn't concerned.

"As long as it makes sense."

Malcolm Jackson, of Barnes, Worstheim and Shuttlecock, puts up a fight that will get him a seat on the top table of the firm's annual Christmas dinner, and his client walks. But while Creston may be free, he is now severely shackled, and Peter Bryan is on the phone to his wife in seconds. "He's had to hand in his passport, no contact with Edwards, and — and you will love this — neither he nor anyone representing him must go within five hundred yards of his wife."

"Brilliant," yips Samantha, and seconds later she's in her car headed for St. John's Wood.

It is an hour and a half from Westchester to the centre of London on a good day, but today is not good — not for Joseph Creston and his crony.

"We should have taken the chopper," he moans to Mason as he thrums his fingers on the leather upholstery in the back of his limousine while they slow for yet another set of road works.

"Sorry, J.C.," says Mason. "But I didn't know if they would let you out."

"I'm going to fight this," spits Creston, boiling at the perceived injustice. "They can't do this to me. I'm going to fight this all the way. Do I make myself clear?"

"Yes, J.C. Very clear."

It is nearly 4:00 p.m. by the time Creston's limousine pulls up at the front of his towering office building, and he's not at all surprised to see the paparazzi setting up shop against a cordon hastily thrown up by his security staff.

"Shall I tell the driver to take us round the back ..." starts Mason, but Creston is in a fighting mood.

"No way. I'm not having some snide reporter saying I weaselled out. I'll front 'em and tell 'em straight out. I've got nothing to hide."

"Mr. Creston ... Mr. Creston ..." yell reporters as they scramble to get his attention when he emerges from his car with a celebrity smile.

"Did you do it?" questions a pushy stringer, and Creston asks for silence with a hand gesture and waits until he is sure he is fully in the frame before pronouncing, "I am totally innocent of all these accusations. My lawyers assure me that it is simply a formality and that the authorities will be forced to drop these scurrilous charges within a few days."

"What are your plans now?" shouts a reporter from the back, and Creston turns to point at his towering edifice.

"Back to work, of course," he says and laughs. "Creston chocolates don't make themselves. Someone has to keep the machinery oiled and the vats stirred."

"Good one," whispers Mason as the two men head for the plate glass doors, then a plainclothes sergeant and two uniformed constables step across the security ribbon.

"Mr. Creston?" queries the sergeant.

"What now?" he spits, dropping his smile.

"I'm afraid you can't go any further, sir."

"What?"

"Sorry, sir," continues the sergeant as if he has never been less sorry of anything in his life. "But I have here a copy of your bail conditions from Westchester Magistrate's court, and I see that you are not permitted within five hundred yards of your wife."

The cameras move in; the microphones are back on; the security guards are getting squeezed.

"Out of my way," fumes Creston, and he gives the sergeant a push. The two uniformed men are on him in a flash and wrestle him to the ground.

"Now," says the sergeant in Creston's ear, while the cameras and microphones zoom in. "Your wife, who I understand is, by reason of the married person's property act, a half owner of this company, is currently in her office together with her attorney. Therefore, you are in breach of you bail conditions."

Mason stands back and buries his head in his hands.

"But," continues the sergeant to the prone man, "I'll assume you didn't know that on this occasion and I'm just giving you a warning." Creston's blood is up and he has no intention of saying thank you as the sergeant continues, "However if you persist I'll have no choice —"

"Mason," yells Creston, calling for backup.

Daphne Lovelace, watching TV at home, can't resist phoning Bliss.

"Daphne ... no ... sorry ..." he says and he turns off the phone.

"Mason," shouts Creston as he's pinned to the ground. "Get in there and get her out."

Sergeant Williams points a warning finger to Creston's right-hand man. "Actually, sir," he says, "as you are acting as Mr. Creston's representative you are also barred from the building while his wife is in residence."

"Get in there," yells Creston, but Mason hesitates, seeing the officer heading his way with deliberation.

"I will arrest you for being an accomplice," warns the sergeant, and then he turns back to Creston. "And I will charge you with breach of bail if he does try to go in. Understood?"

Tracy Jordan, Creston's uptight receptionist, is totally outnumbered by the invading forces and she sits glumly at the reception desk with Clive Sampson for company. She would call her boss, but Samantha Bliss has made it very clear that no action of any kind will be made without Mrs. Creston's say-so.

"Mrs. Janet Creston is taking over as interim company president until her husband has either served his sentence or has been exonerated," Samantha dictated to the woman, adding, "Now type that up and send it as a memo to all departments and representatives."

"I ought to check ..." Tracy started, but Samantha stared her down.

"Not unless you want to start looking for another job in the morning."

Now Samantha says to Janet, "You sit over there," pointing Janet towards her husband's throne, but the terrified woman shies off.

322 *James Hawkins*

"I don't think ..."

"Hey, look at this," shrieks Trina from the adjacent boardroom as she punches a button on a remote control unit to make a giant television appear from a trapdoor in the floor.

"All right, Trina," laughs Samantha, and then she carries on to a bewildered Janet, "We'll give him twenty-four hours to get really wound up, then we'll offer a deal. You get the mansion in Dewminster together with all the household expenses for a minimum of twenty years, an annual six-figure salary, use of the helicopter and Lear jet for a reasonable number of trips per year —"

"Samantha," says Janet putting out a hand to stop her. "Are you sure? It seems like a lot."

"A lot," says Samantha, laughing ironically. "It's nothing after what he's done. In fact there's a very good chance you'll end up with everything if he gets life."

"But it seems so much."

"Janet, you've spent forty years in purgatory because that man murdered your baby. This is only the start. Believe me ... Oh, that reminds me," she adds starting a to-do list on Creston's desk pad, "before we leave we need to get copies of all the accounts, bank statements, transactions, and computer programs, and I'll call in a forensic accountant to see if we can screw that freak in Canada who kept you prisoner."

"I wouldn't mind screwing that freak," yells Trina, now playing with the control for the automatic Venetian blinds.

As the sun goes down in London, Bliss is still furiously writing, but the end is in sight.

"My love ... my one and only true love ... she is coming. I can feel her energy getting stronger as her carriage journeys ever southwards, borne on the mistral as it

sweeps down the valley from the mountains ..." he pens, but his right hand and wrist are stiff and sore. He tries switching to the left but gives up almost immediately.

Yolanda — please come back to me. Please come home, he writes absent-mindedly in the midst of the page and has to scrub out the words for fear that the typist might include them.

"I'll have the rest finished by the morning," he vowed to himself and the girl at the typing agency, but his eyes are drooping; the coffee is losing its grip. His daughter may be right. He may have to finish the final few pages on the plane.

"How's it going, Dad?" Samantha questions using Tracy's phone to wake him at six the following morning, while Janet and Clive are still asleep in Creston's palatial office.

"Where are you?" he queries blearily, not recognizing the number.

"My new office," she answers. "Janet has appointed me the company lawyer and temporary vice-president."

"What!"

"Never mind," she says. "It won't take Creston and his high-priced goons long get back in. They're already applying for an injunction."

"Samantha ... I don't have time ..."

"I know. So where are you with the book?"

"I should have it done this afternoon."

"Good. Don't miss that plane. Caas will meet you at Schipol. He'll have a sign like one of those chauffeur guys. He'll drive you to her place."

"No news I guess."

"Just don't miss that plane, Dad."

"Don't miss the plane," he muses once he's put the phone down. "What's she trying to tell me? What's she saying? Am I too late? Will I be too late?"

He picks up his phone and hits the redial button in a panic.

"What if I'm too late? What if they're already married?"

"Then you will have an even better story. You'll be able to buy me a Porsche for Christmas."

"You're just trying to benefit from my misery."

"It's an ill wind that blows no one any good, Dad," Samantha reminds him, and he grimaces at the pain in his fingers as he carries on:

The mistral, the bitter icy blast from the snow-capped peaks of the High Alps, stings the faces of the carriage driver and his postilion riders as they forge southwards with their precious cargo ...

"Hello, Janet," says Samantha, pouring coffee from Tracy's percolator as the sleepy-eyed woman appears from her husband's office. "Are you ready for the big day?"

"This is too much ..." Janet starts, convinced that she is still dreaming, but Samantha calms her with an arm round her shoulders.

"Hey! Come look at this," yells Trina from the board-room, having stumbled over the button that has slid back the founder's portrait to reveal Joseph Creston's personal safe.

With a busload of forensic accountants and corporate lawyers threatening to drag the contents of his closets onto the street, Joseph Creston and his beleaguered team quickly capitulate, and by mid-afternoon, a beaming Samantha Bliss accompanies her client to the ground floor of the crumbling glass tower.

"You just leave the talking to me, all right," warns Samantha as they head to the front door, where the cameras are waiting, with Trina and Clive in their wake.

"We have reached a satisfactory interim arrangement with Mr. Creston and the Creston company," Samantha announces with muted pride once the hubbub has subsided. "And now, if you'll excuse us, Mrs. Creston would like to return to her Hampshire home, which she hasn't seen for forty years."

"What about Creston Enterprises?" yells a loud-mouthed reporter above the crowd.

Samantha pauses, then leans back into the microphone. "Mrs. Creston has agreed that her husband can retain control for now; however, in the circumstances, she will expect to have considerable say in company policy."

"Fuck … Fuck … Fuck!" screams Creston as he smashes his fists into the seat of his limousine while watching the press conference on television.

"And," continues Samantha, now on her own hobby horse, "as Mrs. Creston is particularly interested in the environment and the welfare of the Third World producers, you can expect some changes."

"Yes," yells Daphne to her television set, and she reaches out to call Bliss on his cellphone.

"The customer you are calling is not available…" a pleasant-voiced computer tells her, so she puts the phone down and goes into the kitchen to make a celebratory pot of Keemun tea.

"Three hundred and eleven pages, ninety-one thousand words, in two days," the typing agency manageress declares proudly as she hands over the document, and Bliss can hardly believe the bulk of the manuscript as he grabs it and heads for the waiting taxi.

"Nice … airport," he says in English, knowing the driver will understand, and he uses the twenty minutes to skim through the script, then he calls Samantha.

"Dad," says Samantha excitedly. "Peter just phoned. Chief Superintendent Edwards has thrown in the towel."

"What?"

"Resigned. Apparently he's done a deal. He's going to plead guilty to the Breathalyzer refusal providing that all the other charges are dropped."

"Oh my God," breathes Bliss as he races to the check-in

desk with his manuscript in hand. "I can't believe this. It's really working." Then he quickly opens his pad and scribbles:

The masked prince, now knowing that he had been duped by the treacherous usurper who called himself king, avenged himself by bringing down the impostor once and for all.

"You must hurry," says the clerk pointing to the concourse clock. "The gate closes in five minutes."

"Right," says Bliss, already on the run, and as soon as he is settled in his seat on the plane he carries on.

The prisoner ripped off his mask, opened the door of his cell, and rowed across the bay towards his great château, the Château Roger. But would he find the woman of his dreams, his one true love, waiting for him? Or would his heartbroken spirit be destined to spend eternity endlessly pacing the halls and corridors of his monumental folly on the promontory overlooking the fortress on the island of Ste. Marguerite?

Bliss's cellphone rings the moment he switches it on in the airport terminal in Holland.

"Caas is waiting for you outside. I've just spoken to him," says Samantha, before asking, "Is it done?"

"Almost finished," yells Bliss as he races towards the arrivals concourse and the end of a quest that has taken more than three centuries.

"Samantha told me what you do," says Caas conversationally as they drive towards the city, but Bliss's heart is in his mouth, his pulse is pounding, and he needs something considerably stronger than brandy to stop his hands shaking.

"Is she there?" he asks, but Caas doesn't know. Is she married? he wants to ask, but dare not.

"Here we are," says the young Dutch lawyer as he pulls into the curb outside a smart tower block. "Apartment one thousand and twenty-four on the tenth floor," he adds, calling, "Good luck," as Bliss climbs out.

I should have brought flowers, thinks Bliss and he checks the street hopefully, but there are no stores.

"OK, this is it," he tells himself and he slips into the building in the wake of a resident and waits for the elevator.

Janet Creston, née Thurgood, is back in the tiny chapel at Creston Hall, crying softly as she caresses her crucifix, the smooth-featured Jesus that she has imbued with the spirit of her firstborn ever since the night that her husband ripped the bronze out of her hand and smashed it into the skull of her crying baby.

"Suffer the little children to come unto me," she prays softly, while Clive Sampson sits next to her with sympathetic tears running down his cheeks, vowing silently to his God that he will spend the rest of his life trying to heal her hurt.

"Hello," starts Bliss as Yolanda opens the door, and he grips the manuscript with white-knuckle force as he holds it out. "I wrote this for you," he carries on, determined that she should have it whatever the circumstances.

Yolanda doesn't move. She's frozen physically and mentally as she tries to assimilate the spectre in front of her, still trying to fathom out whether or not he's real.

"I won't stay if I'm intruding," Bliss carries on as he attempts to see behind her. "Only I just wanted you to know that … I, um … that I love you more than I have ever loved anyone in my entire life. That you have never left my thoughts for one moment since I first met you, and —"

"David," she says, finally getting her mouth to work.

"Just let me finish please," he says blocking her with a hand. "I just want you to know that even if eternity means forever, I have no option but to wait for you."

A thousand kilometres away, on the Provençal coast of southern France, the chilling mistral dies away and the warm westerly pounant ripples the indigo surface of the bay of Cannes.

David Bliss's usual seat is empty at L'Escale in St-Juan-sur-Mer, but Angeline, the waitress, is drawn across the deserted road to the promenade by a strange feeling, and she finds herself peering at the derelict château on the promontory in the twilight.

"Bizarre!" she mutters at the ghostly glow of flickering candlelight in the glassless windows of the old building, but then she shrugs it off with a "Bof" and blames it on the sun, which has just sunk into the distant depths of the Mediterranean sea.

chapter twenty

"Please, David —" Yolanda starts as she waves off the manuscript, but a Dutchman's voice inside the apartment cuts her off.

"Who is that, Yolanda?"

"No one," she replies and is starting to close the door when it is stayed by a larger hand.

"Can I help you?" asks the pyjama-clad man in a heavy accent, and the blood drains from Bliss's face as he tries to hide the manuscript and turn away.

"Sorry, Klaus — sorry," stutters Bliss.

"I am not Klaus," says the man, opening the door wide to reveal a red-faced Yolanda. "I am Jan, Yolanda's husband. Klaus does not work here. He is my business partner."

"Partner ..." echoes Bliss, but Yolanda has come to life and is tussling with Jan over the door.

"Please, David. Just go — please just go," she is pleading as she tries to unglue her husband's hand, but Bliss has a foot in the door as he repeats, "Partner ... Klaus?"

"Yes," says Jan, wrenching Yolanda's hand away and opening the door wide. "Klaus is my associate ..."

"David, just go — leave me alone. Please go ... go!" Yolanda is yelling in the background, but Jan has other ideas.

"I think maybe you should come inside," he says, catching hold of Bliss's sleeve. "It seems that my wife does not wish me to talk to you for some reason."

Beautiful is burning, consumed by the hellish, satanic fires so often prophesied by the Lord Saviour. But the devil that set this conflagration is Wayne Browning, the saviour himself. However, this is no Waco or Jonestown. Pathologists and gagging policemen won't be raking the coals for the charred mortal remains of worshippers seeking immortality. Browning and a few of his most devoted angels have taken off through the forest in search of a new nirvana, while the rest of his dejected brood, a few scrawny children and a dozen wasted women, have lost their wings and walk in a ragged line towards a cordon of flak-jacketed policeman cowering behind cruisers and machine guns.

"Stop there," opens up a Mountie with a bullhorn and the women immediately comply. Then, as the heavily armed men move in to surround the pathetic group, a dozen fire engines with screaming sirens blast their way up the gravel road. But Beautiful is gone, along with all trace of the millions of dollars that the Creston Foundation has laundered over the years.

Caas is waiting with the engine running as Bliss gets back into the car. "So?" questions the young lawyer brightly.

"I thought I could change history," says Bliss with an ironic smirk as he leafs through his manuscript, then he throws it onto the back seat and slowly shakes his head.

"How stupid of me."

"But what about Yolanda?"

Bliss's hand on the young man's shoulder suggests masculine affinity as he offers some sagely advice. "Louis XIV was absolutely right," he tells him. "He always claimed that sacrifice is the only thing that all women desire."

Joseph Creston Jr., receives the news about Beautiful from Mason with a touch of a smile, although he has little to be pleased about. The charity commissioners have joined the tax inspectors to dig through his books, and his lawyers are still trying to contain the flood of lawsuits that threaten to engulf him

"The lack of physical evidence linking you to the baby's death is encouraging," said Barnes, of Barnes, Worstheim and Shuttlecock as he reviewed the murder case, although he was less optimistic regarding the bribing of Edwards and the assault on police.

Bliss's cellphone rings. "How did it go, Dad?" chirrups Samantha, and he finds himself laughing.

"I think I had a very, very lucky escape."

"You didn't get her back?"

"No ... although in a way I suppose I have," he says, knowing that Yolanda is going to have a very hard time with both her husband and Klaus. "I guess I'm going to have to buy you that Porsche after all."

"Oh, Dad," she sighs.

"Don't worry, Sam, nothing about her was real. She was just a mirage," he says breezily, then explains that the captivating image he fell for was just a façade put up by a desperate and deceitful woman, before adding, "Everything she told me was a lie."

"Everything?"

"Yes. She's just a sick, self-centred woman with no conscience. Klaus obviously caught on that she was going to be a nightmare so he ran the other way. She jumped into my bed to make him jealous."

"And it worked."

"No," says Bliss, laughing. "He didn't come. But she still had a couple of weeks to kill before her husband expected her home so she came back to me for a second dose."

"But that's terrible …"

"Actually, no," cuts in Bliss, smiling in relief. "It means that I'm finally free and I can get on with my life … plus I don't have to change history for my novel."

In Vancouver, Trina is back to chasing her guinea pig, while Inspector Mike Phillips still sits on the report linking Dave Brougham with Craddock, Janet's abductor.

Jody Craddock, ex-cop turned private investigator, is still in Hawaii, but no one takes any particular notice of the broken hobo who scavenges the garbage bins alongside the gulls and iguanas on the outskirts of Hilo.

In Dewminster, England, Amelia Drinkwater has stood down from the bench, much to the relief of the local constabulary, and hits the bottle while she awaits a verdict.

The warm Provençal sun lights up the fortress on the island of Ste. Marguerite the following morning as Bliss sits on the promenade in St-Juan-sur-Mer with his pen poised over a plain sheet of paper.

"Daavid?" queries Daisy, appearing from nowhere. "I zhought you had gone."

"No, Daisy," he replies as he gazes towards the Château Roger on the promontory. "I was just chasing a dream." And then he looks deeply into her dark Mediterranean eyes